HIGH STAKES

~~~~~~

"What you said a moment ago, Captain Krake," the alien thundered, "is untrue. Everybody does *not* know that transiting a wormhole is fatal. One of you says otherwise—is that not so, Sork Quintero?"

Sork blinked at the Turtle. "Are you talking about those old scientific chips? But they're just a record of what some professor said in a lecture hall; I don't know, myself, if any of it is true."

"You have told us that these humans believe it to be true," Litlun said severely. "Sue-ling Quong also has said that the chips are authentic. Do you deny the wisdom of your own race?"

"Well, you've been denying it!" Krake put in furiously. "What made you change your mind?"

Silence for a moment. Then Chief Thunderbird said hollowly, "We have not changed our minds. We simply have no choice, because we are *desperate*."

"The best yet of [Pohl and Williamson's] joint efforts, and a commendable addition to either's list of achievements.
—*Science Fiction Chronicle*

THE
SINGERS
OF TIME

Frederik Pohl &
Jack Williamson

SPECTRA™

BANTAM BOOKS
NEW YORK • TORONTO • LONDON • SYDNEY • AUCKLAND

All of the characters in this book are fictitious,
and any resemblance to actual persons, living or dead,
is purely coincidental.

THE SINGERS OF TIME
A Bantam Spectra Book / published by arrangement with Doubleday

PRINTING HISTORY
Doubleday edition published February 1991
Bantam edition / October 1991

ISBN 0-553-29432-6

Published simultaneously in the United States and Canada

PRINTED IN THE UNITED STATES OF AMERICA

RAD   0 9 8 7 6 5 4 3 2 1

To Stephen Hawking

in gratitude for an inspiration he would never recognize and, mostly, for being Stephen Hawking

THE
SINGERS
OF TIME

An Earth human whose name was Augustine once sang in his confession:

"What, then, is time?

"If no one asks me, I know.

"If I wish to explain it to someone who asks, I know not."

———

But one of the aiodoi, who do know that they are also scientists (since the aiodoi know that they are everything), sings instead:

"Time is always.

"Time is all.

"Time is only illusion, but there is no other truth than time."

1

The individual was known as Chief Thunderbird, and he was a Turtle—at least, that was the name human beings had given their benefactors from space. Chief Thunderbird wasn't his actual name, either. That too was simply what human beings generally called him. Properly he was addressed by his title, which was Proctor for Human Oversight. In his own language he had a name, of course, but that didn't matter to human beings. Human people had no hope of pronouncing the shrill squawks and high-frequency hisses of the Brotherhood.

The Proctor turned one wandering eye to gaze down at his companion and gestured with one sinuous, webby claw. "Now, Younger Brother," he said benignly, or as benignly as a Turtle's screech could ever sound, "this will be your main post of duty as Facilitator."

The Younger Brother allowed both his eyes to roam without pleasure over the vista before him. This was the Brotherhood's largest compound on Earth, with its hundreds of human workers and busy trains of matériel converging at the foot of the skyhook. "You will do good business with these beings," the Proctor promised. "Trade is just beginning to expand, now that we have completed the orbit elevator." One eye turned admiringly to gaze up at the cable of the skyhook, receding to infinity overhead. "When I first came here, we had to use actual spacecraft for all lifting in and out of orbit. Of course, the freight costs cut very heavily into the profits."

"It's very wet here," the Younger Brother complained.

Chief Thunderbird was not famous for tolerance toward subordinates. What little compassion he had was rapidly running out. This newcomer did not even look like a proper member of the Brotherhood. He was short. Where Chief Thunderbird stood nearly three meters tall, his carapace sleekly glistening silver and black in the yellow sunlight of this world called "Earth," this new one was half a meter shorter. And he was ugly. Even the color of his carapace was hideous. What could he have been eating to give it that hideous rusty-orange hue? It did not gleam at all. Taking everything together, the best word to describe this Younger Brother was "scrawny." It was hard to believe that he and the Proctor were of the same brood.

Unfortunately, the Proctor reflected sadly, such things happened. When a Mother came to the end of her fertility cycle there was always the probability that some of her last get would be—well—inferior.

The implications of that thought saddened the Proctor. It meant that the Mother—who was his own Mother, too—would have to be replaced soon. But that was the way the world went.

Chief Thunderbird drew himself up and looked around his dominion with—not with pride, no, but with contentment. Senior members of the Brotherhood did not suffer from pride. They had no need for it. They were simply well aware that their great Brotherhood spanned a thousand star systems and brought their treasures to share with lesser races like these humans—profiting greatly from such transactions, of course.

Even on this sorry, soggy little planet the Brotherhood's transactions were vast. Tens of thousands of tons of raw materials filled the cargo carts that climbed into orbit each day along the three great elevators of the skyhook. Of course, those materials were not particularly precious. They were common enough in space; this very solar system had a swarm of asteroids orbiting out past its third planet that were rich in metals and minerals. But it was a great convenience to have a planet of intelligent —well, *fairly* intelligent—beings to collect them and bring them here to the cargo terminals.

"They look so soft," the Younger Brother complained. "Wet, too."

The Proctor turned both eyes on the new arrival. Didn't they teach cubs any manners any more? It was a great condescension for a Proctor to show a newcomer to the planet around in this way—though a welcome one, since it meant his own eventual release.

He made an effort to be indulgent. "Yes, they are repulsive, but you will have no trouble with these humans. They are eager for trade with us."

"Why should I have trouble?" the Younger Brother asked, sounding perplexed. The Proctor for Human Oversight diverted his second eye to glare at him. This cub was simply not civilized. It was not a fitting way to speak to an Elder Brother, particularly one as distinguished as the Proctor.

Anger led the Proctor to say something that was not called for: "I remind you, Younger Brother," he snapped, "that not every creature the Brotherhood has encountered has been as agreeable as these humans."

That found its mark. The Younger Brother looked away with both eyes, shocked and embarrassed at the reminder of the ancient, but never forgotten, Sh'shrane. He muttered, "I had not forgotten, Elder Brother."

The Proctor gave him a brief nod, then waved at the compound with one hard-plated arm, allowing his eyes to roam independently. It was a busy scene, with the endless commerce of the space ladder flowing down to the base from orbit, and thence out to the world of human beings. He gestured at the human laborers and said, "The natives are entirely organic, you know."

The new Facilitator glanced around distastefully at the hurrying humans. "I know. Fragile and wet and primitive, like the Taurs."

"Almost like the Taurs, yes," the Proctor agreed.

"Both species are very wet, and in some ways their physical structures resemble each other. But these Earth humans don't have those disgusting Taur superstitions."

"One hopes not," the Facilitator said fervently, gazing upward reverently with both eyes. "So they do not require improvement?"

"Well, not in the same way as the Taurs, anyway," the Proctor said thoughtfully. The Taurs had presented some serious problems to the Brotherhood, until they had found a way of preventing those problems from arising any more. "These creatures do have superstitions of their own, I'm afraid. You'll see. But they're anxious for trade, and very desirous of our machines—and very impressed, too, by our space technology." He waved an arm toward the majestic space ladder. "Now that this is completed our commerce can really develop, with cargoes leaving all the time. The humans will help us in this. They are quite teachable, with some technological help we can give them. Even without it, some of the humans have even been allowed to operate waveships."

The Facilitator looked shocked, but was now too chastened to say so. He only said, "In the wisdom of the Mother no errors are possible." His tone caused the Proctor to look at him sharply, but the Facilitator was not pursuing the subject. He was staring around him with both his eyes, each roaming independently to take in part of the view, none of it very appealing to the new Younger Brother. "It's so hot and wet here," he complained again.

The Proctor, who knew just how much hotter and wetter it was likely to become as the seasons changed, hid his amusement. "You'll get used to it. Be pleased that you are assigned to work in this compound. The bases for the other two legs of the ladder are even worse. They had to be located in what this planet calls its tropical zone."

The Facilitator sighed, contemplating the years ahead in this soggy, steamy climate. "And this place was one of their 'cities'?" he said, shuddering slightly.

"Yes, they are disgusting," Chief Thunderbird agreed. The mere idea of a "city" was unpleasant: imagine a race that settled itself in vast structures, when the proper purpose of any being is to quest for new gifts for his Mother.

But of course, the humans were deficient in that respect. They did not have a single Mother. "This place was called 'Kansas City,'" the Proctor went on, forming the human words in a way no human could have understood. "It was severely damaged in one of their wars and, really, there was no point in trying to restore it. But it still had transportation facilities available, so we based one leg of the ladder here."

"Wars!" the Facilitator grunted. It was like an epithet.

"Oh, yes, they fought wars. Of course, we've put a stop to all that sort of wasteful physical combat."

"Of course." The Facilitator diverted one yellow-red eye to gaze at the Proctor. "Is there further wisdom you must impart to me in this place?" he asked.

Chief Thunderbird rolled one eyestalk heavenward. "Does the Younger Brother already know everything?" he demanded.

"No," the Facilitator admitted, attempting respect.

"Then the Younger Brother may ask whatever questions are on his mind," the Proctor said benevolently.

The Facilitator groaned inwardly, glancing around. He pointed at a group of workers unloading a flatcar of scrap metal. "I see both humans and Taurs working there, Elder Brother," he said. "Would it not be more efficient to have only whichever race is best at the task employed?"

The Proctor twined his eyestalks negatively. "The Taurs are best at heavy lifting," he informed his companion, "but the humans are more intellectual in some ways. Actually, the humans like Taurs very much, not only for labor but for meat. Nearly all humans now eat Taur flesh."

"But didn't they eat meat before we came?"

The Proctor made a tolerant gesture. "Yes, of course, the meat of their kindred animals. But those animals were not intelligent at all, not even as intelligent as a Taur. They could not be instructed to present themselves for slaughter when ready. They wasted resources, too, since they ate the same grains as humans, whereas the Taurs can of course eat anything that grows as long as they also have a few redfruit in their diet. And, by the way, the humans also enjoy our redfruit—"

But the Younger Brother was showing signs of distress. "I don't much care what the animals eat, Elder Brother," he gasped. "It is very *wet* here."

The Proctor turned both eyes on the Facilitator. But all he said was, "Very well. We will go inside one of the buildings, where it is drier, and I will show you how we care for these humans."

The new Facilitator was doing his best to be courteous to an Elder Brother of high rank. His best wasn't very good. He couldn't help it, though. He was in distress. The physical conditions on this Mother-forsaken planet were appalling, for a Brother used to the waterless comforts of the Mother worlds.

And then there was his own special problem.

The Facilitator was one of the last of the present High Mother's litter. He knew he was physically very marginal among the Brotherhood. Eggs that tested very little farther below standard than his own had not been permitted to develop.

But, although the Facilitator was very young, he was not stupid. That would have been impossible. Physical blemishes were tolerated among the Brotherhood, but intellectual ones never. No Brother with impaired mentality was allowed to survive his first hatching year. The Facilitator was also wholly dedicated to the service of the Brotherhood and the sacred Mother, but of course that went without saying.

All the same, the new Facilitator was not entirely pleased with the assignment he had drawn. Like every young Brother, molting into his final grown-up carapace, he had dreamed of more exciting work for the Mother. To travel around the stars in a waveship, opening new lanes of commerce, finding new treasures to bring home to the Mother—that was what every young Brother aspired to. Not this! He could not help feeling that if he had been just a little more physically prepossessing, his selection would have been entirely different, and much better. To be assigned to this muggy, swampy world to ride herd on a few billion unpleasant aliens was—well, it was the sort of thing you got assigned to, he knew, when you were just a little under par.

Which told him something he was too intelligent to say about the Elder Brother who was showing him around: Just what was the flaw in the Proctor that had landed *him* in this ghastly place?

The Facilitator could see that the Proctor was getting restive. He understood that perfectly. He was getting as bored as his guide, and hungry, too. He was about to suggest a refreshing half hour in the radiation chamber when the Proctor led him into a low building that seemed to be occupied entirely by the soft-bodied aliens. He paused at the door and waved inside. "You will want to observe this institution. It is a hospital," the Proctor explained. "For humans. It is one of the things we have done for them, giving them the benefit of our expertise in medicine and anatomy."

The Facilitator was surprised. "Didn't they have hospitals of their own? I mean, I understood they had machines, and even primitive spacecraft—"

"Oh, *human* machines," the Proctor said, dismissing them all with a wave of one horny claw. "Very crude. Not anything like as good as what we have given them. Their spacecraft, for example, used chemical rockets to rise from the surface of the planet to orbit—you can imagine how weak and wasteful they were, before we brought them the elevators on the space ladder. And their medicine was quite crude. Come inside and you will see for yourself."

It was better in the building than out of it, less warm, less humid, but there were surprises there too. The Facilitator stared at a couple of quiet young Taur males who were working at cleaning, carrying, doing routine jobs, their horns just beginning to bud. "I didn't expect to find Taurs here," the Facilitator said in surprise.

"Oh, yes," the Proctor said, with satisfaction. "Actually, Taurs are one of our most successful exports to this world. The humans like them for manual labor, and of course for food. The humans have been taught all they need to know about how to treat Taurs," he said proudly, "and they are careful to follow our instructions."

"The Mother be thanked for that," said the Younger Brother, with heartfelt sincerity.

"Of course. Now I will show you some of the ways in which we have helped the humans. For instance, this building is a hospital."

"Do they not have their own repair facilities?"

"Of course, but not as good as ours. Here we perform essential services for human beings that they cannot perform for themselves—High Mother!" he finished, with a startled squawk. One of the passing humans had stopped and clutched at the Proctor's claws. The Facilitator's first impulse was alarm, but then reason reassured him that the Proctor had nothing to fear from these moist savages. The human being was proudly showing the Proctor his forelimb, where a crude drawing of some sort of beast appeared to be made directly on the skin.

The Proctor recovered his calm, adjusted the transposer on his arm and spoke to the human. The Facilitator shuddered at the sounds that the Proctor was making. It was an analogue of human language, or as close as the Brotherhood's vocal apparatus could manage. He was going to have to learn that himself, he knew dismally. He could barely hear the corresponding sounds that came out of the transformer, stepped down to frequencies humans could hear. When the human replied, it was only an unpleasant noise.

To the Facilitator's surprise, the Proctor was laughing.

"What is amusing my Elder Brother?" the Facilitator asked, clawed hands submissively bent in the gesture of respect—you didn't have to feel it to show it, and he was aware that the Proctor was annoyed with him.

"This human is a new arrival in our compound," the Proctor explained. "See, he doesn't even have a memo pocket in his skull yet. I suppose that's why he's here, for the operation to install it."

"Memo pocket?" the Facilitator asked.

Complacently, the Proctor touched the spot in his armor where the skull reached the edge of the platen, where his kind inserted data disks to help them with their technological works. "Humans do not possess our natural ganglionic loci, Younger Brother," he explained. "So in order for them to use the memo disks, they have to have one created surgically. That was the first great challenge our anatomists faced, but, fortunately, the specimens our first scouts acquired gave us a good deal of experimental material."

"I do know about the specimens that were collected, Elder Brother," the Facilitator said, wishing the Proctor would get on with it. "Some still exist, I believe."

"I am not speaking of the surviving specimens. I am speaking of those specimens which were too severely damaged for reanimation when acquired by our scouts. By dissecting them, our anatomists learned how to implant memory chips in humans. After that it was simple to perform various kinds of surgery that were beyond the skills of the humans themselves. That is what this hospital is for."

The Facilitator groaned, but not aloud. There was simply no stopping this Elder Brother. The Facilitator had not journeyed all the way from home without cramming his very large and able brain with every fact he could find about his new posting. Humans had possessed only explosive-propelled spaceships and knew nothing of the wave-drive? Of course. Only the Brotherhood had waveships—well, the Brotherhood and that one other galactic race that was best forgotten. The orbital tower that was their elevator to space? Naturally the Brotherhood had made it a high priority to install one as quickly as possible. How else could you carry on large-scale interstellar business?

He raised one scaled claw, hoping against hope to cut

off the flow of educational lecture. "One thing I do not understand, Elder Brother," he said humbly. "What is it about these humans that amused you?"

The Proctor turned both eyes on him. "It is simply that they love us so," he said, gazing down affectionately at the human. "Do you see this thing on his arm? It is called a 'tattoo.' He has decorated his skin with this picture which he believes resembles one of us."

"It is a very poor likeness," the Facilitator complained, darting both eyes at the faded lines of the drawing.

"Oh, it is not really of one of our Brotherhood. The tattoo depicts an Earthly beast which is called 'turtle.'" Of course, his vocal cords made a hash of the human word. "It is what they call us, the 'Turtles.'"

The Facilitator was scandalized. "They are so offensive that they name us after a dumb beast?"

"You do not understand," the Proctor sighed. "Humans have an old tale in their religious lore which speaks of a race between a 'turtle' and a 'hare.' Although the hare can run much faster, it was the turtle which won the race—so, you see, it is a term of respect."

"If the Elder Brother says so," the Facilitator grumbled.

"I do say so. Don't you see? We win the race, in spite of everything," the Proctor said proudly. "We always do."

"Always," agreed the Facilitator, happy to have something to agree with the Proctor on. The Brotherhood always did win. In every contest they ventured to undertake. Or some members of the Brotherhood did, at least. . . .

And it was the Facilitator's fervent intention to be the one who conquered in the next, and most important, one.

At least now they were moving again, the Proctor leading the way. He said, "There are several complex surgical operations now in progress—they come from all over to be helped by the procedures we have brought to their planet. Come, we will observe one of them."

Unwillingly the Facilitator trailed the Elder Brother to what was called an "operating room." He observed a cluster of humans in white, green and lilac robes surrounding a table where another human lay. Then he took a closer look. "But those are humans performing this operation," he said. "Did the Elder Brother not say that this hospital was reserved for cases so difficult that only the skills of the Brotherhood made them possible?"

The Proctor nodded reluctant approval. "You are quick to observe, at least," he said grudgingly. "Yes, those are human surgeons, but the skills they use are those of the Brotherhood. Note the memo disks in their skulls. They are needed, because this is indeed a particularly difficult operation." He turned one eye expectantly on the Facilitator. "Observe the patient. Do you notice anything strange?"

The Facilitator studied the subject, then waved an arm negatively. "What should I notice?"

"It is a *female,*" the Proctor said gleefully. "Half of the humans are female!"

The Facilitator shuddered; the thought of an intelligent race with more than one active female was vaguely repellent, though he had been taught to expect this. "What is wrong with her?"

The Proctor said, "She is 'pregnant.' It is her unborn young that need attention. These creatures bear their young live, like Taurs, and sometimes things go wrong. In this case, she has two young ones developing inside her, but they are malformed. It is what humans call 'Siamese twins.' They are joined at the brain."

"At the brain!"

"Yes," said the Proctor with pride, "but with our memo disk the surgeon will be able to separate them in utero and they will develop normally. That is why she has come here from one of their cities."

"Cities," the Facilitator repeated, shuddering. "Disgusting!"

The Proctor said fairly, "Even the humans find their

cities unlivable, with all their noise and dirt. Therefore it is a good place for us to secure memmie helpers—especially when, like this one, they are in difficulties."

The Facilitator said impatiently, "Why do we trouble with such things? Why not let them deal with it themselves?"

"Oh, Facilitator," the Proctor said in dismay, "have they taught you nothing? It is because we *do* things for these humans that our relations are so successful. We have given them so many things: machines, medical techniques, the Taurs for servants and food, the redfruit to replace their native vegetation, the opening to space through our ladder. These things are our trading stock! We can show the humans that our technology is better than theirs, and in that way cause them to give up their heretical notions."

The Younger Brother squinted up at his superior. "What heretical notions?"

"Fantastic distortion of the Mother's truth," the Proctor told him somberly, "woven into the pseudosciences they call 'physics' and 'astronomy'—that is," he explained, "their own weird ideas of the stars."

The Facilitator was astonished. "What do these beasts know about the stars?"

"They are not really beasts," the Proctor acknowledged justly. "But they do have strangely mistaken notions. Even blasphemous violations of the Mother's laws. Notions of such strange things as multiple dimensions in space-time, as they call it, and something they call 'quantum reality.' "

The Facilitator shuddered. "We must stamp that out!"

"Indeed yes. That program has already begun. Ultimately these heresies will die away, along with those other nasty customs of these humans, like 'nations' and wars."

The Facilitator sighed. "But this will take a long time," he said dismally.

"Oh, no doubt," said the Proctor, at last beginning to

feel at ease. "But you have the time. And now," he said, beaming, "I think you have all the indoctrination you need. Now you can take up your duties and I—I will spend the rest of my duty tour in the orbital station, far from this damp, miserable surface!"

The aiodoi seldom sing of twentieth-century Earth humans, but among those humans is a scientist. This scientist does not know that he is also an aiodos. Nevertheless, at times he sings most poetically to his students, like any aiodos. Then in his songs are certain things the aiodoi also sing:

———

"Now, pay attention, class, because we're going to try to understand what Stephen Hawking means when he says he no longer believes in the Big Bang.

"What Hawking says is that the universe is infinite in time. It has lasted forever. It will go on lasting forever.

"Please understand that this isn't the old Hoyle-Gold idea of continuous creation, which we took up last month. Hawking doesn't believe in creation at all. What he does say is that, every once in a while in the eternal history of the universe, there is a sort of vacuum fluctuation which produces a temporary flux of particles. 'Temporary' doesn't necessarily mean something that lasts for only a short time. It can be quite a long time—I would say, perhaps, in this case for as long as ten to the sixty-sixth years or more. These particles appear, they expand, they condense into galaxies and stars and planets and you and me. Then, over time, they subside again. The vacuum energies return to the zero state and the universe goes on unchanged—until the next eruption.

"Are you following me? Maybe a picture would make it clearer. You can draw it in your notebooks, if you want to.

"For your picture, think of the whole universe as an endless, one-dimensional line.

"Then think of that endless line as hollow. Like a very narrow hose. Better still, think of it as an extremely long, extremely skinny anaconda, and imagine that the anaconda has just swallowed a pig. From outside the anaconda, you can see the bulge in the snake's belly, where the pig is being digested—

"But the pig can't see that bulge in the snake's belly. The pig can't see the anaconda at all, because it is *inside* that infinitely long snake.

"Now think of ourselves as living within that pig inside that snake. Think of us as some smart, tiny bacteria that live in the pig's gut. Maybe we could be something like that favorite, harmless intestinal bug we all carry around called *Escherichia coli,* only a lot more intelligent. In fact, if we *E. coli* are intelligent enough, we might possibly be able to invent some kind of instruments—call them 'radio telescopes,' or something of the sort—that might let us explore the entire pig. We may even be able to deduce, from studying the pig's structure, that there was a 'beginning' to the pig. That would be the point in the snake's body where the curvature of the swallowed pig first begins to appear. We might call that 'the Big Bang.' Perhaps we can speculate that there will also be an end, when the last trace of the pig will be gone and the snake will resume its endless, one-dimensional stretch.

"We can imagine all that. But what we intestinal bacteria can never do is see *past* the outer limits of the pig we live inside, for the body of that pig is our whole perceivable universe.

"If one of us pig-gut fauna happens to be like Stephen Hawking, he may theorize that there could be a lot more of the snake than the pig's body occupies, even if we can't see it. Nevertheless, what we can never do, *ever,* is have any personal encounter with anything before or after the pig. Those areas are forever hidden from us. There may be other pig-universes elsewhere along the snake from its previous meals and later ones, but we can only guess about that. We will never be able to see them, or communicate with them, or have direct proof that they exist.

"For that reason, our bacterial Stephen Hawking will call these other possible universes 'imaginary.'

"In just that way, the living Stephen Hawking of our own world, in fact, describes everything before the Big Bang as 'imaginary time,' along with everything that follows after that temporary swelling of space and time which we perceive as our whole universe. He calls the time we live by—clock time; the time by which we measure our heartbeats and the recession of the galaxies and the rotation of the Earth—'real time,' because it seems real to us . . . since it's the only one we can ever detect.

"But, Hawking says, the universe runs on 'imaginary time.' What appears to us as real is only a deficiency in our ability to see beyond our slowly digesting pig.

"That's all for today, class. Bring your notes tomorrow, because we're going to have an open-book quiz."

———

Thus sang the ancient Earth scientist, who was also a poet, and the aiodoi heard. But here is what one aiodos sings:

———

"Which is the first particle in a flux of infinitely varied particles that has gone on forever?

"Every one is.

"For when each particle first comes to exist, it is, for itself, the first particle that ever existed.

"And what does 'cannot' mean?

" 'Cannot' has only one meaning, and that is that 'cannot' cannot ever be."

2

~~~~~~~

To Sork Quintero, the teachings of the old human scientists weren't heretical. They were *human*, and it was Sork's firm plan to learn everything the human race had ever known . . . as well as, God willing, everything the Turtles knew as well. That made Sork's life even harder than it would otherwise have been. Among other things, the effort cost him a lot of sleep. He didn't have time for much of it, when he put in his hours studying the borrowed old tapes after his day's work for the Turtles was through. It cost him pain, too, because it made his head hurt, especially when he tried to understand what those wild old tapes were talking about. Space. Time. The universe. It didn't mean that these were difficult subjects—as long as he didn't try to understand what the old scientists were saying *exactly*—but what in the world could they mean by something they called "imaginary time"?

When he did try to digest those indigestibles, then his head hurt. Then nothing they said made sense. Then everything the old Earth scientists said was far more alien than the Turtles themselves.

Sork had begun to convince himself that he would never understand the tapes without help. But where was that help going to come from? Certainly not from the Turtles, who would be horrified even to be asked about such things. Not from his twin brother, Kiri, either, because what did Kiri know of such matters?

He wished his twin was awake to talk to, anyway, but when Sork looked into Kiri Quintero's room, he saw that his brother was still bubbling soft snores in his bunk, untroubled by such questions. That was a pity. Kiri might not study these arcane, antique subjects, but Kiri had the power of comprehension. Kiri understood things. Kiri seemed to grasp conceptual matters almost intuitively; his mind functioned in large images—pictures—interactions—relevances. But Kiri was not, when you came right down to it, much help in his twin brother's desperate effort to learn, because Kiri Quintero was very bad at explaining the things he understood to anyone else.

Sork sighed and walked out into the waking-up noises of the Turtle compound, rubbing the back of his head, where the memmie slot sometimes itched. Already the long flatcar trains were rolling in with their cargoes of raw materials for the Turtles. Looking up, Sork could still see stars overhead—and one bright object that was not a star. It slid silently down the heavens as he watched, as bright as Sirius—and, Sork Quintero thought morosely, just as unreachable. But that wasn't fair either, because he recognized the thing. It was human-built! It was the abandoned shell of an old human space station, empty for centuries now, but still an every-night reminder that, once, human beings had ventured into space on their own.

Once. No longer.

————

A gentle mooing from behind made him move aside to make way for a Taur servant, ready to begin his day's work of cleaning in the Turtle compound. "Good morning," Sork said politely, though he knew it was unlikely the immature Taur would understand.

Then he began wandering aimlessly across the compound, trying to sort out the things he had heard. His

head still hurt. And no wonder! Such strange talk! Time
. . . real time, imaginary time, time as a dimension just
like up and down and sidewise—what could such things
mean?

He didn't know. You could not talk about such things
with a Turtle, and no human being seemed interested. If
he had any sense, he reflected, he would forget about
these old lecture chips and concentrate on his real life
here in the compound, working for the Turtles. Certainly
the Turtles would prefer it if he stopped.

And that was the main reason Sork Quintero was so
doggedly insistent on going on.

He rubbed the memo disk scar at the back of his skull
reflectively. Listening to the old lecture chips wasn't like
using the memo disks the Turtles supplied their most
trusted employees. In some ways, listening to the old hu-
man-made chips was better. You had a different kind of
headache when it was over. Most of all, you could actually remember what was on the chip after you finished
playing it. At least, you could if you were lucky. If you
played it over often enough. If you could figure out what
all the strange old words meant.

As to *understanding* all the strange things they said,
on the other hand—

He shook his head ruefully. Understanding the *meaning* of all this talk of "cosmologies" (whatever they were)
and "universes" (as though there could be more than
one!)—that was another matter entirely. He wondered if
he would ever comprehend just what the old human scientists were trying to explain—or if he could ever be sure
that they *did* mean something, instead of just being some
silly pre-Turtle superstition, as the Turtles insisted—
when they would discuss the subject at all.

Sork scratched his chin rebelliously. These centuries-
old human scientists were *not* slaves to superstition! They
had built a great civilization, with no help from Turtles
or anyone else. His own grandfather's grandfather had
seen it!—had lived in that exclusively *human* world of
high technology and freedom, without Turtles, without

Taurs, just men and women living and working together in peace and democracy. . . .

Sork stopped himself there out of fairness, for, as the woman he loved was in the habit of pointing out to him, that wholly human world had not been all that peaceful, or even all that democratic.

Reminded of her existence, Sork glanced at his watch. Sue-ling Quong should be coming off duty now, and with his twin brother, Kiri, still abed he could have her all to himself for the hour or so before his own shift started.

Sork thought briefly of breakfast, then gave up the idea and headed across the compound toward the hospital. Working under the memo disk for the Turtles was stressful enough; coupled with the fact that his head ached already, it would be better to tackle it on an empty stomach.

What Sork did for the Turtles was a form of bookkeeping. His job was to handle complex questions of loading the linear induction cars that swarmed up the space ladder. His choices determined the routing of cargoes to one of the three skyhook landing areas—not the nearest, necessarily, but the one with the most current available capacity.

At least, Sork *thought* that was what he did. He could never really remember what he did under the memo disk. He knew that he was tracking some "values" for the Turtles, but what those values were exactly he could not say.

Yet, the Turtles seemed easy enough to understand— if you took what they said of themselves at face value. Their philosophy was mercantile. They didn't believe in conquest, only in trade. They did, of course, write the rules their trading went by.

Trade they certainly did. Overhead the great space ladder, the Turtles' stairway to the stars, sloped off toward the south and invisibility. As always, there were a dozen cars sliding up and down its cables. Sork looked up at it with his jaw set. Some day, he promised himself, some day he would be in one of those cars, heading out into space the way humans used to do before the Turtles came along. . . .

"Watch it, stupid!" a hoarse human voice shouted.

Sork brought himself up short on the edge of the railroad tracks. A long train of flatcars was coming into the Turtle compound. A uniformed guard, not a memmie—not *even* a memmie, Sork thought—was scowling at him. "Don't slow the train down!" he barked.

Sork didn't answer. He stood there, more or less patiently, while the train clanked and rattled slowly past. Each car held a rusted, evil-looking chunk of metal. Sork thought he knew what they were: tanks and cannon, old, almost forgotten instruments of war. The kind of thing the Turtles had made unnecessary for humans to have ever again.

It wasn't unusual to see such ancient artifacts come in for shipment up the ladder to orbit. It only meant that somewhere on the Earth the Turtles had ferreted out another old armory and politely, insistently, had made a deal to buy its contents for shipment to wherever they forged such things to their own purposes.

Really, the whole compound was a junkyard. Turtles didn't care about appearances. If, here and there, you could see a few patches of greenery you could be sure that they were nothing to do with the Turtles. Such little plantings were invariably tended by humans in their spare time. The only use Turtles seemed to have for growing vegetation was to eat it, but that they did only rarely. The Turtles didn't need to do much farming for food, because the Turtles ate almost anything, organic or not.

As the last car went by, Sork saw a Turtle waiting on the far side, demonstrating impatience by munching at something—it sounded like rock being crushed. Sork recognized the alien from the rusty carapace and yellow eyes—and mostly from the creature's stunted size. It was the one he worked for.

"Hello, Facilitator," Sork said. That was of course the creature's title, not his name—certainly not his unpronounceable Turtle name. Among themselves the humans had given their own names to the aliens—"Litlun" for this one, because he was smaller than the rest.

The Turtle engaged his transposer and spoke. "Which Quintero are you?" he demanded.

"I'm Sork Quintero," he said. "Your records keeper." He tried to move away to avoid Litlun's tart, musky smell. It had an acid hint of lemon rind and a sharp turpentine tang: it was the smell of Turtles.

The Turtle made a sound of annoyance. He turned without a word and stalked away, his carapace rusty brown in the sunlight. Sork knew that the Turtle was confused by the fact that Sork was an identical twin. It irritated him, and seemed to make him dislike both of them. But that was all right with Sork Quintero, because he didn't like Litlun either.

Oddly, the other Turtles didn't seem to, either. But who could understand what Turtles felt?

———

Sork stopped at the door of the office of the woman he loved, frowning. An unfamiliar male voice was coming from within. When Sork peered inside he saw a stranger hovering over Sue-ling's desk. The man had a neatly pointed, curly brown beard on a pink, undepilated face. He looked young, but there was a weary sadness in his brown eyes as he waited for Sue-ling to check something out in her records.

Sue-ling gave Sork a quick smile as he entered and the stranger turned to greet him, hand outstretched. "Hello," he said. "I'm Francis Krake."

"Sork Quintero," Sork said, shaking the hand. It was a strong, hard hand, and the man seemed decent enough. But strangers were unusual in the Turtle compound. "What are you doing here?" Sork asked bluntly.

"I'm asking the doctor here for a favor," the man said. "It's about my crew. We had a little accident, and they're in the surgery topside—up in the orbital station. So while I'm waiting for them to be ready to fly again I thought I'd take a few days to look Earth over, and I've been asking the doctor to keep checking on them for me."

"A few days isn't much time to see a whole planet," Sork pointed out.

Krake nodded doubtfully, as though unsure he were getting the point. "Actually I've seen Earth before," he said. "It's just that it has been a long time."

Sork didn't doubt that. Even the man's clothes seemed queerly old-fashioned, like something Sork's grandfather might have worn. He asked the man a logical question. "Why didn't you bring your friends down here for treatment?"

Krake looked either embarrassed or resentful, Sork could not tell which. "It's not the first time they've been hurt," he said stiffly. "They were picked up by the Turtles at the same time I was, but they were in a lot worse shape —almost dead, in fact." He thought for a moment, then corrected himself. "I guess you'd have to say they were really dead, until the Turtles took care of them. You see, they'd crashed in the Andes. Their limbs were broken, they were suffering from frostbite. The Turtles fixed them up, gave them a lot of prostheses—"

He stopped there. After a moment, he added, "Anyway, the way things are with them now, they do better with Turtle medicine than human."

"Sue-ling's a *very* good doctor!"

"I'm sure she is! I didn't mean to hurt her feelings." The man looked over at her sadly. "I'm just not very good with girls any more," he confessed. "With people at all, I guess."

Sue-ling looked up from the message on her communicator. "Well," she said, "they say your people are doing fine, Captain Krake. And I've asked the orbit crew to keep me informed if there's any change."

Krake nodded. "That's good. I'll call in from time to time, if you don't mind." He hesitated, then confided, "I thought I'd check out my old home. It'll be changed in a lot of ways, but still I'd like to visit it. And is it all right if I leave some of my gear with you until I get back?"

"Of course. Call in whenever you like, and I'll tell you what I hear from the orbit station. And I hope you have a good trip, Captain Krake," Sue-ling said, smiling up at him.

"Thank you." Krake stood up to go, then stopped, staring at the back of Sork Quintero's head. He seemed embarrassed again, but in a different way. "Excuse me," he said, his eyes on Sork's skull, "but you're a memmie, aren't you?"

"Of course I'm a memmie," Sork said, surprised. His hand went up to touch the rubbery lips of the implant socket at the back of his skull. "So's Sue-ling. We almost all are here. Naturally. We can't do any real work for the Turtles without a memo disk implant, how else could we handle their technology? It would be impossible."

The stranger shook his head. "Not impossible," he said, and touched his own, unmarked skull. "Thanks for helping me, Doctor," he said to Sue-ling, and turned away.

―――――――

When Krake had gone Sue-ling gazed absently after him, biting her lip. Sork felt a quick twinge. The last thing he needed was another interesting man to show up in Sue-ling's life. He asked jealously, "Who was that fellow?"

She shook her head. "He's a space pilot, Sork. Can you imagine that? He flies Turtle ships."

"Human beings don't fly Turtle ships!" Sork objected. "He isn't even a memmie!"

"I know, but that's what he says. He has his own interstellar wave-drive ship. The Turtles gave it to him. It has small chemical rocket ships attached—scout ships—so he can land where there isn't any ladder, can you imagine that?"

"Why would they let him do that?"

"For their convenience, of course, what else? He goes to the kinds of planets the Turtles don't like—you know, the warm, wet kind, with oceans. Like the Earth, really."

"And you believe all that?" Sork asked indignantly. The woman he loved gave him an affectionately understanding look. She was a beautiful woman—eyes almond-shaped but intensely blue, skin fair, hair gleaming coppery red—and the look she gave him was fondly tolerant. "Why would he lie to me? He's really interesting, Sork, and I do hope his shipmates are all right." Then, remembering, "And do you know what else he says? He told me he is the oldest human being in the universe."

He stared at her, not comprehending. "He doesn't look any older than I am," he objected, but Sue-ling was shaking her head.

"He's been in space," she explained. "On a wave-drive ship, traveling at almost the speed of light."

"Oh," said Sork, comprehending at last. The Turtle interstellar wave-drive spacecraft moved at a velocity so close to c that the time of their decades-long travel was shrunk to a matter of a few days for those aboard. "It's time dilation! Just as it says on those tapes!"

"That's right." She nodded, then gave him an inquiring look. "Did you come here because you wanted something?" she asked.

"To see you, of course," he said promptly.

She smiled at him, sweetly enough. "Of course. Still, I thought maybe you had another reason—like running out of the astronomy lectures?" And when he confessed that he had, she reached down into her desk for a fresh supply.

Sork gazed fondly at the back of her bent head, where a neat circle of her lustrous, coppery hair had been depilated for her memo disk implant socket. It might have looked ugly to most human beings. Not to Sork Quintero. There was a socket in his own skull, but that wasn't the point; the point was that since the first moment he had seen Sue-ling Quong, just arriving at the Turtle compound when the university she had worked at had closed down, nothing about her had seemed ugly to Sork Quintero.

Sork turned the little box of chip recordings over in his hands wistfully. "I wish I understood what they're talking about in these lectures," he sighed. "Do you think

I could ask one of the Turtles to help me make out this quantum mechanical stuff?"

She looked at him with shock. "Are you insane? Have you forgotten what happened last time?"

"Of course not," he said resentfully. "Litlun threw a fit. Said it was a sign of my essential instability to listen to those blasphemous 'songs,' and threatened to report me if I kept on. Why do you suppose they call them 'songs'? And why blasphemous?"

"What difference does that make? Do you want to be thrown out of the reservation?"

"No, but—"

"But that's exactly what would happen. You know that! The Turtles *hate* that sort of talk! I'm pretty sure that was one of the reasons why they closed my school down, because some of the physics professors were still teaching what they called quantum mechanics. That's blasphemy from their point of view—there's nothing about quantum mechanics in the divine revelations of the First Mother! That kind of heresy upsets them, Sork. I think they'd destroy these tapes if they could think of a legitimate way of getting their hands on them."

"Don't let them do that, Sue-ling!"

"Well, of course I won't," she promised. "But you have to be careful! You know what would happen if you offended their religion. You'd be out of here in a minute! You couldn't be a memmie any more—"

"What's wrong with that?"

She paused, biting her lip. This man was so *infuriating* sometimes! Then, controlling herself, "Be reasonable. What else can you do? Do you think there are any high-tech jobs for humans outside the Turtle compounds? You'd make a rotten farmer, Sork." She shook her head maternally. "No, stay here, keep your mouth shut, don't get tossed out of civilization just because of silly curiosity."

He gave her a challenging look. "If I did get thrown out, would you miss me?"

"Of course I would," she said, summoning up all the patience she had.

"A lot?" he persisted.

"Just as much as I would miss Kiri," she promised.

He left it at that. It was not the answer he wanted, but it was the answer she always gave. Sork Quintero loved his brother, Kiri, in spite of the fact that they were so different. But there were times when he could have wished Kiri Quintero a few oceans away. And those times had started when Sue-ling Quong appeared on the scene.

She was watching him. "Oh, Sork," she sighed, "I'm sorry. I know I'm making trouble between you and Kiri."

"There wouldn't be any trouble if you'd just pick one of us and quit going to bed with the other," he told her brutally.

For a moment her anger almost burst forth. What possessive, self-centered pigs men were! The fact was that she loved both of the twins—and, naturally, did what was right and natural to do when you loved someone. But why did each of them feel he had to *own* her?

Then her sense of humor won out. She grinned. "Could be worse. Look at the bright side, Sork, dear. There's only two of you, and there are plenty of other human women—so count your blessings!" He was looking at her steadily. "I mean," she said, beginning to wonder if Sork's sense of humor was responding to her own, "how would you like it if you were Turtles, a whole race of males and only the one female Mother in all the universe?"

Sork gave the woman he loved a hostile stare. "It doesn't help to joke," he said.

"I'm only saying—"

"I know what you're saying, Sue-ling." He shook his head, suddenly wistful. "I wish you and I could go off somewhere by ourselves, just the two of us."

"Where would we go?" she asked sensibly.

"Anywhere! Anywhere but here, doing anything but working for the Turtles. This life just isn't good enough."

Sue-ling Quong studied him, trying to find some way of soothing his bad mood. "But Sork, dear," she said tentatively, "we're all better off this way. Think of everything the Turtles have done for us." She gestured out the window at the trains of scrap metal. "Look at all those rotten old war machines! I think it's *fine* that the Turtles take them off our hands for scrap. We don't need them any more, because we don't have any more wars. The Turtles have seen to that! And no more terrorists, no more crime, no more addictive drugs—it's a good bargain we made with them, Sork!"

Sork glared at her. "Faust," he snapped. And when she looked puzzled, "Didn't you ever hear of Faust? There was stuff about him on one of the old lecture tapes, before I got into the science ones. This Faust was supposed to have made that kind of bargain with the Devil, and it cost him his soul. No, Sue-ling, it isn't good enough. It never has been good enough."

Then he paused. Sue-ling, knowing this man so well, knew what was coming next. She could almost feel the sensation of Sork shifting gears in his mind, as he switched from one mode of thought to another. "Sue-ling," he said, his voice deeper and huskier, "have I ever told you that your eyes have sunshine in them? They make the whole day dawn for me."

She sighed, not because she wasn't pleased. "Oh, Sork," she said, "go on and get to work. You'll be late. And I'm about ready to sack in."

She put her face up to be kissed and watched him leave her office, pensive. Sork and Kiri, Kiri and Sork! They were so different.

There was no doubt in Sue-ling's mind that she loved them both dearly. She did her best to love them equally, too, though that was harder. It was Sork who usually made it so—aggressive Sork, always demanding what he wanted, which was generally more time in bed with her. Kiri was less demanding.

Kiri was not, however, less loved. She was certain of that. She was certain, too, that the twins loved each other, but it did sometimes occur to her that Kiri Quintero loved his brother a tiny bit more than he really needed to. When Sork demanded, Kiri nearly always gave way.

Yet each touched her heart. Even in the way they spoke to her. Kiri Quintero's most romantic speech to her was "You're beautiful," or, "I love you." Never anything more; and yet if he told her she was beautiful in those same words a thousand times, somehow each time was new. There would be a different look in his eye or quirk of his lips. If Kiri had few words, he made each one do for a thousand shades of meaning. And Sork—

Oh, Sork! Every day he made a new speech. The problem was that she never knew just what kind of speech it would be. There were times when Sork Quintero spoke to her in tones that were so curt as to barely miss being humiliating, the times when he was caught up in some design of his own and lost sight of everything else. Yet other times he could be a poet. He praised her eyes—and Sue-ling knew that, really, she had quite ordinary eyes—but according to Sork Quintero they were stars, they were deep wells of clear spring water, they were sparks of burning flame. Of course, they weren't any of those things. They were just eyes. And her skin was only skin (Peach blossom! Golden silk! Such nonsense!), as her lips were only lips and the rest of her body no more and no less than any reasonably healthy young female of her genetic background should have. It was all wordplay with Sork. Worse, some of it, she was nearly sure, was lifted almost bodily from the old lecture chips on romantic poetry that he had read so assiduously before moving on to other subjects. . . .

Still, it was endearing wordplay. It was meant to please her and, because Sork meant that so intently, it did.

Whereas Kiri—

Hell, she said to herself, getting up from her desk, stop this. There's no point.

Sue-ling Quong knew that sooner or later she would have to give up one of the twins if she wanted to keep either. She didn't dodge that responsibility in her mind, because Sue-ling was a responsible person.

But she knew that she was not the solution to their problems.

Certainly she was not to Sork's. He wanted something that she couldn't give him, perhaps something that the whole world couldn't give him. For Sork to be happy something had to change—radically change, with unimaginable consequences—and Sue-ling Quong could see no chance, anywhere, that that sort of immense change was in sight.

In this, as it happened, she was very wrong.

The great event that was going to change everything for Sork Quintero (and for everyone else in the universe) had already happened.

In fact it had occurred long before Sork began listening to his old lecture chips—even before he and his twin brother had been born, nearly thirty years earlier. The event itself had actually happened longer ago than that, more than seventy-three years ago, in fact. But as the place where it happened was a bit more than seventy-three light-years away in space, and, as the news could not reach them any faster than the speed of light, neither Sue-ling nor Sork nor anyone else on Earth—Turtle, Taur or human—knew about it yet.

But, all too soon, they would.

———

When Sork Quintero went to work he had to leave the human quarters and venture into those colder, meaner, underground sections the Turtles reserved for themselves.

He knew the route well. He could have walked it in his sleep, and sometimes he very nearly did, when he had been awake for hours puzzling over the old lecture chips. But still he gazed distastefully around as he crossed the busy streets of the compound. He was aware of the vast cables of the space ladder, which stretched up and out of sight into the clouds to the south and east of the reservation. There was no hope of seeing the top of the ladder, of course, though sometimes, on a clear night, the eye could follow a cable for a long, long way just after dusk or just before dawn, while its upper reaches were still lighted by the sun which had already set for those on the surface.

Sork Quintero knew when he had left the human areas. The difference was sharp. Now there were symbols of the First Mother all over, the great winged female Turtle figure that represented the—perhaps—goddess of the entire Turtle race. Or so people said. Sork wondered if it were really true that there was a real Mother of all the Turtles somewhere in space. That was another thing that some people claimed, but was it true? Certainly no human had ever seen a female Turtle.

But no one knew for sure. The Turtles did not care to discuss their religion—or whatever it was—with unenlightened human beings.

There were fewer humans in this part of the compound. There were a handful of Taurs, the adult-male castrated kind, all wearing memo chips of their own, none of them paying any attention to Sork Quintero as they went about the business the chips ordained for them. Taurs, of course, were common everywhere on Earth now—great meat animals, almost human in body, bull-like as the Minotaur in the head.

Turtles, however, were not common at all, anywhere but here.

Most Earthmen would have been startled by what Sork was seeing. Most Earthmen seldom saw a living Turtle, and only a few humans were ever permitted the privilege of serving the Turtles in one of their compounds. Most humans would have been dazzled by the noise, the lights, the eerie strangeness of that part of the compound. To Sork Quintero it was an old story. He had spent his entire life in one part of the compound or another, without ever going outside.

That was the price you paid. Human beings who accepted memmie service with the Turtles also accepted the Turtles' rules. When you worked in the great northern ground terminal for their space ladder on the ruins of old Kansas City or any other Turtle compound, you stayed on Turtle territory all the time. The only exceptions were when you were sent somewhere on a Turtle errand, and then you usually were chip-driven and knew little of where you went. The compound was where the Turtles provided food, clothing and housing for their full-time memo disk employees. That was a significant fringe benefit that went with the job—

It was also, Sork thought bitterly, the same fringe benefit that was given to the inmates in any prison. Although working for the Turtles paid well, it was even worse than being in one of those old-time armies. It was not a human life at all.

While outside—

Sork shook his head. He didn't want to be outside, either. He wanted to be *free.*

That thought would have startled most of the humans outside the Turtle compound if they had heard him say it. They felt free enough. After all, the Turtles did not interfere with human activities in any *physical* way. They hadn't outlawed war, for instance. They had simply traded Turtle technology for military hardware until every nation on Earth was overflowing with Turtle aircraft, Turtle ground vehicles, Turtle appliances and Turtle machines—and had nothing left to conduct a decent war with. The Turtles hadn't abolished nations. They had simply insisted on making their trading contracts with smaller political units, and over a generation or two the superpowers had simply dissolved away. Every human being on Earth knew that the Age of the Turtles was a time of unparalleled peace and plenty for most of the human race. Now human beings lived longer and more prosperously than ever. Humans were generally unmolested by the Turtles—not many humans ever even saw one—as long as they didn't interfere with trade.

It was different, though, with those particular human beings who had become memmies.

When you signed up to work in the Turtle treaty compounds as a memo disk employee, your life changed. By human standards, it wasn't even a comfortable life. The Turtles lived cold. The frigid air of their underground parts of the compound were edged with their acrid muskiness. Their odor was as penetrating as menthol, as eye-tearing as ammonia and, when you got too much of it, as foul as an exhumed grave.

But the memmies had something the free people in the outside world never had. They had access to Turtle technology. Almost all of it.

For all the good it did them, Sork Quintero thought savagely. You could operate any Turtle machine, perform every Turtle task, however complex . . . but, once the memo disk was out, you couldn't any longer remember how.

———

Sork knew where his direct superior, Litlun, would be waiting for him. His brother, Kiri, would be in the same place, because the brothers had arranged to work the same shifts so that neither would have an advantage over the other with Sue-Ling Quong. But when Sork arrived at the Turtle "refectory" Kiri was not there yet, and Litlun himself was in a part of the place where neither Sork nor any other human could go.

The Turtle was "at meal."

That was to say, Litlun was taking that part of his daily nourishment which did not involve actual eating. To be sure, Turtles did eat in more or less the same way as humans, now and then. Sometimes they even ate organic food, like Taur steaks, or the tart, heavy globes of redfruit—or simply a clutch of grass or weed or a tree limb that came to hand. More often what they ate was inorganic materials. It seemed that almost any kind of matter could form part of a Turtle's diet, since they did not depend on what they chewed and digested to supply them with energy, only with raw materials to replace the cells of their bodies as they wore out. The Turtles' life-giving energy came from a different source entirely. It came directly from radiation.

For that reason, what Litlun and half a dozen other Turtles were doing was basking. They were lying belly up in a sealed room, with a crystal panel through which Sork could look, but which he dared not pass. He was well aware that the radiation inside that room would kill him. Even the Turtles lay there with their eyes covered by the nictitating membranes that prevented blindness.

The Turtles, however, were soaking the radiation up. It was presumably what they had evolved to live on, ages past, on that mysterious home planet no human being had ever seen. But even through the shielding crystal, the light from the globes on the ceiling of that chamber felt as though it were scorching Sork's eyes.

"We'll have to wait, I guess," said a familiar voice, and Sork turned to see his brother, Kiri.

Genetically Sork and Kiri were identical, but few people would have believed that in looking at them. They were the same height, almost to a centimeter; they had the same jet hair, straight as string and almost as coarse; their eyes were the same piercing black. But they were antiparticles of each other. Kiri was an electron, Sork a positron; they were identical in every respect, save in sign. Where Sork was slow and thoughtful Kiri was always in motion; Kiri was the athlete and the impatient one. "You were trying to make time with Sue-ling, weren't you?" Kiri added, feinting a punch at his brother's shoulder—but grinning as he did it.

Sork dodged automatically. He was sensitive to everything that concerned Sue-ling Quong, most sensitive of all when it came from his brother. The trouble was that in their contest for her undivided love, Kiri had the advantage of seniority. It was he who had first met Sue-ling, at her old school called Harvard, while running an errand for the Turtles. He not only met her, but fell in love with her. When her school was abandoned, it was Kiri who persuaded her to come to work in the Turtle compound.

And then all the complications followed when Sork, too, fell in love with her, and Sue-ling found herself loving both at once.

It made for confusion. Not for the first time, Sork wondered if the Turtles had made a mistake in accepting them for memmie duty. Both of them had volunteered, of course, as soon as they were old enough, but the unusual configuration of their brains had bothered the memmie surgeons. He remembered lying there on the operating table, his entire head numb from the jaw up, his eyes frozen on a point in the operating-room ceiling but his ears missing nothing, while the surgeons debated whether the abnormal configurations of their brains disqualified them for the memo disk implant.

In the long run, the surgeons had decided to go ahead with implant sockets for both of the Quintero twins. But sometimes Sork wished they had not.

He turned his mind away from the familiar track. "I just wanted to get some more study tapes from her," he said, without total truth.

Kiri shook his head in mock reproval. He didn't have to say that he thought it was a waste of time. His expression, his whole body stance, said it for him. What he did say was only, "Memo disks."

"Oh, I know," Sork said wearily, "you think we don't need to *learn* things any more. Just slip in a disk, and then—and then we're somebody else. Like us."

Kiri's face showed compassion. "Well," he said, trying to sympathize with his brother's drives, "what now? Some new theory of how the universe began?"

Sork complained, "It's all so confusing! They keep talking about people I've never heard of and things I can't even imagine, Kiri! Other universes! Black holes, white holes, wormholes—none of it makes any sense to me. Maybe it doesn't make any sense at all," he conceded unhappily. "The Turtles say they don't believe it. Because the First Mother didn't say it. They call it just human superstition—you know, like alchemy, and phlogiston, and the—what did they call it?—the 'luminiferous ether.'"

Kiri shook his head again, seriously this time. "Not the same," he said briefly.

"Well, I know that. This fellow Hawking must've been pretty bright, from everything they say about him, and so was this other fellow Planck. See, Planck said that at certain levels—very small distances, very high temperatures, all sorts of unusual conditions—the regular laws of physics just didn't apply any more. And then others came along and they said that even time wasn't something that could never be changed. Sometimes cause and effect didn't mean anything, because 'effects' could happen before their 'causes' and—"

Kiri's expression clouded. He was looking over Sork's shoulder, into the Turtles' sunning chamber. "Careful," he whispered. "Did you forget they can hear us, inside there?"

The reminder came too late.

Inside the chamber the Turtles were squawking among themselves, some of them rising, stirring, gazing out indignantly at the human brothers.

The largest of the Turtles, the one whose title was Legate-on-Earth, rose and stalked toward the door, followed by Litlun. "You memmies!" Legate-on-Earth barked through his transposer. "One dislikes such foolish human talk! One wonders if you wish to continue in memmie service!"

"Sorry," Sork muttered rebelliously. "I was just talking with my brother—"

"Do not talk of evil things!" the Turtle hissed, and stalked away.

Litlun remained, drawn up to his full height beside the open door to the basking chamber. Sork retreated, not anxious to expose himself even to the splash of radiation that would come through the opened doorway. He waited for the explosion that would come from his boss for talking "heresy" in the presence of the other Turtles.

Strangely, it was muted. Litlun said only, "Why do you waste your time with such songs?"

"They're not really songs," Sork said.

The Turtle glared at him. It was hard to read Turtle expressions at best; Turtle faces were stiff-tissued, darkly rigid, their armored eyes set wide apart and moving independently in a way that still disconcerted Sork.

"They are songs," Litlun insisted, "and wicked ones. They are a Taur disease! A hallucination that affects mature males, rendering them unfit for useful labor and dangerous to their handlers! They are not proper for you—especially because of the circumstances of yourself and your egg mate, which leave you vulnerable to disturbances."

"My egg mate? Do you mean Kiri?" Sork challenged the Turtle: "Are you saying that there is something special about us?"

The Turtle hissed thoughtfully to itself, glaring at him. There was no doubt, Sork thought, that Litlun did know something, almost certainly knew as much as the twins themselves did about the circumstances of their birth.

But if so he was not willing to discuss it. "Forget these songs," he ordered. "Leave them to the Taurs. Now come with me to draw your chips. It is time to begin your work." And then he turned and waddled away, fluffing the radiation-absorbing webs attached to his limbs in satisfaction, like any human patting his belly after a feast.

In the "office" of the Turtle, Sork went to work under his memo disk.

The disk fit easily into the slot in the back of his skull. Memo disks were gold and plastic, and not really disks; the objects were almost egg-shaped in plan section. As with everything the Turtles did, there was a practical reason for that: the shape made sure that there was only one way that the disks would fit into the receptor that had been surgically implanted in his skull.

Sork Quintero was at work instantly, as soon as the memo disk slipped into its slot. The memories and data it recorded were now more a part of him than his own recollections; all the thoughts and worries that had troubled him away from the disk were wiped away.

The work that Sork did for the Turtles was a little bit like bookkeeping, keeping track of all the Turtle exports. It was an important job. Sork's work was quite essential to the mercantile Turtles.

In a sense, this job was a promotion. As a memmie, Sork Quintero's work had been sometimes fascinating, usually exhausting, sometimes physically repulsive. In his nine years in Turtle service Sork had done almost every kind of job, from piloting Turtle aircraft to working in the slaughterhouse detail, slicing up Taur carcasses for the kitchens of the compound. It didn't matter what assignment was given to him. Under the disk, Sork was an expert at them all. Any memmie was, because with the appropriate memo disk in place in his skull, he could do any job the Turtles didn't care to do themselves. Which was almost every job they considered boring, or physically stressful for them in the hot, damp planet of Earth.

So what made Sork a particularly promotable memmie wasn't his skill. The Turtles supplied the skills. What they prized most in a memmie was dependability. So many humans were lazy, or drank when they were off duty, or got involved in personal affairs and came late or sick to work. Not Sork Quintero—

Well, Sork would have had to admit to himself out of fairness, not *often* Sork Quintero. It was true that there had been a time when he had done a good deal more drinking than his brother liked—or that the Turtles ever found out about. But that had stopped when Sue-ling came into his life, because Sue-ling didn't like it either. And it was a fact that Sork was always on time and never complained about his assignments—at least, not out loud where the Turtles might hear. His Turtle masters liked those traits in their servants. That was why they had "promoted" him (of course, it wasn't the kind of promotion that brought him any more money, and certainly not any more power) to helping to keep their accounts, because that was an area very important to the Turtles.

They didn't want any problems there. It never occurred to the Turtles to suspect that Sork Quintero did not want to be a memmie any more.

———

When the day's shift was through, Sork and Kiri left the Turtle work area. Without discussing it, they did what both knew they had been going to do: They headed for Sue-ling Quong's rooms in the hospital area.

Sue-ling had known they were coming, too; so by the time they arrived she was awake, showered, dressed, ready to spend time with the two men she loved. Hand in hand with both of them, she led the way to the hospital refectory. It was breakfast for her, perhaps supper for the two men, but all three had the same thing—Taur steaks, with fried potatoes and huge glasses of fruit juice and, when they were through, cups of hot black coffee.

As the Taur servant filled their cups it mooed politely. Sue-ling said, "Yes, thank you, it was very good."

Kiri chuckled, but it was Sork who put the thought into words. "How do you know what the thing was saying?" he demanded.

"She isn't a thing," Sue-ling said defensively. "Taurs are really quite intelligent, and of course she was saying she hoped we enjoyed our meal."

"Doesn't that strike you as strange?" Sork pursued. "I mean, what is it she hoped we enjoyed eating? Taur!"

Sue-ling shrugged, annoyed. "The fact that they're meat animals doesn't mean we have to treat them like, well, *brutes*! Kseen has been working here in the refectory for two years, and she is really quite sweet. Just watch her—oh, heaven! What do you suppose is the matter with her?"

For the female Taur had suddenly gone down on her knees, mooing in misery. She had dropped the tray of dishes, and when she turned to look at the three humans, the broad bovine face was racked in misery.

"She's sick," Sork declared.

But his brother was shaking his head. "No," he whispered, listening.

And Sue-ling heard it too. There was another sound, barely heard—a wordless keening from far away. It climbed in volume and pitch, and it was dire.

Sue-ling blinked at the brothers, suddenly afraid. "Is that the Turtles who are making that awful noise?" she whispered.

Kiri nodded somberly. Sork said, his voice taut, "If we can hear this much, this far away, they must be screaming up a storm." He didn't have to say that most of the vocal range of Turtle sounds was well outside the frequencies audible to humans.

"I've never heard anything like it," Sue-ling said.

Sork, whose entire life had been spent in the Turtle compound, nodded slowly. "Nor I. Not even when they worship their goddess. This is something brand-new."

"It must be something really terrible to get them so upset," Sue-ling said, gazing at the Taur, now drunkenly picking herself up and staggering out of the room.

And Sork, his eyes suddenly gleaming with a savage light: "You bet it must—and, oh, God, I hope so!"

Where do the aiodoi sing? If one must ask that one may never know, for the aiodoi are not in a "where." Still, their songs are heard everywhere, except in a few places where those who dwell there have never learned to listen, while the aiodoi themselves hear everything, always, even the faint old songs from distant Earth.

————

"If you remember when we talked about Hawking's idea of what we called 'the eternal anaconda of time,' you probably also remember that we mentioned that the universe was born out of 'vacuum fluctuations.' What we didn't do was tell you what was in the vacuum to fluctuate, or how it fluxed.

"There's a good reason for that. The reason is that we don't know the answer.

"Still, we do know quite a lot about vacuum fluctuations in general, and that's what we're going to take up today. To begin with, there's no such thing as 'empty space.' There isn't any such thing as a law of conservation of matter and energy any more, either, except perhaps statistically, over time. The ironclad bookkeeping limitations were repealed by Werner Heisenberg, as a logical consequence of his uncertainty principle.

"According to the uncertainty principle, the conservation of energy doesn't have to be exact at every moment. 'Borrowing' is allowed. At some point temporary particles can be created out of nothing at all. However, they have to be 'paid back' later on by disappearing. The new law allows that they can last for a period, which is written as delta-T, in an amount, delta-E, such that delta-T times delta-E is roughly equal to Planck's constant, which you all of course remember is written as h.

"We don't usually see these particles appearing and disappearing before our eyes. There are several reasons for that: they are tiny; they don't last very long; and we don't usually look in the right place. It would be possible for us to see them, I think, or at least to see very clear proof that they exist, if we had some stable superheavy elements to look at. The heaviest natural element we have is uranium, with ninety-two protons. Even the artificially created elements, the ones that are called 'transuranic,' aren't very much heavier. If we had some really massive elements—say, with atomic numbers of two hundred protons or more—the particles we're looking for could be counted on to appear inside those atoms, and they would have definite, measurable effects on the atoms so we could detect them. As it is, they appear only randomly—but they do it everywhere, and all the time.

"Space, all space, is literally filled with these particles, winking in and out of existence. And that is why space is not truly empty.

"That's another reason why a good many physicists refuse to use the term 'empty space' any more. They even go back to the old idea of the 'luminiferous ether'—well, not really to that; but at least to the notion that there is some sort of universal frame, or what we call a rigging vector field, which pervades all of space. You remember, I hope, that some of those scientists, particularly the old Jagiellonian group, in Krakow, Poland, have ventured to use the word 'neoether' to describe just what the invisible something is that fills the universe.

"I suppose you are now beginning to think that next week we'll be reviving phlogiston and the Philosopher's

Stone. No. We don't go that far. But all the same, we have to admit the notion that there is *something* that exists *everywhere*."

————

But the aiodoi simply sang on, for that song, like all other songs, they had been hearing forever.

3

~~~~~~~

Four thousand kilometers from the Turtle compound at
Kansas City, Captain Francis Krake looked around him
and felt almost at peace.

That was a blessing he had longed for, for a long time.
Just being on an air field revived some wonderful, aching
old memories—the memories of that almost forgotten
Second Lieutenant Francis Krake of World War II. Nineteen years old. The world before him then. There was the
memory of basic training in Miami Beach, flight cadet
school in Mississippi, two-engine transitional training in
Oklahoma—and, in all of those places everywhere, the
dayrooms with their jukeboxes blaring *That Old Black
Magic* and *My Reverie* and all those other soppy, senti-
mental, *wonderful* songs of parted lovers and joyous reunions. There had been real reunions in Krake's
memories, too; the precious forty-eight hour passes with
a friendly pilot to take you home for a day; that last
overseas leave when Madeleine had promised to wait for
her airman to come safely back home from the war. . . .

It did not do to think about Madeleine. Krake knew
that, at last, the wait would have turned out to be too
long.

It didn't do to think of the end of it, either, when
Krake had known for certain that he was going to die
. . . until that incredible stub-winged Turtle scout ship

had appeared miraculously to pull him from the waters of the Coral Sea. They had certainly saved his life. . . .

Or they had stolen it from him, one or the other.

Now here he was, at an air field again. It was his kind of field. It certainly was not an "airport," like that crowded, crazy place at Kansas City where he'd boarded the commercial flight to take him here to New Mexico. This place was relaxed, slow-moving—no giant liners inching toward a takeoff strip, just a few dozen parked light planes and a sign that said "rentals." And when he had phoned that pretty doctor at the Turtle compound to make sure nothing new had come from the orbiter, he entered the rental office. Inside, a shapely young woman looked him over appreciatively and said, "An aircraft? Certainly, sir. You'll want a low-speed, hover-capable two-seater, I suppose? Any particular model?"

Krake shrugged. "Whatever you think best," he said, and glanced away as she gave him a warm smile before leading the way out of the rental shack. He felt embarrassed. It wasn't that he didn't recognize the interest in her eyes. It wasn't that he was no longer sexually functional, either. At least, he didn't think he was—though with all those long space voyages since the Turtles had picked him up, and no human companionship except for Marco and Daisy Fay—and Daisy Fay, though certainly female, being what Daisy Fay was these days—he was no longer entirely sure.

Anyway, there was one thing decisively wrong with this pretty woman. She did not look in the least like Madeleine.

But he followed her with a spring in his step—caused, maybe, by the idea of flying a real airplane again after all the subjective years in Turtle spacecraft. He was prepared to find that these new planes would be a little tricky to fly. You had to expect that, after all these years. Krake thought he might have to taxi around the field for a while, until he got used to the new controls. But it couldn't be too hard. The planes were sure to have wings, flaps, an engine and landing gear; and if you could fly a

P-38 in aerial combat in the Pacific you could fly *any-thing*. . . .

He was wrong about that. It turned out that you couldn't.

When the woman opened the cockpit hatch for him, Krake pulled back in sudden wrath. The controls! There wasn't any joystick, no rudder pedals, no throttles. All there was was a keyboard, like an adding machine. That was it.

"Of course," said the woman from just behind him, her voice as warm as her gaze had been, "you'll need the piloting memo disk. We'll be happy to supply it at no extra charge, so if you'll just—oh," said her voice, its tone now completely different. Krake turned to stare at her. She was looking wide-eyed at the back of his head. "But you aren't a memmie, are you?"

"No," he said tightly.

"Oh," she said, trying to adjust to the surprising new information. "Well, I'm afraid that *all* our planes are adapted for memo disk operation only, sir—"

"Then what do you have that isn't?" he snapped. "A jeep? A bicycle? A pogo stick?"

"What's a 'pogo stick'?" she asked curiously. "But we don't have one, anyway. We do, however, have some surface cars—though not very fast or large ones, of course. But these do have pure manual controls. . . ."

———

So a few hours later, Krake was driving his rented car along the narrow New Mexican road. It wasn't a plane. But it was taking him where he wanted to go, and Francis Krake began to feel at peace again.

He marveled at the things he saw out of the car window. Could this really be the land he was born in? He had been prepared for changes, because they said the climate was all different these days. They said that every year the monsoon rains spiraling up from Baja grew heavier now, transforming the arid plains he had known —but he was not prepared for *this*. It was just as hot as he remembered, but everything else was different. Alders and willows instead of a few isolated cottonwoods, groves of redfruit and fields of corn and soybeans instead of the dry, flat, empty lands of his boyhood, with nothing but sagebrush and mesquite as far as the eye could see.

Francis Krake was not a man given to self-doubt. All the same, he wondered if he should have come on this trip. It could be a complete waste of time—almost certainly would be. Things changed in a few hundred years. There wouldn't be anything left of his childhood home. Certainly there would be no one he knew still alive. There wouldn't even be anything he could recognize.

Still, until his crew members were out of the Turtle hospital, Francis Krake had nothing but time to waste.

He still wished he had an airplane instead of this strange, hot, flimsy three-wheeler. Any kind of airplane —well, no, he thought. Not *any* kind of airplane. He didn't want anything as fast and tricky as the crippled P-38 he'd been flying when the engine died and he ditched over the Coral Sea long ago. Say, one of those slow, easy UC-78s he had flown at the transition school, or even a Piper Cub. Any kind of plane at all would do—

Except the only kind that had been available at the airport at Clovis, New Mexico. The kind that you needed a memo disk to operate.

Francis Krake had no intention of, ever, becoming a memmie.

It was a good thing, he thought, that when the Turtle scout ship fished him out of the drink in 1945, they hadn't developed memo disks for humans yet. They couldn't have, of course, since Francis Krake himself had been their first human—captive? Might as well use that word, he reflected, because it was the only one that fit. They had saved his life and, as far as they could, treated him very well. But they hadn't let him go home.

The woods began to open up as he drove. Now and then he passed cornfields, and one or two plots of what he

recognized as sugar beets. That was all new since his
time. It wasn't cattle country any more. Krake supposed
that there probably wasn't any such thing as cattle country any more, anywhere in the world, not since the Turtles had brought the first herds of that new and better
kind of livestock, the Taurs, to Earth. He did see an occasional cluster of Taurs, placidly munching away at their
graze in the late evening sun, but none of the four-legged,
forty-acre cattle he remembered from his youth. Curiously, there weren't even any human beings in sight. He
had driven for most of an hour without passing a soul on
the road, and hardly a building.

New Mexico had always been thinly populated—but
this was something else entirely.

In all the subjective years of Francis Krake's star
traveling in the service of the Turtles he had thought
about Earth often. Nevertheless, he had not, he realized,
really understood what it had become with the benevo-
lent partnership of the Turtles. He certainly had not expected to find the human race so sparse on the ground.
Had humanity just frozen in its development, like aborig-
ines when Europeans arrived, overwhelmed by Turtle
technological superiority?

He knew, of course, that all military activities had
been terminated. The Turtles did not believe in war, or
armed conquest, or violence of any kind. But what else
had happened on Earth? He knew there were still big
cities—even old Kansas City had been largely rebuilt,
outside the Turtle compound. But how many people, actually, were still left?

On impulse, Krake slowed down. More or less at random he stopped the car by a field planted with soybeans,
not because he was particularly interested in them but
because he was tired of driving. A small herd of Taurs
was methodically cropping the weeds between the rows
of beans, careful not to harm the crop.

The great heads were turning placidly toward him.

"Hello, babe," he said, reaching out to stroke the head of the nearest. It did not respond, merely gazed at him as it placidly munched away at its fistfuls of growing things.

They were ranch stock—each one had a brand on its broad, hairy face, just under the massive cheekbone. He saw with regret that they were all females. If only there had been a nearly mature male with them! The males, up until the point where they were turned into steers at least, were much more alert and intelligent. Some of them made good house servants, or manual workers, before they were sent off for slaughter. But the females had only the most limited intelligence.

Yet they faced the same fate. They were so gentle, he thought. Did they know they were about to be slaughtered?

Surely they did, if what was said about the Taurs was true. Krake had not spent much time with Taurs; there hadn't been any on the scout ship that rescued him from the Coral Sea, and he'd only seen a handful of them in his contacts with the Turtles since then. He wasn't sure what to make of Taurs. Turtles said they were more or less intelligent. (But then why did the Turtles treat them like beef cattle or slaves?) Turtles also didn't like to talk about some things connected with the Taurs, and so Krake hadn't pushed his questioning too far. Something about adult male Taurs being—what? Dangerous? Crazy? Or merely just, for some Turtle reason that only Turtles could understand, offensive to them?

That wasn't the biggest puzzle. The great wonder was why, if the Taurs were as intelligent as people said, they so meekly allowed themselves to be enslaved, herded, castrated and finally butchered for food.

Krake retreated to the shade of a redfruit grove across the road to think about what to do next. In the shelter of the broad, leathery crimson leaves he pulled out the map the young woman had given him in Clovis and frowned over it. "Of course," she had apologized, "this doesn't show *every* little place in New Mexico. But I think the one you're looking for was about—here." And she'd penciled a cross along a road.

The trouble was, he didn't know exactly where he was. This New Mexico simply did not look like anything he remembered. He folded the map. Then, realizing that he was hungry, he plucked some of the fruit. The big, heavy globes were still yellowish, not quite the ruby red of ripeness, and they were more tart than he liked. He tossed most of the fruit across the fence for the Taurs in the soyfield: They probably liked that stuff better than he.

And then the first car appeared on the road.

———

It was really a light, four-wheeled truck. In the back, gripping the roof of the cab, stood a tall young male Taur, still bearing its horns, and the driver was a young woman in overalls and a visored cap.

She pulled up behind Krake's three-wheeler, peering into the grove. "Hello there," she called. "Having trouble?"

He shook his head as he approached, but he was hardly looking at the girl. His eyes were on the Taur. The huge, strange creature was bobbing its head, too. Krake decided it was nearly mature, its horns already sharp-pointed and, even in the sunlight, with a hint of the adult glow that would soon suffuse them. Its purple-blue eyes were fixed on Krake. The space captain jumped back as the Taur vaulted lightly over the side of the truck, sniffing at the strange human.

"Easy there, Thrayl," the young woman commanded. The Taur obediently backed away, and she said, "He won't hurt you, you know."

Krake kept his eyes fastened on the animal. Curiously, he wasn't afraid. There was something about the way the Taur held himself, the way he gazed at Krake out of those immense purply eyes, that was reassuring—almost as though the thing *liked* him.

He turned to the young woman. "I don't know much about Taurs," he began—and then, as he got his first good look at her face: "My God!"

The Taur made a worried noise, and the young

woman drew back. "Is something wrong?" she asked. "Are you all right?"

"All right?" he repeated. Then he shook his head. "I —I was just surprised, that's all. You, uh, you look a lot like somebody I used to know, and it was kind of a shock there for a minute." He collected himself and went on to finish the sentence, still staring at her. "I started to say that I don't know much about Taurs," he apologized. "I've seen them, of course, but we didn't have much contact with them on my ship." She looked even more surprised at that, as though he had said he were unfamiliar with sunrises, or with rain. Then, belatedly answering her question, "I'm fine, I just took a break from driving. My name's Francis Krake. I used to live around here."

"Moon Bunderan," she responded, offering her hand out of the window. She looked at him curiously. "You used to live around here, and you don't know much about Taurs?"

"It was a long time ago."

"It must've been," she agreed skeptically, but she opened the door and climbed down. She was very young, he saw, not much older than the Taur bull who was dancing nimbly around on his four-toed feet, keeping his great eyes fixed on Krake. And she was not, he realized, really very much like the woman he had taken her for at first. On the other hand, she was definitely rather pretty—a fact which was getting more and more important to Francis Krake, in the unaccustomed company of all these humans on Earth—though there was a look of worry in her face that he didn't understand. As she turned to close the door he saw that her hair was brushed smoothly into a pony tail. There was no implant scar on the back of her head.

"You're not a memmie," he said, a little bit startled, a lot pleased.

"No, of course I'm not," she said, surprised in her turn. "Why would I be? We don't have memmies here, except a few in the cities. And," peering up at him, making the same discovery, "you're not either."

He grinned. "Sorry. I said I've been away for a long

time, and at the airport almost everybody I talked to wore a memo disk. I didn't mean anything by it."

She nodded to show she accepted his explanation, and then said suddenly, "I could have been, though. I thought of it once."

He looked at her doubtfully. She said, "It was because I wanted to be a doctor. We used to have one—he delivered me, and he was our doctor for years."

"And he was a memmie?"

"No! That was the point," she explained. "I loved Dr. Tetford more than any other man but my father, and I wanted to be like him. But when he died there wasn't anybody. One of the ranch hands volunteered to take his place. I hated that idea—but he did it; he went to the city, and got a slot cut in his head, and when he came back he had the disks to stick in his skull. Oh," she said, in justice, "he was all right as a doctor, I guess. But he was still the same ignorant herder! And—I just couldn't be like him."

"No, of course not," Krake said, looking at her with either curiosity or sympathy, he wasn't sure which. He changed the subject. "Maybe you can help me. I'm looking for a place called Portales."

She blinked at him. "Portales? But you're on the Portales ranch now."

He blinked back at her. "I'm not talking about a ranch. I mean the town."

She shook her head. "There isn't any town called Portales anymore," she said positively.

"But I used to live there."

"Mister," she said, "nobody's lived there for a *long* time. It isn't even a town anymore. My dad's grandfather said the floods got it a hundred years ago—"

"Floods! In Portales?"

She nodded. "After the Turtles built that undersea baffle in the North Pacific. It was because of the Dry Time," she explained. "My dad's grandfather used to tell us about it. There was irrigation farming here once. Then the aquifers were just pumped dry—no water left at all.

The desert came back. There wasn't any way to live here then, so people just moved away—"

"You were talking about floods, not drought!"

She nodded earnestly. "That was why the Turtles did all that macroengineering. They wanted to make it possible to farm here again—to do us good, you see. So they built the undersea baffle that diverted a warm tropical current past the Aleutians and through the Bering Strait, and—"

"Miss Bunderan," Krake said sharply, "why are you telling me all this?"

She was frowning at him, obviously wondering. "I'm explaining why the town's gone. When the weather really began to change, there were some really bad floods. The whole town just got wiped out. I don't think there's much left."

"I still want to find it," he said stubbornly. "Meanwhile, I need a place to camp for the night."

She studied him appraisingly. "All you want is a campsite?"

"That's right. I've got all the gear in the car. I just want a place to set up my tent." He hesitated, then offered an explanation. "I guess you could say I'm on a kind of a vacation here."

She nodded, then reached a quick decision. "You could probably just camp anywhere you liked around here. Nobody's likely to chase you, as long as you don't start a brush fire or leave too much junk around. If you want permission, you're welcome to camp anywhere on our land."

He looked at her curiously. Flushing, she said, "Well, it's not *our* land, exactly. A Turtle company bought up all the old deeds after they changed the climate—seemed fair enough, people say, because it sure wasn't worth anything before that."

"So they helped you by changing the climate. And now they own the land," Krake said, his tone non-judgmental.

"My dad says it's fair," she said firmly, and that closed the question. "Anyway, he's foreman on the ranch, but right now he's off at the far end with my brothers. I know they'd be glad enough to have you. Our headquarters is just about ten kilometers down the road, at the fork. If you take the left-hand road it'll take you to where the town used to be. At least, I think it will. There's a stream there for water. Tell me, what are you on vacation from?"

Krake turned and looked at her. She was in the shadow of the redfruit grove now, and her face was shaded by the tall rows of trees, the big leaves dark maroon and thick as leather. The air was sweet with the scent of the yellow, bell-shaped blooms, edged with the odd, sharp odor that drifted from the Taurs across the road.

She said apologetically, "Excuse me for being so nosy, but you look kind of lost. Is there something I could help you with, besides finding that old town?"

He shook his head, forcing his eyes to focus on her face again, to make sure that it was not the face he had dreamed of finding again. It wasn't. This young woman was the present, alive and vital in this strange new now.

"That's all right," he said. Then he took the plunge: "I'm on vacation from space, Miss Bunderan. I'm a waveship captain."

She stared at him. "You're *what*? I didn't know that was possible! I thought only Turtles could fly the interstellar ships."

"Almost always," he agreed, "but I'm a special case. This particular ship is chartered to me, for my own use. I earned it, too. The Turtles leased it to me to operate on their behalf, so I could do the things they don't like to do themselves. They don't like actually going down to the surface of planets much, you know, unless the planets are a lot colder and drier than Earth. I suppose that's because of what their home planet is like, but as to that I don't have a clue. I've seen the place from space, but that's all."

"But you've seen a lot of other planets?"

He grinned at her. "Eleven," he admitted. "At least, altogether there were eleven that I actually landed on. If you count the planets I've seen in the ship's screens, from orbit, probably a couple of hundred. They're not all worth landing on, you know."

"Eleven!" she breathed.

He said, "Well, that was over a lot of years. Not that many *subjective* years; most of my travel was at pretty nearly light speed, so time dilation made it go fast. You understand about time dilation—?"

He looked at her inquiringly. She nodded to show that she knew what time dilation meant. "You look young to have done all that," she observed.

Krake managed another grin. "I was born in 1923."

She blinked at him. "I beg your pardon?"

"1923. That's a date," he explained. "It's the year I was born, the way human beings used to count the years before the Turtles came. 1923 was what we called a vintage year for boy babies; I was born just in time for the war."

"War," the girl repeated flatly. It was a word out of the dim past.

"Oh, yes, we had wars then. This was a big one—we called it World War Two—and I was right in the middle of it. The Turtles must have been cruising around the area, checking us out from a distance. Then, when everybody's attention was on the war, they came in for some sampling missions. That was when they picked me up. 1945. I was twenty-two years old. I'd been flying combat for nearly a year, and the war was almost over. I was a fighter pilot, you see. I got shot down in the Coral Sea, strafing a surfaced Japanese submarine."

He paused, remembering that time. "It didn't scare me much right at first," he said. "I thought there was a good chance that somebody from a carrier might pick me up—"

He shrugged. "They didn't, though. Nobody came near me. I drifted a week in a rubber boat before I saw anything but clouds and waves, and then the thing I saw didn't belong to human beings. It was a Turtle scout craft exploring the planet. I don't think saving me was exactly intended as an act of mercy. Turtles don't really operate that way. What they wanted was to collect a specimen of the human race without attracting attention. But they did save my life while they were doing it."

He stared into space. "That was centuries ago by Earth time—not quite fifteen years by my watch and my diary. I guess you know what happens to time when you're traveling near the speed of light—oh, sorry. I asked you that already, didn't I?"

Moon looked at him sympathetically. The man was troubled, she could see. She wanted to touch him reassuringly, but, after all, he was almost a complete stranger.

He thought for a moment, brooding. Then he shrugged. "I tried to learn their language, but that took a long time. They had to develop the transposer first, you see. You know how it is with Turtles and Taurs. Nobody can make the sounds of their languages."

"I can, a little. Taur, I mean, not Turtle," she offered. "Thrayl's a Taur, and he understands me, and I understand him."

He looked at her blankly. "That's nice. Anyway, the Turtles are smart. I finally worked out enough language so I could understand most of what they said in their language, and they could figure out my English. They interrogated me. They—put me to work." He grimaced. "That was the first work I did for them. Helping them understand the human race. I told them all I could about the Earth, because I figured they couldn't make things worse than the war already had." He paused for a somber moment before going on. "And I worked on their ship, and after they saw I could run it well enough they made me a deal. The Turtles are honest traders. They do pay for services. So when they had tested me out and they were quite sure I could handle it they leased me a starship of my own. I've still got it. I've been running it on charters for them ever since, me and my crew."

His voice trailed off. To break the silence, Moon offered, "I never met anybody who'd been in a 'war' before. I think in some ways that's the best part of the Turtles coming—at least we don't have those terrible wars any more. The Turtles don't approve of them."

Krake laughed sharply. "And do you know why? Have you ever heard of the Sh'shrane?"

Moon Bunderan thought for a moment. "N—no, I don't think so—"

"Well, they're why the Turtles don't believe in war," he declared harshly. "Don't think it's some kind of moral superiority for the Turtles. They fought the Sh'shrane when they had to, all right. They just don't *need* to go to war when they're dealing with people like us."

Under the curly beard, Moon Bunderan could see that his jaw was pulsing. "Haven't you noticed?" he cried. "You don't have your freedom any more, either. That's a little detail they didn't bother to tell me when they picked me up—that they were going to take over the planet—and the whole human race along with it!"

Behind them there was a worried, warning rumble from the Taur, and Francis Krake realized he was frightening the young woman. "Oh, hell, Maddy," he mumbled, "I'm sorry. I just got a little over-excited. Tell your Taur I didn't mean any harm."

"Thrayl knows that," she declared. "It's all right." And then, after a moment, "Who's Maddy?"

He blinked at her. "What?"

"You called me Maddy. Is that someone you know?"

He looked away unhappily. "Not anymore," he said. "Not for a very long time now . . . and not ever again."

What Moon Bunderan wished was that she could spend the whole day with this exciting stranger. But it was impossible; she and Thrayl were supposed to be going into town for supplies for her mother, and finally, reluctantly, she let the man from space go about his search for the old town of Portales.

Then he was gone.

Moon didn't want that to happen. On her way to town, she made a conscious effort to keep her mind on him. That wasn't hard, at least at first, for Captain Francis Krake was certainly the most interesting thing that had happened to her in a long time. But that didn't last, and then the nagging worries at the back of her mind, that she had managed to suppress for a brief time, began insistently to come back.

Worriedly, she glanced into the rear-view mirror. She saw Thrayl's purple-blue eyes gazing soberly and insistently into her own. And, sickly, she knew that there couldn't be any doubt about it.

She wouldn't have to tell Thrayl what was going to happen to him. He already knew.

It wasn't fair! But what could she do about it?

Moon Bunderan wished sadly that Thrayl could be sitting next to her in the cab, as he had done when he was smaller. That was another of those things that wasn't possible any more. Thrayl was too big to fit there comfortably any more, but that wasn't the real reason. More important was that it would cause talk if anyone saw. Making a pet of a calf was one thing—silly, of course, but not *wrong*. But it was not all right at all when the calf had become a grown Taur bull, with horns that had already begun to glow with the adult light that soon would be darkened forever. . . .

Moon Bunderan shivered, because she knew exactly what was in store for her pet Taur. She had learned the basics from her childhood at the ranch, and filled in the rest at the university, when she majored in Taur husbandry. Like everyone in her class she had had to take her turn at branding the Taurs and giving them their routine shots. It wasn't at all difficult. What made it easy was the nature of the Taurs themselves. The great creatures came in willingly and lay there, unresisting and passive, while Moon did her work. Sometimes they even patted her affectionately with their hard, three-fingered hands before they left. The young males brought in to be castrated and dehorned were just as unquestioningly cooperative. She had done it herself at college, the huge, powerful Taurs submitting themselves to being manacled on the work table. The manacles were necessary not because any one of them would ever resist, but because the agony of the operation might cause some involuntary shudder or muscle twitch and thus disturb the concentration of the surgeon.

Then, when it was over, the Taurs would get up carefully, made cautious by the pain of their wounds, and leave without complaint.

Just as Thrayl would . . . if she didn't prevent it.

———

In the town Thrayl trotted obediently behind his mistress as she ran her errands. He easily shouldered the great sacks of concentrated feed supplement for the Taur calves, loaded them into the back of the truck, squatted outside the drugstore and the hardware store and the clothing shop as she picked up her list of needed items.

When she came out of the hardware store Thrayl was sitting at the curb with his great legs folded, eyes blank. "Listening to the songs" was how he described it to her, in his own impossibly unpronounceable language, but to Moon's eye it closely resembled what she had heard called "meditation." When she touched his warm, hard shoulder the great purple-blue eyes focused on her at once. He rose quickly to take the sack from her hands.

The shopkeeper had followed her outside. He looked at Thrayl, then glanced at Moon Bunderan, wiping his hands on his apron. "Getting a little too old to keep, isn't he?" he said neutrally.

Moon didn't answer the storekeeper. To Thrayl she said, "Up you go," and as the great Taur lifted himself easily into the back of the truck she nodded good-bye to the man. But the owner of the hardware store was not put off so easily. He had known Moon Bunderan since she was in diapers and was fond of her. He came up to her and put his hand parentally on her arm. "Honey," he said, his voice sorrowful and sympathetic, "I know how you feel. But it's a mistake to make a pet of them. There always comes a time when they have to go. Don't make it worse by putting it off."

Moon gave him a brisk nod. "Good-bye," she said, as politely as she could, getting into the truck and starting the engine. But as she pulled out she caught a glimpse of the storekeeper's eyes, following her wisely, sympathetically.

As Moon drove out of town she was going fast—too fast, she knew, but there was something on her mind.

She had to talk to Thrayl about the thing that was planned for him. She had to do it *now,* she told herself. She had put it off as long as she possibly could, and there wasn't any more time.

But she didn't know what to say to the Taur. She was sobbing softly as she drove along, still speeding, though she knew that speed was no answer to the problem—

Suddenly there was a roaring drumbeat of thunder from over her head.

The truck swerved wildly as, startled, Moon almost lost control. Could so violent an electrical storm have sprung up so quickly? But the sky ahead was almost cloudless above the redfruit groves along the road.

She pulled over to the side of the road as the sound repeated itself—a violent drumming on the roof. It wasn't thunder.

It was Thrayl.

She got out, startled, almost frantic, and gazed up at the Taur. His usually placid demeanor was shattered as he drummed despairingly on the roof of the cab, moaning to himself. "Thrayl! Stop that! What in the world is the matter?" she gasped.

Then he quieted, as suddenly as the tempest had begun. "A bad thing," he rumbled. "It is a very bad thing that has happened."

Moon's hand flew to her throat. "My—my mother?"

But the great head shook somberly. "No. Not a person. Not here. But very bad."

Half reassured, still frightened, she asked, "Then what is it, Thrayl?"

The great head rolled back, the horns thrusting toward the sky, the purple-blue eyes half closed. But the Taur could not find an answer for her. "The smallsongs sing of a bad thing that has happened to the Turtles," he rumbled unhappily. "There is great fear. Great pain. Great—mourning, Moon."

"But it's just the Turtles?" she insisted. He didn't answer that, just shook the immense head. The girl fidgeted for a moment, then forced herself to the thing she didn't want to do.

"Thrayl," she said, "I thought it was something else. About you." She gazed up into the affectionate eyes of the young bull Taur. "Thrayl," she said, speaking slowly and clearly, "do you know what is going to happen to you?"

The Taur stood silent for a moment. Then the great head nodded. He spoke in the Taur tongue, so hopelessly unpronounceable for humans, so hard to comprehend even when the words were known: "It is sung. It is true. It is right." And he gestured sweepingly at his horns, the little apron over his sexual organs—finally at his throat.

Moon shuddered involuntarily. He did know, yet he seemed so calm about it! "But there's more, Thrayl. After they slaughter you, they will—"

She couldn't say the rest of it. Thrayl waited a moment, then pantomimed eating. "So it is sung," he rumbled. "Have heard this song always."

She said fiercely, "But I don't want that to happen! Thrayl, you could hide out in the western plantations! There's plenty of redfruit there, and no one comes there except my own people—I'd always know where they were going, I could warn you. Then, after a while, I could get an aircar and take you somewhere else. Maybe up north! Into the mountains!" He didn't respond, merely looked at her fondly, almost seeming to smile. "But it could happen, Thrayl! It wouldn't be easy, I know. When it gets to be winter again you'll be cold. And there won't be any redfruit plantations there—but you'll be *alive*! I can save you, Thrayl!"

He gazed down at her benignly, with a ghost of a smile in the immense eyes. She waited for a response— waited a long time, until she almost wondered whether he would answer at all.

Then he reached down and touched her brown hair kindly. "Your wish, Moon," he rumbled, and turned away.

————

They were preparing dinner, Moon Bunderan and her mother, but the young woman was not in her customary cheerful mood. Molly Bunderan's eyes turned often to her daughter. The older woman sighed, her heart heavy for the girl. "You're making yourself sick about Thrayl, aren't you?" she observed.

"It isn't *fair*," said Moon.

Her mother thought for a moment, setting the timer for the grill. "Well, honey," she offered reluctantly, "let's see if we can figure something out. Maybe Thrayl doesn't really have to go to the slaughterhouse. Not right away, anyway. I suppose if you wanted your father wouldn't mind if we just dehorned him and sold him to a breeding farm. We wouldn't want to keep him ourselves, of course, but they could put him to stud—"

"No!"

Moon's shout caused her mother to peer at her over her glasses. "I mean," the girl added swiftly, "you know what happens to the studs. They go wild!"

Her mother nodded, acquiescing to the fact of life. Dehorned Taur males who had not been castrated were valuable to ranchers, because they were how the ranchers kept their female Taurs in calf. But an uncastrated, dehorned male quickly lost that placid good temper that marked the Taur race, along with those vestiges of intelligence that made them good slaves. A breeding male had to be kept caged. The females he mounted were always at risk. Often they came out of the breeding pen wounded and bleeding—sometimes even killed, for the fury of the studs was legendary. And no human could ever go near one again, until the physical decline that began with the dehorning reduced the Taur to a raving, raging wreck that it was a kindness to put away.

"I know," her mother sighed. "And it wouldn't keep

him alive very long anyway—you're lucky if you get two seasons out of a Taur stud before you have to put him down, and then you can't even sell the meat."

"I don't want that to happen to him either!"

Molly Bunderan said soothingly, "I know you don't, dear, but some things can't be changed. When the males mature they have to be castrated and dehorned; that's the rule."

"Thrayl wouldn't be any trouble!"

Her mother shook her head. "You hear stories," she said darkly. "Adult male Taurs and human girls—"

"That's ridiculous!" Moon flared. "How could such stories be true? Nobody's ever kept an adult unaltered male Taur!"

"Where there's smoke there's fire," her mother said wisely. "Why, just a couple of years ago, over toward Amarillo, there was that young bull Taur they burned alive—"

Moon shuddered. "I know the story," she said grimly. "I don't believe he did anything. And Thrayl would never hurt me, you know that!"

Her mother turned from the steaming pots to gaze at her tenderly. "I know it's hard for you, Moon dear. I blame myself. I should never have let you make a pet of him."

"But he's *gentle*," Moon begged. "He loves me—not in any ugly way."

"We'll talk about it later," Mrs. Bunderan promised. She patted her daughter's shoulder in awkward sympathy . . . but in her heart Mrs. Bunderan was sure Moon's reasons for objecting to the idea would never matter to her father. What those reasons might really be Molly Bunderan did not even want to think.

She turned back to the practical job of running her part of the ranch. "Vegetables," she said. "What would you like tonight, Moon? Peas and carrots, and a salad? Go find Leesa and tell her to bring in whatever you like."

But she knew that whatever the girl had for dinner that night, the taste would be ashes in her mouth.

———

Half an hour later the men came back from their work at the ends of the ranch. Their hover dropped into the courtyard with a flurry of dust and squawking chickens. The first thing on the agenda was baths for all of them, then they had dinner.

They all ate at once—that was one of the great advantages of having Taur females, like their house Taur, Leesa, to wait on table. The meal was Taur steaks, with vegetables from the little garden the Taur females tended for them. Leesa served them silently, then curled up at the foot of the table to wait for orders, like any good dog.

Moon avoided the female Taur's eyes. It had always been hard for Moon, as a child, to eat the meat of the Taurs they raised, but her father had laughed at her and her mother had insisted, and gradually Moon Bunderan had learned to turn off that part of her mind. Tonight was harder. When the meal was over Moon quickly put the dishes in the washer and slipped out of the house. Her brothers went off in the aircar for an evening in the town.

Then Molly Bunderan sat down with her husband to talk over cups of coffee. He looked tired, she thought. With the boys he had been out in the aircar, inspecting the herds at the far reaches of their land. "Too much rain," he told her. "The streams are up, and we're going to have flooding if we get another big storm. And—" he shook his head—"this afternoon the whole herd was spooked by something. Even the cows took an hour or so to quiet down—God knows what it was."

"We had a little flurry here, too," Molly Bunderan told her husband.

He nodded, considering that, then shrugged. "Well, that's Taurs for you," he said. "They were all all right when we left, anyway. Even the young bulls."

His wife took a deep breath. "That—that brings up something I want to talk to you about," she told him.

Then, when she had her husband's full attention, she told him her worries about Moon and her pet, Thrayl.

"We never should have kept the Taur so long," she said, blaming herself. "It was all right when he was little. She played with him like a doll, remember? Bathing him. Dressing him up. It just seemed like a sweet, little-girl kind of thing. But now—"

He nodded. "Where is she now?"

"Where else? Out talking to him in his pen."

Mr. Bunderan took a long, slow sip of his coffee. Then he said: "It's too bad, Molly, but we don't have any choice in the matter, do we?"

"It's just that she's so attached to the animal," his wife said.

"And there's no better time than now to end it. No, Thrayl's getting too mature. He's got to go off to be fattened. Next time we have a shipment for the feedlots." He glanced up at the date clock on the wall to see when that might be, then nodded. "There's a shipment tomorrow," he said heavily, "and that's as good a time as any."

The human poet sang on, while the aiodoi listened kindly through the more perfect music of their own everlasting singing:

———

"Let's talk about whether the universe is symmetrical.

"We all hope it will turn out that way, but if we want to find the truth about that, first we have to establish some universal frame of reference. That's where those people we were talking about at the Jagiellonian University in Krakow—Heller, Klimek, Rudnicki—come in. They discovered that this universal frame—or rigging vector field, as it is sometimes called—sounds so much like the old idea of an 'ether,' you remember, that they refer to it as a neoether. But, whatever you call it, you have to have *some* frame from which to measure whatever symmetries may be.

"It turns out that the larger the frame, the better the case looks for symmetry.

"In fact, although velocities of individual stars within galaxies, and of individual galaxies within clusters, vary very widely, the velocities of massive galaxies at the center of clusters vary quite linearly with their red-shift distances, at least within the error bars for measurement. This (say Heller, Klimek and Rudnicki) means that there is indeed some indication of an overall law that describes both nuclear particles and the largest bodies in the universe, for the correspondence is to the velocities of fundamental particles—and that, they say, is 'one more proof of Nature's kindness toward Earthly cosmologists.'

"We'll talk about some of those other proofs before long because, trust me on this, class, before you get through you're likely to think that we human beings have indeed had some special gifts from—Nature. Or God. Or Whoever it is you want to credit with doing the things that make it possible, or even maybe inevitable, that people like you and me could sit in this room discussing them now."

———

To the aiodoi that was a pleasing song, but not a new one, for they had heard that song forever, and would go on hearing it forever, for that was known to be the nature of great songs always.

4

Sork Quintero stared around in astonishment. Every Turtle he could see was groveling on the ground, all of them keening together in that awful collective moan of misery. Even more surprising was what he saw happening only a few meters away. There a great Taur had lumbered over to lower himself gently to his knees beside a grieving Turtle. Amazingly, the Taur was stretching out one hard, three-fingered paw to touch the Turtle's carapace in sympathy. . . .

Even more amazingly, the Turtle was allowing it.

Sork turned to his brother in bafflement. "What's happening to them, Kiri? They act like they're all going insane!"

Kiri Quintero gazed at his twin. His expression was of a peaceful sorrow, a feeling too immensely sad to be felt as pain. But there was something else in his expression, too, and it annoyed Sork to recognize it. It was pity. Pity for Sork himself. Kiri was sorry for his brother.

"Damn it, Kiri!" Sork exploded. "Don't start that I-know-something-you-don't! Tell me what's going on?"

His twin spread his hands. "I would if I could, Sork," he said reasonably. "I can't. I only know that it's a terrible tragedy, and it's happening on the home world of the Turtles."

"But that's more than seventy light-years away!"

Kiri sighed patiently. "Don't you learn anything from those old lectures? It's all the same, Sork. Time is an illusion."

Sork groaned. More double-talk! "Kiri," he said warningly, "I can put up with your foggy talk most of the time, but what's going on now is serious. Look at those guys!" A couple of the moaning, writhing Turtles were levering themselves ponderously to their feet, trudging slowly and hopelessly away toward the Turtle quarters. "Something *big* is going on, and I want to know what it is!"

Kiri looked at his brother in surprised understanding. "You're enjoying this," he said.

Sork shook his head, scowling. "No, of course I'm not—Well. Maybe I am, in a way. If whatever this is is bad for the Turtles it might be really good for *us*. But how can I tell, when I don't have any idea what's driving them so bugs? Anyway," he said, "let's find out where they're going and see what they do."

But as he turned his brother put his hand on his arm. "What is it, Kiri?" Sork demanded sharply.

His twin said, "Sue-ling should be through with her surgery by now. We ought to get her and take her with us."

Sork gritted his teeth. He knew how deeply he loved Sue-ling Quong . . . but why was it always his brother who remembered to consider her feelings?

———

At first, Sue-ling missed the full impact of what was happening. She was under the disk, and her mind was fully occupied with the work she was doing. When Sue-ling Quong worked under the memo disk, her scalpels went exactly where she wanted them, she could read every sign of color or flaccidity or size of every organ like words on a printed page, the location of every blood vessel was clear in her mind, the whole opened body of every patient was as familiar to her as the palm of her own hand. Dr. Sue-ling Quong was a first-class surgeon by anyone's standards. She had proved that at the university medical school, before the whole university was declared obsolete and terminated. But under the memo disk, she was more than that. She was superhuman.

There were two things wrong with that. The first was that when she came out from under the disk, she had no memory of what she had done while it was implanted. All she knew of her own skill was what she saw, later on, in the taped records, and then, as, wondering, she watched herself on the screen, she could only marvel at how much better she was than she had ever been before.

The other thing was worse: it was her realization that all her long years of training were a waste of time. Sue-ling had bitterly opposed closing down the medical school, but she had lost the fight. Schools were now a frivolity. Her decision to come to work in the Turtle compound had been a last resort. She might not have come simply because that exciting new man, Kiri Quintero, had urged it, but there was a more important reason. She was determined to find out just what it was like to be a memmie. She had found out, all right. And now she had to concede that it had made eminent practical sense; for with the disk implanted any warm human body could be as good a surgeon as she.

She instructed the nurses to close and, retreating to the door of the operating theater, reached up and removed the memo disk. Then everything swam around her. At once there was that terrible thudding headache, and she saw, without pleasure, that the nurses were nodding to her with admiration as they readied the patient to the recovery room.

The human administrator of the hospital was standing in the doorway. "He'll be fine," she said. "You did a great job."

"Thanks," Sue-ling said. And then, looking around the room, "What's going on, Lucille? I thought there were some Turtle observers here when I went under the disk."

The administrator said, "Oh, you wouldn't have known, would you? There was some sort of announcement about half an hour ago, and every Turtle around went racing off. Funny thing. I've never seen them show what I could really call emotion before, but this time they were really spooked. There's a meeting going on right now, matter of fact." She turned to go. "Anyway," she called over her shoulder, "your patient is going to get well now."

Sue-ling nodded ruefully. No one could object to being told she had done a good job—even if she didn't really know what the operation had been.

As she came out of the surgery she found the twins waiting at her door. They were looking out over the compound, and for a moment she could not tell which was which. Then they turned to greet her, both faces brightening at the sight of her, and then there was no doubt. Excitement, worry—that was certainly Sork. And the serenity on the face of the other twin belonged, beyond doubt, to Kiri. It was Kiri who spoke first. "We thought we'd take in that Turtle meeting," he said amiably. "They're really all shook up about it, whatever it is, so let's go on over to the arena."

Sork was moody again on the way over, gazing irritably out at the always present trainloads of materials going toward the lifts of the space ladder. "Look at that," he said jealously. "You know what those big chunks of structural steel are? I do. They're pieces of rocket launch towers—*human* launch towers."

"Which nobody uses any more, naturally," Kiri pointed out blandly.

"But we *could* use them! We did, once. Human beings used to go into space on their own. Now we're not allowed to any more!"

Sue-ling said, "Of course we are, Sork. Some of us are, anyway."

"Sure—a very few—as passengers! On Turtle ships!"

"But the Turtle ships are so much better," she said reasonably. "There isn't any need for ours."

He glared at her, and might have answered with words he would regret, but he was spared. They were at

the Turtle amphitheater and the time for conversation
had run out.

And—thought Sue-ling—just about in time. If only
Sork wouldn't squabble so much—

Or if only Kiri were Sork.

Sue-ling sighed. One day soon, she knew, she would
have to make up her mind which of the brothers she was
going to cleave to, as the old people put it so strangely,
and which she would shun.

But she planned to put that day off as long as she
could.

————

When Turtles met formally, the place where they
gathered was an arena, a little bit like an audience chamber, something like the great hall of a temple. The place
was built to the heroic Turtle scale, and it was filled with
a seething, muttering crowd of the aliens. Sue-ling saw
that the areas where their memmies were allowed to observe were only sparsely occupied. Most people didn't
care what the Turtles did, Sue-ling thought—probably
because it was so hard to tell what was on their minds
anyway.

She led the brothers to seats in the human area. Those
seats were a concession to the short size of human beings
—and to the fact that human beings needed something to
sit down on. Turtles never sat. They couldn't. Their anat-
omies did not bend at the hips. But the presence of seats
was the only concession the Turtle designers had made to
the needs of their vassals. The steps and the platforms
were Turtle-sized, far taller than any normal human being would have designed. Altogether, the vast, chill cav-
ern of a room was overwhelming. The walls were
immense gray granite blocks, and they climbed higher
than a human found comfortable to the dark-shadowed
vault of the roof. A pair of massive square pillars rose to
flank the tall dais where the leaders would appear, and
between them hung a gigantic, dimly glowing image of

the Turtle deity, a hundred times the size of the little emblems that were all over the compound.

Sue-ling gazed at the image with renewed interest. The Turtle deity was always represented as a wide-winged female. It was the only female Turtle any of them had ever seen. Real Turtles—the male ones, anyway—never had wings, she thought. Why did they show her like that? And she was depicted as descending from the sun (but not at all Earth's sun—too dim and too reddish in color) to bring new life for them.

It was a pity, she thought with detached interest, that the Turtles were so unwilling to talk about their origins or their home planet—especially about their religion. If religion was what it was. . . .

But then, so much about the Turtles was still a mystery.

Sue-ling felt very strongly that the coming of the Turtles had been a blessing for the human race. Well, she *usually* felt that way—except when she had been listening to Sork Quintero. Sork was one of the few who doubted that.

When the Turtles first showed up, a hundred years earlier, the human race had been angry, belligerent, frightened—mostly frightened—at the sudden presence of these creatures with better science and unfathomable plans.

Yet the Turtles had seemed to know just how to quiet human fears. Sue-ling blinked as it came to her just how that had been possible: It was people like Francis Krake, captured and carried away for study, from whom the Turtles had learned what to do. Undoubtedly Krake had told the Turtles enough about humanity to pave their way. So when the Turtles at last showed themselves to the human race they made their intentions clear at once. They came as traders, they proclaimed in their radio broadcasts from orbit. And trade they did. *Wonderful* trade, that benefited all of humanity. Without compulsion. Without threat. The Turtles carried their way simply by making humanity offers it could not refuse.

She looked around her curiously. No Turtles had appeared yet on the dais. Next to her, Sork was saying to his brother, "On the tape they were talking about something they call the 'anthropic principle,' Kiri—ever hear of it? I don't understand it very well, but it has something to do with the fact that our universe is *exactly* what we need to permit human life—and, I guess, Turtle life and Taur life, too."

"So? We're here in this universe, aren't we? Naturally it's just right for us."

Sork was shaking his head. "No, it's more complicated than that. See, the universe could have been quite different, they say."

"Shut up and sit down," his brother commanded. "The Turtles are getting ready to do something."

The aiodoi did not laugh, but they could be amused. As they heard the song of the Earth scientist who was almost an aiodos they might have smiled tenderly, for the burden of the song was so sweet, and so touching, and so childishly, basically wrong.

"Today we're going to take a little excursion into history. We're going to go pretty far back, in fact as far back as the beginning of our universe.

"To make it easier to comprehend, we're going to do it in three stages, in the same way that human history is handled. As you undoubtedly remember from your humanities classes, human history is divided into three parts —prehistory, ancient history, modern history—and we're going to make the same three divisions in the history of our entire universe.

"I have to caution you first that this does not square with the Hawking notion of imaginary time and endless universes popping up and dissolving. It doesn't contradict it, either. But for this session we will think only of the universe that we think of as beginning with the Big Bang.

"In this schema, what we will call modern universal

history starts about fifteen billion years ago, which is to say, about one second after the Big Bang itself.

"By then everything is pretty well decided. Protons and electrons have already formed; the matter-antimatter mutual annihilation has taken place, leaving the excess of what we call normal matter that we observe when we look around us. All that happens after that first second is that nuclear processes begin to happen, plasmas condense into galaxies and stars, planets are formed and, after a while, living things begin to evolve—just routine stuff. The modern history of the universe isn't really that interesting. It's all cut and dried, you see; the time when all sorts of 'decisions' are up for grabs is *before* the end of that first second.

"So let's forget about those fifteen billion years of modern universal history, and get to the interesting stuff. We'll do that in our next session, because I've got plans for the rest of this one. Take out your pens and papers, please, because I'm throwing you a quiz."

———

And the aiodoi sang on, almost laughing at the sweet, sad, time bound creatures who believed in such a word as "history."

5

As soon as her mother was asleep Moon stole out of the house and moved silently toward the pen that held Thrayl.

He was alone there. Moon's father had taken him from the common pen with the cows as soon as the Taur's budding horns began to develop. The rest of the breeding herd were sighing and stirring in their own pen on the far side of the thornbush barrier, but Moon slipped past without waking them.

In the light of the full moon the girl could see the sleeping Taur. Thrayl was lying in a corner on a nest of redfruit branches, his great horned head pillowed on one arm. In sleep his broad face was as innocent as any baby's.

"Thrayl," she whispered.

At once the great eyes opened, fastening on her. He rose with that quick Taur grace, the crooked little legs moving as smoothly as any dancer's. "Moon," he rumbled, almost purring affectionately—the Earth word came humming from his lips, like the mewing of a cat. She saw, with a poignant mixture of sadness and delight, that his horns were brighter in the moonlight, lovely with rainbow hues. The horns dipped as Thrayl bowed his huge head in greeting.

"Thrayl," she whispered again. Her voice was shaking, but determined all the same. "Thrayl, it's time for us to go now."

"Go." He mewed the English word softly. "Moon? Do you do well to do this?"

"Yes! I do very well, Thrayl, because I'm going to save you!" At least for a little while, she added bitterly to herself. She took one warm, solid arm to hurry him along, and he let her guide him, patiently agreeing. She unlocked the gate with her penlight and hurried him through the moonlit hedge. The air was cool and still, and Thrayl's warm odor filled her nostrils—a little like the aroma of new hay when it was cut for bedding in the stalls, a little like the scent of pines in the mountains. It was his very own, the good odor she remembered from the times she used to bathe him, when he was still a tiny calf.

Beyond the hedge they came into the redfruit grove where they used to play. Those trees were old now, gnarled and dying, weeds grown tall in the shadows under them. Thrayl's horns glowed brightly in the darkness under the trees, almost bright enough to show their way —or to betray them, Moon thought, if anyone in the house should wake and come looking for them. They walked more slowly there, close together but not touching. She was oddly shy of physical contact with him. Remembering how she used to pet him, she could hardly bear to touch him now.

He stopped short as they approached Moon's workshed, where she cared for injuries to the livestock—and where, sometimes, her brothers had dehorned and castrated young bulls.

She thought she understood what was in his mind. "No, Thrayl," she explained in annoyance. "Don't be afraid. I'm not going to do—that—to you. I've just got to remove your brand—or, better, change it to something else. Do you understand? It's just in case anyone sees us."

He stood silent, his head swaying as his sweetly glowing horns thrust this way and that, listening to his songs. In the Taur tongue he rumbled softly, "The song is not of fear."

"What then, Thrayl?"

"The song is of a terrible loss," he hummed.

She peered at him with sudden fright. Standing in the shadow of the twisted old redfruit trees, lit with the glow of his own horns, he looked so wonderful and splendid that she was trembling with love and worry. "What loss, Thrayl?" she whispered. "Have I lost something?"

His huge hand pressed her shoulder, hard and reassuring. "The song is not of humans," he said. "The song is full of faraway pain."

She sighed in relief. "Oh, it's just that Turtle thing that had you so worried today. Well," she said practically, "we can't deal with things that are far away, can we? But we've got to get moving. Mother locked the truck, so we're going to have to do a lot of walking before daylight, Thrayl. But I'll be with you."

The great, hard hand stroked her head. "I sing of being with you," he rumbled. "But I sing too of terrible loss and pain."

―――――

Beyond the hedge they came into the redfruit grove where they used to play. Past their best years, some of the trees were gnarled and dying, with weeds grown tall in the shadows under them.

Moon led the way by the light of Thrayl's horns. They were walking more slowly now, close together but not touching.

Moon said suddenly, "Thrayl? Your horns are so bright now."

"Bright," he rumbled, solemnly agreeing.

"Do they—do they *feel* any different?"

He was silent for a moment, considering. "Power," he said at last. "Ears when they shine. Eyes when they shine."

"You mean you, well, hear and see through them?"

"No," he said flatly. "Only the songs. Nothing on Earth—only the great sad pain from far away."

"Where?" she whispered. "How far away?"

"Nowhere far," he said mournfully. "No far, no when. Nowhere."

Then he stopped short, the horns casting this way and that.

Alarm suddenly flooded through Moon Bunderan. "What is it, Thrayl?" she asked. "Is there someone there?"

"Friend. Yes."

"A million miles away?" she asked bitterly—worriedly.

"No. A good smallsong, Moon, but also sad—and, yes, very near."

———

Half a kilometer away, Captain Francis Krake was sleeping badly that night.

It wasn't that his mission had failed. Indeed, he had met with more success than he could have hoped for. Certainly he had found the place where the little town of Portales used to be, though it was only the weed-ground mound in the middle of the old courthouse square that proved he was in the right place. Nothing else survived. No buildings—unless you counted something that looked curiously like a great bomb shelter, in the general area of the old college. Only that, and the stones of an old burying ground between the redfruit groves.

Krake had not lingered in the old cemetery. He did not want to find a stone with a name he might know. So he had made a quick trip to town to call the pretty memmie doctor back in Kansas City—no news; but at least no *bad* news—and then back to his campsite.

The trip was a waste, he told himself. But what difference did it make? He decided to start back the next morning. There was nothing to keep him here any longer.

He had stopped to rent a video set in the town, more to help him waste this wasted time than because of any curiosity about what was going on in this strange, foreign, human world that was no longer his own. But then he had been caught by the news stories. They had upset him. Turtles failing at their jobs, neglecting their assignments—total confusion, it seemed to Krake. And what wild rumors!

Could it be true that the Mother had somehow disappeared?

The thought was incredible. Krake tried to imagine the feelings of the Turtles if anything happened to their Mother. Yes, of course, sooner or later even a Mother would die—though the Turtles had never been willing to speak much on that subject, at least they had admitted that. But nothing would change, really. The death of a Mother was a time of great, complex ritual. One of the nymphs would be allowed to mature—a male would be selected to father the next brood—and the Turtle ownership of the galaxy would go on unperturbed once more.

That would *always* go on. Nothing, Krake told himself, would ever interfere with Turtle commerce . . . and wondered whether the thought made him pleased or depressed.

He did not really want to think about the Turtles.

He wished them no particular ill—but no particular well, either. True, they had not harmed him in any physical way. Indeed, they had certainly saved his life, for that had surely been lost on that rubber raft in the Coral Sea if their scout ship had not come along. But the price he had had to pay was high.

Every night since then, Francis Krake had gone to sleep with the consciousness of guilt on his mind.

He turned over, trying to put these matters out of his thoughts. There was no reason, he told himself, why he should be wakeful. If he had been disappointed at finding so little left of the town that had been his home, he had had no real hope of finding more than that. And he lacked nothing for his comfort. The rented camping gear was high-tech stuff that made him—at least, that should have made him—as cozy in the tent as he had ever been in his ship. The pop-up tent's memory fabric had immediately assumed the shape best fitted for his comfort. He had cooked a meal with self-heating pans, and if he had also built a fire outside the tent, that was more for the pleasure of looking at it than for any need. There was an incinerating toilet, and a thermo-constant blanket that made night chill irrelevant.

Moreover, you didn't need a memo disk to operate any of it.

Fretfully, Krake scratched the side of the tent. Where his touch stirred to life the phosphors built into the fabric of the tent, a gentle glow sprang up, softly illuminating the inside of the tent.

He slid his feet into his boots, rose and stepped outside, looking fretfully around. A gentle sighing of breeze in the redfruits, a faint purring from the stream down the hill—apart from that the woods were silent. Overhead the Moon was ivory-bright. Squinting, Krake thought he saw a glint of metal in the Moon's lower hemisphere—was it, he wondered, the human Moon base that the Turtles said had been abandoned there? It was still wonderful to Krake to think that his own race had somehow stretched out into space on its own, with no help from Turtles or anyone else—but, of course, that was all history. There was nothing left of that human presence in space. Krake knew that once there had been all sorts of human-built communications and surveillance satellites in orbit—but the Turtles had removed most of them, because they endangered the elevator cables of their skyhook.

Given a choice, Krake told himself justly, between a scattering of satellites and the entry to the galaxy that the Skyhook offered, obviously the Skyhook was a better bargain. But, all the same, he wished something important still remained in space that was entirely, and independently, human.

He craned his neck toward the south and east, hoping for a glimpse of the Turtle orbital station at the top of the Skyhook, where his crew were waiting for their next tour of duty. He couldn't see a thing. He knew, though, that the Turtles had their own remote orbiters and that they could certainly see him—see his campfire, at least; just as they had seen his downed plane and life raft, and so much else, all those years ago.

He stirred restlessly. Sleep was far away. The wind was picking up, and the Moon was disappearing into a growing mass of cloud. He wondered if it was going to rain, after all. There were sounds in the brush all around him—

Krake froze, bolt upright, listening.

Not all those sounds were the wind! He fumbled in his pack for his flashlamp and turned it on, looking toward the stirrings in the brush.

Two figures were coming out of the woods along the stream, and one of them was certainly not human.

Krake listened intently, ready for whatever might be coming. They said there wasn't any crime any more on Earth, but he had never believed that . . . certainly did not want to risk having one of those rare crimes happen to him. . . .

"Captain Krake?" It was the girl's voice, the one he had met along the road. "Captain Krake? It's me, Moon Bunderan. Will you help us, please?"

———

The Taur was deep in meditation, paying no attention to the talk of the humans. Krake crouched on one side of his little campfire, staring across the flames at the girl who looked so much like the woman he had left behind so long ago. He was shaking his head in astonishment at what she was asking. "But I can't take you anywhere, Moon," he said. "Where could we go? I have no home here on Earth. You certainly don't want to go with me on my ship, do you?"

"I do! *We* do! Please take us anywhere where Thrayl will be safe," she begged.

He grimaced, half amused at her obstinate assurance, much more than half determined to save her from a serious mistake. "You wouldn't say that if you knew what it was like in a waveship, Moon. It's terribly lonesome. There'd just be me and my crew—no," he said emphatically, to keep her from arguing, "that's out of the question."

"Then take me to the orbit station with you!"

He said reasonably, "That's no good, either. The Turtles won't let you stay on their orbiter, Moon. Even if you got there, they'll just notify your parents, and then they'll come after you. And I won't be staying there myself; I'm going up to my ship as soon as my crew's ready, and then —off. Somewhere. Wherever there's a job for me."

"But they'll hurt Thrayl," she sobbed.

"You told me yourself that he doesn't mind—"

"I do! I mind *terribly*."

He sighed. Had there ever been a time when he could talk easily to a young woman? If so, that time was long gone. He did his best: "You don't know what you're asking, Moon. Are you prepared to leave your family permanently? Once you get in a starship you've left everybody you know on Earth forever."

She looked puzzled in the light of the fire. "Forever? But can't I come back to Earth?"

"To Earth, yes," he said bitterly. "I've just done that. But it's not the same Earth you come back to, Moon. Time dilation makes sure of that."

"I know all that, and I don't care! They don't need me any more. My brothers will stay on the ranch, that's the only thing they really care about—except going into town to look for girls. And I'm Thrayl's only friend. If I don't save him, who will?"

The girl thought for a moment, then added honestly, "I don't want to stay here anyway. I want a bigger life than this, Captain Krake."

"Bigger how?"

"I don't know that, exactly," she admitted. "I just know that it's time for me to go."

He gazed at her helplessly. He could see nothing but difficulties, though he found himself longing to help. "I guess," he said at last, "I might be able to figure out a way to take you as far as the Turtle compound at Kansas City—"

"Oh, yes! Thank you! That would be wonderful!" At least for a beginning, Moon added to herself.

He gave her a suspicious look. "But I don't see how

we could really get away even with that, because we can't take commercial air transportation," he pointed out. "If your family knows you've run off, they'll have reported it. The authorities will be watching for you and Thrayl."

"There must be some other way!"

"I don't know of any."

"Sure you do. Your car." She pointed triumphantly to the three-wheeler pulled up under the trees. "We could drive the car to this space ladder."

Krake stared at the huge Taur. Even squatting on the ground in his "listening to the songs" posture, he was almost as tall as Krake himself. "What, the three of us in that little thing? Including *him*? It would take us days to get there if we drove!"

She said sturdily, "That's no problem. I can drive, too, so we can spell each other. Go straight through. And Thrayl can curl up in the back—we could cover him with your blankets, maybe."

"My camping gear has to go in the back!"

But Krake knew it was a losing argument for, when push came to shove, he could not resist those eyes. And what, he asked himself, were a tent and some odds and ends worth, after all? Why not just abandon them here, forfeiting the deposits? The money didn't matter.

And as to the things themselves, he would never need them again. Not in space. Not at all, unless he ever returned permanently to Earth . . . and Francis Krake had long decided that that he would never do.

The Earth singer sang on, trapped in his error, unable to sing the truth that even the error revealed:

———

"You remember our last class, I hope. In it we said that we are going to divide the history of the universe—our own personal universe, that is, the one we can experience, at least in theory—like the history of the human race, into three eras: Modern, Ancient and Prehistoric. We've already dealt with the modern era, which is to say the part beginning one second after the Big Bang.

"Now let's look at Ancient History. Don't get hung up on proportions, though. In human terms, Ancient History goes back several times as far as modern. That isn't true of the ancient history of our universe. It lasted only a little less than that one second.

"Even so, an awful lot of things happened in that second. We can divide even the Ancient History of the universe into several eras. Ancient History starts at ten to the minus-43d power seconds, and the first part of it is the Grand Unified Theory, or GUT, Era. That goes from ten to the minus 43 to ten to the minus 37 seconds, which is to say that it lasts altogether for a little less than 1 divided by 10,000,000,000,000,000,000,000,000,000,000,

000,000 seconds—that is, it is just under one ondecillionth of a second.

"That doesn't sound like much. Well, it wasn't. But it was enough to set the foundations for the Grand Unified Theory, and that's quite a lot.

"After the GUT era, things happened a little slower. Then we have the era when the hadrons begin to form—that runs to about a millionth of a second, which doesn't sound like much, either, but it's a *lot* more than an ondecillionth—and then the considerably longer era when the leptons begin to form, which uses up the rest of that first second of Ancient History. That's not too interesting, either.

"It is the GUT era, and the time before it, where the big events happen.

"The GUT era of ancient universal history is a time of very high energies and consequently of very heavy particles. It is also the time when space itself can be said to begin to exist.

"Now, some of you may be raising an eyebrow at that. You may have some dumb questions stirring around in your mind. For instance, how can there be anything before there was space for it to be in, you may ask.

"Let me show you why that's a dumb question. Space implies some kind of *structure*. The smallest structures we know, and we think probably the smallest structures that exist, are at the Planck length, which is somewhere around 10 to the minus 35th meters.

"But space does have a *structure*. It isn't a seamless nothingness; it is something like a collection of tiny, Planck-length cells. Sometimes we call that basic, underlying structure of everything 'the spacetime foam,' because at those very early epochs we can't even distinguish the dimension of time from the spatial dimensions.

"So that's the GUT era. It is the time of ultraheavy particles and spacetime foam; and that's all we need to say just now about Ancient History."

———

And the aiodoi sang sweet and complimentary songs of how pretty that song was, as a human might of a two-year-old's first attempt at carrying a tune . . . and how childishly wrong.

6

~~~~~~~

If Kiri Quintero had been allowed the control of his own body he would have delighted in what he was doing. He was flying! After four grueling days in California, doing some sort of research for the great, golden Turtle they called Yellow Bird—his proper title was Defender of God —he was on the way home, but rest was still forbidden. Kiri was under the memo disk. He wasn't released until the big Turtle aircraft was already settling in for a landing at the Kansas City skyhook compound, and then he was too bone weary even to glance out the window at the scene beneath.

He got up wearily as the plane's doors opened, and was pushed rudely out of the way by Yellow Bird. With a hostile squawk the great Turtle shoved past him and disappeared. Kiri Quintero followed more slowly, stretching his aching limbs. It was already dark, and a hot, muggy night, with no stars in the skies. He wanted to go to bed, but he wanted even more to see his brother and the woman they loved.

He suspected he knew where he could find them both, and he was right.

As he walked along the hall toward Sue-ling's apartment he heard his brother's voice, crackling with anger, then almost drowned out by the shrill squawks of a Turtle. That was odd; Turtles rarely came into human quar-

ters. But when he reached the door, there the Turtle was
—Litlun—hard arms waving, squawking furiously at
Sue-ling and Sork through his transposer. "Do you pre-
tend you do not have recorded blasphemous material?
You cannot, for one knows this to be true, so you must
not refuse to sell it to me! Come, set a price, for one
wishes to have it!"

Sue-ling put a quieting hand on Sork's shoulder and
addressed the Turtle herself. "I don't know anything
about blasphemous material, Facilitator," she said stead-
fastly.

"It is," he blared, *"infuriating* when a reasonable
commercial offer is rejected for no reason! If you behave
so badly we must reconsider whether your services will
continue to be needed here."

Sue-ling shrugged. "That's up to you," she said.
Then, studying him, "It might help if you told me why
you want it."

"That is not your concern!"

"And it isn't your material," she pointed out.

Litlun glared wordlessly at her with both yellow eyes,
his claws drumming angrily on his belly shell. Then, with
a frustrated hiss, he turned and stalked violently out of
the room.

Sue-ling followed him with her eyes, then shook herself. "Hello, Kiri, dear," she said belatedly.

It was a greeting, at least, and more than Kiri got
from his twin. Sork, too, was gazing after the Turtle. "He
really wants those astrophysics chips," he said thoughtfully.

"I see that," Sue-ling said. "But why?"

"It has to be something to do with what happened to
their Mother. Maybe they think she fell into a black hole
or something—"

"The whole planet?"

"Why not? It couldn't be just that one Mother died.
That happens over and over, and they just let another one
take over. I'll bet that they want to know more about
black holes, and they think human science can tell them
what to do." He grinned savagely, delighted at the

thought of Turtles conceding they needed human aid. Then he added, "But if that's what really happened, I think she's *gone*. Nobody on the lecture chips ever said anything about a way to get out of a black hole."

Sue-ling nodded doubtfully, then was distracted by the fatigue lines on Kiri's face. "Where've you been?" she asked. "You look like you've been working too hard!"

"I was. Yellow Boy commandeered me," Kiri said. "We've been in California for five days, at a hospital, checking out a lot of old research material in the medical records—I think."

Sue-ling looked puzzled. "What did a Turtle want with human medical records?"

Kiri spread his hands. "How can I know? I was under the disk the whole time, almost. Yellow Boy had me going through all the records of the hospital genetics department—I didn't know what I was doing, of course, but from things the Turtles were saying to each other on the way back I think that was what it had to be. And—" Kiri hesitated, always unsure of offering his intuitions to others—"I do have a theory. A guess, anyway."

"Which is?" Sue-ling demanded.

"It's only an idea—but what I think they were trying to figure out was whether there was some procedure that could recreate a female Turtle by modifying a male Turtle's genes."

"But that sort of thing is just another kind of sacrilege to them!" Sork said wonderingly.

Kiri grinned wearily. "So the Exarch told us when he found out what we were doing," he agreed. "I never saw the Turtles so upset! They were squawking at each other on the phone like back-fence tomcats."

Sue-ling said, thinking it out as she spoke, "I don't think trying to modify a male into a functional female would work, anyway. I'm pretty sure the Turtles have never done that kind of work themselves and, although genetics isn't my field, I never heard that anybody on Earth ever managed to create a female out of male genes for any kind of animal. Maybe they really are getting desperate."

"You bet they're desperate!" Sork said with glee. "And we're not going to help them! I'm going to take the lecture chips away and hide them, in case Litlun figures some way of getting them away from you. They're *human* science, not Turtle, and we're going to need all the human science for ourselves!"

Kiri looked at his brother. "What are you talking about?"

Sork said, "Don't you understand? What's the life span of a Turtle?"

"How would I know? I think somebody said around seventy-five years, but—"

"But that's only a guess," Sork agreed. "All the same, we know they die *some* time. And in seventy-five years— maybe less!—they'll all be dead. There won't be any Turtles any more. Well, a few—as they keep coming back from time-dilated trips, now and then. But they won't matter, and then who's going to be the dominant race in this galaxy?"

Kiri blinked at him. "You mean—us?"

"Who else?" Sork demanded. "The Turtles are going to die out. Whatever future there is in this galaxy, it belongs to us!"

Kiri stared at his brother, trying to make all these concepts fit together. "But *we* can't travel around the galaxy," he said reasonably. "How could we? We don't know how to operate wave-drive spaceships."

"We'll learn. Besides, some human beings can already!" Sork said triumphantly. "Francis Krake, for one, and Sue-ling had a message from him yesterday. He's driving back here right now."

"Driving?" Kiri asked, astonished.

Sue-ling shrugged. "Don't ask me why, but yes, that's what he said. I expect he'll get here tomorrow. Only—" she bit her lip—"I wish I had better news for him about his crew. The Turtles in the orbit station are all going crazy, too—they aren't really attending to business. I hope his crew's all right."

"Is something wrong with them?" Kiri asked.

Sue-ling spread her hands. "I don't know. Last time I

tried I couldn't get an answer from the orbital station at all," she said, "and that has *never* happened before."

———————

When Sork left them for some business of his own, Kiri Quintero lingered behind.

Sue-ling's expression was pleasantly receptive. Cheered by the look on her face, Kiri asked her, "Tonight? I've been gone a long time."

"Tonight," she said softly, "would be a very fine idea. I've missed you, too."

So placid Kiri Quintero was almost excited with the pleasure of anticipation as he strolled back toward her room a few hours later. He knew what was forthcoming. She would be wearing the yellow silk robe he had once managed to buy for her in New Hong Kong, when there on some never-to-be-clearly-known errand for the Turtles, and her sweet body would be fragrant with the Spanish scent she loved. It would be a wonderful night together—

It would not. Voices told him that when he was in the hall outside. Sue-ling was not alone, and the person with her was his twin.

A man who discovers his lover in the arms of another man has many options—tears, fury, violence; perhaps suicide, if one believes the romantic novel to represent truth. Kiri Quintero did not choose any of them. He stood there in thought for a moment, trying to listen to the words from inside—there was, after all, the chance that his twin had stopped by just for a moment, perhaps to pick up some more of his old lecture chips. But that did not seem to be the case. Although Kiri could not really make out the words from inside, he could surely hear the tone—Sue-ling protesting, Sork persuading, Sue-ling objecting, Sork insisting . . . and finally Sue-ling surrendering.

Kiri sighed, turned around and went back to his own room.

He knew that Sue-ling thought he yielded too often,

and in too many ways, to his twin. Perhaps it was true. But Kiri Quintero had always been happiest when Sork Quintero was happy, too.

All the same, he slept poorly that night. When he woke he automatically listened for the faint whisper of his brother's audio chips from the room next door, and was not surprised when he didn't hear it. No doubt Sork had chosen to stay the night.

That didn't really trouble Kiri Quintero, exactly. Though he loved Sue-ling, he was not jealous of her. Perhaps one day she would finally give up their ménage à trois and settle on one of the twins. Perhaps then she would marry him. Perhaps it would be his brother she chose. Whichever happened would be right . . . and, in any case, he would go right on loving Sue-ling Quong.

Kiri rolled over on his back and gazed peacefully into the darkness of his room. Poor Sork! Where Kiri saw symmetries, congruences, interlocking relationships and resonances, Sork saw only problems. For Kiri Quintero, he always knew that every part belonged to the whole, and the whole was all of its parts. Sometimes the patterns he perceived were pleasing, but sad. Sometimes they were just pleasing. Kiri Quintero's nature was not to worry about whether the future would be good or bad, or about whether whatever was happening at any moment was right or wrong, for whatever was *was*.

All these things Kiri Quintero knew as certainly as he knew that his heart beat and his lungs drew breath—and that one day both heart and breath would stop and he would die—and that there was nothing in that knowledge, in any of it, to cause fear or sorrow.

If there was one thing that Kiri Quintero regretted it was that his brother did not seem to understand this self-evident law of nature. If it had been within his power he would have tried to help his brother—to share with him his own vision of the rightness of what was so. To share it with the whole world, if he could.

But it was Sork Quintero, not Kiri, who had the skill with words. Kiri's lofty peace was all internal. He had no way to share it.

Kiri hadn't known that he had at last fallen asleep until he heard his brother pounding on his door. "Kiri? Wake up, it's morning. Sue-ling just got a call from that space captain. He's in the compound, and he's brought somebody with him."

Kiri sat up, still groggy. "Who?"

"I don't know that yet, do I?" his twin snapped pettishly. "That's what I'm going to find out. I'm going over to meet them at the western gate. Come after me when you're awake, all right?"

"All right," said Kiri, yawning. Somehow the brief discontent of the night before had gone away, as it always did with Kiri Quintero. He stretched placidly and then, comfortably, not at all rushed, rolled out of his bed and headed for the sanitary. There was no reason for haste, after all. Whatever was there would still be there when he got there.

It was still early morning when he strolled out toward the gate, and turning out to be a sultry, lowering day—the kind that all Turtles despised. Few of them were in sight. Few of *anybody* were in sight. The bustling compound at the base of the space ladder had turned into a ghost town. The long trains of scrap metal were motionless and abandoned, and there was an eerie silence where for so long there had been the drumming bustle of Turtle trade.

As Kiri approached the gate he caught a glimpse of a group of people gathered around a three-wheeled surface vehicle. One of the group was his brother, all right, along with that captain from space. With them was a human female, but it was not Sue-ling Quong. She was a young girl Kiri had never seen before and standing behind her, looming over her, was, yes, a *Taur*. Not just a Taur, but a male, with developed horns. Kiri blinked and started toward them, but as he turned in their direction a Turtle stepped out from behind a halted freight car to challenge him. Kiri was surprised to see that it was the rusty brown pigmy called Litlun, evidently lurking there to look at the humans.

One of Litlun's eyes turned to Kiri, and the Turtle instantly activated his transposer. "Stop there, Quintero! Which are you?"

"I'm Kiri Quintero, Facilitator. Not," he was careful to explain, "my brother, Sork, who is the one you believe to possess some disapproved recorded lectures."

The Turtle rolled his yellow eyes at him. "One does not speak of such record chips," he said, like a reproving teacher. "Their possessor does not wish to sell, and they are not of importance. One cannot concern oneself with commercial matters at this time."

Kiri's eyes almost popped. Litlun couldn't concern himself with *trade*? A *Turtle* couldn't? So it was all true!

But the Turtle was still speaking. Litlun gestured toward the group at the gate. "Is that creature not an adult male Taur?" he asked.

"Oh, I don't think so," Kiri said automatically. "Not an *adult* because, look, he still has his horns—" Then he took a better look. "Well, he does *look* different from most of the others," he admitted.

"One may have a use for such a Taur. Go and find out, please," rapped the Turtle, and turned back to the shelter of the motionless car.

Kiri's calm was threatened at last by surprise—not least because, for the first time in his memory, he had heard a Turtle say "please" to a human being. But the real surprise came when he got closer. The great bull-headed creature standing by the three-wheeled surface car was fully horned, and even in the light of morning Kiri saw that the horns were faintly glowing.

His twin turned to him. "You took your time," he said accusingly. "Look, you stay here with this girl and her Taur—don't let anybody bother them."

"Who would bother them?" Kiri asked reasonably. "Where's Sue-ling?"

"Back at her office, of course," Sork snapped. "That's where Krake and I are going, to see if she can get any news of his crew. Oh, don't argue with me now, Kiri,"

Sork went on as his brother opened his mouth. "We're in a hurry!" And the two of them left, leaving Kiri face to face with the young woman and the Taur bull.

The girl was studying his face. "You two look a lot alike," she said, discovering. "Are you brothers?"

"Twins," Kiri told her. "My name is Kiri Quintero."

"I'm Moon Bunderan," the girl said, extending her hand. "This is my friend, Thrayl. He can shake hands with you, too, if you like."

"Of course," said Kiri, though his tone was more uncertain than his words. But when the Taur reached down and took Kiri's hand in his own hard, three-fingered fist, the skin was warm, the pressure friendly. "Nice to meet you," Kiri said, looking up at the huge-eyed, massive, horned head. The horns really did glow with a light of their own.

Then the Taur spoke. It was a hissing, buzzing sound that Kiri could not understand at all. "I don't speak Taur," he said apologetically—apologizing to an animal!

"He only said that he thinks your smallsongs are good and that he hopes your horns grow strong," the girl translated. "It's kind of what Taurs say, like—well, like 'Nice to meet you,' I guess." She sat suddenly on the hood of the car. "I'm sorry," she went on. "I'm really tired. We've been driving for days—all the way from New Mexico. And it was kind of—"

She hesitated, looking into Kiri's eyes as though wondering whether to trust him with a secret. Evidently she decided she could, for she finished, "Kind of scary. Because we were hiding, really. You know, a lot of people are afraid of grown-up male Taurs, and some of them might've wanted to hurt Thrayl."

The bull Taur suddenly blared a sort of muted roar and danced around, lowering the huge head, the horns pointed back toward the place Kiri had come from. "Oh, *Lord*," Moon Bunderan breathed in excitement. "Look at that, Mr. Quintero! Isn't that a *Turtle*?"

Kiri looked around. Litlun had drawn closer, his frill quivering as both yellow eyes were fastened on them.

"Why, yes. His name's—well, we call him Litlun. Because he's smaller than the rest of them, you know."

"He's smaller? Then the others must be as big as Taurs! And he looks excited about something."

It was true that Litlun was waving his boneless upper limbs and cawing to himself as he came. The Turtle turned one eye on Kiri Quintero. "Well?" he demanded through the transposer. "Is it not true? Isn't it indeed an adult male Taur?"

The young woman shrank back. "Oh, don't let him hurt Thrayl! He's only just becoming mature. He's not dangerous at all!"

But Litlun wasn't listening. He ignored Kiri Quintero, barely glanced at the young woman with one eye in passing. All the Turtle's attention was focused on the Taur. Litlun stopped dead in front of him, both eyes now firmly fixed on Thrayl's horns. One of the Turtle's boneless arms reached out to touch a horn.

Thrayl pulled back. There was a warning rumble from the Taur, and the horns seemed to brighten with a reddish light.

"Please, Mr. Quintero," the girl said worriedly. "That Turtle is bothering Thrayl—he's not used to having anyone touch his horns. Except me, of course."

The Turtle spun around and glared at her. He barked something, but he was speaking so rapidly that even the transposer did not make him comprehensible to her. "What's he saying?" the girl said, backing uneasily away.

Kiri frowned in surprise. "He—he wants to buy your Taur. He asks how much you want for him."

"Oh, no!" the girl cried. "I won't sell Thrayl! That's why he and I are running— That's out of the question," she said firmly. "Tell him. Say thank you, but Thrayl isn't for sale."

Kiri didn't have to translate, because Litlun got the message. The yellow eyes blazed angrily as the Turtle boomed away again, this time more slowly. "One will pay anything you ask," he squawked. "One wishes to have this adult male Taur."

"No! Please make him understand. I don't want

Thrayl dehorned, turned into meat—or breeding stock, either."

A rumble from the Turtle. "One will not physically harm the animal in any way."

"I don't believe you!" Moon Bunderan said fiercely.

Kiri cut in. "Well," he said reasonably, "I've never known a Turtle to lie, or break his word. They're honest traders, Miss. If he makes a deal he'll keep to it."

"*No.* Thrayl and I are going with Captain Krake in his ship, and that's the way it's going to be!"

The Turtle hissed furiously, the eyes wandering in all directions. Litlun opened his parrot-beak mouth to speak, then changed his mind. He closed it with a snap and stormed away.

Moon Bunderan gazed fearfully after him. "What's he going to do?"

Kiri shook his head. "I never saw him so excited. I don't know, Miss Bunderan. They are acting pretty strange these days—why, just last night he was trying to buy some old recorded Earth lectures from Sue-ling Quong." He felt an unhappy sense of confusion—unusual for Kiri; but there were suddenly all these strange bits of data that must fit together somehow—but how?

The girl put her hand on his shoulder, looking up at him. "Will he try to take him away from me?"

"Oh, no," Kiri said in surprise. "No, he won't do that. The Turtles never *take* anything. It's all fair and square commerce with them. But," he added seriously, "I'm afraid it looks as though Litlun really wants your Taur. And the Turtles generally find a way to get what they want."

*To the third song of the Earth poet the aiodoi listened
with compassion and perhaps even pride, for error was giving way to understanding, and the song began to ring
beautifully as it went on.*

———————

"For the last time I remind you that our division of
universal history into three eras, like the divisions of human history, is really only an analogy. But it's a good
one, I think, and now we will come to the important part.

"It's time for us to say what we know about the universe's prehistory.

"As with the prehistory of the human race, from the
first African Eve—or whoever it was—to the beginnings
of history, or at least of legend, the prehistoric part is far
the most important. For human affairs, that prehistory
lasted for hundreds of thousands of years. The prehistory
of the universe is a lot shorter. All the same, it is the most
important part.

"Still, it won't take much time to tell it, for what we
know about the Planck Era—that is, the first ten to the
minus-47th seconds after the Big Bang, which we will
call the prehistory of the universe—is, basically, nothing.

"That doesn't stop us from *needing* to know. It only

makes it impossible for that need ever to be satisfied. We can't see back past the Planck barrier. Maybe nobody ever will. We don't know the detail of events.

"What we do know is that somewhere in Planck time —or maybe some of it happened in the GUT time which was the beginning of the Ancient History, we can't really be sure—all the rules for our universe were set.

"That is to say, all the 'wave functions' (as you might call them) were 'collapsed' into exact, hard numbers. Values which could have been almost any value at all suddenly became fixed values. That was when, for instance, it was 'decided' that *pi* would then and forevermore equal three-point-etcetera instead of, maybe, seven or some other number; when Planck's constant and the fine-structure constant and all the others became rigid facts instead of some possible other values.

"From that point on, everything else was pretty much decided.

"You might say the program for our universe was written then; everything since then has just been the running of the computer. If we could somehow catch a glimpse of that primordial computer program we would understand a lot of things that are now shrouded in doubt. . . .

"But we can't, and perhaps we never will."

———

And the aiodoi sang on tenderly and with compassion, and the song they sang was of hope.

7

~~~~

Sork Quintero didn't follow Sue-ling into her office to try to check on the well-being of Captain Krake's crew. He had something more important to do.

Sork wasn't good at making plans, and he knew it. Planning anything complicated always involved so many factors that Sork was sure to leave something out, forget some detail. It took the full concentration of all of Sork's quite high intelligence to perceive a goal and devise a way to get to it—and then it took endless, repetitive going over and over every possible relevant fact before he could be sure he hadn't overlooked something.

His brother Kiri, of course, could see a whole tree of relevances in a single glance and unerringly identify every bond. If Kiri hadn't been his brother, Sork Quintero would surely have resented him intensely.

On the other hand, what Kiri could not do was act. In that quality Sork was superb. Once he had a plan complete he could not be swerved from it.

The plan that was forming in Sork's mind was certain to be—he *thought* it was certain to be—both sensible and complete. But to make sure, he stalked impatiently back and forth in front of the hospital, rehearsing his arguments; and when Krake came out, followed by Sue-ling Quong, Sork aggressively positioned himself in their way.

"You're Krake," he said, making sure. "You're going to your ship."

The space captain looked at him curiously before agreeing. "Yes, that's where I'm going," he said, "as soon as I make arrangements for Moon and her Taur—if that doesn't take too long. I've got to see how my crew is coming along. The Turtles up in the orbit station aren't saying much!"

Sork wasn't listening. Impatiently he put his hand on Krake's chest; the space captain looked surprised, but didn't resist. Sork gestured at the desolate scene around them.

"You must help us. Look at those things!" Sork cried, waving an arm toward the abandoned cars of scrap. "Isn't it appalling? I've watched them go for years—all sorts of things that belong to humanity—gantries from the abandoned space launching sites, giant magnets from supercolliders, all sorts of old research equipment, and it's all disappearing into space. The Turtles have stolen our science!"

Sue-ling was frowning at him. "Please, Sork. The captain has other things on his mind. That stuff is all out of date anyway. Nobody bothers with those things anymore, because Turtle technology is better."

"Turtle science belongs to the *Turtles*!" he snapped at her, and back immediately to the waveship captain. "Krake, please! You've got to help us!"

The space captain was doing his best to be patient with this intense young man. He was not succeeding. "That's all very well, Mr. Quintero, but there isn't anything I can do about Earth science, is there? What do I know about it? The last time I was on Earth nobody even *thought* of going into space, and I never heard of these— what do you call them—supercolliders and all that. It's my crew I've got to care for."

Sork would not be diverted. He said firmly, "Listen. If the Turtles are all going to die off, then we must learn how to travel in interstellar space ourselves. That's where your duty is."

Krake gave him a hostile stare. "My duty?"

Sork sighed and spelled it out logically for this obstinate man. "It *is* your duty, because you're the only human being who knows how to fly a turtle waveship! Human science was picking up a lot of momentum before the Turtles came, even if you didn't see it yourself, with rockets and computers and—"

Krake stopped him, puzzled. "Computers?"

"Machines that solved problems. Machines that helped people *think*. Only once the Turtles showed up with the memo disks, nobody needed computers any more. So now all those things are lost. We're going to have to learn to use Turtle technology to get our birthright back, and that's where you come in. Take us along to space!"

He stopped there. He had put forward the case with total logic; now it was up to Francis Krake to respond.

But the waveship captain wasn't responding. Krake looked around at the others, as though seeking their help in dealing with this persistent man.

Sue-ling Quong broke the silence. "I think," she said hesitantly, "that Sork's right in a way, Captain Krake. You are a pretty special resource for the human race right now."

Krake was aghast. "But Dr. Quong! What are you getting at? You don't want me to take you along into space, do you?"

"I do!" cried Sork, answering for her. "We all do!"

Krake looked at him as at a child who had asked to be handed the Moon. "You're as bad as Moon Bunderan. You simply don't understand what you're asking. Once you take off in a wave-drive ship at relativistic speeds you're *committed*. It's a one-way trip in time. You'll be leaving everything!"

"Yes, of course," Sork said impatiently. "For a period we will, until we return to help humanity to be reborn."

"For a *long* period of time! It may be centuries. Why do you think I never came back to Earth before this? Because as soon as I had been in space a few weeks, while the Turtles were still interrogating me and the others, I discovered that everybody I had known on Earth was old or dead. Decades had passed. My crew and I were forgotten."

"But you see, Krake," Sork said flatly, "we don't have anyone to leave behind."

"There's Kiri," Sue-ling put in. Sork blinked at her.

"Oh," he said, "I'm sure Kiri will come with us. He always does."

———

And of course Kiri agreed at once, comfortable with doing whatever his brother chose for them to do, content to explore a new facet of the always fascinating whole that was life. The real surprise was that the young woman from New Mexico insisted on joining them. She was immovable on the subject. "You must take us! I can't stay here, Captain Krake—I'm afraid of that Turtle they call Litlun. What if he finds some way of taking Thrayl away from me?"

"He can't do that," Krake said, trying to reassure her —and trying, for one more time, to prevent her from making a terrible, irrevocable mistake . . . though inside him there was a part of his heart that leaped with pleasure at the thought of having flesh-and-blood human companions again. Especially a young female one who looked more and more like the long-dead Madeleine. Then he added, thinking it over, "Well, I don't think he can take your Taur away from you, anyway—"

"But you never know, with Turtles, do you?" She pressed his arm persuasively. "You say we'll just be gone a few weeks, but fifty or a hundred years will have passed? By then maybe there won't be any more Turtles."

"Not many, at least. They won't be running things anymore, there won't be enough of them."

"Then there won't be all those memmies, doing better than ordinary people can?" She turned to gaze up at the kind, broad face of her Taur. "Then maybe we won't have to follow their orders about Taurs anymore, will we?"

Krake studied them, the tiny girl and the great

horned beast. Prudence fought longing in his mind. Prudence lost. "If you're all sure this is what you want, then—" surrendering—"all right."

Moon searched his face. "Are you sure?"

Krake, who was not at all sure—who had been surprised to hear his own mouth form the words "all right" —grimaced. "Let's just do it before I change my mind," he said sourly. "We'll need extra food, more supplies— well, we can arrange all that at the orbit station. We'll take a car up the space ladder."

"Right away," Moon Bunderan said firmly.

"Well, why not?" said Krake, smiling at last. "Get your things, whatever you want to take with you, and we'll be on our way."

"All I need to take is Thrayl," Moon said, patting the Taur's broad back. The Taur turned and mooed at her, his great horns glowing bright. A cloud crossed her face as she listened.

"What did he just say?" Sork demanded.

She said slowly, "I don't entirely understand. He was listening to his song, and sometimes when he tells me what the singing was about I don't know what he means. He seems to think that we're doing the right thing, that it's *important* we go with you. But there's something else, too. I think—" She hesitated, then finished. "I think he said that because of what we do everything will change, in ways we cannot now understand."

———

The funny thing, Sork thought, was that in the turmoil around the loading area he was almost sure he had seen the Turtle, Litlun, scurrying into an earlier car. Why would the Turtle be heading up to the orbiter? But, Sork told himself perhaps he was wrong; it had been only a fleeting glimpse, and when he thought of mentioning it to the others he decided against. It would only worry Moon Bunderan, to no purpose.

And he had so much on his mind already! He was actually tingling with excitement—literally, tingling—it was almost as though an electric shock were teasing his body, raising the short hairs on his arms. It was the same feeling he had felt just before he took that first, needed drink—back in the days when he needed drinks to survive, before Sue-ling Quong showed up and gave a new purpose to his life. He didn't want a drink now. What he wanted most he was actually about to *have*!

Sork could hardly sit still in the space ladder lift car as it slid up the cables toward the orbit station. They had been lucky to get space in a car, with so many Turtles going up to orbit with all sorts of strange possessions. The car reeked of the little knot of Turtles that shared it with them, clustered in their own corner. It was an odor that tickled the nostrils, almost stinging, like menthol but tinctured with something repellent, like an opened grave.

Sork craned his neck to see out the window of the elevator car. Disappointingly, there was little but clouds to see. The orbit station itself hung high above, tethered by its three lift cables to Kuala Lumpur, the west coast of Africa and Kansas City. Its central location put it sixty thousand kilometers over equatorial Brazil. Of course there was no hope of seeing it from the lift car yet, and there was nothing to see below but the curve of the Brazilian bulge into the broad Atlantic Ocean. Even that was almost obscured by the clouds.

Sork Quintero sank back into his uncomfortable perch. The lift cars had been designed for Turtles, not human beings; Turtles who were half again as tall as humans, and whose leathery carapaces did not bend in the same way as human bodies. And the thrusting of the car as it pulled itself up its long hundred-thousand-kilometer lift didn't help. At first it had been like being perched on the edge of a tall, uncomfortable desk, with someone twice as heavy as himself riding his shoulders, for the acceleration of the car, too, was set to Turtle standards, not human. But then it had slowed somewhat—or the thrust of acceleration had been eased, Sork did not know which—and now they could at least move about.

He patted the pouch at his side. There had been no time to pack. There also had been little in the way of possessions for any of them worth the trouble of packing. He had insisted on taking all Sue-ling's old university lecture chips—as much out of spite, to keep them from Litlun, as for any use he could see for them.

Next to him the young woman from New Mexico was scribbling on a notepad. Peering over her shoulder, Sork could see that it was a long letter to her parents, to be mailed, no doubt, from the orbiter. The girl was weeping silently as she wrote, and her Taur had rested a hard, warm hand on her shoulders protectively.

Sork looked the creature over with distaste. It was impossible to read expression on that broad, branded face, but the Taur was moaning softly, musically, to himself, his eyes fixed on vacancy. Sork hoped it wasn't going to be airsick. It was a mistake to bring that animal along, Sork was sure; but the girl had been so insistent—

On a compassionate impulse he reached down and touched her arm.

The Taur's eyes came into quick focus, and the great horned head turned warningly toward Sork. Sork hurried his words, as Moon Bunderan looked up inquiringly, "I thought you'd like to see where we're going. We'll be coming in sight of the orbiting station soon, and you've never seen it, have you?" Nor had he himself, of course, except in pictures.

"Thank you, Mr. Quintero," the girl said with polite interest. She put down her pen, dabbed at her eyes and said brightly, "It's a wonderful thing, isn't it? The space ladder, I mean. The Turtles certainly gave us some wonderful inventions."

"But it isn't!" Sork cried. "I mean the skyhook *isn't* a Turtle invention—or not just theirs, anyway. Human beings had thought of the space ladder long ago, way before the Turtles came."

"Oh, really?" She pondered that. "Well, then, if it's so useful, why didn't we build one ourselves?"

Sork flushed. "It was just too big an engineering project for our resources—then. Oh, we certainly would have done it, sooner or later. But the Turtles had a big advantage."

"They're more advanced scientifically, yes," the girl nodded.

"No, that's not what I mean. It's true enough, but it's not the most important reason. I admit the space ladder has to use some very high-tech materials, cables with a tensile strength that's pretty remarkable, but our scientists would have developed something that would do. No, what made it hard for us to build a ladder like this was the cost."

The girl looked disbelieving. "You mean there wasn't enough money?"

"Not just the money cost, though that would have been spectacular. The important thing was the cost to the environment. Every gram of material in the ladder—cables, cars, orbital station, machinery, everything—and that comes to billions of tons!—every last gram would have had to be mined and manufactured on the surface of the Earth. Then it would have had to be launched from the surface to orbit. It wasn't the building of the ladder that was too hard. It was getting all that stuff into orbit—in the cargo bays of rocket ships! With ten times the mass of fuel having to be lifted for every gram of cargo, and all those terrible rocket exhausts messing up the stratosphere. But the Turtles, you see, had the big advantage that they *started* in space. They didn't have to fight the gravity well to assemble the orbiter. They built it out of asteroid iron and cometary-nucleus materials, and all those things were already in orbit. The Turtles manufactured the whole skyhook, cables, cars and all, right in space!"

"Oh," the girl said, nodding. "I see." Then, that subject finished, good manners directed that she find another. She gestured around at the three Turtles who were sharing their car. All of them were busily strapping themselves in. "What's happening?"

"We're getting close," Sork told her. "We'd better buckle in, too."

And then, as they fumbled with the straps, "There it is!" his brother shouted, his face pressed against the crystal.

All of them leaned as far forward as they could. The station itself was now in sight, seen from below and rapidly approaching. It was well worth looking at. The orbital station was not a single object. It was several score capsules linked together with cables and passages—like beads on a string, but jumbled together as though the necklace had been squeezed into a tightly interlocking ball.

Sork took it upon himself to be tour guide for the young girl from New Mexico, loosening his safety straps to see better. "Some of those things are the living quarters for the station Turtles and the working parts of the station," he informed her. "They don't have wave-drives. They don't have propulsive capacity at all, not even reaction drives. They don't go anywhere, just stay there as a base. But the other things you see—the things that, some of them, look kind of like peanuts? Those are real ships. The little round ones are the orbital shuttles and workships; they're rocket driven and they don't go very far. But the big ones shaped like peanuts—do you see the ones I'm pointing at? Those are interstellar wave-drive ships."

"I see," Moon said. Then, pointing, "What about that one over there? It's got some kind of design on it, do you see? The red and white stripes, the blue with the white stars?"

"I can't see," Sork complained—and then the car seemed to lurch as abruptly it decelerated. Sork clutched for the webbing and almost missed it. It was the space captain, Francis Krake, who reached out with one strong arm and kept him from flying into the cluster of disapproving Turtles, glaring and murmuring at them.

"Thanks," Sork muttered, hastily lashing himself in.

"That's all right," Krake said. "You were asking about the insignia?"

Sork looked up at him. "What insignia?"

"On the ship you were looking at. The red, white and blue? That's my ship, the *Golden Hind*. That thing painted on the side—I had it put there. It's an American flag."

Of them all, only Krake had been off Earth before. Getting out of the lift car every one of them found himself stumbling and swaying. "Microgravity," Krake warned, grinning. "You'll get used to it—but make sure you're holding on to something every chance you get until you do, all right? Now, let's see if we can find Chief Thunderbird and get my crew back." He started to turn away, then paused, looking at Sork. "Are you all right?" he demanded impatiently.

Sork licked his lips. He felt so *odd*! As though he were floating—but not floating serenely like a cloud in a summer sky, but uneasily slipping, sliding—Sork had never been at sea, but he recognized the term "seasickness." "I—think so," he said hoarsely, and then corrected himself. "Well, not very," he admitted.

His brother was no better off than he, and Moon Bunderan was holding tight to the arm of her Taur, her face mirroring interior problems of her own. Sue-ling looked at the brothers with worry. "It's not serious, you know," she told them. "It's just what's called vestibular disorientation. Try not to move your heads any more than you have to; moving around shakes up the little ear canals." But Sork saw that she was showing signs of strain herself.

"Oh, hell," Krake said, exasperated. "Come on, let's go to the surgery. You'll feel better if you keep doing something. Anyway this won't last too long . . . I hope," he finished, in a lower voice.

Sork swallowed and tried to obey orders. Moving about in microgravity was a whole unlearned skill for him, but he saw how Krake pulled himself along by railings, hardly bothering to walk at all. Hazily, Sork was aware of his surroundings. He noticed, in a dim way, the unnatural stillness of the orbit station: There were great lashed-down mounds of supplies, redfruit seed and machinery and all the myriad commodities the Turtles traded to Earth. But they were not being transferred to the down cars that would take them to the surface of the human planet. They were simply sitting there, and the few Turtles in sight seemed dazed, or obsessed—some wandering at random, some hurrying recklessly about. The shock that had disabled the Turtles on the surface of the Earth had clearly reached here too.

There were no other human beings in sight, but Sork hadn't expected any. Everyone knew that the whole orbit station was Turtle territory.

Sork did his best to follow the instructions of the expert. They helped a little. By holding his head as rigid as possible, and especially by fixing his eyes on things as far distant as possible, he managed to still most of the uneasiness in his belly. He felt Krake's encouraging hand on his shoulder. "Almost there," the waveship captain said, and Sork nodded gratefully.

Then Krake stopped short.

Sork saw that a Turtle half again as tall as Litlun, twice as tall as any human, stood commandingly in their way. His shell was ruby red, his beak black and hooked as he challenged them.

"That's Chief Thunderbird—the 'Proctor,' they call him," Krake whispered. "He's in charge of the port. Let me do the talking."

As they approached, the Turtle gave all of them a withering glance from each eye. He addressed the space captain. "You," he stated, engaging his transposer to make his words intelligible, "are the one who is permitted to captain one of our ships. Who are these other creatures?"

"My new crew," Krake said without hesitation. "I've added a few for—for special purposes. They are Kiri and Sork Quintero, Sue-ling Quong, Moon Bunderan. I will require additional supplies for them. At least twice the usual quantities."

The huge Turtle's roving eyes scanned them all again before he spoke. Both locked on Thrayl, gazing mildly at the Turtle. "One has heard of this Taur," Chief Thunderbird said. "It is an adult male, but neither castrated nor dehorned."

"Thrayl isn't dangerous!" Moon Bunderan said quickly. "I promise he won't do any harm."

The eyes swiveled briefly toward her, then focused on Sork and Kiri. "Quintero and Quintero," the Turtle said musingly. "One has heard of these humans as well." Then the eyes returned to Francis Krake, and the Turtle said, "It is permitted. Additional supplies are appropriate and will be installed. It will be done at once."

"Fine," Krake said. "Now, what about my crew? Are they ready to travel?"

One of the huge Turtle's eyes remained on Krake, the other seemed to wander at random. Once again the Proctor took his time about replying. "They are," he said at last.

Krake said suspiciously, "What are you hiding? Is something wrong I haven't been told?"

The Turtle shrugged the massive carapace indifferently. "Nothing is 'wrong.' It is simply that certain events have caused unanticipated changes in large-scale planning," he squawked. "Your crew has been summoned. As soon as they arrive here you may proceed to your ship, for it is necessary to leave soon."

Krake glared at him, puzzled. "What do you know about when it's time for my ship to leave?"

The Turtle did not answer, but simply turned and stalked off. Krake scowled after him, until Sork Quintero, who had been glancing from one to the other, touched his arm. "Is he always like that?" he asked.

Krake shrugged irritably. "I don't know him that well. I never even saw him until I came in a few days ago, with Marco and Daisy Fay needing attention, and I certainly don't see that he has anything to do with when my ship leaves."

"What about your crew?" asked Sue-ling.

"I wish I knew! I guess the only thing we can do is wait here at the Proctor's office until they show up," said Krake, tugging angrily at his beard. He was obviously very displeased.

Sork Quintero said, "If you want my opinion, Krake,

you're handling this all wrong. Why do you let that Turtle push you around?"

Krake turned the scowl on Sork. "And what is it that you think I should do?"

"Why—just go to wherever your people are and pick them up—"

"Where's that? Where's the place where my crew is?"

"How should I know that?" Sork said, sounding indignant. "You're the one who's supposed to know his way around this place."

"Thank you. I wish it was true. I've been here exactly once before in my life, and only for a couple of hours then," Krake pointed out.

"So we're just going to stand here, doing nothing?" Sork blustered. "God, Krake! If that's the way you run your ship, maybe we're better off with the Turtles after all!"

"Sork, Sork," said his brother, distressed. "Captain Krake, too—let's not argue like this."

"Kiri's right," Sue-ling seconded. "Sork, don't get so belligerent, please. Remember, we're all going to be together in a small ship for a long time, so we'd better work at getting along."

Sork stared at his twin and his love, the picture of offended innocence. "What did I do?" he demanded. "I was only saying that it's stupid to be just standing here. If that hurt your feelings, I'm sorry."

Then Kiri put his hand on Sork's shoulder to quiet him. Kiri was studying the space captain's face. "Francis," he said, his voice gentle, "is there something wrong that you haven't told us?"

Krake flushed. He tugged at the beard for a moment, then said, "I guess there is something I should have mentioned. Well, not anything *wrong*, but anyway there's something *different*—about Marco and Daisy Fay, I mean. My crew."

"What about them?" Sork demanded suspiciously.

Krake ran his fingers through his cinnamon-colored beard. "They're a little unusual," he said.

"Unusual how? Do we have to drag it out of you? If you've got something to say, then say it!"

Krake held up a mollifying hand. "All right, you've made your point. It's just that, you see, when we were—rescued—or kidnapped, whichever way you want to look at it—both Daisy Fay and Marco were in really bad shape. They'd been in a plane crash, and then, to make it worse, they were trapped in an avalanche. They had it all —frostbites, broken limbs, terrible internal injuries—it was a miracle the Turtles were able to keep them alive at all."

Sue-ling said sympathetically, "We know what great surgeons the Turtles are—they're where I get the memo disks I use myself."

Krake nodded. "Exactly. Or, I mean, that's not exactly what I was going to say. Remember, when the Turtles worked on us they'd never dealt with human beings before, so they had to—well—sort of figure things out as they went along. And—"

That was as far as he got. There was a lowing sound from the Taur, whose horns had begun to glow in prismatic colors, and Moon Bunderan said softly, "Oh, my dear Lord! What are *those*?"

Around a bend in the hall came two figures. Sork gasped as he saw them, and even Kiri caught his breath.

They did not look at all human. They were two hard-shelled, egg-shaped bodies, one glinting of copper, the other the black of Japanese lacquer. Each had eight boneless, prehensile limbs protruding from the globular body, all of them writhing at once. Two large eyes—Turtle eyes, not at all the eyes of human beings—gazed out at the newcomers from the ends of flexible stalks. And, strangest of all, there was something like a video screen on the belly of each shell, and each screen showed a friendly, animated human face.

"Hello, Francis," said a voice from the copper-colored one. The face on its screen was that of a young woman, fresh-faced and eager. The machine turned to the others in the group. "I'm Daisy Fay," it said.

"And I'm Marco," said the other, the voice human

enough to sound embarrassed, the face on the belly screen a dark-skinned man with an engaging, diffident smile.

Sork whirled on Francis Krake. "And these are your *crew*?" he demanded.

Krake sighed. "I tried to tell you," he said. "They've been like this ever since."

Though the aiodoi are not of space and time, it is of space and time that they sing, and it is to the smallsongs of space and time they hear (for they hear all songs, always and everywhere) that they listen most closely . . . even though so many of the smallsongs are sad, or angry, or simply wrong.

———

"Today, class, we're going to talk about a different kind of history. We discussed the three ages of mankind briefly, and the three ages of the universe in a little more detail. Today we're going to discuss the three ages of mankind's *understanding* of the universe. That's history, too, and you can write it in three words. The three words are:

"Caprice,

"Causality, and

"Chaos.

"Those are the three big Cs.

"The first C was the age of Caprice, and it lasted the longest time, maybe a million years. That was the time when everything was a superstitious marvel. For all that time, people thought that the Sun rose, the lightning struck and the wind blew not for any natural reason, but simply at the Caprice of some supernatural being—or beings. Sometimes the people thought there were any number of them, maybe one for every rock and tree and cloud.

"Some of the things that happened were really important to the people. If the rain didn't fall at the right time, you got no crops. If the Sun disappeared in an eclipse, you would do anything to get it back.

"So primitive man did his best to make deals with these Capricious supernatural entities. They sacrificed harvest grains to them, or animals, or sometimes their own children. They made love in the furrows of their fields to encourage the harvest gods to be fertile—whatever it took. Or whatever kind of bribe or inducement they thought it might take.

"Then some people got a little smarter. The smartest of them, way back then, were the ancient Greeks. They got an idea in their heads. Suppose, they suggested, things didn't really just *happen* because of some supernatural Caprice. Suppose there were *laws* that governed things like the procession of the seasons, and the movement of the planets about the sky, and everything else in the observable world.

"Suppose, in other words, that everything had a Cause.

"That is the state of mind that we now call 'scientific.' It began about six centuries before Christ, in the Greek settlements on the west coast of Asia Minor. It was the first notion of Causality, and it lasted for two and a half thousand years.

"The Greeks carried the burden of the Causality idea for almost half that time. Then the rest of the world began to get the idea at, oh, let's say, about the time of Copernicus. By then we began to have all those great minds trying to figure out just what Caused things to happen—people like Kepler and Galileo, Robert Boyle and Christiaan Huygens—Isaac Newton, one of the greatest of them all—Dalton, Carnot, Faraday, Maxwell —right up to Albert Einstein and his lifelong search for a

Unified Field Theory that would explain the Causes of *everything*.

"All of them were looking for the same thing, you see. They were trying to figure out the rules by which A interacted with B to produce the state C. All Causal, by their basic nature.

"Then things began to go a little sour for Causality, because along came Planck, Heisenberg and Stephen Hawking to tell these great seekers that they had been looking in the wrong place.

"In the *right* place—in the place where first explanations had to be found—Causality broke down. There were events which did not have specific, identifiable causes. Some kinds of information had to remain forever unknown. Some processes, in short, were intrinsically Chaotic . . . which meant that no matter how much you knew about the state of System X today, you had no way of predicting what its state would be tomorrow.

"That's when Chaos came along. It wasn't welcome. People like Einstein really hated it. 'God does not throw dice with the universe,' he protested, and Hawking came back with his famous riposte: 'God not only throws dice, he sometimes throws them in places where they can't be seen.' "

———

And the aiodoi, who saw all always, sang:
"Of course.
"No one can see what is never there."

8

Kiri Quintero looked placidly at the thing with the copper-colored shell that was approaching him. "Hello," it said in a warm female voice, extending a tentacle to take Kiri's hand. "I'm Daisy Fay. It's just wonderful to see human beings again—besides Francis, I mean."

To Kiri's mild surprise, the tentacle felt warm and soft, not metallic at all. "Hello," Kiri said. "I hope you'll excuse my friends. We just didn't know exactly what—uh—"

The biomech laughed. "What we looked like? Francis didn't tell you, did he? Well, I know we're a surprise to you. We were pretty much a surprise to ourselves when we woke up the first time! But the Turtles have done a good job, especially now, considering what it's been like for them, the last few days. Chief Thunderbird's a righteous tyrant, when he wants to be, and he usually does. But he made sure they checked us over and got us in shape for the next mission."

Beside Kiri, his twin brother said, shuddering, "Like that kind of shape?"

"Like still being alive," the girl said softly, "and that's more than we would have been without their help. Would we have done as much for one of them?"

"I hope not," snarled Sork Quintero.

A stalked eye turned toward him, the face on the

belly plate still smiling. "I don't think we've met yet," said Daisy Fay. And the introductions went around—as if they were, Kiri thought, any new couple coming to a party.

"We're both glad to meet you all," said the one called Marcos, "but, Francis, don't you think we should head for the ship?"

"I don't know where it is," Krake confessed.

"Of course you don't, Francis, but we do," the girl said. "Lead the way, Marco!" And as they started off, she slipped a tentacle fondly into her captain's hand. "Anyway," she said, "I'm dying of curiosity. What's this mission Chief Thunderbird's been talking about?"

Krake turned to stare at her. "Mission? What mission are you talking about?"

The biomech hesitated. "I thought you'd know, Francis," she said. "Chief Thunderbird told us we had to be ready for some big deal—do you mean he hasn't told you what it's going to be?"

"He has damn well not," Krake snarled. The pretty face on the belly of the biomech looked sympathetic.

"Oh, Francis," she sighed. "You're getting all upset again, aren't you? I'm sorry I mentioned it. Anyway, we'll be at the ship in a minute—"

"And then we're out of here," Krake said flatly, "and then it doesn't matter what kind of plans the Turtles have!"

But in that he was quite wrong.

———

For Kiri Quintero, the situation was becoming uncomfortable. He could sense conflict and pain—Francis Krake's worries, his brother Sork's confusion and fear, Moon Bunderan's apprehension over the fate of her pet Taur. Kiri wished he could ease their unhappiness. There was no need for it! Everything which was right would go on being right; that was an immutable truth. Kiri wished he had the words to convey that certain knowledge to the others. Not all the others needed explanations, though.

Kiri had a strange feeling about that, wholly unexpected and not at all logical. It was ridiculous, really—at least, Sork would surely say so—but Kiri felt sure that the dumb beast who was with them, Moon Bunderan's Taur, shared that tranquil understanding.

That was impossible, Kiri Quintero told himself firmly . . . knowing that it was not.

Then they turned a corner, and they were there. Through a crystalline window in the wall Kiri Quintero could see the odd-shaped waveship with the even odder "American flag" painted on it. "Home at last," said Krake, smiling for the first time since talking to the huge Turtle. . . .

But the smile froze when they opened the port, for someone was there before them. Two Turtles were standing there inside the ship, waiting for them.

One of them was that same Chief Thunderbird they had met in the corridor. The other was rusty brown, with bright yellow eyes that roved around them all, and Moon Bunderan cried out when she recognized him. "You may enter the ship," said Litlun, the Facilitator. "You took a long time to get here. It is time for us to leave."

That was more than Captain Francis Krake could stand.

He growled in rage, hurling himself into the doorway, dwarfed by the armored bulk of the two Turtles but giving not a centimeter. He glared up into Chief Thunderbird's hard-beaked face. "What are you doing in my ship?" Krake demanded.

The Turtle glared at him with his ruby eyes, then rasped through his transposer: "Do not speak foolishly. We must begin the voyage now." The Turtle gave him a fleeting glance from one eye, the other roaming around the group. "The presence of this Taur is required, also its keeper and the Quintero Sork. Other human persons may depart this ship if they wish, for they are not needed."

"Not needed," Krake snarled, simmering with anger. "What do you have to say about what's needed? You have no right here, either of you. Get off my ship!" he shouted.

Litlun drew himself up to his full height, his narrow-beaked head hostile. "It is not your ship," he squawked in the gurgly, chirpy Turtle language, his transposer converting it into frequencies humans could comprehend. "It is only leased to you."

"But the lease is part of a *contract*—it's good as long as I work for you Turtles! I was promised that. Won't you keep to your agreement?"

"Do not question the instructions we give you!" Litlun thundered, but Chief Thunderbird intervened.

"Wait," he squawked, and with one sweeping movement turned off both transposers. The two Turtles hissed and gurgled at each other for a moment, then the Proctor turned his transposer on again. Sweeping the group with his eyes, he declared, "There is no quarrel here. There is only an agreement to be made."

"The hell you say," Krake snapped, and Sork Quintero put in:

"You certainly can't make the Taur and Moon Bunderan go with you. That's kidnapping!"

"There is no kidnapping here, Quintero," hissed Litlun. "Listen to the Proctor as he explains!"

And Chief Thunderbird, drawing himself up, said majestically, "There is simply a sharing of assets. You have certain things which we need, this Taur and the lecture chips."

Sork's jaw dropped. "How do you know about the chips?"

"Foolish person," the Turtle squawked, "do you think we are not aware of what you carry in those bags? Of course we know! And you have these things which we require, while we have what you want, this ship. We will form a partnership."

"Partnership, hell!" snarled Krake. "It's my ship, as long as I'm working for you!"

"You *are* working for us," Litlun thundered. "This ship is required to take the Proctor and myself on a voyage on Turtle business—the most important Turtle business there can ever be!"

"What business?" Krake demanded.

"There is no necessity for you to know that. There is only one question: Shall this be with you or without you? None of you humans are needed, Francis Krake. Both we Brothers are competent to pilot this vessel without you."

"And you won't even tell us what we're going to do?"

The Turtles hesitated. One eye of each turned to regard the other, but neither spoke.

Krake swallowed unhappily, gazing around. At his look, his crew stirred. Daisy Fay said tentatively, "He's right about that, Francis. It's basically their ship, and any Turtle can run it."

And Marco said, "We'll fight them if you want, Francis, but that's true."

Krake surrendered. "If I have to take your orders to keep my ship, then I'll take your orders," he said sourly. "Under one condition. Answer the question."

Both Turtles bristled. Then Chief Thunderbird swept the transposers off again, and the two Turtles bickered for a long moment in their own language.

At last Chief Thunderbird turned his transposer back on. "We have decided that you may retain your title," he squealed. "You will, however, follow our instructions. First you are to undock this ship. As soon as we are at suitable distance you will engage the wave-drive."

"You weren't listening," Krake accused. "You have to answer our question."

Each Turtle turned an eye again toward the other. It was Chief Thunderbird who spoke first. "Our destination is the Mother planet," he squawked.

"Or," Litlun added painfully, "the place where it used to be."

"Then what?" Krake insisted.

Hesitation. Then Chief Thunderbird took over. "We cannot give you an answer at this time. First we must conduct certain researches—"

"What kind of researches?"

The huge Turtle was losing patience. "We will inform

you as needed!" he screeched, and added, "It is enough for you to know the purpose of them. It is the greatest and most sublime purpose in the universe. You are privileged to be allowed to share in it; for what we propose is to restore a Mother to the Brotherhood!"

Sweetly the aiodoi sang on, and listened on, and sometimes almost laughed at the smallsongs they heard.

———

"When we were talking about particle formation some of you had trouble reconciling the wave-particle duality. I suppose by now you've got the duality question pretty clear in your mind, or anyway if you haven't you're probably flunking out of the course so it doesn't matter. Now I want to try something else.

"Let's put the 'wave' part of the duality out of our minds for a minute, so we can talk about another little peculiarity of the particle considered only as a particle.

"When you think of the electron as a particle, you probably envision it as small, hard and round—like a tiny version of a planet like the Earth. That's all right up to a point. The point where it stops being all right is when you start to rotate the particle.

"Let me give you an illustration.

"Suppose you took a slip of paper and bent it into a ring, gluing the ends together.

"Then suppose you took a bead that was the size of an electron—you can't possibly do this, of course, but we're just *supposing*—and you made a slit in it so that you could thread it onto the paper ring. (It would have to be a very *small* paper ring, of course.) Let's say this little electron-sized bead has distinct surface markings— maybe it looks like a globe of the Earth—so you can always tell which part is facing you: You're looking directly down on Ecuador. The particle's North Pole is toward your head, its South Pole is toward your feet.

"Got that so far? All right, now let's do our mind experiment.

"If you slide this bead all the way around the ring of paper, when it comes back to its original position you are looking down at Ecuador again. The bead has turned through 360 degrees and it's exactly as it was before. Anybody who didn't see you turning it would have no way of knowing it had been turned at all. There is no test anyone can apply that can tell whether or not it had been rotated. So it doesn't really matter, in any objective sense, whether you've spun the thing around through 360 degrees or not.

"That isn't the case with an electron.

"If you wanted to perform the same experiment with a real electron, rather than with an electron-sized bead, you would have to make the paper ring a different way. That is, you would have to give the paper a half-twist before you glued the ends together.

"Doing that, of course, turns the paper ring into what's called a Moebius strip.

"So now you can do your mind experiment, and you will see that something funny happens. When you slide your electron around the ring to its original position, it's not quite the same. You're still looking down on 'Ecuador,' all right, but the rest of the globe is all screwed up. It turns out that now the North Pole is where the South Pole used to be. The thing has been turned upside down.

"It's still possible to get it straightened out, but now it requires an extra step. If you want to return it to its original state, you have to slide it around the Moebius strip *twice*. Then it's back the way it started and, again, there is no test anyone can apply that can show it was rotated at all.

"So in a certain sense, from the point of view of an electron, a circle doesn't have just 360 degrees, it has 720.

"Does that confuse you?

"Good! Let me just remind you of what Niels Bohr said, long ago: 'If a man does not feel dizzy when he first learns about the quantum, he has not understood a word.' "

———

And, greatly amused, the aiodoi sang:

———

"What is there to understand?

"What is so is so. What is so understands itself, and that is all there is."

9

For Sue-ling Quong, this was becoming a real adventure. It was exciting! It made her feel young again—as young as Moon Bunderan, or even younger, for the girl from New Mexico seemed to be able to take all in her stride . . . while Sue-ling was experiencing one thrill after another. When she looked around the control room of *The Golden Hind* she was not only impressed, she was startled, as well, and even delighted, like any tourist visiting a wondrous place never seen before.

The heart of a waveship was certainly impressive to look at. There were banks of controls—two separate sets of them, it seemed, though for what reason Sue-ling could not guess. Though it was a large room it was crowded now. The two Turtles and Moon Bunderan's Taur took up more space than anyone else, but the little band of human adventurers now numbered seven—well, Sue-ling thought, assuming you included as human these odd new robotic things that said they were Francis Krake's crew.

But some of the pleasure and excitement were spoiled for Sue-ling Quong by the childish, abrasive, deplorable way everyone was acting! She was almost ashamed of her friends—well, when you came right down to it, she admitted to herself, only two of them. Kiri as always was quiet and generally placatory; Moon Bunderan and the two robotic crew members were mostly listening. The offenders, really, were Francis Krake, veins starting out on his dark temples as he shouted at the two Turtles—though Sue-ling had long since lost track of just what it was the captain and the Turtles were arguing so vehemently about . . . and, yes, that problem child, that loved one who was so seldom lovable, Sork Quintero. He was so *up*! She toyed with the thought that perhaps he'd started drinking again—but where would he get liquor on this spartan waveship?

Willing to do anything to stop the bickering, Sue-ling marched up to Sork, took his arm, pulled him away. "What's the matter with you?" she demanded. "Can't we just get started without all these cat fights?"

Sork stared at her unbelievingly. "But didn't you hear what that big Turtle's saying? He wants us to find their missing Mother—or get them a new one, or something. They're really out of their minds now, Sue-ling. I thought Litlun was crazy when he was trying to buy everything in sight—the Taur, the lecture chips—but this is *really* loopy."

Sue-ling interrupted him. "I've been thinking about that. Are they all connected?—the Taur, the chips, this trip?"

Sork blinked at her, trying to wrestle this new datum into his overriding plan. "I don't know," he said at last. "That's not what I'm worrying about, anyway. What's on my mind is—what if they succeed?"

Sue-ling gazed at him, not understanding. "Yes?"

"Don't you see? Litlun wants us to help him keep the Turtle race alive—but that's not what we want! If they all die off it will be the best thing that ever happened to us!" Sork turned to his brother and Moon Bunderan, drawing near them to get away from the storm center. "Isn't that true, Kiri?" he demanded.

Even Kiri's calm had been frayed by the squabbling. He gave his brother a tired, forgiving smile and said gently: "Whatever is right will happen, Sork."

Moon Bunderan turned and looked up at him. "Are you sure of that, Kiri?"

"Very sure," he said positively, though his face was still strained.

"Oh, I hope you're right," the girl from New Mexico told him. "But I'm still afraid of that little one. Why do you suppose he wants Thrayl?"

Sork made a sweeping-away gesture, dismissing all such questions at once: "Turtles! Who knows why they want anything? What matters is what *we* want. Shall we help the Turtles survive?"

The little red robot thing named Marco was scuttling over to them. "Friends," he called out, the face on his belly smiling up at them, "it looks like we're going to be on our way. I suggest you all hold onto something for undocking!"

"Have they settled what they're going to do?" Sork Quintero demanded.

"Settled?" The face was laughing now. "No, you can't say anything's really *settled* . . . but we're taking off anyway!"

———

In the control room the Turtles had moved to one side, out of the way. Francis Krake was at one of the control boards, looking irritated but determined. Daisy Fay McQueen was at the other board. "Screens!" Krake called, and Daisy Fay touched a button with one of her long tentacles.

Sue-ling caught her breath. The walls around the control room blinked and disappeared! She was looking at a view of the space around the *Hind,* almost as though there were a transparent band circling the control room.

"It's all right," Marco whispered, seeing her surprise. "Daisy's just turned on the external screens so we can see what's happening—there aren't any windows in a wave-ship, you know. But the screens are pretty good, aren't they? Now the captain's going to start the undocking."

So he did. "We go," called Krake, moving some toggles on his board.

Sue-ling grabbed at one of Marco's tentacles as the

floor seemed to lurch under her. Outside, she saw the umbilical to the orbit station they were moored to. No longer! Tie clamps were parting. Lax cables dropped away and were automatically reeled in to the station. Set free from its moorings, *The Golden Hind* drifted clear.

Sue-ling winced in the sudden blaze of eye-straining light as the docks of the orbit station burned behind them in the light of the naked Sun, an ungainly tangle of tanks and valves and connected passageways.

"Board green," Daisy Fay called, and took her fingers off the board. Off in a corner Marco turned a smiling face up to Sue-ling Quong.

"That's it," he announced. "Now we'll start the mass-drive as soon as we drift clear of the structure. Then we have to move out of range of the station before we go into wave-drive. It'll take a little while."

Uncomfortably, Sue-ling remembered to let go of his tentacle. "Thanks," she said. "Is that all there is to it?"

"Well, all for just now," he said. One of his eyes turned, gazing around the room. "We haven't got you settled yet, have we? Would you like me to show you to your quarters? There'll be time before we go into wave-drive."

Sue-ling, grateful, said, "Oh, I'd like that—but I don't want to miss when we do that, you know."

Marco was chuckling. "You mean miss the experience of knowing when we go into wave-drive? Oh, I wouldn't worry about that, Sue-ling. You'll know, all right."

———

On the way to Sue-ling's quarters they passed the cubicle where Sork was busily listening in again to the old lecture chips. "Are you sure you don't mind doing this, Marco?" she asked. "Missing the lectures, I mean?"

The face that looked up at her from the belly screen looked a little embarrassed. "Well, a little," he admitted. "But Sork promised to let me borrow them later on. I don't sleep much, you know—don't have to sleep at all unless I specially want to. So I have the time. And actually I've been really fascinated by all that old stuff." He hesitated, then turned an eye to look at her. "I wished when I was a boy that I could be an astronomer," he confessed.

"You're better than any astronomer now. You actually go out and *touch* these other worlds," she told him, and wondered if she meant it.

And yet, funnily, she did. Sue-ling was beginning to believe that whatever had happened to Marco had not been all loss. With his eight tentacles to pull him along, he scampered through the walkways of the waveship like a mechanical dog.

And that was another strange—but, really, very nice! —sensation for Sue-ling Quong, to be in the company of this funny-looking robot who said he was a human being. On balance, she was pleased to be with him rather than the others just now. As a practical matter, she wanted to know where she was going to sleep. As an emotional one, she was glad to be away from the constant, draining squabbles in the control room.

"You want to get to know these sections of the ship, Sue-ling, because you'll have to spend a lot of time here. At least while we're traveling on rocket drive you will," Marco called, one eye wobbling back to look at her as he led the way. "These parts are pretty well shielded, but even here you need to be careful sometimes, if there's a solar flare or anything."

"Solar flare?" Sue-ling repeated questioningly.

"That's a sudden flux of radiation from a star. Of course, you only have to worry about it when we're near one, like now. Usually when we're traveling we'll be in wave-drive and pretty far away from any star—it's a big universe, you know. Not that even a solar flare could do us any harm in wave-drive, for that matter. Anyway, the Sun isn't flaring right now." Marco gestured casually around with a couple of his tentacles. "All these areas are shielded against radiation. Daisy Fay and I don't care; we're not very sensitive to radiation. But Francis is. When the Turtles had the *Hind* they used these spaces for cargoes that might have been damaged by radiation."

"What kind of cargoes would that be?"

Marco's tentacles writhed, and the picture on the belly plate shrugged. "I would guess they were mostly living things of one kind or another. The Turtles wouldn't need shielding themselves, of course. They *thrive* on radiation. Now, take a deep breath, Sue-ling. Can you smell anything?" Both eyes turned to regard her.

Sue-ling sniffed thoughtfully. Then she nodded. There was indeed a faint, sour reek in the air. "I think so. Like something spoiled."

"That's it. I can't smell anything any more," Marco apologized, "so I can't tell for myself. But Francis used to complain that there was always a stink in this part of the ship. It comes from something the Turtles were hauling, I guess." He hesitated, the eyes roving around to study Sue-ling's face. Her eyes were fixed on him. "Is something the matter?"

Embarrassed, Sue-ling cleared her throat. "I was just wondering—" she began diffidently.

The machine-man laughed out loud. "I know what you were wondering. You want to know how I came to look this way, don't you?"

Sue-ling flushed. "I'm sorry, Marco. I don't want to be rude."

"Don't worry, Sue-ling. You won't hurt my feelings asking about it. I know what I look like. I can't say I *enjoy* it, really. But it's a lot better than being dead. And that was the only other possibility for me."

The face on the platen looked grim for a moment, then relaxed. "It was a long time ago," Marco said. "I guess Francis told you about the Turtle scout ship that was exploring the system, a couple of hundred years ago. . . ."

She nodded. "They found him adrift in the Coral Sea and picked him up."

"That's right. But Francis wasn't the only one they picked up." The tentacles and eyestalks moved restlessly, and the face on the belly plate looked somber. "I think the war frightened the Turtles," Marco said. "They don't like wars, because of what the Sh'shrane almost did to them a long time ago—"

"Sh'shrane?"

"They were the ones the Turtles did have a war with, long ago. I don't know much about it," he apologized. "It isn't a subject the Turtles like to talk about. But the Turtles lost that war, I think. I guess when they saw a good, big war going on on Earth, the Turtles couldn't help wondering whether this unruly new race of aliens— us—might be a problem for them. So they took samples. The samples were always individuals who were right at the point of death, like Daisy Fay and Francis and me. And they always did it where it was safe, in places where their scout ship could not be seen or detected by the primitive radar of the time."

"And that's all they took? Just the three of you?"

"Oh, no. Altogether they picked out twenty-two specimens—some of them corpses, some of them so near death that even the Turtles couldn't save them. We're just the only ones that survived. I was lucky—I guess," he finished.

Sue-ling listened attentively, particularly interested in the medical aspects of his story. "Francis was the only one in good health then. Of course, he was going to die of exposure if they hadn't taken him."

Sue-ling thought wonderingly of how the Turtles had managed to create artificial bodies for the two who could be saved, using the nineteen cadavers for dissection and study. That was how the Turtles had been able to develop the memo disks, Marco said.

Evidently there were Turtle medical skills they had not seen fit to pass on to their humans . . . although, on second thought, she wasn't entirely sure of that. Perhaps, she mused, they were embodied in memo disks and it simply happened that she had been using them all along without knowing she was doing so. . . .

She was startled to feel Marco Ramos's tentacle on her shoulder. "What is it?" she demanded, suddenly alarmed.

"I just wanted to tell you," the machine-person said

reassuringly, "that I hear Daisy Fay coming. I didn't want her to startle you. She's got someone with her."

The someone was Moon Bunderan. "I thought I'd find you here," Daisy Fay told her partner. "We got tired of listening to them argue, too."

Sue-ling impulsively put her arm around the younger woman. "Where's your, uh, friend?" she asked.

Moon shook her head. "Thrayl's in one of his moods," she sighed. "He's just squatting there with the others, not paying any attention to them. I think he's worried because his songs are all mixed up and confusing."

"He's not the only one," Daisy Fay said morosely. "I don't know what's happening, either. The Turtles have some kind of plan, and they insist on carrying it out—and Francis is telling them it's his ship, and it's all a mess." Her tentacles writhed. "The big thing," she said, "is Chief Thunderbird has decided he's the captain."

"Oh, *hell,*" said Marco. "That's really going to tear it."

"Already has," Daisy Fay sighed. "Naturally Francis says there's only one captain for *The Golden Hind* and that's Captain Francis Krake. Heaven knows how they'll sort it out. Meanwhile we're just floating around in space, till they come to some agreement."

The robot-woman's tentacles floated around, and her face looked up at the humans. "Anyway," she said, "we've got some time before we go into wave-drive. How would you like it if Marco and I showed you around the rest of the ship?"

———

For Sue-ling everything was beginning to seem dreamlike. None of this was part of her old familiar life! Nothing had been, really, since the day her university had closed down and she had come to the Turtle compound in the hope of something more important to do with her life. But to be here—in a Turtle wave-drive spaceship!—with these strange half-human robots for companions—not to mention a pair of Turtles—and, by every token, on the verge of a trip into deep space, with the knowledge that everyone she had left behind would be dust by the time she saw Earth again—

It was all simply too strange.

With Moon Bunderan, she followed the two robot-people down the empty passageways of *The Golden Hind*. There was nothing familiar here at all. She gazed uncomprehendingly as Daisy Fay, tentacles awave, gestured at two huge black cylinders looming above a passage. They were decked with a maze of knobs and colored lights. "Those are the antimatter generators," Daisy Fay said proudly.

"Antimatter," Sue-ling repeated, frowning up at the glowing board.

"That's what we use for the mass-drive," Marco Ramos put in. "The ship has two drives—mass reaction for short trips and docking maneuvers, and also for landing on a planet when we have to. Mass drive is just a kind of rocket, if you know what a rocket is."

She nodded. "Human beings used to use rockets to travel in space."

Marco gazed up at her ruefully. "So they tell me. It was all before my own time, of course—or after. Anyway, those early rockets were all chemicals. Like big firecrackers. These are a million times more powerful."

"But of course," Daisy Fay chimed in, "they're no good at all for interstellar travel."

"Right," Marco agreed. "For that we have to use the wave-drive. We'll show you the wave-drive stuff in a minute, but let's finish up here first. Do you know what antimatter is?"

His eyes weren't on Sue-ling but on Moon Bunderan, who was gazing around with awe. "Well, yes," Moon hedged. "At least, sort of—"

"It's common matter turned inside out," the robotman explained. "The electric charges are all reversed: the shells of the atoms are positrons, instead of electrons; the cores are antiprotons. Antimatter would be a deadly explosive if it got free—but it doesn't.

"You see," he went on, warming up, "when antimatter meets the normal stuff it reacts. The unlike charges cancel into gamma radiation. These generators simply create it by reversing a few of the charges in a stream of fuel atoms. Then the new antimatter reacts instantly with the normal atoms in the same stream, the mass converts to energy and it comes out as electrical power. That's our mass drive: electrical rockets."

Moon nodded as if she understood. Satisfied, Marco charged ahead. They went through another passage, tugging themselves along by holdfasts, and came out on the naked curve of the hull. "We're taking a chance here," Daisy Fay warned, "because we're out of the shielded section of the ship. But this is where the mass-drive thrusters are, and the wave-drive equipment just aft of this compartment." Sue-ling felt the air colder here, and it was alive with a faint vibration from the dark metal all around them.

"The mass thrusters," Daisy Fay said, waving a tentacle at a maze of thick pipes and humming machines. "The pumps and the energy exchangers, where the exhaust mass becomes a superheated plasma that goes out through the external rocket nozzles."

Sue-ling stood staring, until she saw the others moving away. She hurried after them, caught up as Daisy Fay was indicating a web of heavy cables that spread to a thick, bright metal ridge that curved around the hull.

"The wave-drive," Daisy Fay said with satisfaction.

"I don't understand the wave-drive at all," Moon Bunderan declared positively.

"No, of course not," Marco said reassuringly. "I don't really understand it myself—but I know it works. Of course, you can't really see much of it. Do you know what particle-wave duality is?"

"No," said Moon flatly.

"It's simple enough. Particles and waves are just two aspects of the same thing, you see," Daisy Fay put in. "The drive turns our particles into waves, and we travel at the speed of light. Of course, we can't use the wave-drive for launching. That's why we're out here, away from the orbit station. We have to get well away from the docks before we can shift into it."

"Will it hurt?" Moon asked, observing with pleasure that her voice did not quaver.

"Oh, no. Anyway, it shouldn't." Daisy Fay's eye-stalks tipped back and forth like shaking heads. "The effect is hard to describe, because of our language and the way we've learned to think. Even the terms 'particle' and 'wave' don't fit quantum reality. You'll probably know when we shift—"

"You *positively* will," Marco laughed.

Daisy Fay turned a warning eye on him. "But don't worry about it. Different people feel it differently," she said.

Sue-ling stirred herself. "Differently how?" she asked.

"Well," Daisy Fay began, considering, but was interrupted by a blare: Francis Krake's voice, coming over the ship's internal communications system.

"Marco, Daisy Fay!" he was saying. "Take your places for wave-drive entry!"

"We'd better get back in the shielded room," Daisy Fay said, and her voice seemed to smile. "You're going to have to start learning how to run the ship if you're going to be part of the crew, because it seems we're on our way. I won't have to try to explain how it feels. You'll find out soon enough!"

The songs of the aiodoi are heard by many, in many places, and often they are loved. The aiodoi sing frequently to the Taurs, and the Taurs love to hear them. The aiodoi do not sing to humans, because the humans cannot hear. Nor do they sing to the Turtles, who will not listen. But the aiodoi themselves always listen to the smallsongs from everywhere, and when they listen it is always with love, even when they listen to the childish babblings from Earth.

―――――

"I talked about rotating an electron last time because I wanted you to get ready for some other rotating phenomena—not just in space, but in space-time.

"I have here in my hand a bust of Abraham Lincoln. Look it over. It has three spatial dimensions—top/bottom, left/right and back/front. Since I am now holding it what we call 'upright,' I share those dimensions and directions with it. My 'up' is the same as Honest Abe's 'up.'

"Now let's rotate it ninety degrees—standing old Abe on his right ear, as you see. I have rotated it on its back/front axis, and now the bust is lying on its right side. The direction I would call 'up' is now 'left' to Abe. Contrariwise, what is 'up' to Abe Lincoln is now what I would call 'right.' But that doesn't cause any real confusion.

The only people who are confused would be outside observers. Both Abe and I see clearly that up, right, back, front and so on remain in the same direction as ever—relative to our own individual selves.

"All that is such simple stuff that you don't even need to think about it . . . in three-dimensional space.

"But we're thinking now about space-time, and space-time has *four* dimensions. The other dimension is past/future; it is the dimension of time.

"So, while in 3-D space we had a choice of three axes to twist the sucker around on, now in 4-D space-*time* we have a choice of four.

"When we rotated Abe's bust in 3-D, his left/right became our up/down. But what if his left/right now becomes our past/future? Nothing's going to look different to Abe. He still sees left and right as left and right.

"But how does he look now to us?

"I'm going to leave you with that question for a while. We won't come back to it for a while, but when we do I'm going to relate it to the proposition we call 'CPT invariance.' "

And the aiodoi sang:
"What is so is so.
"What is right is right.
"That is the real and the only invariance."

10

~~~~~~

What Sue-ling Quong felt was excitement, what Sork Quintero felt was savage joy at the prospect of attaining his life's ambitions, but what Sork's twin brother Kiri Quintero mostly felt was relief.

Kiri's relief was not complete. It was tainted by the passions he could still feel floating around the control room, even though the main disputants had finally agreed —if not on any long-range covenant, at least to stop their bickering for a while. It had been hot and heavy for a while there. Kiri himself had found his peaceful calm fraying, and even Moon Bunderan's Taur had been restive, tossing the great horned head and lowing from time to time in unhappy protest as the fight went on.

Now there was a break. Kiri looked up as Sue-ling and Moon came in, with Krake's half-human crew. "Over here," he called to Sue-ling. "We're going to go into wave-drive—and we're all going to get our first lesson in space piloting!" He nodded toward Francis Krake, who raised his head from one of the control banks long enough to glower up at them.

Sue-ling looked around uncertainly. "What's been going on here?" she asked.

Kiri slipped a reassuring arm around her, enjoying the warm, solid feel of her body. "Oh," he said, aware of his brother's eyes on them but not looking toward him, "those three have been going around and around for the last half hour." He jerked a thumb toward the two Turtles, standing immobile as granite, flanking Krake at the control board. "I guess the Turtles won," he added, lowering his voice, "because Krake finally threw up his hands and said he'd take off. But they didn't really agree on anything, I'd say. I think that's what he's so ticked about."

"May I?" Daisy Fay said politely, and Kiri moved out of the way to permit her to slip her ungainly metal body into the space where the board operator's seat should have been. "Thanks," said Daisy Fay, turning one eyestalk toward him. "Did anybody tell you what we do here?"

Kiri shook his head. "They were all too busy fighting," he said.

Daisy Fay chuckled. "I think we're going to see a lot of that. Anyway, this position is only the state-of-the-ship board. It doesn't actually fly the *Hind.* All you do here is watch out for signal lights. If any of them turn red, then there's trouble." The pretty face on the plastron grinned up at him. "But none of them ever have," she added.

"I didn't know the Turtles used red for a warning color," Sue-ling put in.

"Far as I know, they don't. This is *our* control room. They designed it to our specifications and put it into the shielded section when they leased the ship to Francis." One eyestalk twisted around to look at Francis Krake. "Captain?" she called. "Are we ready for wave-drive insertion?"

Krake didn't look up. "Board green," he called, his eyes fixed on the controls.

"Green," Daisy Fay repeated. Her fingers danced over the board for a moment, and Kiri Quintero felt a sudden lurch as the mass-thrusters gave *The Golden Hind* a gentle nudge. "Correcting orientation," Daisy Fay called. In an undertone she explained to Kiri, behind her, "We want to be pointed in the right direction."

"Locked on course," Krake called from the other board.

Daisy Fay's tentacles moved rapidly across the board. "Stand by for wave-drive," she said, her eyestalks glancing up to look at the screens. Kiri could not help following her glance. It was a startling spectacle. Earth appeared behind the orbit station, no more than a thin blue crescent. The Sun rolled into visibility, but diminished by the screens to no more than a tarnished copper coin.

"Wave-drive on," cried Francis Krake.

And the bottom dropped out of Kiri Quintero's stomach, and he felt himself falling.

———

In Kiri's dream he was being held tenderly by a woman who was not Sue-ling Quong. She was not really a woman at all. She was a red-shelled monstrosity that had seized him with blood-colored tentacles; and when he opened his eyes the dream was no dream at all.

"It's all right, Kiri," said Daisy Fay McQueen's reassuring voice. "I know it felt pretty strange, but it was only the shift to wave-drive. It must've hit you hard."

Kiri pushed himself free of her embrace, surprised again to feel himself of a normal weight. "It did," he said dizzily, staring around. He wasn't in the control room any more but in a tiny compartment with a bunk in it. "I —I thought I was falling—" He found himself covered in sweat, and let the woman in the hideous machine help him to lie down on the bunk. "Why are we in gravity again?" he asked plaintively, looking up at her.

"We're not, really. The sensation is just an artifact of the wave-drive." Daisy Fay touched a control, and screens like the ones in the control chamber appeared around the room. "We're picking up speed now," she told him. "There's Earth, and over there—" (Kiri blinked at an impossibly crimson disk, shrinking from sight.) "—that's Mars. The colors are the way they are because they've red-shifted because of our velocity. Of course," she went on, lecturing as to a child, "we don't really see them. We don't have anything material to see with any more. Our own wave train is transparent; radiation passes right through us. But instruments can still pick up interference effects, and that's what we show on the screen."

"We're *going*?" He pushed himself erect.

"That's right, Kiri," the metal-woman said, waving her tentacles affirmatively. "Now you'd better get some sleep. I'm on shift in four hours, and you're supposed to come with me to learn how to pilot a waveship."

He gazed up at her uncertainly. "All right," he said, and started to turn away. Then he stopped himself, out of the habit of a lifetime. "Where's Sork?" he asked.

The face on the belly plate looked away. "Why don't you just go to sleep, Kiri? I'm sure Sork's all right."

Kiri was wide awake now. "No! Answer me, what's he doing now?"

The face on the belly plate looked sympathetic. "Honestly, Kiri, I don't think he's in any trouble . . . though I doubt he's enjoying it. He's—he's gone off with the Turtles. They're questioning him about something, Kiri. I hope he's all right."

————

A hundred meters away, Sork was hoping the same thing about himself. It wasn't that he was afraid for his safety. Though the two great Turtles hawked and shrieked threateningly, Sork was reasonably sure they would not descend to any physical act on his own person. That was not Turtle style.

For that matter, Sork wasn't afraid of anything very often. Not even when he had good reason to be. Fear simply was not a part of his makeup. But he could be troubled, and often enough was, and what troubled him in this particular situation was that he could not interpret what the Turtles were after. Their questions kept coming back to the old quantum-physics lectures Sue-ling Quong had brought from her old school.

The worst thing was that he couldn't fit it all into a sensible pattern. He wished Kiri could help him, and knew he could not—and wished for half a moment for a drink of Scotch that would help ease that familiar confusion in his mind; but he put that thought away as soon as he discovered it in himself.

It wasn't fair! He had planned so *carefully.* Sork had done the precise thing that needed to be done: anticipated a situation, worked out a plan, decided how to handle it. Accordingly, "Yes," he said, almost as soon as they brought the subject up, "I am willing to give you access to the tapes as a commercial arrangement, under certain terms."

Chief Thunderbird rapped severely, "We do not speak of other 'terms.' Also, mere access is not enough. You must furnish more."

"What more?" Sork asked.

The Turtle seemed embarrassed. "You have heard many of these tapes. There are certain words and concepts in them which are unfamiliar. One requires that you help us by explaining them to us."

"Help you," Sork said meditatively, enjoying the sudden feeling of power—how long had it been since any human heard a Turtle ask for "help"? He said, "I'm willing to do that, but I ask you again, what terms do you offer?"

The Turtles turned an eye on each other, one each on Sork Quintero. "No additional terms are required. It is a pooling of assets, as agreed," screeched Chief Thunderbird.

"Oh, no," said Sork, confidently shaking his head. "We have no agreement here. What assets do you contribute? There must be something in exchange for my services; that's the Turtle way."

"Your services are only to make possible our use of the chips, and those are not your assets, Sork Quintero! They are the property of the human female, Sue-ling Quong!"

Sork was ready for that one. "Sue-ling and I have already pooled assets," he said, not entirely truthfully. "I speak for both of us."

The Chief turned both eyes on him in baffled rage,

then turned off the transposers for a moment. Sork waited while the two Turtles hawked and hissed at each other. Then Litlun turned to him. He spread his webbed paw, counting off items on his talons:

"These are what we offer: Food. Air. Water. All the things you humans require for survival. The Brotherhood is furnishing these assets to you in exchange for the ones we request." And, as Sork began to scowl: "If you do not wish to accept these terms it will be necessary for us to remove you and Sue-ling Quong from this ship."

"At a suitable place, of course," added Chief Thunderbird. "One on which it is possible for you to survive, though perhaps not in as much comfort as on your own planet—and, of course, there would be no guarantee that you would be returned to your Earth at any specific future time."

Sork cursed to himself: It had all seemed so logical when he thought it out in private! Leave it to the Turtles to find some way of ruining things! He tried to imagine what it would be like to be set down on some strange planet. He couldn't. It was simply too far out of his experience. But what he was sure of was that the thing he wanted most, the thing he had planned for—to learn how to pilot a spacecraft—was within his grasp in *The Golden Hind,* and if he let that chance slip away. . . .

He tried desperately to take command on the discussion. "But—" he began, floundering for the right words. "But—but why do you want these tapes? You said they were heretical. I think one word you used was 'obscene.' "

"That does not now apply," screeched Litlun. "Because of the great peril the Brotherhood now stands in, we must conquer our revulsion at—certain things."

"Which are no concern of yours, Sork Quintero," Chief Thunderbird pointed out. "It is only necessary for you to confirm to us that you accept this pooling of assets for mutual benefit."

And there the argument rested—for an hour and more, Sork battling for some advantage, the Turtles grimly holding their position.

The situation became more and more puzzling to Sork the more he thought about it. It seemed that the Turtles were tacitly admitting that all this possibly "blasphemous" (but certainly weird) quantum-anthropic-whatever-you-called-it stuff was in some way "real."

But if that were so, that raised some hard questions. For instance: If the lecture stories were true, then the science involved had to have been known to the inventors of the wave-drive. But if the Turtles denied the science . . . then how had they built the waveships?

When he tried to ask that of the Turtles they were fierce in snapping at him. "Do not ask questions on matters which are not your concern!" thundered the Chief.

Sork stared at him in loathing and defeat. What made it worse was that for some time now he had been smelling food cooking somewhere. It had been a long time between meals.

Litlun squawked ferociously, "There is no need for further discussion, only for your answer! Do you accept our terms? Or do we alter course to set you down on some other world?"

Sork sighed and surrendered—almost. "All right. I will do my best to explain what the lecture chips are about."

"Good! Then this is agreed," Chief Thunderbird said. "Our first session will begin now."

"But I'm *hungry*," Sork wailed, but the Turtle only said:

"Now."

———

When Sork at last was allowed to return to the control room he wasn't surprised to find Francis Krake there. The surprising thing was that Krake wasn't the one who sat at the control board. Krake was off at one side of the room, busy taking food out of a heater; it was Moon Bunderan who, under Marco Ramos's watchful stalked eyes, was sitting there at the controls. Her great Taur was squatting beside her.

As Sork came in the animal looked up quickly, but then the great purple-blue eyes went blank and the head swayed away from him again.

"Hello, Sork," Moon cried, pleased with herself—then seeing the look on his face. "What's the matter?" she asked quickly.

Sork shrugged. "What are you doing?" he asked.

She said proudly, "I'm driving the ship! Not that there's anything to do," she added honestly, "but Marco says I've picked up enough to see the warnings if anything went wrong. . . ."

"You're doing fine," Marco assured her. "How's the chow coming, Francis? I bet Sork would like some too."

The space captain grunted and began dumping containers of hot food into dishes, handing them around. "Thanks," said Sork, realizing just how hungry he was. But as he began to lift his fork toward his mouth he saw that the shelled creature who was Marco Ramos was eating too—ladling food into a slit in its shell with as much evident gusto as any hungry human.

One of the eye tentacles turned toward him, and Sork could almost have thought that it had a humorous twinkle. "Oh, yes, we eat," Marco told him. "We have complete digestive systems. Would you like to know how we go to the bathroom, too? It's simple. There's this hatch—"

"Please!" said Sork sharply.

Moon Bunderan looked at him, then changed the subject. "This Taur steak is really good, Captain Krake. You know how to broil meat—oh," she said, looking at his plate. "But you're not eating any."

"I don't eat Taur," Krake said flatly.

Moon stared at him, not comprehending. "But it's so good," she said.

Krake nodded, fixing her with a stare. "And you do eat it, don't you. In spite of how you feel about Thrayl?"

Moon stopped chewing. "Now, that's not fair!" she protested unhappily. "Thrayl is my friend. The others, the ones who are slaughtered—they're dehorned steers, you know; they aren't intelligent!"

Krake gazed at her soberly, then turned away without speaking. Moon appealed to the others. "Isn't that true, Sork? Taurs *are* eaten. That's what they're raised for, isn't it?"

"Of course it is," Sork Quintero reassured her.

Then he turned to Krake. "Why are we going to the Mother planet?" he asked.

The space pilot laughed angrily. "You don't know? But it's your fault."

"My fault? What did I do?"

"You let Litlun think you knew all about white holes and wormholes and all that. Now he's got the idea that that's what happened to the Mother planet."

Sork blinked at him. "But what's the point of that? If the planet's destroyed, it's destroyed, isn't it?"

"Ask Litlun," Krake said shortly. "Anyway, that's where we're going." He rubbed his bearded chin. "What I'm hoping," he said, "is that once we get there he'll see how hopeless it is and then he'll let us go our own way. Meanwhile, that's our destination."

Sork opened his mouth to confess what deal he had made with the Turtles, but closed it again. The only person he had to confess to was Sue-ling Quong, not this spaceman. He asked a question instead. "How long will it take to get there?"

Krake gave him a look of surprise. "I thought you knew that all waveship trips take about the same time—a few days at most."

"That's *it*?"

Krake shook his head. "You haven't understood time dilation, have you? When the ship is in wave-drive it is traveling at the velocity of light. Time is maximally dilated. That is," he explained, "as far as we're concerned, it simply *stops*. To travel a light-year takes one year of elapsed time, yes. But that's the galaxy's time. We don't feel it. That's why waveship navigation is so tricky; you don't know how long you've been traveling, except by instruments."

Sork was beginning to forget his disagreeable interview with the Turtles. Fascinated, he asked, "And you can teach us how to read these instruments?"

"Of course," Marco Ramos called. "That's what Moon's doing now. Come and learn too!"

———

When you are in the process of achieving your heart's desire other things dwindle in importance. Exhausted as Sork Quintero was, hungry as he still was, he was *flying*. He was piloting a *spaceship*. He was living out in his real life the most unattainable hope of his dreams, and it was all *real*. Sork wore a foolish smile on his face as he sat there, now and then remembering to take a bite of the sandwich in his hand.

Yes, it was true. The instruments before him were the veritable control-board toggles and dials of an authentic waveship. It didn't matter that there was nothing to do, really, since there was no reason to change course in mid-flight. He was where he had wanted to be, and nothing else existed for Sork Quintero at that moment. It wasn't until Sue-ling Quong had put a friendly hand on Sork's shoulder that he realized she had come into the room—and a moment after that before he remembered what he had to tell her.

Then the dream collapsed. He looked up into her friendly blue eyes and swallowed before he spoke.

"Don't get mad," he said, "but—" He had to swallow again before he could finish, dismally, "I told the Turtles I'd help them understand the lecture chips."

She looked at him with astonishment. As she opened her mouth to ask a question, he forestalled her. "It was the only thing I could do, Sue-ling. I couldn't help it. They threatened to put us off on some out-of-the-way planet if I didn't."

"Have you given them the chips?"

"No! I didn't *give* them anything . . . but I played a couple of them with them, and I tried to explain what some of the words meant." He cleared his throat unhappily. "What else could I do?"

She looked at him thoughtfully for a moment. Her lips had been open to speak, but now she closed them firmly. She needed to think before she said something she might regret . . . and, she thought irritably, how often was it that she had to do that with Sork Quintero.

"Did I do wrong?" he demanded. Sue-ling shook herself.

"No," she said, "I suppose not. Actually, I think we all have to hear those chips now, Sork."

His brows drew down in a question. "Why all of us? You surely don't mean everybody—even that child from New Mexico?"

"Even Moon," she said. "Even her pet Taur, if she wants him to." Sue-ling gave a nod for emphasis that made her coppery hair swing around her head. "If there's anything important there, we should all hear it—and try to figure out what it means. When's your next session with them?"

"After I get some sleep. I convinced them I just couldn't go on without it . . . although," he began, his expression changing.

She cut him off. "That will be fine. I'll tell the others what we're going to do. Now I think you're right about the sleep; you look like hell. Go put your head down until I call you."

He looked at her in a different way, but not a way that was unfamiliar to Sue-ling. "Absolutely," he said, putting his hand gently on her cheek, and she knew what was coming next.

He pulled her toward him, nuzzling against her hair. To the top of her head he whispered, "I do need sleep, but what I need most of all is to make another dream come true. Do you know what that dream is, dearest Sue-ling? I've had it for years. It's just the two of us, you and I, sharing the space between the stars as we love each other, and go on loving each other, and—"

She pulled away and put a gentle finger on his lips. "No, Sork," she said kindly.

He jerked his head away from her hand, his expression wounded. "But— But it's my *turn*," he said childishly.

She bit down hard on her lip before she answered. Then, drawing a breath, she said, as quietly as she could, "Three things, Sork. First, you're wrong. The last time I made love it was with you, not Kiri. Second, nobody gets a 'turn' with me. I'm not a playground toy, and you're not a child—or shouldn't be. And, third, no. Just *no*. Go get some sleep. We've got a lot to do before we get to the Mother planet."

There are songs that the aiodoi listen to very carefully, for they touch on things that the aiodoi know well—even when they come from an ancient poet-scientist who was scratching at only the outermost surface of the meaning of his song:

———

"We've talked about some curiosities of dimensions. Today we're going to talk about forces.

"If you want a definition of a 'force,' try this: 'A force is that which makes things do things.'

"For instance: If you hold a magnet over a pile of paperclips, you can pick the clips up. The force that makes the clips cling to the magnet is called magnetism. If you turn on a switch and send a current through a bulb, you get light. That current is the force that is called electricity.

"Those two, however, aren't two different forces. They are only one. A long time ago scientists proved that they were only manifestations of the same thing, which is called the electromagnetic force.

"That's one force. There are, in all of nature as we see it today, only three others.

"The second force is the one that holds you to the

surface of the Earth and keeps the Earth from flying into space away from the Sun. That one is called the force of gravity.

"Then there are two other forces. You don't notice them much in everyday life, because they mostly have to do only with things that go on inside the structure of atoms. They do exist, though. Their names are 'the strong force' and 'the weak force.'

"I am not, at least not right now, going to tell you about the ways in which these four forces relate to each other. Right now they seem to be quite different—although, actually, some scientists have tried to write equations which link them together; that was one of the things that drove poor Albert Einstein to distraction in the last years of his life, because he thought he should be able to do that, and he wasn't.

"Long ago, though, they weren't different at all.

"If you remember your plate tectonics courses, you'll recall that once there was a time when most of the present continents of Earth were joined together in one big continent called Gondwanaland. They didn't stay joined together. As the plates migrated the continents split apart, and as a result we have the map of the globe that we all know and love so well today.

"In somewhat the same way, those four present-day forces were once a single force.

"That was a long time ago—back in Planck time, way back at the beginning of our universe, only the flicker of a gnat's eye after the Big Bang itself. At that time there wasn't any separate force called 'gravity' or 'electromagnetism.' There was just one force that included all of them, and it has a name.

"Its name is 'superforce.'

"What is the superforce? It is the basic and overriding force in the universe. It is the force that can do anything to everything. It is what generated everything we know and see everywhere. As Paul Davies says about it, the superforce 'is ultimately responsible for generating all forces and all physical structures.' If we could control the superforce, there is *nothing* we could not do.

"So says Paul Davies. But then he goes on to say that to achieve the superforce you need to attain what he calls 'the Planck energy'—more energy than you can imagine —and that, he says, is impossible.

"But wouldn't it be pretty if we could?"

———

And the aiodoi sang lovingly:
"Why not?"

11

"The name is *superforce* . . ." the voice of the long-gone professor was saying, and Sue-ling Quong was forcing herself to listen to every word. Whether she understood them or not was another question entirely. There was nothing in her education that had prepared her for this—or, of course, in anyone else's, either.

Nor were the surroundings conducive to concentration. Francis Krake had insisted on keeping the view screens on—"I have to *see* where we're going, dammit!" —and so what Sue-ling's eyes could see was the picture of her shipmates hovering around the player, and behind and around them all the great silent spectacle of the galaxy, with all its stars and dust clouds and clusters. Her shipmates looked like gods in a vast, empty heaven.

Or like pitiful living creatures, trying to comprehend what only a god could really understand.

Francis Krake was next to her, almost dwarfed by the bulk of the two Turtles on his other side. Krake looked sad, Sue-ling thought—or maybe just thoughtful, for it was hard to discern expressions in the dim light—but behind him the fierce parrot beak of Chief Thunderbird was grimly thrust forward in concentration. Or in revulsion. Sue-ling wondered which it was, and what could be passing through the mind of a Turtle as he forced himself to listen to this quantum-mechanical anathema. The Turtles had complained furiously against being compelled to share the lectures with the whole crew—out, Sue-ling thought, of pure embarrassment.

Or else simply because they were Turtles.

Krake stirred slightly, frowning in thought. Impulsively, Sue-ling put her hand over his in sympathy. He gave her a surprised, abstracted glance, then he returned his attention to the lecture.

Now why, Sue-ling wondered, did I do that?

Then she caught Sork's glare directed toward her. Guiltily—and annoyed at herself for feeling guilty—she withdrew her hand and sat up straighter to listen . . . just in time to hear the lecture come to its end.

When the chip went silent no one spoke for a moment. Then the Taur lowed softly to its mistress, and Moon Bunderan stirred. "Are those things they're talking about all real?" she asked, wonderingly. She waved at the panoply of stars all around them. "I mean, does all that talk have anything to do with *that*?"

Queerly, it was the giant Turtle, Chief Thunderbird, who responded. "That is a proper question," he squawked through his transposer. "What is your answer, Sork Quintero?"

Sork gave him a belligerent look, then turned it on Sue-ling. "Ask her. She's the one who gave me the chips."

Chief Thunderbird turned one red eye on Sue-ling. "Well?"

She shrugged. "Those chips came from my university, after it was closed down. Sork has my agreement in giving them to you."

"We do not seek your agreement," the Turtle told her. "That is assumed. What we need is quite different. It is necessary for us to know about the source of those information chips. It is Sork Quintero's opinion that they were genuine and represent actual scientific theories of humans. Do you concur in this?"

"As I've told you, the chips are exact copies of lectures from our astrophysics department at the university. Does that answer your question?"

"It does not," rasped Chief Thunderbird. "Does what they say represent *truth*?"

"I can't tell you that," Sue-ling said firmly. "I don't know anything about astrophysics or cosmology or quantum effects—I was a med school student. But I did know some of the faculty members at the university as personal friends, and, yes, as far as I know—as far as they knew— the lectures represented serious theories about the subject."

"Theories can be wrong," Litlun put in, seeming unhappy.

"Of course they can. That's why they're theories," Sue-ling replied.

Sork Quintero spoke up. "That's what I've been trying to tell you," he said sulkily. "That's what human beings call the scientific method. Scientists make a theory to try to explain something that is happening. Then they look to see if the theory predicts certain effects or events, and then they conduct experiments to see if those effects happen. If they do it's a good theory. You can even assume that it's right—that it's a *law*—at least for the time being. But it's still only a *theory,* and sooner or later you may find some other phenomenon that doesn't fit; then you have to make a new theory."

"That is very unsatisfying," Chief Thunderbird rumbled.

"It's the best we can do," Sork said. "Now, what about you? Isn't it about your turn to talk now?"

Chief Thunderbird's claws scratched warningly across his belly plate. "One does not take your meaning, Sork Quintero," he rasped.

Sork said, "I mean we have a right to know your reasons—not to mention all the other things you're keeping from us. Why you care about these lectures, and where are we going?"

"And what did you want with Thrayl?" Moon Bunderan put in.

The big Turtle's limbs were flapping ominously as he listened. He opened his beak to screech, but before he got a word out Kiri said, quite calmly and judiciously, "They are right, Proctor. We can't help you if we don't know what you need."

That stopped Chief Thunderbird. He squawked to himself, then turned off his transposer, and he and Litlun screeched at each other at length. It went on for quite a while, and the odd thing about it, Sue-ling thought, was that, although they were certainly agitated enough, they seemed more frightened than furious.

At last Litlun engaged his transposer and spoke. "This is very difficult for us," he said—quite unnecessarily. No one was in any doubt of that. "We agree that we must speak to you of things that have never been spoken outside the Brotherhood, but—" Litlun stopped, plucking nervously at the hard shell of his plastron. "But we do not know certainly what things we must share." He swiveled both eyes to Francis Krake. "Captain, when will we arrive at our destination?"

Krake gave his crew an inquiring glance. "Daisy Fay?"

"We'll be there in about twenty-two hours, Captain," the machine-girl told him.

Litlun waved both horny arms in a slow affirmative gesture. "Then I propose this," he said through the transposer, one eye inquiringly on the other Turtle for approval. "Let us postpone these questions until we see what we find at the Mother planet. If it is as we—" he paused, clucking to himself before he was able to speak the frightening thought—"have reason to believe," he went on, dodging the pain of specificity, "then we will share all our thoughts with you. But until then, allow us to wait." He hesitated again, then managed to get out that very un-Turtlelike word: "Please."

Astonishingly, Sue-ling was touched. "Of course," she blurted, but Sork's shout overrode her.

"No!" he cried. "That's not good enough!"

"But it is all we can do," Litlun said—or moaned; even the flat voice of the transposer seemed to be pleading.

"It isn't," Sork said. His voice was hostile, and he didn't even look at the others for concurrence. "You've kept too *many* secrets, and you've kept them too long. We don't even know why your Mother matters so much to you!"

There was a startled, shocked hiss from both Turtles at that. Sork blinked at the intensity of the reaction, and his twin quickly put in: "Sork doesn't mean to offend against your religion—"

"It is not a *religion*," Chief Thunderbird blazed.

"Well, whatever it is. The thing is, we just don't understand the severity of this crisis for you."

Transposers off, the two Turtles shrilled and croaked at each other for a moment. Then Chief Thunderbird turned the transposer back on. "We will tell you what we can," he said sourly. "What do you specifically wish to know?"

"Everything," Sork snapped.

"There is no need for you to know 'everything'!" He paused, then made himself go on. "It is enough for you to know that we are all brothers—almost all of us still alive, born of a single Mother. So our loss is grievous."

"She must have a lot of kids," Marco Ramos piped up. He drew a scathing look from Chief Thunderbird.

"The Mother," he said severely, "produces some two eggs a minute, for all of her blessed fertile life."

"Which is how long?" Sue-ling asked.

"There is no need for you to know that," the Turtle stated.

"But after a while she does die? And then what?"

More agitated squawking between the Turtles. Then it was Litlun who said, "Then a nymph is caused to mature. She becomes the new Mother, and a new Brotherhood begins."

"And where does this nymph come from?" Krake began, but the Turtle scratched his belly plate warningly.

"That is not a proper question," he decreed.

"It's the question I'm asking, though," Krake said stubbornly.

More conferring in squawks and hisses. Then, grudgingly, Chief Thunderbird spoke. "A very few of each Mother's eggs are female. Some are allowed to develop.

Others are . . . not." And the parrot beak snapped shut.

"There will be no more questions on this subject," Litlun decreed, but Sork Quintero was shaking his head.

"Wrong," he said. "There's at least one more, and we want an answer. Why don't you simply do what you usually do and let a new nymph take over?"

This time there was no discussion. Both Turtles stood silent for a moment, eyes wandering aimlessly, before Chief Thunderbird said slowly, miserably, "This time there are no nymphs left, either."

————

An hour later, Sue-ling was in her little cabin, doing her best to go to sleep. She wasn't really tired but, medically speaking, she was aware that it was sleeping time, and she wanted to be fully awake for their arrival at the Mother planet.

What kept waking her up wasn't the excitement of the trip, and the tragic fears of the Turtles. It was Sork Quintero. It wasn't good for him to get so tense and argumentative. And she was not able to get out of her mind his quick, sardonic remark as she left him: "If I can't have what I want, maybe a drink would be second best."

And then, of course, she had had to spend half an hour with him, talking him out of it. She resented the imposition, kept asking herself why she had bothered. She knew, as a doctor, that the only person who could keep an alcoholic dry was the alcoholic himself.

And yet, he was so *sad*. Finally she took herself off, consoling herself with the thought that there wasn't anyplace for him to get a drink on the ship. . . .

When she woke to the sound of hammering on her door frame she began to suspect she had been wrong about that. She got up, pulling a robe around her—it wasn't really a robe but a long tunic she had borrowed from Francis Krake, and she thought she could detect his masculine odor in it—and stumbled to the curtain door, her hair undone, her eyes swollen from sleep. When she pulled the curtain door back she was not surprised to find herself blinking into the reddened eyes of Sork Quintero.

"What do you want?" she asked fuzzily. "I was sound asleep."

"I need to talk to you. Let me in."

She stood silently regarding him, wrinkling her nose as she caught a whiff of his whiskey breath. Then she shook her head. "I just got up. I need to get cleaned up and dressed. You can wait out here if you want to." And slid the curtain closed in his angry face.

———

Time was when a young woman about to face an interview with a lover—by the looks of it an unpleasant interview—would have spent at least an hour on makeup and hair and choosing just the right dress.

Sue-ling was not of that generation. If she had been, she would still have been forced to make compromises, given the sparse resources of *The Golden Hind*. She rinsed herself off in the spray chamber, pulled on a clean coverall and glanced at herself in the mirror. She did go so far as to pull a comb through her hair, but that was it.

But she did it all in slow motion, because she was determined not to let Sork Quintero hurry her into anything. When at last she let Sork in he plumped himself down on the edge of her bed, sliding the door closed behind him. He glared at her silently.

"All right," she said. "What's this all about?"

"You know damn well!" Sork snapped. "I'm not stupid."

She said, controlling her patience, "And what is it that you're not stupid about?"

"Francis Krake! I've seen the way you act around him, and it isn't fair to me. To us," he corrected himself. "Kiri's as upset as I am."

"I don't believe that, Sork."

"Then just believe that I'm hurting over it!"

Sue-ling gazed at him blankly. "What are you talking about?" she asked, her tone purely wondering. "Francis

Krake is the captain of this ship. We're all stuck in here together. We have to get along—"

"You don't have to get along that well!" Sork said resentfully. "You've kept Kiri and me on the hook for months now. You always said you would marry one of us—"

"I said I *thought* I would—"

"You made us believe that was what you intended! And now here comes this new man, and you're hanging on his every word, following him around—anybody can see that you think he's pretty fascinating."

Sue-ling said, as simply and clearly as she could, "I've never even kissed Francis Krake. He hasn't shown any signs of wanting to kiss me, either. There is no 'relationship' to discuss—and, Sork, I'm astonished at you. I didn't expect this kind of jealousy from you."

"It's not *jealousy*," Sork began heatedly, and then stopped himself. "All right, it's jealousy," he admitted, looking astonished at a new discovery. "But what did you expect? We've waited a long time for you to make a choice between us, Sue-ling."

"Why does this have to come up now?" she asked plaintively.

Sork said angrily, "Why *not* now? Why not settle it before you get too deeply entangled with this Krake character and we both lose out?"

"Oh, God," said Sue-ling, raising her palms to her temples, "don't you think you're a little crazy? Here we are out in space, on this mystery cruise to nowhere, and all of a sudden—"

"It is definitely not all of a sudden," Sork corrected her. Then he took a deep breath. "Sue-ling," he said, his voice firm, "you know I love you. So does Kiri. It *hurts* not to know who you're going to choose."

"But Sork, dear," she said, trying to make her voice as kind and loving as she felt . . . or thought she felt, "don't you see that it's hard for me to choose? We've been very close together, all three of us. To pick one of you means refusing the other, and how can I do that? What would it do to the three of us?"

"What's it doing now?" Sork snapped. "No! Decide, Sue-ling. Pick me, or pick Kiri, if that's the way you want it to be. But, please, do it *now.*"

"I can't," Sue-ling whispered.

"You must," said Sork. "You can flip a coin if you want to do it that way. But, one way or the other, it's time for you to make up your mind."

———

Later on, on her shift at the state-of-the-ship board, with Francis Krake standing approvingly behind her, Sue-ling was very conscious of the fact that he was so close.

But there was nothing wrong with that, she told herself. To think anything else was simply foolishness. There was no reason why she should let Sork's jealousy make her self-conscious about what was a perfectly normal, not at all sexual, relationship between colleagues and friends. To prove this to herself, she moved a bit closer to Krake as she concentrated on the screens and the ship.

The sight the screens displayed was spectacular. Since the ship was in wave-drive, the walls of the control chamber had disappeared entirely. From Sue-ling's point of view, they seemed to be inside a huge, hollow globe that simulated the midnight of space.

She looked around wonderingly, trying to understand what she saw. She did have some idea of the Turtle technology involved, because Captain Krake had explained it to her. The navigation system had to keep track of thousands of stellar reference points—most of them stars, but some of them actually distant external galaxies themselves—as benchmarks. Automatically "fingerprinting" each object by analyzing its spectrum, the system could consult its datastore and pinpoint the location of *The Golden Hind* anywhere within hundreds of light-years of the Turtle planet. She could see the results on the screen.

The view was not static. The star patterns were changing as she watched. The Milky Way and the Pleiades and a few giant stars stayed the same, but the burning

Sun of Earth had long since dimmed behind them until she lost it. Slowly, the nearer stars crept past the ship and slid into new constellations.

Krake touched her shoulder. "We're almost there," he said, pointing. "See that object? That's the Turtle star. I'd better start calling the others so they can be here when we shift into mass-drive."

Sue-ling studied the frosting of stars in the area Krake had indicated. It wasn't rewarding. No particular object looked any great deal different from any other. "Well, it didn't take us long to get here," she observed. It wasn't until she noticed that he wasn't responding that she looked up and saw the expression on his face.

"It took seventy-three years," he said simply.

She swallowed, raising the back of her hand to her lips. "I—forgot," she whispered.

Krake nodded somberly. "It's easy to forget," he said. "But that's the hard fact. We're committed now. It's been seventy-three years since we took off, and most of the people we left behind are dead now—and everything will be all changed, in ways we couldn't have guessed." He watched her expression for a moment, then said gruffly, "Tough idea to get used to at first, isn't it? Well, there it is." He leaned forward to the communicator again. "Excuse me for a minute while I let the others know we're coming into mass-drive range."

Sue-ling found her eyes blurring as Krake spoke into the ship's communications system: "Marco? Daisy Fay? We're almost ready to power down from wave-drive. Report in, please."

Seventy-three years. . . . Sue-ling wasn't listening, barely noticed as he turned back to her. Seventy-three years.

What they had done, she saw at last, was one of the few truly irrevocable acts of her life.

Krake said, with sympathy, "It hits you hard at first, doesn't it? But here we are. I'll zoom in on the Turtle system so we can get a better look."

She forced herself to pay attention as Krake began to explain what she was looking at—anything to take her mind off those eternally lost years. There was, she saw as Krake pointed it out, one single pale fleck that began to stand out as that section of the sky swelled as though it were racing toward them. *(Seventy-three years!)* Then she saw that the star was double. *(And almost everyone dead!* She shuddered and forced her mind to focus on what she was seeing.) Krake was pointing out that one member of the double was a hot blue point, the other a misty disk. He upped the magnification still more, and now the fuzzy disk showed thin blue plumes jutting from its hot blue-white center. It spun so fast—or seemed to—that her eyes could make out the motion, as the blue-lit plumes wound into spirals around it, joining into a wide ring of creeping fire.

"There's a black hole at the center of that," Krake said grimly. "You know what a black hole is? Sork does; we've talked about it. A black hole is the last cinder of a giant star that's gone supernova. What we see is the accretion disk around the black hole. Of course, you'll never see what's left of the star itself; that's why it's a black hole."

"Then what's that light coming from?"

"I told you. It's the accretion disk. Some matter gets trapped in the black hole's intense gravity field. Then the matter is torn into hot plasma as it falls closer to the hole —and that is really mean stuff, Sue-ling. The radiation from it would kill us, right through our shielding, if we went into orbit too close."

Sue-ling gazed at the frightening object, trying to take it in. "And the other star?" Even magnified, it was only a hotter, brighter point.

"That's a queer one, too. It's a neutron star, Sue-ling. It's more massive than our sun, but only about a dozen kilometers through. Probably it went supernova too, some time—they must have traded mass with each other until both went up. But that one was just a little smaller, so it didn't go all the way to black hole . . . not that either one of them is anything you want to get too close to."

She turned and looked up at him. "And the Turtles *live* there?"

"It's their home," he confirmed wryly. "You'd think nothing could survive in a system like that, wouldn't you? But the Turtles do. They love it." He reached for the controls again, saying, "Wait a minute—let's see if we can screen out the stars and get a look at their planet—"

As the screen blurred something touched Sue-ling on the back of her neck. Startled, she turned and saw the mech-woman, Daisy Fay McQueen. The face on her belly screen was smiling up at Sue-ling, and trailing behind Daisy Fay was her crewmate.

But Marco Ramos wasn't smiling. Both of his tentacled eyes were fixed on the Turtle star, as he said sharply, "What's the matter with the screens, Francis?"

Sue-ling turned quickly back. It didn't look to her as though anything were wrong, but she did see that something like a vast shadow had settled on the fringes of the image. The angry dot of light from the companion had winked out, the furious haze of blue light was covered over, and that part of the screen had gone almost black. Sue-ling saw only a pale powdering of more distant stars in the background.

But Krake too was scowling. He looked around at the others who were beginning to come into the control room, answering to his summons. "Where are the Turtles?" he demanded.

"They're on their way, Captain," Daisy Fay reported. "What's the matter?"

"It's funny," he complained. "At this distance we should be able to pick up the Turtle planet, but where is it?"

"What does it look like?" Sue-ling asked, squinting as hard as she could at the screen.

"Not much of anything," he said absently, looking around for the Turtles. Then he turned back to her. "All I can tell you is what I've seen from space. It's a bare world, Sue-ling. No green. It doesn't even have ice caps. It looks dead."

"And the Turtles *live* there?"

"Some of them still do, yes. Or did. They all come from there originally. They aren't human, you know. That radiation would fry us in a second, but it's mother's milk to them—it's most of what they live on." But he was paying little attention to their conversation, speaking only with half his mind. The rest was trying to be patient until the Turtles arrived.

"Captain?" Marco called. "I bet I know why they aren't here. They've got screens of their own in their quarters—I'll bet they're watching from there, just to be private from the rest of us."

"And cooking up what they want to tell us," Sork snarled—startling Sue-ling, who hadn't seen him come in. He looked distinctly hung over, she saw, and was not surprised.

"Maybe so," Krake said worriedly, peering at the wall view. He shook his head. "I've seen the planet on other trips," he said, exasperated. "I've even landed on it —sort of."

She looked at him in surprise. "I could have sworn you said you hadn't."

"It wasn't really much of a landing," he explained. "I dodged down and back—they warned me the radiation from the accretion disk would be deadly if we were unprotected. The neutron star's not quite as bad, but it's bad enough; so we had to take precautions. But I had to land to transfer cargo." He stared somberly out at the scene in space. "See, the black hole and its accretion disk are several light-days away—a safe enough distance, unless you get caught in a flare. We stayed in the shielded parts of the ship, unloading by machine, but the important thing we did was to come in at night. We brought *Hind* in down the cone of shadow, where it was shielded, to the orbiting station for their Skyhook. Then we did what we had to do, and got out of there before the orbiter was exposed again."

"It sounds dangerous."

He looked at her blankly. "Oh? Well, a little maybe, but that's not what's worrying me. What I'm worried about is where the damned thing is. I *know* I've picked the planet up from farther out than this."

And then, as the two Turtles at last appeared, despondently pulling themselves into the room, he appealed to them. "What's wrong? Are our instruments screwed up?"

It was Chief Thunderbird who answered. "The instruments are working perfectly, Krake," the Turtle boomed, the grating voice like a dirge. "The situation is as our worst fears. It is our entire sacred Mother planet that has disappeared. There is nothing left of it at all."

Among the songs the aiodoi sing is a song which speaks of oneness, and it goes:
"It is all now.
"It is all ever.
"It is all one."
And sometimes among the songs the aiodoi hear there is a song which echoes their own, even when it comes from a small voice on a distant world.

———

"Now suppose these notions of Stephen Hawking and all those other people are true, and our universe is only one of many—maybe of an infinity of them. Is there any way that one universe can make contact with another?

"The answer, surprisingly, is 'yes.' It may not be a *practicable* way. But *theoretically,* yes, there may be a point of contact; it's what Hawking and others called a 'wormhole.'

"According to Hawking and Roger Penrose, the trouble with wormholes as a doorway to other universes was that they were surrounded by an impassable barrier called the Cauchy horizon. It was theoretically possible that *something* could pass the Cauchy barrier, but only if you didn't care what shape it got through in. Hawking and Penrose thought that the Cauchy horizon would destroy anything that entered it with one giant pulse of infinite energy.

"That was kind of discouraging to would-be universe travelers.

"But then Kip Thorne took a closer look at the problem, and came up with good news. The barrier wouldn't be all that destructive in one special case that he discovered, and that was where the wormhole had been formed from so-called 'exotic matter.'

"That inspired a couple of English scientists, Felicity Mellor and Ian Moss, to dig a little deeper into the question. Sure enough, they discovered that you didn't even need exotic matter. All you needed was a closed universe.

"The mistake their predecessors had been making lay in the assumption that the universe was flat and open. That made their mathematics easier, but it hid the truth from them. There was, after all, no a priori reason to make that assumption. There was no evidence that the flat-open universe corresponded to physical reality. When Mellor and Moss did the problem over with the more plausible closed-universe assumption, they found that the problem of the Cauchy barrier had disappeared.

"So the way was open for anyone to go through a wormhole and come out in another universe. . . .

"Well, that's not quite true. There was one little remaining problem.

"For that kind of a trip, the first step was the hardest. You had to do one of two things. In order to travel through a wormhole, you had to make one to travel through. Or, if you couldn't find any way to make a wormhole, you had to find a way to get to where some wormhole was."

———

And the aiodoi sang on:
"And that is the way to reach from the near to the endless.
"Do it!"

12

What puzzled Moon Bunderan most was that, although it seemed clear that the planet they were aiming toward no longer existed, the Turtles had not given up. They were demanding—no, it was even more astonishing than that; they were almost *pleading*—for something more.

What that something more was Moon could not say. She had begun listening to all those old lecture chips with the others, but none of them seemed to relate to any reality she had ever experienced, and all too many of them were worrisome.

Thrayl, for instance. What did the Turtles want with him? He looked up at her from where he sat cross-legged on the floor, his gentle eyes concerned. "There is nothing to fear, Moon," he rumbled. "I hear no ill songs for you."

"What about for you?" she demanded. "What are the Turtles going to do with you?"

He was silent for a moment. Then he said, "They will do what they must, Moon."

"And what will that be?" But he didn't answer, only took her hand in his and closed his eyes again. Moon fidgeted, ill at ease. This whole situation, she thought, was getting too weird for comfort. She held tight to Thrayl's hard, comforting, three-fingered paw for reassurance. It was the only reassurance she had when these

—"beings"—she had gone off with were shouting and squawking at each other.

The fact that they were out of wave-drive now was some consolation. At least in the control room she wasn't surrounded by that frightening sphere of stars and empty space. Only the panels that circled the room were lit, but what they showed was almost as unpleasing to Moon Bunderan.

The strangest thing of all was that none of this stressful weirdness had affected Thrayl. As far as Moon could see, her Taur was quite content. He was gazing peacefully up at that awful great swirl of evil light that was called a "black hole," huge in the lower left-hand corner of one screen—still fiercely bright, though it had been dimmed by the instruments so that its brilliance didn't wipe out everything else in view. Thrayl was even rumbling softly to himself—"purring," Moon called it. She took solace from that fact. If Thrayl was at peace, no real harm could be very near. . . .

Or so Moon Bunderan hoped.

No one else was contented, though. The two Turtles were jabbering to each other, transposers off, and both Sork Quintero and Captain Krake were studying the screens with worry on their faces. When Moon stirred, Krake glanced at her. He smiled, though it was a worn, tense smile. He waved a hand at the screen. "See our present problem? I mean the ships?"

Moon squinted at the screen. There was nothing resembling a waveship, only a faint dusting of green in one spot, hardly visible. "Wait a minute," he said, "I'll brighten the ID signal." As he touched the keypad, abruptly, the dusting turned into a flock of what looked like little green birds, all around the place where the Mother planet should have been. They were tiny, bright triangles, green as the grass in her own mother's little front yard.

"What are they?" she asked.

"Turtle spacecraft," Krake said briefly. "The bright spots are ID markers projected from the navigation gear. They aren't light, you know. You couldn't see them with the naked eye. They're signals, so one ship can know when another is nearby."

"There are dozens of them!"

He nodded. "They're orbiting something. Do you see what it is they're orbiting?"

She peered hard. Then shook her head. There was nothing there—nothing except, maybe, just possibly—"Is there something there, in among them?" she asked. "That little sort of, I don't know, squiggly thing that I can hardly see?"

Krake nodded somberly, staring at the same object. More than anything else, it looked like a flaw in window glass. "That's it," he said. He peered more closely at the object, looking disgruntled. "I'm not surprised that you don't know what it is. I don't either. I'd say it was a little black hole, except there's no accretion disk around it. I know what *should* be there, though. The Turtle planet. But it's not there."

"I think it might be what they call a wormhole," Sork Quintero said abruptly.

Moon turned to look at him sharply, wondering if he were making some kind of joke. He saw her expression, and laughed sharply. "Oh, not like a hole in an apple, Moon," he said. "There aren't any real worms in space. But in those old tapes the scientists talked about something like this—about the way a black hole might produce a kind of tunnel through space—or, no, not *through* space exactly, but—"

He stopped, shaking his head irritably. "I don't understand it," he complained. "The Turtles keep asking me about it, but all I can tell them is what's on the tapes —that some people thought these 'wormholes' were actually a kind of gateway to another universe. If *that* means anything. . . ."

Moon blinked at him. "How can there be more than one universe, Sork? I thought a universe was, well, *everything* there was."

He laughed again. "See what I mean? All of this stuff is just too confusing to take in. Maybe it's all nonsense, I don't know. The Turtles seemed to think so, until just now—"

He broke off, suddenly realizing that the Turtles had stopped their private bickering. Both were listening to him. He said quickly, trying to placate them, "I didn't mean to say anything to offend you."

Chief Thunderbird turned on his transposer. "You cannot offend truth," he said somberly. "But truth—"

Litlun finished for him. "Truth has many guises," he said.

"That is right, one believes," rasped Chief Thunderbird, glowering up at the screen with both his eyes. "That place is where our holy home used to be, and now it is gone!"

"And if that is indeed what this human calls a wormhole, perhaps that is where it has gone," Litlun confirmed, glaring at Sork Quintero, who was looking haggard from the long ordeal of his questioning.

Sork shrugged angrily. Captain Krake cleared his throat. "Well, then," Krake said, "that's that, isn't it? What should we do now, turn around and go back to Earth?" A wordless squawk from both Turtles was answer enough. He said, puzzled, "Well, what else can we do? I don't mean to sound insensitive—I know what it means to you. But if the planet's gone, it's gone, isn't it?"

Both pairs of Turtle eyes were on him now—angrily, Moon thought. "The planet has gone *somewhere,*" Litlun corrected him. "If what Sork Quintero says is true—"

"Hey, no!" Sork cried in alarm. "I don't know what's true and what isn't in this stuff—I only told you what the lecture chips said!"

"If it is true," Litlun rasped on, ignoring him, "then this is perhaps a wormhole, and in that case there is much to consider."

"And on that," added Chief Thunderbird, "we must meditate in our own quarters. We will return with our decision when we can."

"Wait a minute!" Krake cried. "What do you mean, 'decision'? We have to talk—"

But they were already gone. "What the hell?" Krake

said, in general. "What kind of decision are they talking about? Sork? Do you know?"

Sork Quintero was gazing after them. Then he blinked and looked at Krake. "Do I know?" he repeated. "No. All I can do is guess, and I don't want to do that . . . because it scares me."

Krake fixed him with a hard stare. "Hold it there, Sork. I don't care if you're scared out of your mind. I want to hear what you think."

"It's only a guess," Sork said obstinately.

"Damn it, Sork!"

Sork shrugged. "I think they think the Mother planet has slipped through that wormhole and disappeared into some other universe." And when he saw the looks Moon and the captain were giving him: "And I think they want to follow it."

"Is that possible?" Krake demanded.

"How the hell do I know that?" Sork asked reasonably. "Ask Moon. Ask her Taur, for that matter—they know as much about it as I do!"

Krake was puzzling over the new thought, hardly listening. Then he looked up. "Wait a minute. I thought the lecture chips said these wormholes only lasted for a skillionth of a second—and, real time, it's almost a hundred and fifty years now since the planet disappeared—"

"The chips also said that wormholes were too tiny to be seen," Sork reminded him, and waved to the immense curvature on the screen. He was smiling as he turned back to Krake. "Meditating," he said, "sounds like a good thing to do right now, doesn't it? I think I'll do some myself—if I can find something to help the meditation along."

————

When Sork was gone, Moon Bunderan asked the captain, "What did he mean about that?"

"He's been hitting my whiskey," Krake told her.

In alarm, Moon said, "But Sue-ling says he shouldn't drink!"

Krake cut her off. "He's a big boy, Moon. He can make his own decisions." He shook his head, dismissing Sork. "I don't know what to do," he complained. "I thought the Turtles would want to contact those other Turtle ships, at least. I wish I knew what they've got on their minds."

Moon shivered without answering. She gripped Thrayl's reassuring paw more tightly and Krake, seeing, pursed his lips. "You're lucky," he said somberly. "At least you've got your pet to comfort you."

Moon said seriously, "Thrayl is not my 'pet,' Captain Krake. He's my friend."

"Well, sure. I didn't mean any harm," Krake apologized. Then he cleared his throat. "There's something I've been meaning to ask you. Please don't take this the wrong way—but about you and Thrayl—?"

Moon stood up straight. "Are you asking me if we're doing something together that we shouldn't? That's the way my mother would have put it."

"Oh, no! Really. Nothing like that, only—"

"Only you can't help wondering, can you?" she said sharply. Then she relented. Sounding sad, she said, "A lot of people had that idea. That's why they might have burned him alive if they'd caught us. But Thrayl really is my friend, Captain Krake. He's like—" She paused, considering how to say what she meant. "He's like a child. I saw him born, you know. He was the size of a kitten— young Taurs are tiny—and I was only about eight myself. I used to play with him like a doll, bathe him, sing to him —he heard my songs long before he heard any of the ones he says he listens to now. I'd rock him in a doll cradle, and read to him. I taught him to talk and to read! Taurs aren't stupid, you know!"

"I didn't know he could read," Krake said humbly.

"He can do all sorts of things. Only—well, Taurs are different, you see. A lot of things that are important to us just don't interest Thrayl. He's like a—" She flushed, having trouble getting the word out—"He's like a kind of, well, saint."

She reached over and stroked the huge head. "I kept

you in the house until you were too big, didn't I, Thrayl?" The huge eyes seemed to smile with love. "He would die for me, Captain Krake. I know that. And he knows that I would do anything for him, too."

Krake studied the two of them for a while, then glanced toward the door. His expression changed again. "That's not really what I wanted to ask you, though. Why do you think the Turtles want him here?" he demanded.

Moon shrugged. "I don't understand Turtles at all," she declared.

Krake shook his head, baffled. "I think it has something to do with those songs he listens to. What do you know about them?"

"They're beautiful," Moon said positively. "Thrayl told me so, only—well, he can't tell me what they're like, exactly, because he doesn't have the words. He says there aren't any words that he can translate for me, not in his language or ours; they're just beautiful. And he began hearing them as soon as his horns began to grow." She stroked the massive head absently. "He says that the thing he fears most is the thought of something happening to hurt his horns. It isn't being slaughtered and eaten that scares him, you see; he doesn't seem to mind that. *I* do! But Thrayl wasn't afraid of being slaughtered at all. What he was afraid of was losing his horns, because that would mean losing his songs."

Krake was staring up at that faint pucker in the screen, his brow furrowed. "Do you suppose it could be those songs that the Turtles want to know about?" he asked. "Can Thrayl . . . well, foretell the future, or anything like that?"

Moon gave the question serious consideration. "I would say no," she said finally. "Not exactly. There have been times when Thrayl seems to know that something is wrong. Or dangerous. Or that there was trouble of some kind ahead. But I don't think the songs are really about *us*. They're sort of from outside. I don't know where 'outside' is, either," she added, forestalling Krake's question, "but I think it's right outside of *everything*. Maybe outside the whole universe."

Frowning, Krake nodded slowly—not to show comprehension, Moon thought, but only to show that he had heard the words. She didn't blame him for that. Thrayl's songs were, well, *funny,* and she knew she didn't comprehend what they were about herself.

She was glad when Daisy Fay and Marco appeared in the doorway. "My turn to relieve you, Cap'n," Marco said, the face on the belly plate grinning cheerfully up at his commander. "What're the orders?"

Krake glanced up again at the blur on the screen. "No orders," he said. "We just wait." He pulled himself erect. "Maybe I'll look in on Sork, keep him from getting too drunk—maybe I can get more sense out of him. You look as though you could use a little rest, too, Moon."

"I'm not sleepy," she objected.

But when Daisy Fay said amiably, "I've got some tea in my room, if you'd like some," Moon jumped at the chance. Anything was better than sitting in this cold, impersonal control room, waiting—and not even knowing what you were waiting for. Besides, she was curious about the machine-woman's living arrangements.

But as they were leaving, Moon paused at the doorway. "Captain Krake? They really are important, you know," she said suddenly. "Thrayl's songs, I mean."

"I'm sure of that," the captain said wearily. "I only wish I knew *why.*"

———

Daisy Fay McQueen's quarters were a surprise to Moon Bunderan. Pictures on the walls—landscapes from Earth mostly, and photos of what looked like some big city from pre-Turtle days, all skyscrapers and crowded streets and automobiles. There were flowers in fixtures on the walls—not real flowers, Moon saw, but there probably wasn't any real way for Daisy Fay to grow her own on the waveship. Then, while Daisy Fay was setting a funny little pot to boil and getting out cups, Moon said, with a shock of surprise, "You don't have a bed?"

"Moon, hon, what would I do with a bed?" There was laughter in the machine-woman's voice. "We're not in the shielded area, either, in case you didn't notice. Marco and I don't need shielding, at least not most of the time—we're almost as good as Turtles that way. Now don't worry," Daisy Fay added quickly, waving a couple of arms reassuringly as she saw Moon Bunderan's sudden expression of concern, "there's nothing near enough for its radiation to hurt you." The machine-woman set the cups on a shelf before moving over to the side of the chamber and pulling a bench down out of the wall. "But I do like to keep some reminders of when I was a fully organic human," she sighed. "I had this put in so Francis could be comfortable when he comes here. You can use it, Moon."

Moon sat down diffidently. Beside her, Thrayl squatted cross-legged on the floor, his eyes on Daisy Fay McQueen. Moon rested her hand affectionately on the broad space between the horns on his head, scratching gently into the fine short fur. To make conversation, she said, "I guess the Turtles took pretty good care of you, back on the orbit station?"

The face on Daisy Fay's video screen looked a little embarrassed. "Well, yes," she said, and then added, "To tell you the truth, Moon, there wasn't much wrong with us, really."

"But Captain Krake said you were being, well, repaired."

"Sort of maintenance, yes," Daisy Fay admitted. "That wasn't the real reason we didn't go down to the surface with him, though. We just—didn't want people staring at us." Absently she stroked her round body with a tentacle. "I know we look pretty funny, Moon. You can't blame the Turtles, though—they used themselves for models, I guess."

Moon cleared her throat. "Daisy Fay? Do you mind if I ask you something?"

"Not a bit," said the machine-woman cheerily. "I

even know what you want to know. How we got this
way, right? It's all right. I'm sort of proud of it, in a way
—I'm the only female half-robot human in the universe,
right? And it beats being dead." She squatted down on
four of her eight tentacles. Like Moon, she reached out
gently with one of her arms and rested it lightly on the
Taur's massive shoulder. Thrayl blinked at her but made
only a faint, friendly sound deep in his throat.

"It was during the war," Daisy Fay began. "I was a
reporter for a Chicago newspaper—do you know what a
newspaper was?"

"For telling people what was happening in the world?
Before they had videoplates?"

"That's right. I wasn't very experienced at it, but
most of the men were away in the service and they had to
give even a young female cub like me a chance. They sent
me down to South America to report on how some of the
other countries were planning for life after the war. And
I had to fly across the Andes—that's a mountain chain in
South America—"

"I know where the Andes are," Moon assured her.
"They're still right in the same place."

"Yeah. I suppose they would be. Anyway," Daisy Fay
said, her tone suddenly harsh, "we crashed."

"Crashed? The plane fell out of the sky?"

"That's right—remember, Moon, this was a long time
ago. Planes weren't all that reliable then. There were six
of us in the plane, an old DC-2—that's a kind of small
commercial propeller plane. Marco was the copilot.
While we were trying to pick our way through the passes
a storm came up and we flew right into a mountain."

She stopped for a moment, only her tentacle gently
stroking the Taur's shoulder. The face on her belly plate
looked sad. Then she made a sudden movement of her
tentacles and went on. "It wasn't anybody's fault, you
know. Least of all Marco's; he wasn't even at the controls
just then. But there we were. The pilot was killed outright, and so were two passengers. The only other passen-
ger, a woman, was badly hurt. So Marco and I tried to
get her down the mountain in a litter, because we knew

she'd freeze to death out there, at that altitude, in the blizzard. . . ."

She stopped. The gentle waving of her arms slowed, as though saddened. "Well, there was an avalanche. We were carried down the mountain. Buried under snow. Really messed up—both Marco's legs were broken, and so was his back. He couldn't move. I was a little better off— just one arm broken, but it was a compound fracture and it hurt like—well, we were in bad shape. And freezing, of course. Our only hope was the Mae West radio that we'd carried with us."

"What's that?"

"A Mae West? It's a kind of portable radio—you powered it by hand cranking it. But that wasn't a good chance, because we were in a high valley, and the radio wouldn't go through mountains."

She made a sound that was almost a laugh. "It turned out that it didn't have to. I didn't expect any planes would find us, and I was right about that. They didn't. But then down came this funny-looking thing—it looked like a banana with tiny wings, long, and a little bent, and it was shooting out pale blue flame from the bottom. I thought I'd died, or was dreaming—well, you know what it was."

"The Turtles?"

"Right the first time! It was a Turtle scout ship. Believe me, when I saw what was coming out of that ship to pick us up I thought I was *really* crazy! And then I passed out—and when I woke up again I was like this."

"So the Turtles turned you into a—" Moon bit her tongue to keep from saying the next word.

"They *repaired* me," Daisy Fay corrected. "They did the best they could, Moon. Marco and I were among the first human beings they'd ever seen. They knew what *Turtles* were like, which is why they sort of used themselves as a model for rebuilding us—but what did they know about human anatomy then?"

"They learned from experimenting on you?"

"That, and the cadavers. Mostly from the cadavers." Daisy Fay sounded sad. "Because not everybody they tried to save survived. We were lucky." She roused herself, her tentacles waving gently. "But the tea's ready now, Moon. How do you like yours?"

———————

Curiously, Moon Bunderan found herself relaxing in the warmth of Daisy Fay's friendship. It was almost like being home again, sitting in a friend's kitchen—not that this waveship cabin was in any way like a New Mexican kitchen, or Daisy Fay at all like the friends of her life back home. But it was all so comforting—

Comforting, at least, until she saw what Daisy Fay was doing with her tea. She must have gasped, because the eyes swiveled toward her.

"Sorry," Moon managed to get out, averting her eyes. The robot-woman had fastidiously opened a little hatch just under the video screen and with two tentacles delicately poured a bit of the tea into it.

Then the face on the belly screen smiled up at her. "I'm sorry," Daisy Fay said ruefully. "I forget how funny it must look. The food tastes just as good, though.

You see, Moon," she said earnestly, "we're still human. Our brains, most of the circulatory and digestive system, all the glands and so on—they're all still inside here. It was only the peripherals of our bodies that were totally destroyed."

Moon pushed her luck one step farther. "And, uh, can you and Marco—?"

Daisy Fay sighed. "I wish," she said regretfully. "No, that's as far as our biological parts go. We can't have sexual relations. The Turtles just never bothered with that part—I guess because they just didn't understand that human beings might have a need for such things. They never do it themselves, you know—except for the Mother and the one-in-a-billion lucky male who gets the chance when a new Mother's ready. And it—" she hesitated. "It's really a pity," she said, "because you should have seen Marco before the accident. He was *gorgeous*. He wasn't really tall. I think I had an inch or so on him when I was wearing heels, but that didn't matter. Marco was beautifully built, with those soft brown eyes—the kind of Latin lover we used to hear so much about, back in those days. Oh, I had a real case on him, all right. I wouldn't have been on that plane if I hadn't. And then we crashed, and that was the end of that. We never did get a chance to make love. . . .

She was silent for a mourning moment. Then the face on the belly screen brightened again. "But at least we're alive," she said staunchly. "And we're together!"

———

Later on, affectionately feeding her Taur, Moon shivered, thinking about how "lucky" Daisy Fay McQueen and Marco Ramos had been. "I don't know, Thrayl," she murmured, rubbing the soft spot between his horns. "It's better to be alive than dead, sure, so that was good luck. . . . But what kind of life is it for Daisy Fay?"

The Taur, squatting beside her, turned his huge purple-blue eyes on her but did not stop delicately munching at the redfruit in his hard three-fingered hands.

"When you come right down to it," she went on, "what kind of life is it going to be for us? These are all good people we're with, Thrayl, I'm sure of that—well, not counting the Turtles, I mean. I don't understand the Turtles real well. But Captain Krake and the others—I trust them. Only all this is getting pretty scary."

The Taur mooed gently at her—not a word, just a sympathetic sound. It was all she expected—or needed; this was the way she had talked to Thrayl when he was a tiny calf, bringing him all her little problems, not needing answers from him only the comfort of his listening ear. She smiled, feeling better.

Then, finishing the last of his redfruit, the Taur stood up, gazing at her expectantly. "Time to go to see what the others are doing?" she asked. "The Turtles are taking so long—I wish I knew what they were thinking about." She sighed and took the huge, hard hand. "We did the right thing, Thrayl," she told him seriously as they walked toward the control room. "We couldn't let them maim you, could we? But, oh, I'd be really happy if I just knew what was going to happen next."

But an hour later, when she did know, she wasn't happy at all.

Though the aiodoi are not guardians, they do observe. Sometimes what they observe makes a song for them to sing, sometimes only a song they hear; for they are aiodoi, and singing is their life.

————————

"You remember we were talking about interuniversal travel through wormholes, and we said there were a couple of tough problems that faced any prospective voyager.

"One thing you could do would be to find a wormhole and go there. You're not likely to find one in Low Earth Orbit, of course, because a wormhole is enough like a black hole that you'd have a hell of a problem with gravitational attraction. It would tear the Earth into confetti, even if there weren't also the certainty of damaging radiation from its accretion disk. So there surely isn't one nearby, or we'd know it.

"So if you want to reach a wormhole, you definitely first have to invent some kind of really fast spaceship to take you to where one is.

"That sounds all right, as long as nobody actually asks you to *build* one. It isn't. The bottom-line trouble with trying to find wormholes is that they are extremely hard to find. You can't see the things. They're very small

—ten to the minus thirty-third centimeters in diameter, give or take a bit—and they don't last very long ordinarily, say ten to the minus forty-third seconds.

"That's to say, your average wormhole is about the size of a typical quantum fluctuation in the structure of our universe. The wormholes, if they exist, are in fact quite indistinguishable from the 'space-time foam' which is the basic structure of everything.

"Still, if you are lucky enough to find one of the things at all, there are some neat things you can do. And even if you can't find one, perhaps you have another shot. Maybe you can make one—or make an existing one big enough, and long enough lasting, to do you some good.

"Some people at Cal Tech figured out a theoretical way of using the Casimir effect for that purpose. A man named Alan Guth, with the help of two people named Edward Fahrl and Jumal Guven, said you could perhaps do the job by heating a volume of space to about ten to the twenty-seventh Kelvin—here, I'll write it on the board for you—

"1,000,000,000,000,000,000,000,000,000 Kelvin

"—or, alternatively, you could compress some matter a lot—down to black hole densities, far denser than even a neutron star.

"If you were able to do either of those things, then you really might have something. At those figures, a wormhole might well open up, and, if Mellor and Moss are right, you might even be able to send something through it. Not matter, probably. But *something*.

"Lots of luck if you decide to try."

And the aiodoi sang on:
"What is luck?
"There is no luck.
"Luck is the chance that something may happen.
"And everything that may happen does."

13

Marco Ramos thought he had never seen his captain so angry—or worse than just angry: he was *baffled*. Captain Krake was almost inarticulate, dancing around as he fought to get the words out. He had even forgotten, Marco thought, to get the wave-drive normalized; they would never be able to get into the wave configuration again if that weren't done first. But just listen to him: "You're insane," Krake was shouting as he squinted up at the hard-armored bulk of Chief Thunderbird. "We can't take this ship through a wormhole! That's suicide."

"It is without previous experience and therefore dangerous, yes," the Turtle rumbled. "One is a child of the Mother, however. One must sacrifice personal interests for our brothers."

"That's fine for you, but we're not Turtles!"

"You have accepted our gifts," Litlun squawked severely. "You have entered the service of our Mother; you too are bound by her needs."

"But the Mother is dead," Krake said brutally. "Face it, Litlun."

"Do not call me by that name!" the Turtle screeched, raising himself up to full height.

"Then don't talk like a fool," snarled Krake. "Everybody knows that if you get too close to a black hole you die. Even you—Facilitator."

There was silence for a moment, while one of Litlun's eyes turned to meet one of the eyes of Chief Thunderbird. Ramos felt one of Daisy Fay's tentacles reach out to hold one of his own for comfort. He turned one eye toward her reassuringly—though not at all confident in himself that there was any reason to be reassured. Then Marco cleared his throat—or made the noise that would have signified that, if he had still had a throat to clear. "Captain?" he ventured. "If we're going anywhere, we need to renormalize the wave-drive—"

"Then do it!" thundered the bigger Turtle.

"Well, sure, Proctor," Marco said, "but there were some funny fluctuations in the drive before. This is an old ship, you know," he added persuasively. "It might be about due for a general overhaul. We could contact some of those other Turtle ships for help—"

"No!" squawked Litlun. "It is not our intention to contact those other Brotherhood vessels!"

And Chief Thunderbird added suspiciously, "One is not aware of any unusual fluctuations. Go and do your work; then come back and report to us." Then he turned to Captain Krake. "What you said a moment ago, Captain Krake," he thundered, "is untrue. Everybody does not know that transiting a wormhole is fatal. One of you says otherwise—is that not so, Sork Quintero?"

Marco and Daisy Fay, on their way to the wave-drive chamber, tarried to look at Sork, as everyone else was doing. Sork blinked at the Turtle. "Me?" he said. "Are you talking about those old scientific chips? But they aren't me talking, are they? They're just records of what some professor said in a lecture hall; I don't know, myself, if any of it is true."

"You have told us that these humans believe it to be true," Litlun said severely. "Sue-ling Quong also has said that the chips are authentic. Do you deny the wisdom of your own race?"

"Well, you've been denying it!" Krake put in furiously. "What made you change your mind?"

Silence for a moment. Then Chief Thunderbird said

hollowly, "We have not changed our minds. We simply have no choice, because we are *desperate.*"

———————

As soon as they were outside, Daisy Fay turned to Marco. "Is there really anything wrong with the wave-drive?" she demanded.

The face on his screen shook its head. "Not as far as I know, but I wanted to give Francis an excuse in case he needs it. Let's get it renormalized, anyway."

She followed him down the hall. "I hate it when Francis gets so apoplectic," she murmured.

"He's got a lot to get apoplectic about," he told her. He stopped in front of the entrance to the chamber. "Whatever happens, though," he said, "somebody's got to take care of the store. Let's balance the wave converters."

It was a relief to be doing something familiar, adjusting the output potentials in the generators to prepare for the next leap into wave-drive space. But Daisy Fay turned on the intercom, and they could hear the angry voices from the control room. Everybody was in the argument now, Krake bellowing, the two Turtles thundering, Sue-ling and the Quinteros trying to get a word in when they could. Only Moon Bunderan and her Taur were silent.

Daisy Fay sighed. "Everything's so mixed up," she complained. "What should we do, Marco?"

"We'll do whatever the captain wants us to do," he answered at once. "What else?"

She said seriously, "Maybe you had the right idea. Maybe we should disable the wave-drive generators—just until Francis gets things under control . . . or the Turtles give up the idea."

"Not without orders from the captain," Marco said at once.

"No, of course not." She sighed again. "Sometimes I wish they'd left me in the snow to die," she said wearily.

Ramos turned both eyes to stare at her. "Never say

that! Still," he added softly, "sometimes I remember what life was like—before."

She waved her tentacles in agreement. "So far away—so long ago. Are you sorry, ever?"

"Sorry that the Turtles rescued us? Never!" he said staunchly. "It's better to be alive than dead."

She looked at him for a long moment before speaking. "But that's the question, isn't it? Are we really alive, Marco?"

"You know we are! Well," he qualified, "not in the same way as—before—maybe, but we're alive all right." His eyestalks turned toward her, and the look on the face on his belly platen was serious. He said, "In a way, this isn't just life for me, you know! It's almost—heaven. It's what I dreamed of as a child. I've told you why."

Daisy Fay turned one eye on her companion, the other busy on the dials as they worked. In the background they could hear the shouting from the control room, words like *wormholes* and *other universes* and, most of all, Krake's raging voice refusing to do what the Turtles were demanding. "Tell me again, Marco," she whispered, her voice almost shivering.

He touched her slick red shell affectionately and obediently began the old story, the one that told of their humanity—so easy to forget these days, especially when you caught a glimpse of yourself in a mirror! "I was a poor farmer's son," he said, by rote. "Back in Chile, in our old Twentieth Century. I was growing up to a life of —nothing. No money. No hope, except trying to scratch a living out of the soil."

"I know," the girl murmured, touching his hard shell with one supple arm.

"But when the clouds lifted I could see a mountaintop far away. There was something on it that looked like a snow-white bubble, the most beautiful thing I could see. They said it was called an 'observatory.' They said astronomers worked there, exploring the universe through their telescopes—and, oh, Daisy Fay, I wanted so badly to be one of them! I'd go out in the pastures at night and lie on my back, gazing up at the stars—the Southern

Cross, and Alpha Centauri and all of them. . . . There was another boy in my town, a storekeeper's son. He had more money than I did, but he was interested in the same things. The two of us ordered some materials through the mail. I didn't have any money, but he paid for them and I did most of the work, and we built a little telescope. God, Daisy! That was so wonderful, looking at the moons of Jupiter and at the Great Nebula in Orion, and the Magellanic Clouds. . . . And then I got a chance to go away to school in the Army and they made me a pilot. I studied navigation, and I wondered if my country would ever let me go to college when I got out, maybe study astronomy—"

He laughed. "It didn't work out that way, of course. I probably never would have got to college, anyway. But the Turtles did the next best thing for me, didn't they? Now I don't just look at the stars—I go out and roam among them!"

"And this is what you call heaven?" Daisy Fay asked wonderingly.

"It's close enough for me," Marco told her seriously. "At least—considering that we lost a lot of options when the plane crashed." Gently their eyestalks kissed and parted. "It isn't just the stars, Daisy Fay, they're only one part of this heaven. The other part is the one that's really important, and that's having you here with me. I remember watching you board the plane," he whispered, his limbs shuddering. "You were so beautiful!"

"I was just an ordinary woman, Marco," she told him, but not very insistently.

"You were the most beautiful woman I had ever seen! And that's why this is heaven, Daisy Fay. I have my childhood dream—and I have you!" They clung to each other for a moment, lovingly and hopelessly.

Then a raucous screech from the passageway interrupted them. "Ridiculous humans!" rasped Chief Thunderbird. "Why are you not tending to your work?" The Turtle quickly scanned the generator panels, then said, slightly mollified, "One sees you have balanced the converters and there is no indication of irregularity. Come, then! It is time for us to act!"

————

Sork Quintero was saying, for the thousandth time it seemed: "Yes, the old scientists said it was possible for a black hole kind of thing to be a way of getting into another universe. They called them 'wormholes.' Yes, I suppose it's possible that that's what happened to your planet, and, yes, I suppose we could follow. But, dear God, I *beg* you, don't try it!"

"We have no choice," said Chief Thunderbird, stalking into the room. "Come, the wave-drive is ready. There is no reason for delay."

Sork licked his lips, staring at the two Turtles. "But don't you remember what the tapes said? Wormholes—if there *are* such things as wormholes—aren't permanent fixtures. They open and close."

"That is not true, because there it is!" squawked Litlun in triumph, gesturing with a webbed claw at the curious spot on the screen.

"There *what* is? How do you know it's the same one? Think it over," Sork begged. "When did the planet vanish? *Almost a hundred and fifty years ago!* Time enough for the message to reach Earth and for us to get back here!"

Chief Thunderbird drew himself up. "This fact is known," he stated.

"But is it understood?" Sork demanded. "Even if all this stuff is right—and we don't know that!—that could be an entirely different wormhole, that might lead somewhere else entirely!"

"This is only speculation, and in any case does not matter," squawked Litlun.

"Hey, wait a minute!" Krake put in. "It matters to me! Sork's right. If we don't know that's even the same wormhole—"

"What we know," Chief Thunderbird declared, "is that there is a *chance* it is the thing we seek, and that by entering it we can save the Mother. Therefore we will do it."

"The hell you say," cried Krake. "You can't make that decision for us! We'll decide that question democratically, by a vote."

Litlun squealed in rage. "What is 'vote,' Captain Krake? It is not a matter of *voting* when the future of the Brotherhood is at stake!"

"Voting is how we humans decide what to do," Krake said angrily, "and there are more of us than of you on this ship, so our rules decide. Come on, everybody! Vote! Everybody who says we don't do this crazy thing, raise a hand!"

His own hand was the first up, followed loyally by a tentacle each from his crew, Marco and Daisy Fay. And, a moment later, by Sork Quintero. Krake waited only half a second before shouting at the others: "What's the matter with you? Kiri? Sue-ling? Moon? Vote, goddamn it!"

Chief Thunderbird roared triumphantly: "They agree with us! Very well, we will be bound by this vote! Now raise hands, those who would take this risk to save the Brotherhood and the sacred Mother!"

And his own hard arm shot up, and Litlun's . . . and then Sue-ling, her voice low, said: "I'm sorry, Sork, but I think they deserve their chance." As she raised her hand, Kiri shrugged and joined her, avoiding his brother's eye.

"Four to four?" Krake whispered unbelievingly. "But you're out of your minds, all of you—well, what about you?" he challenged, glaring at Moon Bunderan.

But she wasn't looking at him. She was looking up at the face of the Taur, her expression worried. "I—I don't know," she whispered. "Something's wrong. Thrayl? What is it?"

The Taur didn't answer. His eyes had the glazed expression of his trance states, listening to the voices.

"Come on, vote!" Krake rasped. But Chief Thunderbird cried triumphantly:

"She is not voting for you, Captain Krake! Therefore

there is no 'majority,' and we will proceed. Younger Brother, direct this ship to the wormhole!"

"The hell you will!" Krake raged, and turned to grab for Litlun as the Turtle was already at the control board, setting a course for the wrinkle in space.

Krake was not in time.

The Taur's expression cleared. Soundlessly he fixed his huge purple-blue eyes on Krake and moved forward, faster on his bowed little legs than Marco Ramos would have believed possible. The Taur caught the helplessly struggling Krake up in his hard arms and held him there.

"Do it!" shouted Chief Thunderbird triumphantly, and Litlun tapped out a swift combination on the keys; and the flare of light told them that *The Golden Hind* was entering wave-drive.

————

"Call your damn animal off!" Krake begged Moon Bunderan in fury, struggling against the Taur's iron grip. But Moon was shaking her head helplessly. Krake blinked as the transition flash lit the simulated sky. As soon as it was over he could see that the Turtle's course had been right on target; they were driving directly toward that terrible wrinkle in space at light speed.

"Stop it, please!" Krake begged, writhing uselessly in Thrayl's arms. "We can't do this! You're endangering my ship! Marco—Daisy Fay—stop him!"

"No one is to stop this process!" Chief Thunderbird roared. "It is for the salvation of the entire Brotherhood and our sacred Mother!"

Krake swore violently to himself as he watched. The accretion disk of the old black hole was whirling, crawling away as they dropped toward the wormhole. Accelerating to light speed, their subjective time slowed almost to a stop, he could see the wrinkle expanding, and the clustered green ship beacons bloating too. Krake heard a low-toned moan from Thrayl—of agony or delight, he couldn't tell.

"It's too late, Francis," Daisy Fay said, her voice trembling. "We're too close now. We have to go in—and through—or we'll get torn apart."

The dome went black, all but that strange wrinkle, Thrayl's horns glowing milky white against the darkness. Krake felt the Taur shudder in a kind of ecstasy. Across the cabin, what Sue-ling Quong felt was a sort of shock in the deck beneath her feet that rocked her with a wave of nausea. Blind in the internal darkness of the control room, she clutched at Sork and Kiri.

"The wormhole," she heard Sork's whisper from close beside her, and even in that moment she could not escape the morning-after sourness of his breath. "We're in it. . . ."

For Moon Bunderan it was a giddy feeling, as though she were plunging headfirst into a widening whirlpool. The wormhole brightened before them until it filled one whole side of the globe, its center an ebony pit, ringed with faint spinning spirals of tenuous gas.

The darkness lasted only an instant. . . .

And then, without warning, the whole sky shone!

Ten thousand suns blazed out all around the slender bridge, above it and below. Krake glared at the spectacle, almost sickened; no human being had ever seen a sky like that before. The falling sensation had vanished. Though there was no physical sensation, something in his unadapted sensory systems was crying to him that he was rising—zooming—soaring into that burning splendor of stars, away from the maelstrom of fire that was the wormhole. He could still see it behind them. Its center was a blinding pit, ringed with spinning spirals of glowing gas and dust. A vast blue plume trailed out of it toward them.

There was a rapturous moan from Litlun at the controls. "We're through!" he rasped. "We've followed the sacred Mother!"

"My God," Sue-ling Quong whispered. "And we're still alive."

Krake bellowed and pulled away from the Taur.

"We're alive, all right," he roared, "but what's happened to my ship? Look at that thing!" In the screen behind them a vast accretion disk spun ominously, but receding rapidly as they drew away.

"Do not interfere, Krake! Attend me, Facilitator! Where is the Mother Planet?" Chief Thunderbird croaked eagerly. "Can you see it on the screen?"

But Litlun was gazing in shock at his navigation board, sparkling with evil red error signals. "Something's wrong," he said in dismay. "What has happened, Elder Brother?"

Krake shouted in wordless anger at what the instruments were telling him about the condition of his ship. Drowning him out, Chief Thunderbird screamed, "Have you damaged the navigation? It is inexcusable!"

"No, no," Litlun said feebly, his yellow-red eyes wandering about helplessly. "One did nothing wrong! But—see for yourself, there are no reference points, nothing is as it should be."

"Fool! Of course not! This strange notion is true; we're in another universe, and certainly there are no familiar reference points! It is the Mother planet you must find, not some distant star!"

"But, Proctor," Litlun sobbed, waving his arm at the screen around them. "Don't you see? There are no navigation beacons. There is nothing to guide us. The Mother planet—its entire network of navigation satellites and beacons—it is not here."

"Marco?" Krake snapped, turning to his crewman.

But Marco said helplessly, "I'm still trying, Captain, but—I think he's right. I'm not getting any beacon readings at all."

"Keep trying," Krake ordered. It was only instinct speaking though. Half to himself, he said, to no one in particular, "There's not much chance."

Chief Thunderbird glared madly at him for a moment, then seemed to collapse. With a wordless howl of despair he fell against the wall, pounding his carapace against it. "Failed," he moaned. "We have failed."

For a moment it seemed the huge Turtle was on the verge of some catastrophic action—suicide, perhaps; or an apoplectic fit, if Turtles could have such things— even, almost, as though he were going to attack, physically *attack*, Francis Krake. Or Sork Quintero, or Kiri, or even Chief Thunderbird's own Younger Brother —anyone, almost, it seemed. Krake had never seen a Turtle so excited. The coppery eyes were revolving wildly, the claws drumming furiously against the belly plastron. . . .

Then the Taur spoke up. It wasn't a word Krake could recognize, hardly more than a loud, commanding bull's bellow. Everyone turned to him and Moon Bunderan. "What did he say?" Chief Thunderbird rasped at the girl.

And hesitantly, bewildered, she said, "I think what Thrayl said was, 'Not yet.' "

———

Not yet, Krake thought to himself in the sudden silence that fell in the control room. Not yet! Did the stupid creature possibly mean that there was still a chance? Or did he mean something else entirely, something that only a Taur could understand? He opened his mouth to ask an angry question . . . and closed it again, for Marco Ramos was waving agitatedly to him from the control board. "Captain?" he said, his voice shaking. "Look at that."

Krake followed the machine-man's stare to a corner of the board. It was at absolute maximum magnification, the tens of thousands (no, now it was hundreds at least!) of blue-white suns almost blinding him. But there, among them, almost hidden in the brilliance—

It was faint, but it was undeniably green, and it had the characteristic Turtle delta shape.

"The Mother planet!" Litlun squealed, almost hysterical. "One may yet win through!"

"I'm not sure of that, Lit—Facilitator," Marco said

quickly. "It looks to me like a ship signal, not a planetary beacon."

"No matter!" cawed Chief Thunderbird, miraculously revived. "Where there are ships of the Brotherhood, then we will find our Mother! Krake! Set course for that beacon at once!"

The aiodoi never fear the future, either for their own sake or for the sakes of those whose songs they listen to, for the future and the past are all one to them. They are not trapped within time. The aiodoi are not trapped within space, either, for they live within all dimensions and none, and they listen kindly to the yearning songs of those who are.

"We've talked about the four dimensions of space-time, but I ought to tell you that that's really pretty old-fashioned stuff. A lot of the current cosmologies need more than four dimensions to make sense, especially the group that are called 'Kaluza-Klein' theories.

"In order to talk about Kaluza-Klein theories, we should start by saying what a Kaluza-Klein theory is, or maybe even by saying who these two guys, Kaluza and Klein, were in the first place.

"Long ago—in 1919, to be exact—Theodor Kaluza was what they called a 'privatdocent.' There's no exact American equivalent, but it was sort of like being a teacher in a junior college. It was the kind of job that didn't have any serious academic rank. Basically Kaluza was the sort of person who teaches the freshman courses no serious scientist wants to be bothered with.

"He wanted more for himself, so on the side he tried to do some real research of his own. When Arthur Eddington gave Einstein's relativity theory its first observational support—that happened, you remember, in his expedition to view the 1919 solar eclipse—Kaluza felt there was something in this 'relativity' idea that would repay some serious investigation. So he began looking into the mathematics of it.

"I have an idea of my own about the reason why Kaluza was particularly attracted to the Einstein theory. I think it might have been because he knew that Einstein, too, had started out as a privatdocent, and look where the man was now! Anyway, Kaluza tried to figure out just how Einstein's relativity theory worked when expressed in formal mathematical terms.

"It seemed to him that it worked best if you brought in some extra dimensions.

"With all his best efforts, it didn't work as well as he might have hoped, though. The equations wouldn't quite balance. What Kaluza didn't know was that there was a flaw in his theorizing. The place where he went wrong was that all of Kaluza's ideas had been unquestioningly based on the classical view of the universe.

"You can't blame him for that—after all, so were Einstein's! But, as time went on and scientists began to get a better handle on what 'reality' was like, it became obvious that the classical view was wrong somewhere.

"For instance, take the way light is generated by electrons changing orbit within an atom. That was an observable fact, but the classical theories about it didn't square with the observations. Classical theory said white light should be emitted—a mixture of all colors, all across the rainbow, uniting to form what we perceive to be 'white.' It didn't happen that way, though. Each excited atom produced its own specific colors—you know that's true if you remember that that's basically how we can tell what elements are in a star, when we turn the spectroscope on it, by the particular colors associated with each excited atom.

"Then along came quantum mechanics.

"Quantum theory told us that electrons couldn't revolve in just any old orbits. There were certain forbidden orbits, and the electrons were restricted only to the permissible ones. Then it all began to make sense, and it became possible to understand why sodium atoms, for instance, radiated only yellow light instead of all the colors of the rainbow mixed together as white.

"So, as quantum mechanics got popular, a Swede named Oskar Klein tried putting Kaluza's ideas of extra dimensions in quantum mechanical form . . . and, voila, the Kaluza-Klein theories were born. About a million theorists have been playing with them ever since.

"That's what a Kaluza-Klein theory is. It is a quantum mechanical theory which invokes extra spatial dimensions to explain the relations among particles and forces. In a Kaluza-Klein theory there aren't any zero-dimensional points. Each 'point' that we perceive as a simple location, without extension in any direction at all, is actually something that we might try to visualize as a little circle; and the circle goes in other dimensions.

"How many dimensions are involved?

"Ah, well, let's not limit ourselves here. We don't quite know how many we have to have. There are some theories which require twenty-six spatial dimensions to work. They don't all need that many. Kaluza himself only needed four spatial dimensions—plus the dimension of time, making his formulation five-dimensional in all.

"Personally, I like the ones that have nine spatial dimensions—plus time, making ten spacetime dimensions in all—but a lot of people who are just as intelligent as I am—well, almost, anyway—prefer eleven. So take your pick. There isn't any right answer—or, anyway, if there is one, no one knows what it is. So you don't have to worry. I promise that you'll never get that question on any quiz from me."

To all of that the aiodoi listened, tenderly amused; but there was one aiodos who sang strongly of something else:

"The song of elsewhere is a good song.

"But for those who live in no elsewhere,

"There is an elsewhere that can do harm.

"And we are part of their elsewhere."

And the rest of the aiodoi were troubled as they sang.

14

What was certain was that the voyage to that pale, distant Turtle beacon was going to be a long one. A day or two at least, Krake told Sue-ling, and did not dare to tell her how many years of "imaginary" time those days would encompass.

Now that there was time to spare, Krake took up some unfinished business. He had not forgiven Thrayl—or Thrayl's mistress. Although he tried to keep his tone level, there was an edge to it as he turned to Moon Bunderan. "Now I want you to answer some questions for me. Why did you let that animal keep me from saving us?"

The Taur only gazed gently at him. Moon said staunchly: "Thrayl had a reason. Thrayl always has a good reason for everything he does, only he can't always explain what they are."

"Good reason! What good reason could he have for risking my ship—not to mention all our lives?"

"Do not address this Taur in that fashion," Chief Thunderbird said severely.

"If it were not for the Taur," Litlun seconded, "we would not have found the trail of the Mother planet. One knew one was right to bring the Taur along. It is proper to praise him now."

Sue-ling blinked at the Turtles. Something was going

on that she had not expected—and something that Chief
Thunderbird was finding interesting, too, because she saw
one of the huge Turtle's eyes slowly revolve to fix on his
Younger Brother. Krake, however, was not interested in
subtleties. He opened his mouth to address them, but was
distracted by what he saw behind them. He craned his
neck to see Daisy Fay, seated at the control board and
looking agitated.

"What's the matter?" he demanded.

The machine-woman waved a few tentacles at the display. "I don't know, Francis. What do you make of this?"

The captain pushed his way between the giant Turtles
to bend over her. "What is it?"

Daisy Fay stabbed out with three or four arms, pointing to several different readings on the chart. "I'm trying
to establish reference points, Francis—you know, distant
galaxies to use as benchmarks, to compare nearer stars
with. But they—"

"Foolish human woman!" Chief Thunderbird snarled.
"Why do you bother with such things? It is the sacred
Mother planet you should be seeking!"

"I know, but—"

"Do not dispute!" the Turtle said peremptorily. "It is
simple! You must find a single planet. It cannot be far
from the wormhole."

"And you must find it quickly," Litlun put in, shivering with a sudden thought, "because if the planet came
through by itself it is in terrible danger—it has lost its
sun! No radiation to feed the Mother and her young!"

Krake looked at him sourly. "With all the radiation
from all those stars? Anyway, there's nothing like a solitary planet in the range of our instruments," he told
them, his face drawn. "And look at what Daisy Fay has
discovered. Those benchmark galaxies? The navigation
instruments have been marking them, and do you see
what the frequency analyzers say? Each one of them is
shifted into the *blue.*"

There was total silence from everyone in the chamber.
Moon dared to break it. "I don't understand. What difference does it make what color a distant galaxy is?"

"It means," Sork said hollowly, "that this is a dying universe. The blue-shift means it is not expanding; it is collapsing."

Captain Krake said tightly, "Worse than that. This whole space is flooded with dangerous radiation."

Sue-ling watched the captain critically as he tried to control himself—there was a good chance of a cerebrovascular accident there, she thought, if he didn't calm down. She put her hand on his arm in sympathy, but he seemed not to notice.

"We of the Brotherhood do not fear this," Chief Thunderbird said in contempt.

"But *we* do! It would kill us. If those old lectures mean anything, this whole universe is collapsing, and as it does it is heating up, producing more and more radiation—"

Chief Thunderbird turned both burning eyes on Captain Krake. "Weak wet things," he said, dismissing them. "That is of no importance. We will not stay here for billions of years, to watch it contract to the single point again, as your legends would have it. We will not be here any longer than we must to find the Mother planet!"

He gabbled majestically at Litlun, and then both Turtles turned to leave. Puzzled, Sue-ling called after them: "But aren't there things we still need to talk over?"

"Talk?" rasped Litlun. "No, what is the purpose of talk when we are on the way to the Mother planet? It is our time to rejoice."

"And we rejoice only with our Brothers—even with the excessively ambitious ones," Chief Thunderbird added, one eye rotating around to glare at Litlun.

Krake looked after the Turtles as they left. "Now, what do you suppose Chief Thunderbird meant by that?" he asked the ship at large.

Sork shook his head. "Turtles," he said, as though that explained it all. "It's funny, though," he added, his tone more wondering than sneering. "After the way they've treated the Taurs, now they make this one a hero!" He hiccoughed slightly.

Sue-ling couldn't hold back her accusations any longer. "Sork, you've been drinking!"

He didn't deny it. "Sometimes that's the best thing to do, my love. Maybe you should try it, too. I think we may all need a drink for what comes next."

Sue-ling was puzzled. "What's that?"

Looking drunkenly clever, Sork said, "What will happen when the Turtles find their Mother planet doesn't exist any more? Don't you remember what I told them? I warned them about what that man called Hawking said: You could perhaps travel through a wormhole—I guess we proved that for him now, since we did—but the gravitational forces would destroy any matter that passed through. And what would come out on the other side, he said, would be spaghetti."

"Spaghetti?"

"Exactly. All twisted and curled and shapeless. That's what Hawking meant: Organized matter can't survive such a trip and stay organized. If the Mother planet did fall through a wormhole, it came out as unrecognizable fragments."

Sue-ling wrinkled her brow. "Sork?" she ventured. "How can that be, when *we* went through ourselves, safely enough—didn't we?"

"Safely?" Sork sighed thoughtfully. "I wonder what 'safely' means now."

Krake said dangerously, "Don't play games with us, Sork! Answer the woman!"

"Oh, it's no game. It's just that what Sue-ling said is irrelevant. The planet was matter, and so it was destroyed. But we weren't in the form of matter. We were in wave-drive—in the form of waves, not solid particles—when we came through the wormhole, so we survived. No," he said, shaking his head, "you can forget about trying to find that planet. It doesn't exist anymore."

He was staring into space, almost like the Taur listening to his songs, and the look on his face was strange. Puzzlement—as though pondering a chess problem;

worry—as though unsure that a great plan could work; and sadness. Then he shook himself.

"Heigh-ho," he said amiably. "It's going to be a long trip, and we're going to have to wait to the end of it for a lot of the answers. So I'm off to sleep." He gave Sue-ling a hooded glance. "Care to come and join me, my dear? No? Well, I thought not."

And he was gone.

Sue-ling said urgently, "Kiri! Stay with him, will you? He's drinking again, I'm sure of it."

Kiri gave her a patient look. "And you want me to stop him?"

"More than that, if you can! Find where he's getting the liquor from—smash the bottles—"

Kirk sighed and turned to follow his twin. But at the door he paused. "No one can be with him all the time, Sue-ling," he said. "He has to follow his own life. He's no better off than any of the rest of us, you know. It's the only life he has."

———

Sue-ling was gazing after him, biting her lips. Krake watched her for a moment, then turned to his crew. "Marco, Daisy Fay—you're in charge. Sue-ling? Come along with me. I think I know where he's getting it."

Sue-ling allowed herself to follow; and then, in Krake's quarters, she saw the answer. He rummaged for a moment in a private cubicle, then looked up, apologetic. "Mystery's over," he said. "It was my liquor. I had half a case of Scotch there. I should have locked it up, I guess, but I never thought anybody would steal it."

Sue-ling's expression was bitter. "You can't trust a drunk with liquor," she said, turning away. "I'd better find him before he drinks it all up."

Krake stopped her with a restraining hand. "You aren't Sork's keeper. Let his brother take care of him," he commanded. She hesitated, very conscious of his touch. "Why do you worry so much about him?" he asked.

"I worry about both of them!" She bit her lip, wondering what to tell this new man who had suddenly appeared in the established pattern of her life. "They're rather special."

He scratched his brown beard, studying her. "I suppose former lovers are always special."

She gave him a frown. How dare he say 'former'? But what she said was, "It isn't that. It isn't even just that they're twins. They're almost like mirror images of each other, Kiri careful, thoughtful, a little slow to act, and Sork—"

"Sork rushing in where wise men fear to tread. I know," Krake said, and changed the subject. "Why don't we just take it easy for a while? I'd offer you a drink, but the bar's dry just now."

"I don't need a drink," Sue-ling said, glad not to be made to pursue the subject of Sork and Kiri Quintero. "It's nice just to relax."

"So I find it," he said seriously. "Especially with you, Sue-ling."

In Sue-ling's opinion, there hadn't been much relaxation in the times she and Francis Krake had been together so far. Nor did she feel entirely relaxed just then. "Maybe we should be getting back to the others," she fretted.

"Why?" he asked reasonably. "If we've got anything at all now, it's time. Marco and Daisy Fay can take care of anything that comes up."

"I suppose so," she said absently. She was responding to his words, but the private part of her mind was more taken up with the fact that he had put his hand on hers. She looked down at their hands, then up into his eyes again. "Francis? Is this the way men started to make sexual overtures in 1945?"

He flushed. She could see that he was nervous, but he didn't take his hand away. "One of the ways, anyway," he agreed, "at least as far as I can remember."

Sue-ling nodded thoughtfully. "Moon Bunderan is pretty interested in you."

"She's a child. I've never touched her."

"It might be better," she said, "if you didn't touch me right now either, Francis."

"Maybe not," he agreed gloomily, and released her hand. "I'm sorry, Sue-ling. I told you, I've forgotten how to get along with girls any more. I understand women about as well as I understand Turtles, and that's damn little."

She looked surprised. "But I thought you did understand Turtles! You've been dealing with them for—centuries."

"For a couple of years," he corrected, "and most of that time it was just Marco and Daisy Fay and me. Hell, I don't even scratch the surface of understanding Turtles. How did they come to have waveships, for instance?"

Sue-ling looked surprised. "They're very intelligent. I suppose they just invented them, somewhere along the way."

"Without ever studying quantum physics? And they never did, you know; it was blasphemy to them—until now, when they're desperate. And what about their history? They don't talk much about it, but every now and then I hear a name, or some kind of hint—there were those people they called the Sh'shrane that they fought against long ago. Real baddies, the Turtles say—but what was the war like, and who won, and where are the Sh'shrane now? I don't know! Hell," he said, shaking his head, "I don't know all that much about human history, for that matter. I didn't go to college, you know. I joined up when I was nineteen, and you didn't get much chance for education in the 188th Fighter Group. I know the names of a few great people—Charlemagne, Julius Caesar, Abraham Lincoln—but what do I know about what they did, or why?"

"You must know something," Sue-ling pointed out. "After all, you named your ship for a pretty famous one."

Krake looked pleased. "Oh, you recognized *The Golden Hind*? Yes. That was kind of a romantic idea, I guess. I suppose I got it from my mother. She was English born, married my father in the first World War, and she used to tell me stories of the great Englishmen. Especially Sir Francis Drake."

"And you're Francis Krake with a 'K.' "

He grinned ruefully. "Not by accident—that's what she named me, you know, Francis Drake Krake, but it wasn't one of her best ideas. It sounded funny. I had a lot of trouble with the name in school."

She was laughing. "I can see why."

"He was a great man, though," Krake said loyally. "The greatest of the English sea captains. He roamed the world in his flimsy little sailing ships, hundreds of years before I was born. I wanted to be like him when I grew up." He looked shamefaced. "When they sent me to fly in the South Pacific I—I thought of myself as covering the same ground he had. I knew that I wasn't the first, like him, but I still had that vision of myself exploring unknown places—"

"Which is exactly what you're doing now, Francis," she pointed out.

"Yes," he said, and stopped there.

"So you've achieved your life's ambition," she went on, feeling as though she were floundering, not sure why, beginning to have an idea.

"Not all of it," he said. His eyes were searching hers, though he made no move to touch her again.

Sue-ling sighed. "Oh, hell," she whispered, and reached out for him, and then there was not much that needed to be said by either of them. As it turned out, Francis Krake had not forgotten everything about human women. Sue-ling began to wonder why she had never made love with a man with a beard before . . . then to wonder whether there was such a word as "trigamous" . . . and then she was not wondering at all, or even thinking on any conscious level, but concentrating on what was happening to her lips, limbs, pelvis and torso, almost hearing, but resolutely not listening to, the tiny voice that, shocked, was whispering to her that this would surely make trouble.

It surely did trouble one member of *The Golden Hind*'s crew right away. When Moon Bunderan next saw Francis Krake and Sue-ling Quong together they were not touching each other, nor was what they said to each other unusual in any way, but Moon's first glimpse of them caused her to straighten her back and bite her lip.

Thrayl noticed immediately, of course. The Taur touched Moon's shoulder with his warm, sympathetic paw, rumbling affectionately. Moon took her eyes off the pair and looked up at him. "It's all right, Thrayl," she told him. *Had* to be all right, she went on to herself. She had no claim on the space captain, nor did she have any right to censure Sue-ling Quong for anything the woman chose to do. (But two men ought to be enough for anyone, she told herself rebelliously.) She wasn't even angry at either of them. Sue-ling was so beautiful, with her copper hair and wide blue eyes—any man would want her!

While she, Moon Bunderan, was so incurably *young*.

She sighed and abandoned the subject. She could see that she was not the only one who had detected something different between Sue-ling and the captain. Tensions were building up between Sork and Francis Krake. At least Sork was not drinking at present. He wasn't entirely sober, either, maybe, but perhaps there was a limit to what you could expect from him under these stressful conditions.

No matter what else went wrong, Moon told herself staunchly, she still had Thrayl, her best and most faithful friend, so she took herself away with the Taur, trying all over again to discover what his "songs" were all about.

Annoyingly, she could not get Thrayl to explain any of his actions. He didn't refuse to answer her questions—Moon was quite certain that the great, gentle Taur would refuse her nothing, ever. But his answers were worse than the questions themselves. The worst of the answers were to questions that began with a "why," for the only answer to those, ever, was, "The songs bade me, Moon. The songs are always true."

"But can't you tell me if they say what's going to happen to us? Do they say if the Turtles will ever find their Mother planet?"

The purple-blue eyes turned away from her. "The smallsongs do not speak of that," he rumbled.

"Then why did you make us go on?"

"The smallsongs speak of that need, Moon. There is no reason for us to stop. There is no other place where we should be."

She shivered. "Damn . . . it . . . to . . . hell," she said, carefully spacing out the words, as Thrayl gazed down at her. "I didn't think it would be like this! I was hoping—oh," she said, trying to remember what all those vague hopes had been, "hoping, I guess, that I could just get you safe, and then go on with my life. I certainly didn't want to let you get slaughtered!"

"Your wish, Moon," the Taur lowed softly.

"I know it's my wish! It should have been your wish, too! What do you want from your life, Thrayl?"

The great eyes looked perplexed. "Want?"

"Don't you know what you want? I do! At least, I used to think I did." And then swiftly, as Thrayl's eyes seemed to twinkle down at her, "I don't mean a *person*. I mean for a *career*. I think I'd like to be a doctor, like Sue-ling Quong. She's a wonderful woman, and she does fine things. Saving lives, helping people—well, I mean, that's what I'd like if we ever get to where there are any *people* again. But—I don't know."

She thought for a moment, looking up at the terrible splendor of those uncountable blue-shifted suns all around them. Then she shook her head. "I don't want a hole drilled in my skull, though, and I don't know how I can ever do all of that any other way." She shook herself and smiled down at the Taur by her feet. "That's my ambition, anyway, Thrayl. What's yours?"

"Ambition," the Taur repeated, as though tasting an unfamiliar flavor in the word.

"I mean, what do you *want*?"

"I do not 'want,' Moon. I simply 'am.' With you, I am happy, Moon. There is no more to 'want.' "

———

When the source of the beacon was clear on their opticals the sight gladdened no eye. "It's just a ship, Captain," Marco reported. "There's no sign of any planet anywhere around."

"I told you," Sork Quintero remarked, to no one in particular—and no one responded.

"And it's just floating there," Daisy Fay added. "It's not in wave-drive, not even in mass-drive. Their scout ship's still attached, but we're not getting any signal from either ship. All we get is the beacon, and that's really low powered."

"Communicate with the vessel!" Litlun commanded.

"We already tried that, Facilitator," Marco said, sounding almost sympathetic. "It doesn't answer."

Chief Thunderbird was accepting no compassion from humans. He thrust his beaked face forward aggressively. "We will board and investigate this vessel," he declared.

The face on Marco's belly screen showed sudden excitement. "Can we do that, Captain?" he asked eagerly, eyes turning to Francis Krake. "You know you can't go out in space here yourself, not with all that hard radiation around, but the Turtles and I will be fine—"

"Not you," snapped Litlun. "One doubts your fitness for this environment, but we will suffer no harm. The intense radiation will allow us to go into anaerobic state, requiring no atmosphere." Both wild eyes swiveled to Krake. "*We* will board it with no humans accompanying us. This is a Brotherhood concern only."

And to that they would admit no argument. Regardless of protestations, with no further word for anyone, the two Turtles trooped into the scout ship, where it lay nestled in its bay along the belly of *The Golden Hind*. A moment later the people they had left behind felt the lurch as the scout pulled free.

"Poor bastards," Sork Quintero said, sounding almost as though he meant it.

Sue-ling gave him an appraising look. "You mean you're sorry for them because they'll find out the planet's gone?"

"Hell, Sue-ling, they're not that stupid. They know that already; they're just going through the motions now."

Krake confronted him. "And what are we supposed to do?"

"Why," Sork said easily, "we're no better off than they are, are we? We've lost the wormhole, you know. There's no way for us to go back. Even if we could find the place again, I'll bet it's closed up—how many years of universe time have we been going now?"

Moon Bunderan shook herself as the Taur lowed gently in her ear. She gave him a perplexed look, then said: "Thrayl says we shouldn't try to go back. He says we are just to go on; it's what the songs tell him."

"Oh, fine," said Sork, with a nod that managed to look sarcastic. "We've done so well following his songs so far."

No one answered that. Then Marco, who had been listening uneasily to the conversation, lifted his eyes to the screen. He spoke up: "They're at the ship, Francis."

Even at maximum magnification, the *Hind*'s scout looked no bigger than a toy as it came to relative rest near the other waveship. The people in *The Golden Hind* saw the scout nudge slowly closer until it was almost touching. Then it hung motionless for a time.

"What are they doing, Captain Krake?" Moon Bunderan asked worriedly.

Sork answered for him. "They're trying to lock on, of course. And failing—of course."

"Why are you so sure of that?" Sue-ling asked him, and again it was someone else who answered.

"Because there's no one alive in that ship," said Kiri

Quintero, his voice gentler than his words. "I think we all knew that. They would have responded to signals if there were anyone to do it."

Daisy Fay said sharply, "Look at them now!"

The two Turtles were coming out of the lock of their scout ship. At that great distance even the great Turtles were barely visible as they came creeping naked out into the burning light of the surrounding stars. Sue-ling shivered at the thought of those scorching rays, though she knew that the Turtles would take no harm from them—might even enjoy the influx of energy. Then, tethered to their own scout, the two Turtles swung themselves to the other scout. They crawled around it for a moment, conferred with each other, then eased themselves over to the hull of the silent waveship itself.

Moon Bunderan gasped as there was a sudden flare of tiny, white-hot sparks from the hull of the waveship.

"They're cutting their way in," Krake said somberly. "I guess you were right, Sork."

Sork Quintero nodded absently. Then he yawned. "I think I'll take a little nap," he said. "They'll be poking around there for a *long* time before they come back . . . and, after all, we already know what they're going to find."

Long it was. Long enough for Krake to begin muttering to himself about the length of time they were hanging free in space, this heavily irradiated space saturated with energy from the onrushing stars. He had ordered everyone to stay inside the shielded compartments of the waveship, which perhaps preserved their health but did little to improve their tempers in the crowded conditions. But Krake kept a worried eye on the instruments. If they let themselves be exposed to that radiation indefinitely there would certainly be serious leakage even through the shielding. . . .

As soon as the muffled clank of the scout told them

the Turtles had returned, Krake was at the lock, waiting for them. "Well?" he demanded.

Chief Thunderbird was first to come through, bending his parrot-beaked head to avoid the top of the lock. He stopped short, holding Litlun behind him, and his eyes roamed around the chamber.

He spoke at last. Even through the transposer his voice seemed flat, lifeless, despondent. "You wish to know what we discovered," he said. "There is no reason to conceal it from you. Every Brother on this waveship is dead."

"Long dead. *Very* dead," Litlun added, drawing a sour look from Chief Thunderbird. But the Proctor went on:

"Although none of the crew of this waveship survived, they left a log. It stated that the vessel had been in wave-drive, near the planet of our Mother, when the object we called a 'wormhole' opened up. Both they and the planet were swept through, and they saw—" The voice halted for a moment, but when it resumed it was as unemotional as ever. "They saw the planet break up into tiny fragments, like a shower of dust. That was all. The Mother planet is . . . gone."

"Oh, Proctor," Moon Bunderan said impulsively. "I'm so *sorry*."

The great red eyes peered at her, but all the Turtle said was, "We wish now to consult in privacy, the Facilitator and this one."

As he moved away Sork laughed. "What's to consult about?" he called after their backs. "Gone is *gone*."

Litlun, following his Elder Brother, paused to regard Sork. When he spoke it was with dignity. "There are some things which we wish to say only to each other. Still, there are data of interest to you as well, one believes," he said. "The entries in the ship's log ended fifty-four years after they entered this universe—"

Sork's eyes opened wide. "Fifty-four *years*?"

"—but the log itself," the Turtle continued, unheeding, "continued to record dates for some time after that. For a long time, Sork Quintero. Perhaps you should consult your lecture chips about this. The last entry was nearly eleven hundred years later."

He turned to leave, but one eye rolled back to look at them. "It appears," the Turtle declared, "that there are some anomalies concerning the passage of time in this universe."

If there are any songs the aiodoi enjoy almost as much as their own, they must be those songs in which some smallsinger comes close to making a great song, a song of which even an aiodos might be proud . . . a song which comes close to capturing great truth. And indeed one such song is heard by the aiodoi, and they rejoice at what the Earth person sings.

"We suspect, you will remember, that there can be more dimensions than our senses observe in the universe we live in. We can suppose, too, that there are more universes than ours; Stephen Hawking showed how they might be formed out of vacuum fluctuations, and there's no reason to believe that our personal vacuum is the only one that ever fluctuated.

"Some people would disagree with that, I know. Wittgenstein, for instance, said, 'The existence of other universes is not a predicate'—by which he meant, as I'm sure most of you can figure out, that there wasn't much point to speculating about possible other universes as long as we couldn't detect any consequences of them.

"Well, Wittgenstein was a truly grand old guy, but I'd like to do some speculating anyway.

"What I want to speculate about is what's called 'the Everett Many-Universe Interpretation.'

"You know that quantum theory tells us that there's no *fixed* way for a particle to move from Point A to Point B. Instead there are a whole bunch of ways, which you can represent on a diagram by lines; when you've got all the lines drawn in they look like the braided pigtails some of you have hanging down your backs, and such drawings are called 'Feynman diagrams.' We don't a priori know which path the particle will take; so we describe the 'sum over histories' clutch of possible paths as a 'probability wave.'

"A long time ago, back in 1957, a man named Hugh Everett had an idea about these probability waves.

"He pointed out that every time a probability wave collapses—that is to say, when we actually *observe* a particle's passage—we suddenly have a definite, measurable state, where before there were only degrees of probability.

"You can think of this process as a kind of an election poll, if you like. *X* many people say the electron is at Point A, *Y* many others say it's at Point B, Point C and so on. Probably, as in most polls, there are a lot of 'Don't know' and 'No opinion' votes. But then the election ballots are counted, and all those quantal *opinions* are instantly converted into a single positive *fact*. Once the vote is in—or once the observation has been made—there isn't any more 'probability.'

"Consider how this affects what we know about, say, electrons. In more or less that way, all we can say about the electron *wave* is that there is a certain chance it is here or there or wherever. You can draw a kind of Gaussian curve of the possible locations where it might be, but you don't know where in the curve the damn thing really is. But once we make the actual measurement we're not talking about a *wave* any more. We're talking about a *particle*. The wave function collapses. It is therefore certain that the electron is known to be at Point A, and it is no longer possible for it to be at Point B or anywhere else.

"That's where Everett asked his big question:

" 'Why is that impossible? Why can't it be at *all* the points?'

"To put it in a different way: What if the electron is actually at Point A, and actually at the same time also at Point B—*but in different universes*?

"What if each time some quantum uncertainty is resolved, the universe splits into two identical copies—almost identical; except for that one fact, which is the different position of the electron?

"That's the notion that is called 'the Everett many-universes' interpretation of the quantum theory.

"There are other possible interpretations. The one that most people accepted for a long time was the one that may have come from Niels Bohr. That one is called 'the Copenhagen Interpretation.' It says that there are two realms of 'reality,' the small, or quantal, realm, and the big, or classical, realm—and never the twain shall meet. We don't have to worry about quantal reality, in the Copenhagen view, because we can never experience it.

"For me, I do worry about it, and I propose to make you worry about the Everett interpretation, too. It has other names, some of which help to explain it. Some people, like Paul Davies, prefer to call it 'the world-ensemble.' By that Davies means the collection of universes, infinitely large in number and always increasing, each of which differs from the one 'next' to it by a single quantum event.

"Of course, a single quantum event right now wouldn't change much. Our universe is pretty set in its ways, and we almost certainly wouldn't even know that that event had happened. Maybe later on that quantal event might somehow turn out to mean that somebody would be born who otherwise wouldn't, or a war would be won rather than lost—you can imagine all that sort of thing for yourself.

"But, even if we concede that such a thing wouldn't make much difference now, it hasn't always been that way. There were critical times in the history of the universe when a single quantum event might have had *big* consequences.

"If it had happened in the critical moments around Planck time, when the fundamental values that describe our universe were determined, it could have made so big a difference that in one universe living things like ourselves could develop, while in another no life at all would be possible.

"Perhaps out of all the myriad possible universes, all coexisting and all equally 'real'—there's only one in which life like ours could exist.

"Of course, if so, we know which one that is. It has to be the one we are in—because, otherwise, we wouldn't be alive to be in it.

"What I have just said has a name, too. It is called 'the weak interpretation of the anthropic principle,' and we'll talk more about what that means in our next class."

———

And while all the aiodoi were rejoicing in the song, one aiodos was singing another song. It was not a rejoicing song. It was not a fearful song, either, because the aiodoi have no need to fear anything . . . but it was a song of concern, and almost of pity, for certain smallsingers who were acting out the song of the Earthly scientist.

15

~~~~~

For Marco Ramos, the worst thing about the way his world was turning out was not that they were lost. "We weren't going anywhere anyway," he whispered to Daisy Fay, trying to console, "so what difference does it make?"

It wasn't very good consolation. She didn't answer. Worse, she wasn't responding at all—had even turned off her belly screen, so that there was no visible face to scan for feelings on the cherry-colored pumpkin that was all that was left of the woman he loved. Marco sighed. She hadn't done that in a long time; only did when things were so bad for her, inside that metal-jacketed mind, that she could not make herself share. It was, he told himself —not for the first time—a great deal worse for her than for himself. After all, what beautiful woman could stand being eternally trapped in the shape of a Halloween goblin? And Daisy Fay had been so very beautiful. . . .

He did the best thing he could think of to do for her. He let her be, and focused his attention on what was going on around him. Things were bad enough there, too —the despondent Turtles locked in their own quarters and refusing communication; the Quintero twins unusually silent; Moon Bunderan almost weeping as she sat beside her Taur. Marco didn't like the way Thrayl was looking, either. The great bull head was drawn in lines of fatigue and unhappiness, and those beautiful bright horns were a sickly gray.

And the captain was in a cold rage of frustration, and taking it out on Moon Bunderan. "Why should we listen to that animal?" he demanded, his beard jutting out accusingly. "I can't set a course without some kind of destination!"

Moon said stubbornly, "Thrayl says we don't have to go to a destination. He says we just have to *go* and the destination will come to us."

"That," Krake said flatly, "is *stupid*." He turned to Sork Quintero, sober now and withdrawn. "And what about this funny business with time? What do your lecture chips say about that? How can it be that the old Turtle ship registered hundreds of years passing?"

Sork said, "I suppose it has something to do with time dilation." Sork did not sound in the least sure of himself, Marco thought. "Or else," Sork added, "maybe it has to do with the fact that we're in an old universe now—collapsing instead of expanding—maybe time runs backwards here?"

"Time *can't* run backwards!" Krake said savagely. "Talk sense!"

Marco made that throat-clearing sound before he ventured, "Francis? Maybe we should all listen to some more of those chips, maybe find some explanations there?"

His captain transferred his angry glare to him. "Right! And we'll just hang here in space while we're doing it? Christ, Marco! That might be all right for you and the Turtles, but the rest of us can't handle the radiation seepage that's coming right through the shields."

"Then maybe we should go into wave-drive," Sue-ling Quong put in hesitantly.

"Fine! Going where, exactly?"

Moon Bunderan answered him. "I told you what Thrayl says, Captain. He says that doesn't matter, just so we *go*."

"And I've told you that that is *stupid*. . . ." And the circular arguments went on and on.

Marco sighed. He glanced at Daisy Fay, still remote in her internal worries and confusions. He reached out and linked one tentacle with hers. She didn't resist, but she didn't respond, either.

A sudden thought struck him. He pondered it for a moment, then said, "Francis, this is getting us nowhere."

"And where do you think we should get?" Krake demanded.

"That's up to you, Francis. You're the captain. But as long as we're just sitting here, there's something I'd like to do."

Krake gave him a weary look, but all he said was, "What is it?"

The face on Marco's belly plate was suddenly eager. "All that stuff outside—I'd like to see it."

Krake's expression turned puzzled. "Look away," he said, waving a hand at the screens.

"No, Captain, that's not what I mean. I want to get outside the ship," he explained. "I want to watch what's happening out in this universe for myself. Not on a screen. I want to see the real thing."

Sue-ling said quickly, "But, Marco, that's dangerous. The radiation out there can be lethal!"

Marco waved a reassuring tentacle at her. "Not for us, Dr. Quong. We're almost as good as the Turtles when it comes to radiation—and they soak it up." He felt a stirring of Daisy Fay's touch on his, and gave her a quick look. It was true; she was beginning to respond again. The face had reappeared on her belly screen, looking puzzled, looking sad—but looking like Daisy Fay once more.

Sue-ling said uncertainly, "But don't you need to breathe, at least?"

"Of course we do, but we can take air tanks, and we'll seal our shells—we'll be all right. And it's important to me! I want to go out onto the hull and see for myself." He hesitated. Then, "You see, Sue-ling, ever since I was a kid in Chile I've wanted to know about these strange things. And nobody—*nobody!*—has ever had this chance before. And I want to observe it with my own senses, not through the simulations on the screens."

"And I," said Daisy Fay, suddenly coming to life, "want to go along." Her clasp on Marco was strong. "Please, Francis! Say we can do it! There's nothing to lose, and if we're all going to die here anyway—" She hesitated, and the face on her belly seemed to swallow. Then she managed a smile. "At least, then we won't have lived for nothing."

———

Outside the lock the two machine-people clung together, tentacles intertwined, eyes roving over the frightening sky. Daisy Fay snapped their tethers tight, for fear that any motion might send them plunging outward—downward—into that vast maelstrom of swarming suns. She knew that she was afraid. But, gazing out into those swelling clouds of glowing gas with Marco by her side, she was also beginning to be—well, very nearly—content once more.

The only thing missing, she thought, was that with their shells sealed against the vacuum, their air coming from the tanks they held in one spare tentacle each, it was impossible for them to talk. Yet what was there to say? Stalked eyes open wide—wider than any human's, because those Turtle-built optics could read frequencies far outside the human optical range—they saw the gamma radiation from far suns exploding, watched the near stars that were fattened with infalls of condensing gas and dust. It was frightening, yes. But it was also spectacularly, inconceivably beautiful.

And she felt Marco's firm, loving touch on her body as they huddled together, limbs intertwined . . . and that was all that mattered.

When she looked back to check their tethers, she could see, in the light from that ocean of stars, the pallid shape of that American flag Krake had insisted on painting on the hull of *The Golden Hind.* It was a reassuring sight, in a way, with its memories of home . . . but a saddening one, too. She faced up to reality. Never again, she told herself, could there be any hope of returning to that old and long lost America. . . .

But the next thing she told herself was that that chance had disappeared, long ago, on the freezing side of an Andean mountain. She nestled closer to Marco's hard, reassuring shell and let that thought slip away. Whatever would happen was going to happen.

For this present moment, she could see that Marco was happy, his eyes darting around, his tentacles quivering with excitement. Most important of all, they were together.

How long they hung there, silent and content, neither Marco nor Daisy Fay knew . . . until there was a rasping vibration from the hull of the ship. It wasn't mechanical. It was a sound, coming to them through conduction in the metal.

They stirred, eyestalks turning to look at each other in wonder. Then both realized that the sound was a voice —slow and hoarsely deep, carried by the vibrations of the hull to their own bodies. It had to be Krake's, Daisy Fay was nearly sure, and quickly deduced what had happened. The captain had rigged a speaker to the hull to reach them. Ponderously slowly, it was saying: "Come . . . back . . . inside. . . . We're . . . going . . . to go . . . into . . . wave-drive . . . again . . . at once."

———

Back at the controls, Daisy Fay at her own position at the other board, Marco was happier than he had been in a very long time. That enriching view had been worth all the fears and pains and losses; the young South American boy that he had once been would have gladly died for such a sight, and his grown-up avatar had not forgotten the yearning.

There was a new sense of purpose in the rest of the *Hind*'s people, too. Daisy Fay was herself again, Sork Quintero wholly sober. Even the Turtles were standing there—dour and silent, yes, but somehow it seemed that

Kiri had wheedled them back into the society of their shipmates.

Marco turned for orders. "Course, Captain?"

"No course," said Krake, surrendering to the inevitable, managing a sardonic grin. "We're doing what the Taur tells us."

And when Marco gave Moon Bunderan a questioning look, she said, "Thrayl's really sick, Marco, but I think I got the drift of what he was trying to say. He said we didn't have to be traveling *to* a place. We won't be traveling to a 'place' at all, but in *time*. I'm not real sure I understood all of it, though; that kind of talk is hard for him," she apologized, "because Thrayl doesn't usually think that way, but it's what he meant. I'm sure of it."

"He means traveling in time, all right," Sork said suddenly. "I think I know what he's talking about—time dilation! Remember? Photons don't have clocks. Time stops for us in wave-drive, but it goes right on in the universe outside. So maybe Thrayl thinks if we just keep going long enough something big will happen in the universe. . . . Ask him, Moon," he begged. "Ask him if that's what he means!"

Everyone else waited while she spoke, softly and lovingly, to the Taur. Thrayl was silent for a long time. When at last he answered he hardly lifted his head, and his voice was a bass moan.

Moon looked confused. "He's very sad," she said. "He keeps hearing songs of pain and danger that hurt him."

"Time!" Sork snapped. "What did he say about that?"

"I think he said you were right, Sork. I think he said a time was coming when something would happen . . . only," she added, the look of bewilderment getting stronger, "I don't think he meant 'coming.' It almost seemed as though he meant 'returning'—but time can't return, can it?" she pleaded.

Krake looked more unhappy than ever. He looked for help toward the morosely silent Turtles, but they were not responding—unless Litlun's faint movement of one clawed hand was assent.

Krake made up his mind. He took a deep breath and gestured to the crew manning the boards. "Wave-drive, Marco," he said. "Wherever we're going, we might as well get on our way."

What the Taur hadn't said—or couldn't—was how *long* they would have to travel to get to wherever, or whenever, they were heading for.

That was a hard pill for Captain Francis Krake to swallow. He sat glaring up at the screens, ignoring everyone else. When he looked away he saw nothing that pleased him. The two Turtles had retreated again for more of their private discussions—or mourning. Sork Quintero was at the other board, gazing abstractedly into space, while across the control room Sue-ling was sitting alone, silent and strained, and she was resolutely avoiding Krake's gaze. Krake swore silently to himself. What was the matter with the woman? What had happened between them in his cabin was something warm and wonderful in his memory—what had changed her?

He started when Marco Ramos spoke to him. "Tough mission, Captain," the machine-man said, trying to be reassuring. "We'll be all right, though. The *Hind*'s a good ship, Captain—and she's got the best captain in any universe!"

"Captain," Krake repeated tightly, unwilling—no, unable—to accept even kindly reassurance. "What the hell am I captain of, Marco? Do you know what this ship is? It isn't *The Golden Hind*. It's *The Flying Dutchman*, cruising forever and going nowhere, with no way home."

"Captain—" Marco began, but Krake was shaking his head.

"Don't you see? We're in a ghost ship. That's what wave-drive is. It makes us a sort of phantom, an energy wave flying at the speed of light and cut off forever from anything real, and I'm the one who got us into this. If I'm a captain, I've got a crew of fools!''

His voice was louder than he intended. Even Sork looked up, giving the captain a puzzled glance. He seemed about to speak, but then closed his mouth and returned to his deep study. Marco's eyes wandered uncertainly about, then he turned away silently; and that was another pain in Francis Krake's heart. He had let his temper get the best of him again. There was no reason for him to insult loyal Marco Ramos, especially not when his anger was all at himself. . . .

With maybe a little left over for Sue-ling Quong.

She was looking at him now—she and everyone else in the control room—but he could not read the expression in her eyes. What Krake wanted most was to talk to the woman in private. If only she would leave the control room, he thought, he could follow her, ask her what the matter was, maybe even see her look at him again as she had, just hours earlier, in his bed.

Of course, there was an alternative. He considered the new thought carefully and with some surprise. He didn't have to wait for her to decide to leave. He could go over to her now, ask her to step outside with him for a private word.

But Krake had been quite right about himself in one respect. He really was not very good at getting along with women any more, and while he was making up his mind the opportunity passed. The two Turtles came back into the control room and stopped at the doorway, their eyes roving about.

Then Chief Thunderbird engaged his transposer. "Captain," he said portentously, "we have something that we wish to say to you."

Krake turned toward them, surprised. "Yes?" he said.

Chief Thunderbird said, "The statement we have to make is of importance." And he stopped there, as though having trouble getting it out. He had everyone's full attention now. Sue-ling's eyes were on the Turtles, Sork had come out of his abstraction, Marco Ramos and Daisy Fay McQueen had swiveled their eyes around to get a better look at the Turtles. There was something strange about their bearing. Both of them had crossed their forearms across their platens, almost as though protecting themselves from something.

"We're waiting," Krake said testily.

The great Turtle's eyes roamed unhappily around the room. Then he seemed to sigh, and said, "We are aware that our mission has caused unnecessary troubles for you."

"Damn right it has," Krake exploded. "I should have my head examined for letting you drag us off on this silly chase."

"No," corrected Chief Thunderbird. "It was not silly. We do not regret our mission. It is evident that it has failed, but it was not wrong. It can never be wrong to work to save our Brotherhood! It is a different truth that we wish to express." He seemed to take a breath before continuing. "We acknowledge that, had we not interfered by coming to your planet, you human beings might have progressed in quite a different way. It is possible that you could have been exploring our own universe now, in search of new worlds and new opportunities of profitable trade even if—" His voice broke, even through the transposer, but he rallied and went on. "Even if the Brotherhood no longer may exist. But that is not the fault one wishes to confess. What we have done is something else."

He hesitated, looking dismally at his Younger Brother. Litlun made a slight gesture with one clawed hand, as though in sympathy. Then Chief Thunderbird plunged on. "We have come to see that some of our opinions have been unfair—"

Litlun engaged his transposer. "Have been wrong," he said succinctly.

"Yes, they have even been quite wrong," the Proctor admitted. "Your Earthly science is not an abomination. Indeed, one now believes that it contains truths which we have never acknowledged. My Younger Brother—" he waved one paw at Litlun—"joins me in the wish to state that we consider it to have been an error to discourage independent human scientific research."

The beak clamped grimly shut there, as though the distasteful effort of confession was over. Behind him Litlun stirred again.

"There is also the Taur matter," he reminded his Elder Brother.

Chief Thunderbird made a sound like a groan, but he jutted his jaw forward and said pugnaciously, "Yes, one must also discuss the Taur matter. We consider that our treatment of them, too, was an error." He glared pugnaciously at everyone in the room, and then he seemed to feel he had said everything necessary. He turned abruptly and waddled toward the doorway. Litlun turned to follow, but Sork interrupted.

"Hold it there," he said, astonishment battling with anger in his tone. "What are you saying? Is it possible that you are *apologizing* to us?"

Litlun continued as though he had not heard, but at the doorway he stopped. Then, slowly, he turned back, both his eyes seeking Sork's.

"Yes," he said, and was gone.

———

"What a strange thing for any Turtle to say!" Sue-ling said to the room at large.

"And what a weird time and place to pick to say it," Daisy Fay agreed. "Maybe, now that they think we're all going to die, they're just trying to ease their consciences?"

"That's really wonderful of them, when it's too damned late to do any good," Krake said bitterly, and Sork grunted agreement.

Moon Bunderan spoke up. "I think it was nice of them to do it anyway," she said. "It must've been really hard for them, especially for that big one! And, oh, Thrayl! Did you hear? They as much as said they shouldn't have been treating all you Taurs the way they've done!"

Thrayl didn't answer. From his board, Marco Ramos turned both eyes to inspect the Taur. The sight was not reassuring. Thrayl's great horns were pallid, almost life-less, and the huge purple-blue eyes were clouded. Al-though the Taur was far larger than Moon, it seemed to Marco that he was leaning on her. Nude except for the apron, Thrayl's covering of red fur was unkempt, his limbs trembling.

Krake was looking too. He gave a short laugh. "I don't think he even hears you, Moon. That's marvelous. Considering we're following his orders, he doesn't exactly inspire confidence, does he?" He began to walk around the control room, looking at each person in turn. "What do you think, Kiri? Are we all as crazy as I think we are, driving full speed ahead to nowhere? You haven't been talking much; don't you have an opinion?"

Kiri spread his hands. "We do what we have to do. We haven't had many choices, Francis," he said mildly.

"How well you put it," Krake remarked. "What about you, Marco? You've known me longer than these people. Am I losing it, letting a Taur take over?" He didn't wait for an answer but turned to Sork Quintero. "What about you? You haven't been much help. Isn't there anything in those lecture chips that you can pass on to us?"

Sork looked up at him, then rose. "There might just be, Krake," he said, his tone thoughtful. "I think I'll go listen to some."

"Fine!" Krake said sarcastically. "Then we'll know what's going on, right?"

"I'm not sure of that," Sork said. "But it's worth a try. I think we need to find some explanation of—that." And he waved a hand at the screens.

Krake looked around, puzzled. There were still the myriad suns, brighter than any stars had ever been in the home universe. "What are you talking about?"

"Oh, haven't you noticed?" Sork said. "Keep an eye on the stars for a minute. You can actually see them move now. I never saw that before, did you? And I'd really like to know what it means."

He gave them all a bland smile, and disappeared. Marco Ramos swiveled his eyes to the screens. "My

God," he said. That frozen sea of stars was frozen no more. And next to him Daisy Fay cried:

"Look, Marco! Everything's speeding up!"

Without words, Marco stretched one tentacle out to intertwine it with one of Daisy Fay's. The screen was almost solidly bright now. Even when Krake, scowling, adjusted the frequency controls to shut out most of the light of the collapsing universe around them, the scene in the screens looked like one of those false-color shots of a star, mottled with spots and flares, and all in motion even as they watched.

There was a moan from the Taur.

"What is it, Thrayl?" Moon Bunderan demanded sharply, gazing up into the mournful, racked face. He lowed into her ear, pointing, and she turned to search the screen.

"I see it!" she cried, pointing. "Captain Krake, do you see there, where it's brightest? Thrayl says that's our way out."

Marco turned both eyes to try to find what the Taur was talking about. In that sea of fire almost everything was spectacular—but, yes, even in that luminous inferno there was one spot that stood out, not like one of those little flawed glass distortions like the one they had plunged through, but something vaster, brighter, more ominous.

"Is it a wormhole?" Krake demanded sharply.

Moon said, her voice trembling, "I don't know what a wormhole is! Neither does Thrayl, I think—but he says we must go into that thing."

Krake gnawed his lip. "Where'd Sork go?" he demanded. "I need to know what that is! Marco?"

The face on Marco Ramos's belly screen was grave and drawn. "I'm not sure, Francis," he said, his voice taut. "But remember what Sork said about time in this universe? Going backward? If he was right about that, and if the universe—any universe—began with a big explosion . . . then how does it end?"

Krake stared at him, uncomprehending. "With everything coming together again?" he hazarded. He glanced around, bewildered, settling on Moon Bunderan. "What does the Taur say?" he pleaded.

She was listening to Thrayl's slow, faint murmurings, her pretty face wrinkling in concentration. "He just keeps on repeating the same thing. His songs say we must go into it, Captain Krake."

"But that's not just another discontinuity," Krake said. "It's—it's *big*. I don't know whether the *Hind* could survive it!" He shook his head. "No! Get Sork," he commanded. "I'm not taking this ship into that thing on the word of a Taur!"

But Marco Ramos lifted his digits from the control board. "Francis," he said soberly, "we don't have a choice. We're going in whether we like it or not. *Everything* is! We're being sucked down into it with everything else. . . ."

And the truth of what he said could no longer be argued. The motion on the screen was picking up speed, the great whirlpool of light was growing hugely . . . they were falling, falling. . . .

If the sight had been spectacular before, now it was terrifying. "We're watching a universe die," Daisy Fay breathed, her eyes trembling as she stared at the screen. "Look at the instruments! We're getting into a steep gravitic gradient—and so is everything else!"

For the universe was tightening around them like a closing fist, as stars and gas clouds hurtled into the burning whirlpool around the great black hole.

"Captain," called Marco Ramos from the second board. "We're getting more background radiation—heat, too! The *Hind* wasn't built for this kind of stress!" And, indeed, outside the entire sky was becoming incandescent.

"It's all speeding up," Kiri murmured. "Sork's lecture chips were right."

Krake swore under his breath and turned to Moon Bunderan. "Your Taur," he snapped. "Is he sensing anything?"

"I don't know. He's terribly sick," Moon said wretchedly. "But he says we must go on."

"Go on where?"

She looked at him helplessly. "Just where we're going, I guess," she said. . . .

And then they were in it.

————

When the shock came it was like being destroyed and born again. The whole great ship groaned and shuddered. Something crashed. Moon heard Thrayl moaning softly to himself, as though in pain. There was a tearing, shattering moment of topsy-turvy transition. . . .

And Moon found herself lying on the floor, her head throbbing. Somewhere Thrayl was whimpering, but she was too dazed to look for him. Krake stood over her, clinging to the control console, yelling, "What the hell did we hit?"

"Nothing, Francis," Marco gasped, scrambling back into sight from wherever he had been. It took him a moment to recover his voice. "It couldn't have been anything material, or we'd have been vaporized."

"It felt like a rock!"

Marco said, "I think it was magnetic fields, Francis. They'd be powerful in the contracting plasma—"

Then shock stopped his voice. The control room had gone dark. The screens winked out. That angry disk was gone, with all the blazing gas clouds and crashing suns.

"Where are we?" Krake gasped. Thrayl moaned again, and Krake's voice sharpened. "Marco! Get the lights back on again!"

"Right, Captain!" Marco began, but Daisy Fay's voice came urgently.

"Wait, Marco! There's something out there. Marco, you've got the screen dimmed down—turn the sensitivity up again."

Marco hesitated, torn between a direct order from his captain and Daisy Fay's common sense. Common sense won out. He adjusted the screen.

At normal sensitivity it was true. The screens were

not entirely black. There were tiny distant wisps of light, thousands of them.

"My God," said Krake after a moment of staring. "Those things aren't stars. Look at the shape of them. They're distant galaxies! Marco, can you get us a distance fix?"

Marco obediently reached out for the instrument adjustments—then, realizing the impossibility of obeying the order, he dropped his tentacles back. "We can't do that, Captain," he said soberly. "How can we measure their distance? When we're in our own space, the way to range an external galaxy is by red-shift—but how do we know what the shift is here? And we don't have enough of a baseline for triangulation."

"The only clue we have," said Daisy Fay, her voice low but level, "is their brightness. And that means, Francis, those things are *very* far away. It—it looks like we're alone in a lot of very empty space."

Krake took a deep breath. Then he was in control of himself again, and of the ship. "Turn on the lights," he ordered again, and this time was obeyed. "Marco, what does your board say about the condition of the ship? That was quite a beating we gave the *Hind;* did we come through all right?" And when Marco reported that there was no structural damage, no failure of systems, "All right, how about all of you? We were thrown around a lot —anyone hurt?"

Sue-ling rubbed her arm. "A couple of bruises, Francis," she said ruefully. "Do you suppose the Turtles are all right?"

Krake said, "They're pretty tough. Still, Daisy Fay— go check them out. And what about Sork?"

"I'll go, Francis," Kiri said, moving faster than usual for him. Krake nodded.

"All right. Let's see what we've got. Evidently we went through this end-of-the-universe thing and came out in a new one. I don't know why there aren't any stars nearby, but we can figure that out later." He paused, calculating. "When Sork comes back, we'll ask him what he thinks. Maybe we can get some help from the Turtles, too, and—Moon? What does Thrayl say now?"

She was holding the great head in her arms. "He's very sick, Captain," she said wretchedly. "He can hardly talk at all now."

"Ask him! He was the one who told us what to do—I want to hear what he has to say now, and—"

Krake stopped suddenly, listening. Then they all heard it: a call from outside the room. "Help me!"

Sue-ling Quong reacted first. "It's Kiri! Something must have happened to Sork!"

And when they got there, the facts were beyond argument. Kiri Quintero, his face ashen, was carrying his twin brother in his arms. Sork was limp, obviously unconscious. His face was bloodied, and his head was lolling at an angle it should never have had on his neck.

"He was thrown against a wall," said Kiri. "I think he hit his head. Sue-ling, is he dying?"

He didn't have to ask her that. Sue-ling was already beside them, carefully touching Sork's ruined head, lifting an eyelid to peer inside, listening for a pulse. When she looked up at last her face was somber.

"I don't know, Kiri," she said. "He needs surgery. And he needs it right away."

An Earth human who was not a scientist at all, but wondered greatly and was therefore a poet, sang this song while the aiodoi listened and were moved:

———————

"I have to make a confession before we get into this session. See, I can stand superstrings and Grand Unified Theories and quarks, but do you know what beats me? The thing we were talking about last time. The anthropic principle, that's what beats me.

"Remember what they say about all the basic constants of the natural laws of the universe—Planck's Constant, and the numerical value of pi, and the relationship between gravity and electromagnetic force and all those things. What they say is that all these specific values came about just by chance, right at the time of the Big Bang . . . *early* after the Big Bang, that is; back on the other side of the Planck wall, ten to the minus forty-third seconds, when everything was still plastic. Before the Planck barrier, all the forces were one—gravity, strong force, electromagnetic, weak force—they were all part of what we could call the 'superforce,' which we'll talk about at more length another time.

"And they also say that those numbers we call 'constants' didn't have to be constant at all. They could just as easily have been other values entirely. Pi could've been seven, instead of three point et cetera. Gravity could've been stronger than the electromagnetic force, instead of nearly two thousand times weaker. Even the law of inverse squares didn't have to be what it is. After all, you can generalize it as a power law of n minus one, where n is the number of dimensions of a space—we have three spatial dimensions, and that's why our exponent is two, and we get inverse squares. Kaluza's four-dimensional space would be quite different; the law there would be inverse *cubes,* and planets would fall right into their stars.

"There are an infinite number of other possibilities. But the scientists who tell us all this also say that if any of those alternative things had happened to be true, we wouldn't be here.

"Life couldn't have evolved; maybe even matter couldn't have evolved. And they say the chances are millions to one *against* us. In all probability, those randomly determined values would, most of the time, have turned out to have been such that we would never live.

"So that's what they call the 'anthropic principle.' It comes in two flavors, strong and weak.

"The weak anthropic principle is the one we talked about last time. It just says, wow, how lucky we are that the dice fell in just the way that would allow us to show up.

"The strong anthropic principle is even spookier. It says that such long odds are too long to be taken seriously. Such one in a zillion chances just aren't going to happen. So there must be some causal connection between those long-ago random fluctuations and us—which seems to mean that, by gosh, we are what made the universe what it is.

"One or the other has to be true . . . but which one?"

———

The eternal aiodos sang on:

"Why, yes.

"Naturally. Of course."

But among them one aiodos hardly sang at all, for he was listening to the faint and fearful songs of some persons who were now discovering some of those alternative possibilities to be real.

16

~~~~~~

There wasn't any sick bay on *The Golden Hind*. Francis Krake had never seen a need for one. He had no interest in ever having Turtle surgery for himself, with the examples of Marco and Daisy Fay always before him, and those two, of course, never got sick.

What the ship did have was all sorts of hospital-type supplies, a lot of them, scattered here and there among the cargo. Krake and Kiri Quintero went on a hasty hunt to round them up, with the assistance of the two Turtles in lugging the supplies to the improvised operating room. The Turtles were not greatly interested in the fate of one human being, not with all the weight of their woes burdening them, but they did help. Perhaps it was a kind of penance for them, Moon Bunderan thought. She had been drafted to help locate the supplies, with Thrayl shambling half-dazed behind her. Then, with Sue-ling tenderly supporting Sork's lolling head and Marco and Daisy Fay efficiently carrying the main weight of him, they took Sork to what had once been a cargo chamber. It would suffice for an operating theater, Sue-ling thought. It had the necessary advantages of good lighting, air that no one had breathed in lately and a flat surface to put him on. The compartment was not in the shielded portion of the ship, but when Kiri anxiously raised the question of radiation exposure Krake said flatly, "We're still in wave-drive, Kiri, and anyway, radiation from what? Take another look outside."

Sue-ling was already rummaging in her kit for the appropriate memo disk. Before she put it in she checked out the equipment. "Asepsis lamps, right, anesthesia, that's good, surgical instruments, sterilizer—I'm going to need help, though," she said. "Daisy Fay, will you give me a hand? And—Moon? Didn't you tell me you'd had veterinary training?"

"But I've never treated a *human*!" Moon Bunderan objected, looking thunderstruck.

"Doesn't matter. Meat's meat, when you cut it, and anyway I'll be doing the complicated parts. Scrub up. All the rest of you, get out of the way," Sue-ling ordered, and slipped the memo disk into the slot in her skull.

———

Moon could see that the people not directly involved were glad enough to get away from the scene. It wasn't just revulsion at the prospect of blood; she knew that all of them were looking forward to the chance to talk over what had happened to their ship, or to make their guesses about what sort of place they were in now. And, after the first shock, Moon Bunderan was glad enough to stay and help out. She accepted the doctor's orders without question. How could she not? A human life was involved.

There was something else, too. For Moon, the scene in the sickbay of *The Golden Hind* was like a childhood dream come true. The surroundings were crazily wrong, of course—racing through the nothingness of a strange universe in a lost waveship, all her world thoroughly lost behind her. The only loved, familiar thing was Thrayl, squatting, head bowed and silent, in an overlooked corner of the room. But those dreams came flooding back. All those long sessions in the veterinary school, when what her heart wanted was to be a *real* doctor, a people doctor—those were adolescent fantasies, she had told herself at the time, and almost forgotten them. Now all those long-ago yearnings were becoming real. She was actually doing it!

Not that she was herself a doctor, no. That was too much even for a dream. Sue-ling Quong was the surgeon, not Moon; Moon was not even the official nurse, because Daisy Fay McQueen was the one who had the familiarity with the ship's small (but adequate) resources—as well as limbs enough to handle anesthesia and half a dozen other chores at once. But Moon was right there to assist them both, scrubbed up, masked and gloved, custodian of the scalpels and other instruments.

There wasn't much blood when Sue-ling deftly lifted a flap of Sork's shaved skin from above his temple, not even when she began cutting through the skull itself, though the harsh stink of burning bone was unpleasant. Moon took note of it, then put it out of her mind. It was a real human life that was at risk here, and her feelings had to be forgotten. She could see that Sork Quintero was in bad shape, breathing strangely, his eyes half open but unseeing. Without immediate surgical intervention he might easily die, Sue-ling had said, before she scrubbed and inserted her memo disk.

That had been the strangest sight of all for Moon Bunderan. She had never seen anyone under the disk before. She glanced out of the corner of her eye at the masked face of the surgeon wonderingly. Was it really her friend Sue-ling Quong who was standing so tall there, cutting and drilling the skull of her lover—maybe of her *former* lover?; Moon was beginning to wonder just what the relations were becoming—anyway, carving into Sork Quintero's helpless flesh and bone with her memmie-precise skill? It didn't look like her, behind the cap and surgeon's mask. When she spoke, the voice didn't really sound like hers, either. "Suction," snapped Sue-ling, in a flat and commanding tone that Moon had never heard from her before, and instantly Daisy Fay, anchoring herself firmly with a couple of her tentacles, was using another to direct the gurgling little tube into the incision in Sork's skull, to pump away the oozing blood that was obscuring Sue-ling's view. "Careful!" warned Sue-ling. "Don't touch the brain!"

Daisy Fay was certainly careful. For that matter, Moon was careful, too, as she handed over a scalpel or a sponge. As careful as she had ever been in her life . . . and beginning to dream again, too. This was not so different from operating on a calf or a ram! It was not impossible. . . .

It was not impossible, at least, if she were willing to do what Sue-ling Quong had done, and allow her own skull to be opened, as Sue-ling had opened Sork's with her buzzing little drill, for a memmie implant.

Moon shuddered involuntarily, and got a warning look from Sue-ling.

How long the surgery took Moon could not guess—hours, probably. She was too keyed up to keep track of time . . . but then it was over. "We'll leave the skull open," the surgeon decided. "We may have to go in again; but we'll suture the scalp now."

And then, when gauze had hidden the top of Sork's head and Daisy Fay was left to, very gently, fit a kind of helmet atop it to guard it from accidental bruises while Moon put the instruments in the sterilizer, the surgeon stood back. "He's stable. I think he'll be all right for now," she declared, "but that clot was in a tricky place and if another one should form he could be in bad trouble. We'll have to watch him for a while."

And then the surgeon lifted her hand to her memmie socket. As she slipped the disk out she blinked and seemed to reel dazedly for a moment before she caught herself.

Then Sue-ling Quong looked wonderingly at her friends. "Wow," she said, rubbing her suddenly aching head. "Is the operation over? Is Sork all right? How did I do?"

————

They left Kiri standing guard over the unconscious Sork, warned to call Sue-ling if there was the slightest change in his condition. Sue-ling herself went off to catch as much rest as she could, the large problems of *The Golden Hind* out of her mind as she concentrated on her patient. Those weren't Moon Bunderan's immediate concerns, either. Wearily she washed herself up after the operation, wondering how it could be that there had seemed so little blood in the operation itself, and yet so much on her hands and gown? And all the time, she was keeping an eye on Thrayl, stretched doglike on the floor behind her. When she turned to look at him, he did not meet her eyes. "Thrayl?" she ventured. "Are you feeling any better?"

Even then he didn't look up. When he answered his voice was low and wretched. "The smallsongs are not happy here, Moon. They hurt," he said.

"How do they hurt, Thrayl?" But, however she pressed him, he would not explain. When she lost patience and went back to the control room, he got up and followed her, still sunk in apathy.

There Daisy Fay came to greet her. "There's news, Moon," the machine-woman said, the face on her belly plate smiling. It was no more than a tentative smile, hopeful rather than reassuring. But it was still a smile, when Moon Bunderan had begun to forget that there were things to smile about. "It isn't as bad as we thought in this place! There are stars here, we just couldn't see them!"

Litlun moved his arms reprovingly. "We do not know that these are stars," he croaked, correcting her. "They are objects, yes."

"They're damned big objects," Krake said, his tone more baffled than hostile. It wasn't hard for Moon to deduce that she was coming in on a continuing argument —but what else had this whole trip been but arguments? "Show her, Marco."

"Right, Francis!" Marco Ramos said, and began tapping on the keyboard. "We made a systematic search, Moon," he told her. "There's nothing that we can detect in the optical frequencies, but when we switch down in the infrared—look."

As soon as Marco made the frequency shift, the screens were speckled with tiny dots of light. To Moon it looked like a sky, all right, though an impoverished one —not like the dense shoals and reefs of stars in their own universe, not even like the bright nighttime skies over her own ranch, almost as poor as a night sky in town, when the bright lights drowned out the heavens.

"We can see more of them with magnification," Marco pointed out, "but they're pretty faint. All they radiate is low-level heat—but they're there, all right."

"They have to be stars," Krake said flatly. "Maybe this is an old universe and the stars are almost dead."

"Or they could be brown dwarfs," Marco offered, "though I don't see how brown dwarfs could exist unless there were some really big, bright ones, too? And I can't find any useful data about brown dwarfs on the lecture chips."

Krake ordered. "Turn up the magnification. Give us some close-ups."

The images on the screen swelled and shrank again as, obediently, Marco moved the magnification area across that vast, dark sky. It looked, Moon thought, almost like some nearsighted reader sweeping a magnifying glass across a printed page. But Marco's best efforts showed very little. At utmost magnification, the objects were still simply points of warmth in the frigid cold of this universe's space.

"That's all there is. Just heat," said Marco, working at the board. "I'm not getting anything else, Captain. No optical frequencies, no ultraviolet, no radio—nothing but low-grade heat, and not much of that."

"Puzzling," crowed the Turtle, Litlun, uneasily. "One has never encountered such objects before, except—"

"Except what?" demanded Krake.

Chief Thunderbird cut in. "The Facilitator means only that there are stories of such things," he squawked harshly. "From very old times. Not well documented. Of no help to us now, certainly."

Krake gave him a hard look. "If there is something, I

want to know it," he said. Litlun muttered in the larger Turtle's ear, but Chief Thunderbird only waved him away.

"It is not relevant. As a matter of more importance," the big Turtle squawked, "what has the Taur to tell us of this?"

Diverted, Krake turned to Moon Bunderan. "Good question. What about it, Moon?"

The girl from New Mexico shook her head worriedly. "Thrayl isn't saying anything, Captain Krake. He's still in some kind of trouble."

"He looks all right!" Indeed, the needle-sharp horns were again glowing with a subdued iridescence, though the great purple-blue eyes were clouded.

"It's his songs," Moon said. "If I understand him, he's hearing a different kind of song now, one he's never heard before. It's—repulsive to him. And it drowns his true songs out."

Krake said angrily, "That's not good enough, Moon. This situation is all his fault! If he hadn't interfered we'd still be in our own universe."

"I can't help it, Captain. Neither can Thrayl. There's something here that hurts him. He says the smallsongs are evil, and they drown out the good ones." She looked at the Taur with woeful eyes. Then she said, "Captain? Can't we get home somehow, even if Thrayl can't help?"

Krake tugged at his beard unhappily. "I don't see how," he said.

"But isn't there any chance at all?"

Krake looked at her with compassion. "Oh," he said, trying to soften the blow that could not be softened, "I suppose there's always a *chance*. But the odds are stacked against us. If I understood what those old scientists were saying, there are many universes, maybe even an infinite number of them."

"We can't just keep trying different ones?"

"Moon," he said patiently, "I don't even know how to get out of this one. If Thrayl could guide us, then maybe, with a little luck, we could find another wormhole. But even if we do, how can we know what it would lead to? My guess is it would probably take us farther from Earth, not nearer. With an infinite number of possible chances—all but one of them wrong—how likely is it that we could blunder back home?"

There was silence then, until Daisy Fay spoke up. "We're all still alive, though."

"And—we could be in a lot worse shape than this, I think," Marco put in.

"Worse how?" Moon asked.

Marco said slowly, "At least this universe hasn't killed us outright. I've been listening to a lot of those old lectures, and they talked about all kinds of possibly different universes—places where the physical laws were different from our own."

Krake was looking at him with new interest. "Yes?"

"Well, Francis," Marco said, "as Daisy Fay says, here at least we're alive. But what would've happened if we'd blundered into one of those where life—our kind of life anyway—would be impossible? Where the laws that allowed atoms to form and chemical reactions to happen didn't apply, so we couldn't eat or breathe or digest food? Or we could find ourselves in one where the physical constants just happened to be a little different in some other way, so stars never formed, or formed early and died before life had time to evolve."

Moon offered, "Couldn't we just move on to another universe then?"

"Through what kind of gate? How could we do that if stars never formed in the first place? Without stars, how could there be black holes? Or wormholes?"

The Turtles were listening uneasily. Krake gave them a quick look, then returned to Marco Ramos. "I think I see what you're saying. But then, if there weren't any wormholes at all, we couldn't have come to a universe like that in the first place, could we?"

Marco thought that over. "I guess not. Still, what if there had been some other kind of change in the basic physical laws? Something that would have altered the binding force of atoms, so that we'd simply disintegrate as soon as we entered that one?"

"What you're saying," Krake said, trying to follow, "is that there's a real danger every time we go through a wormhole? That the next universe we wind up in might kill us?"

"That's what the chips say, Captain," Marco confirmed. "Of course, they could be wrong."

Krake gave him a sour grin. There was nothing to say to that. If the chips were wrong they had even less to go on—and already, without Thrayl, they had next to nothing.

After a moment Marco turned silently back to his keyboard, searching sector after sector of the speckled sky. Daisy Fay shook herself. "I think I'd better take over in the sick bay," she said. "Kiri can probably use some relief."

Krake nodded to her absently. He had almost forgotten about Sork, lying near death a few dozen meters away—had even almost forgotten about Sue-ling Quong. He wished she would wake up. He wanted very much to talk to her, in private. There were things they had to say to each other, he thought.

Although Francis Krake knew that his ideas of sexual morality were several centuries out of date, he also knew that even in New Mexico in 1944 the fact that a man and woman had happened to make love once did not necessarily imply any kind of commitment (though actually, in that time and that place, it had come close). Sue-ling Quong didn't owe him anything, he told himself. But then he rejected his own statement, because he felt strongly that at least he was entitled to a friendly look, even a word or two in private. That was how it had been with Madeleine, long ago; there had been days of sharing that delightful secret, public decorum and, each night, a few hours of private bliss. That was how a love affair should be! But this woman simply would not even meet his eye. . . .

He rubbed his bristly beard irritably, and hardly

heard Marco Ramos's voice until the machine-man called him again.

He blinked at Marco. "What did you say?"

"I said look at the screen, Captain. I've located an object that's not so far away."

The Turtles were clucking excitedly to each other as everyone turned to see what Marco had found. It was worth looking at. It wasn't a mere point of light; it was an actual disk. On the screen, it was the size of an apple, a sphere that glowed with a dull, cindery red.

"What is it?" Krake demanded.

"I don't know, but whatever it is, it's relatively near," Marco insisted. "Of course, we don't know what its actual size is. Still, if it were a normal star we wouldn't get this kind of resolution at any distance over a light-year or two."

Krake looked around. "I wish we had Sork here. Any ideas about what we're looking at, anybody?"

"It is possible—" Litlun began, but his Elder Brother overrode him.

"We have no knowledge of this," Chief Thunderbird squawked, glaring commandingly with both eyes at the other Turtle. "No such star has ever been observed in the records of the Brotherhood. It is an entirely unfamiliar object." Litlun opened his beaked mouth to speak again, but thought better of it and simply waved his stubby arms helplessly.

Krake gave the Turtles a puzzled look, but from his board Marco was being insistent. "We could get closer, Captain. Then we might be able to figure it out."

"For what?" the captain demanded. "Is this just to satisfy your curiosity, or do you think that might help us find our way home?"

"Captain, I don't know if anything's going to do that, so why not take a look?"

Krake sighed and looked around. Then he nodded. "Go for it," he ordered.

———

Wave-drive travel was a great leveler of distances; the short trip to the vicinity of the darkly glowing cinder would take only a matter of hours, nothing like proportionate to the vast billions of light-years they had already traveled in only days.

Krake thought of sleeping for a bit, then vetoed the idea; there was too much on his mind. The Turtles departed for another of their angry gabbling to each other in private. Kiri appeared briefly, then went off to sleep, and Sue-ling came in, rubbing her eyes, just back from checking on Sork Quintero.

"How is he?" Moon Bunderan asked at once.

"He's still unconscious," Sue-ling told her, "but his vital signs are good. I think he'll be all right."

"Thrayl and I will watch him for a while," Moon decided.

"That's good," said Marco. "Then Daisy Fay and I can get something to eat."

"Shall I start something for you?" Sue-ling offered, gesturing at the food warmer.

"Oh, no, we'll eat something in Daisy Fay's room," Marco said. He didn't say why. Actually, he had two reasons. One was that neither he nor Daisy Fay liked to eat when their shipmates were watching. The other was simply that it looked to him as though Krake wanted to be left alone with Sue-ling Quong.

Marco turned both eyes on the lady doctor. Sue-ling looked pretty nearly exhausted to him—maybe from the ordeal of the surgery she had just performed; or maybe, Marco thought, from something else. He didn't know what was going on between Sue-ling and the captain, though he was beginning to get a pretty good idea, but there was obviously some kind of trouble. That didn't matter to Marco Ramos. Whatever happened, he was staunchly on the captain's side anyway. He paused one more second, looking for something to say that might take the captain's mind off his burdens. Then the face on his belly screen grinned ruefully, for the only thing he could think of to say was certainly not in that category.

He said it anyway. "Don't forget about the supplies, Francis," he said, and was gone.

Sue-ling looked after him. "What did he mean by that?"

Krake rubbed his stiff, short beard. "When we were looking for medical supplies Marco noticed we're running a little low on food. The Turtles didn't stock us up to cruise forever, with this many people."

"I thought Chief Thunderbird promised to take care of it," Sue-ling said.

"That's what I thought, too. If I had a suspicious nature, I might think the Turtles would be happy enough to see us all starve—then they'd have the ship to themselves. They can eat just about anything at all—even the bulkheads, if it came to that, I guess. But actually, I think the Turtles just didn't expect this kind of a trip, any more than I did." Then he took a deep breath and looked her in the eye. "What's the matter, Sue-ling?" he demanded.

She didn't answer right away. "Nothing that's your fault," she said at last. "I just made a mistake."

"The hell you did! What we did wasn't any mistake. You're not married to Sork Quintero—"

She grinned at him. It was not a happy grin. "Or Kiri," she pointed out.

He shook his head angrily. "I don't care how many people you've been sleeping with. You're not obligated to either one of them, Sue-ling!"

"But I really am, Francis," she said. "I love them, and that's all the obligation anybody needs, isn't it?"

He couldn't help asking, knowing he would regret it as soon as he said it, "If that's how you feel, how come you went to bed with me?"

"Yes," she agreed, "that's exactly where I made my mistake." When she grinned at him this time, there was real humor in it along with the sadness. "I didn't say they didn't drive me crazy sometimes. Sork! Half the time I'm with him I wonder what's wrong with me, that I put up with his temper and his drinking and his bossing me around. And Kiri—well, he's so *passive*! Sometimes being with him is just about like being all alone. But—well, here's where the test is. I can't imagine living the rest of my life without either of them."

"And what about me?"

She looked at him with affection and regret. "I like you very much, Francis," she said. "But, you see, I haven't got addicted to you."

————

When the time was close to coming out of wave-drive most of the ship's complement was back in the control room—lacking only the Quinteros, Sork still in his coma, Kiri once again by his bedside.

Krake looked up at that slowly swelling ocher disk on the screen, then turned to Moon Bunderan. "After we've all satisfied our curiosity, we'd better get out of here. Is your Taur going to be able to help us?"

"He would if he could, Francis," Moon said earnestly. She reached down to touch Thrayl, again slumped on the floor beside her. "I don't know what's the matter with him. He not only can't hear his songs anymore—the real ones, I mean—he's hearing something else that hurts him."

"What?" Krake demanded.

Moon said fretfully, "He can't seem to say. It's like anger and pain, all at once. Like someone screaming and screaming in his ear."

"Poor thing," said Sue-ling, but her tone was abstracted and her expression sad. Moon looked at her speculatively, wondering what had gone on in the last few hours. Whatever had been between Sue-ling and Francis Krake, it seemed to have gone badly. The captain was controlling an interior anger, and Sue-ling—Moon wished she knew what Sue-ling was feeling. As a doctor Sue-ling had been so machine-like sure and efficient at the operating table, and yet now, as a human woman, she seemed so vulnerable.

Of course, now she was only herself, not a puppet of a Turtle memo disk.

There was no jealousy in Moon Bunderan any more. Her heart went out to this woman whom she admired. Whatever was troubling her, Moon wished she could ease it. Impulsively, as Sue-ling passed her, Moon reached out a hand to touch her. Sue-ling looked up sharply and Moon, trying to find words that would help, said, "You were wonderful in the operating room. I—I envy you. I wish I could be a surgeon."

Sue-ling looked at her for a long, remote moment. Then her eyes seemed to come into focus and she smiled. "You could be, you know."

Moon said unhappily, "But I don't want to—well—"

"Become a memmie, like me?" asked Sue-ling, her face hardening again. But it was only for a moment. "But I was a doctor before I became a memmie, Moon. You could learn. You're still young. You could even start now, if you wanted to; I've got some of my medical texts with me, and I'd be glad to help you with them."

Moon's smile was like a sudden sunrise. "Really?" But then she looked down at the Taur that was gazing mildly up at her as he lay across her feet under the control board. "But what would I do with Thrayl? If we got back to Earth and I did go to medical school—"

And stopped, because she had suddenly remembered what a very big "if" that was.

————

When they were coming out of wave-drive, close enough to the strange darkly glowing object that Moon thought she could actually feel heat from it, Kiri Quintero peered in. "Sork's resting quietly," he reported. "Can I leave him so I can watch what happens?"

"Absolutely not," said Sue-ling firmly, but then she proposed a compromise. The chamber they had converted to an operating room didn't have proper hospital facilities, anyway; why not bed him down right here in the control room? There would always be someone to keep an eye on him, and, she said, someone *must*. That left no room for argument. Still unconscious, snoring faintly from time to time, he was strapped onto a cot in the control room.

When the transition flash came Sork did not even stir. Sue-ling was fussing with the sheet that covered him at the time—not because there was any need for it, just for the sake of something to do to help him. That wasn't like her, she told herself. Even less like the normal Sue-ling Quong, she discovered that she was weeping. She didn't understand what it was that brought those slow, endless tears trickling to her cheekbones. She didn't like it, because it was a confession of weakness, and so she concealed it from the rest of the *Hind*'s crew. But there it was.

No one noticed, for everybody else in the control room was staring at the screens, fully occupied in trying to figure out just what it was that they were seeing, through all the myriad sensors the ship had to offer.

What struck Sue-ling about the gathering in the control room was that, for some strange reason, nearly everyone seemed—well—seemed to be once more *alive*. That was the only word that occurred to her. The despair that had blighted them all in the collapsing universe had melted away. It was crazy, she thought. They were not a centimeter closer to home, or even to anything that looked like a habitable world.

But even the Turtles were perking up as Marco waved a couple of tentacles at that great red coal blotting out half the sky. "Captain," he called, "I'm going to try straight optical frequencies now."

"Do it," Krake agreed. And the screen changed. The tiny distant wisps of galaxies reappeared. The red disk was gone. Nothing was left of it at all, except a sort of shadow that blotted out some of those distant cloudy spirals.

"There's still no visible light at all," Marco reported with satisfaction. "This star radiates only in the infrared; that's why we're not seeing anything."

"That is not a star," rapped Chief Thunderbird positively.

Krake looked at him curiously. The Turtle was drumming his claws apprehensively across his belly, and Litlun was twitching nervously beside him. "Do you know something we don't?" Krake asked the Turtles.

"One knows only that that cannot be a star," said Chief Thunderbird, and Litlun chimed in:

"Such things no longer exist."

"What do you mean, 'no longer'? And what is it, if not a star?"

But it was Marco Ramos who answered. "Francis, I think it's an artifact."

There was a squawk from the Turtles, and Daisy Fay put in, suddenly excited: "Hey, yes! I know what you mean. There was something about that on one of those old chips!"

"That's right, Daisy Fay," Marco said, the face on the belly screen nodding eagerly. "It was just a quick mention but I remember it, because it was pretty nearly the only thing those professors ever said that I thought I really understood. What one of them said was that a really high-tech civilization would want to have a lot of energy to keep itself going, and the best way for them to get it would be to capture *all* the energy from a star!"

"Capture it how?" Krake demanded.

"By building a kind of wall around the star!" Marco cried. "Closing it in, not letting one bit of its energy escape to be wasted in space. The only thing that would get through the wall would be the low-level radiation left over—just heat!—after they'd used the high-level stuff for —well, for whatever they wanted to do with it."

Krake stared up at that ominous black shadow. "You mean that thing's a hollow shell? With a star inside it?"

Marco shrugged. "What else could it be?" he asked.

"And there are all those others just like this one," Daisy Fay put in eagerly. "Remember how many of them we saw on the screens? Millions of them, Captain, maybe billions! A whole galaxy—or a billion galaxies!—that have been inhabited, and tamed, and every star in every one of them turned into a living machine for—for someone, Captain."

Krake shook his head, pointing to the wisps outside the obscuring disk. "But what about those other galaxies?"

Marco waved a tentacle, like a shrug. "I don't know that, Captain. Maybe they haven't been colonized yet— I'd say that's unlikely, though. Maybe they're just so far away that the light from them just shows the way they were before these—people—got around to colonizing them."

Sue-ling was beginning to feel a vertigo worse than the shift into wave-drive. "Excuse me, Marco," she began. "Does that mean—are you talking about a whole *universe* inhabited by a single highly advanced civilization?"

"Why not?" Marco demanded, his tentacles fluttering in excitement. "Oh, Captain! We've discovered something *wonderful*!"

And even Sue-ling began to share the rising excitement—almost as though everyone were beginning to have hope again. The Turtles croaked at each other for a few moments, then Chief Thunderbird engaged his transposer. "One should exercise great caution in dealing with advanced beings," he said, and Sue-ling noticed wonderingly that the Turtle seemed nervous.

"But what if they could help us get home?" Moon put in. "Maybe even help you with—with your problem."

More jabber between them. Then the big Turtle said, "One insists, however, on caution."

"All we want to do is see if we can talk to them," Krake said reassuringly—"if, that is, they exist at all."

"Right!" cried Marco Ramos, and others echoed it— until Kiri Quintero's voice rose above the rest.

"Hold it," he said sharply. "There's one more thing I want to talk to the Turtles about first."

Krake stopped on the point of giving the order to try communicating. This from *Kiri*? Who never raised his voice, who almost never spoke at all? There was a puzzled silence from everyone, until Daisy Fay broke it. "What's that, Kiri?"

Kiri turned to glare up at Chief Thunderbird. "My brother wanted to ask you something before his accident. Since he can't do it, it's up to me. What I want to know—before we go any farther—is, did you mean what you said?"

Chief Thunderbird paused, eyestalks firmly on Kiri. "One always means what one has spoken," he said stiffly. "What particular statement do you mean?"

"You said," Kiri persisted, "that you Turtles were wrong in discouraging Earth science. Was that just talk, or will you do something about it? If we get out of this, will you do better?"

The great Turtle hesitated, then turned to Litlun. There was a raucous, unintelligible squawking between them, with much waving of limbs, until Chief Thunderbird turned on his transposer again.

"Such questions are not for one Brother to decide. Such decisions belong to the entire Brotherhood," he said.

Litlun echoed him. "This is true. All must agree."

"But," said Chief Thunderbird, "if we were to succeed at last and find a new Mother—"

They looked at each other speculatively. "Then," said Litlun, "one of us might well become the new consort, I think. That would make a difference, for the Mother's consort always has much to say."

"But only one of us," said Chief Thunderbird, both eyestalks fixed on Litlun.

Kiri grinned at them. "Good enough," he said. "Or good enough for now. All right. Go ahead, Captain Krake."

Krake opened his mouth to ask a question, then shrugged. "All right," he said. "We're all agreed, then? We have to find some way of contacting these people—if there are any—in these star shells?"

"I don't think that will be necessary," said Marco Ramos.

Krake scowled at this new voice in the discussion. "Why not?"

Marco shrugged. "If they're as high-tech as they have to be, they'll have some kind of instruments keeping tabs on the space around them, won't they? And they are not likely to miss the phase shift of a ship coming out of wave-drive. No," he said comfortably, "I think we've already advertised our presence."

"Then why haven't they responded?"

Marco spread his hands. "Time, Francis," he said. "Time for the signal to reach them. After all, we're probably a couple of hundred million kilometers from that object—how long is that in light-travel time? Maybe ten minutes? So it would take them at least that long to discover us—about as long," he finished, grinning sunnily around at them, "as we've been here."

Krake reined himself in. "Then," he said, managing to be civil, "you think we should just sit here and wait for them to come to us?"

Marco didn't answer. He only shrugged again, and was silent.

There was a sudden bellow from the Taur. He clutched his horns, suddenly burning bright, rocking the great head back and forth as though in agony. Moon cried, "Thrayl's hearing something! Something *bad*!"

And on the screen there was a sudden bright eruption of green light—another—then another, and more. All at once there were a dozen of them suddenly winking out at the periphery of the great dark shell.

"I think they've found us," Daisy Fay remarked composedly. "Isn't that the signal of a wave-drive ship?"

And then there was a scream of mortal terror from Chief Thunderbird. "One has made a terrible error!" he squawked, his tone hysterical. Then he snatched the transposer off and dived toward the control board, shoving Marco violently away, as his stubby claws poked at the keys.

On the screen, the green flares developed red circles around them that pulsed angrily, like a warning sign.

And both Turtles at once were screeching in horror. "Use your damned transposers!" roared Krake, but even before they did Sue-ling had recognized one word, repeated over and over again by the frantic Turtles:

"Sh'shrane! Sh'shrane!"

The aiodoi, though they sing all, also hear all. Some of the smallsongs they heard were doleful, and some were painful, and some were tinged with fear; yet they sang on, and did not neglect such other songs as that of the old Earth scientist/poet.

———

"If you take seriously that anthropic-universe idea we were talking about, you're probably going to be asking yourself some logical questions.

"Okay, you say. I'll buy into the idea that this particular universe we inhabit couldn't just *happen* to be so neatly adapted to the needs of intelligent living things like us. Fine, but if that's true, where did it go wrong?

"That is, here we are, sitting on one measly little planet of a third-rate star, which is only one of the two hundred-odd billion in our own galaxy alone, and God knows how many more in all the other external galaxies.

"So why is it just us? If the design of the universe was so hotsy-totsy for smart living things, shouldn't there be some others around somewhere?

"That's a fair question, and people have been asking it for a long time. The question even has a name. It's called 'the Fermi question' after an Italian scientist who was the first one to ask in public, 'Where *is* everybody?'

"A lot of scientists took the question seriously, and a bunch of good ones began spending time looking for an answer. One place to look was in the zillion flying-saucer stories that went around in those days, so some scientists began investigating them. It was a dead end. Out of all the tens of thousands of reports of sightings and abductions and what-all, they never found *one* with any solid evidence to prove it—and an awful lot that were clearly the work of loonies or cheats.

"Other scientists begged or stole time on radio telescopes, and they listened devotedly, day after day, for some sort of non-random message from Out There. They never heard one, though.

"Later on, a man named Freeman Dyson, an Englishman who became an American, had a different idea. Dyson said he thought that any truly advanced technological race would probably be enough like ourselves that it would want to do a lot of high-tech things, and that if so it would need energy to do them with. Where would it get that energy? Why, said Dyson, the best place would be to trap the radiation from their nearest star. What he thought they might do was take all the planets in their solar system and grind them up and rearrange them as a hollow sphere, putting a kind of wall around the star. That way they could use all the star's highest-level energy for their industry—or whatever—and let the waste heat radiate away from the outside of the sphere. So Dyson asked that infrared astronomers keep their eyes open for such weakly radiating infrared objects, which came to be called 'Dyson spheres.'

"So a lot of astronomers did that . . . but they never found any Dyson spheres.

"What it all adds up to is that Fermi's question is still unanswered.

"If you want my personal opinion, the answer's pretty simple. Where is everybody? There isn't any 'everybody' but us. We're all alone in this great big universe."

And the aiodoi sang:

"To seek forever, and never to find, that is to fail.

"To seek for a while, and then stop seeking, that is also a failure; but it is a failure of the self.

"To seek and fail when the object of the search is almost at hand—that is sorrow."

17

~~~~~~

Francis Krake couldn't help himself. When he saw the giant Turtle roughly shoving Marco out of the way to take over the controls of the *Golden Hind* he leaped forward with a roar.

Chief Thunderbird didn't surrender the board willingly. He cawed frantically at Krake as he resisted, striking at the captain with his clawed forelimbs, but Krake would not be denied. Although the Turtle was half again his height and much more than twice his mass, it was Francis Krake who wound up with his fingers on the board.

Krake knew that he wasn't being sensible. There was nothing he could do at the controls that the Proctor couldn't do as well. Krake knew that the Turtle was at least as good a pilot as he, but that didn't matter. *The Golden Hind* was *his ship*.

Krake turned his back on the bleating Turtle. He absently rubbed at the blood on his forearm, where the Turtle's claws had broken the skin. Krake swore monotonously to himself, staring up at the screens as the simulated sky began slowly to revolve around them. Both Turtles were screeching at him all the while, transposers forgotten, but Krake wasn't listening. The ship was turning too slowly! Yet he knew it couldn't be helped. There was no way to make the turn go faster. A waveship was not a fighter plane; it couldn't stop and turn and reverse, skittering all over the sky like the P-38s and P-51s Krake had flown in the South Pacific. It was like a vast liner. All you could do was change the direction of thrust, and the resulting vector would slowly, bit by bit, alter the direction of travel.

Litlun finally remembered to turn on his transposer. "Run, Krake!" he begged. "Get away from them quickly, please!" And Chief Thunderbird, fumbling with his own speaking machine, echoed:

"Quickly! For one believes they are the Sh'shrane!"

"I'm going as fast as I can," Krake said tightly. He took one second to glance around the chamber. Sue-ling was crouched over her patient, her face white with worry, Moon holding tight to her crushed-looking Taur, the others simply waiting. Then he returned to the screens. The red and green blotches were still coming in their direction —more ships than ever, he saw, scowling—but not directly at them. The oncoming ships were displaced a few degrees to one side now, and the angle growing.

Krake allowed himself one final oath. Then he turned around, tugging at his beard as he glared at the two Turtles. He said flatly, "We'll miss them, I think. There's nothing else we can do now, so let's hear some truth from you two! Who are the Sh'shrane?"

The Turtles were silent for a moment, their eyes wandering at random. Then they exchanged glances and Chief Thunderbird spoke for both of them.

"They are our ancient destroyers," he said, tolling the words like a dirge. "They killed us by the thousands, and now we are helpless in their midst."

As the Turtles began to speak, Sue-ling lifted her head. "Sork's worse," she said briefly. "Kiri! Please get my bag—hurry!" And, at a moan from Sork, she bent down to him again, her eyes wet.

Krake saw, but had no time to observe. He took his

eyes off Sue-ling Quong and turned to the Turtles. "All of it," he grated. "Everything you haven't told us already!"

Chief Thunderbird said, his bearing hopeless but still with some dignity: "There is little to tell. It was many Mother-lives ago. We were conducting our business without harm to anyone—" Krake barked a sardonic laugh at that, but the Turtle went on unheeding—"when our ships began to disappear. Then fleets of other ships began to appear on our screens. They were not like ours, Krake. They were far more maneuverable, and—they were armed."

"So were ours," Litlun put in despairingly.

The Proctor turned both eyes to glare at him, then surrendered. "Yes," he admitted, "one must say that is true. True at that time—which was many, many Mother-lives ago. Our armaments made no difference. Their weapons were better than ours, and so were their ships."

Out of the corner of his eye Krake saw Kiri Quintero hurrying back with Sue-ling's supplies. She wrenched the bag open, found her memo disk and slipped it into the slot in her skull. Krake looked away, unwilling to see her go under the spell of the disk. "What else?" he demanded of the Turtles.

"There is no 'else,'" Chief Thunderbird squawked. "They attacked us. We resisted. They defeated us—over and over. They even approached the holy planet of the Mother Herself!"

He stopped there, wrapped in silence and fear. Krake gnawed a strand from his beard. "Well?" he demanded. "What then?"

Chief Thunderbird drummed restlessly on his belly plate. "They went away," he said at last.

Krake stared at him. "What do you mean, 'went away'? First they attack and beat you—then they just *leave*?"

"That is the case," the Proctor agreed. "You are puzzled, one sees. Yes, that is appropriate. We too were puzzled; the records of the time show long debates, questions, speculations—but there is no answer to those questions, Krake. The Sh'shrane simply went away."

"Until now," said Litlun unhappily.

Krake shook his head, and turned to stare up at the growing cluster of red and green markings on the screen. There were at least a hundred of them now, he saw, but their pattern was spreading out, fanwise, like the spray from a garden hose being turned across a lawn.

"Proctor?" Moon Bunderan ventured. "Are you sure these things on the screen are the—the Sh'shrane?"

"The instrument readings are the same," Chief Thunderbird said simply. "Those are the indications of their ships." He might have said more, but there was a sudden, low bleating sound from the Taur.

"Wait," Moon said, putting her ear close to the great bull head to listen. Then she looked up. "Thrayl says it is true. They are the same."

"How the hell does he know that?" Krake demanded, but Litlun was gabbling already.

"Of course they are the same! And they are most terrible, for they are not living things at all."

"Machines," said Chief Thunderbird. "They are machines. Not the same as the Brotherhood, not like the Taurs, not even like humans. They are only machines."

"And they *kill*," said Litlun, his eyes rotating fearfully.

Krake sat back, puffing out his cheeks in frustration. "Are you telling me they're robots or something like that?" he began. "Because if you are—"

He didn't finish. Marco interrupted him. "Captain?" he said. "Look at the screen."

Krake turned to do it, and his eyes widened. There were as many of the blotches as ever, but they seemed smaller, paler than before. And in the moment he watched they were beginning to disappear.

Krake took a deep breath. "Well," he said, "whatever they are, it looks like we've lost them."

"One is not sure of that," Chief Thunderbird said despairingly.

———

Screens back on the infrared, Krake could see the great, ruddy coal dwindling behind them, and nothing at all of those frightening "Sh'shrane" ships. He left Marco at the board with orders to keep running—not because he thought it was the best thing to do, but because what better choices did he have?

Sue-ling Quong had removed the chip from her skull again and was hovering over her patient, Moon Bunderan at her side. "Get some rest, Sue-ling," Moon urged the older woman. "I'll watch him."

"He's lost sensation in his left side," Sue-ling fretted. "There might be a clot—I think I'll probably have to go in again."

"Not the way you are," Moon insisted. "You didn't have enough rest to go into a surgical operation again. Get some more sleep—I'll watch over Sork." She turned to look sadly at her Taur, who was slumped against a wall, his great eyes open but unseeing. "I can watch two patients as well as one," she said.

Sue-ling was suddenly remorseful. "I've been forgetting about Thrayl. I'm sorry, Moon. He looks like he needs help, too."

"There isn't any help I can give him," Moon said sadly. "He refuses food, water—he refuses everything, even to talk most of the time. When he speaks at all he talks about great pain and a kind of crippling anger that I just don't understand."

"But at least I should check him over!"

"Oh, Sue-ling," said Moon, half amused, half exasperated, "what do you know about Taurs? I've tended them all my life, and I'm telling you it's nothing physical with Thrayl."

Sue-ling looked doubtful, but Moon was firm. "Captain Krake," she called. "Please make her get some more rest." And, surprisingly, Sue-ling submitted, and it was only when Moon was watching them leave together that she began to wonder if she had made a mistake.

Long before they reached Sue-ling's room, Francis Krake was wondering the same thing. He could feel himself getting ill at ease. "I don't really have to escort you,

Sue-ling," he said. "I do think you ought to rest a little more, though."

But she said, "Please. I'm not going to sleep, Francis. I have to check Sork again in an hour." She sat down on the edge of her bed, then leaned back and closed her eyes. For a moment Krake almost believed that she really had dropped off, but just as he was about to leave quietly she spoke again.

"Sork isn't doing well at all. I think he's paralyzed on one side."

"So you'll have to operate again?"

She opened her eyes and regarded him. "If I thought I could do any good, do you think I'd be loafing around here? I just don't have the tools. If we were on Earth I could do lots of things—transplant fetal tissue, perhaps, or maybe repair the damage with microsurgery. But what can I do on this ship?" She shook her head. "But if he continues to get worse, I'll have to try, anyway."

She sat up, putting that thought out of her mind. "So talk to me, Francis. Tell me what's been happening. What were those things on the screen that had the Turtles so frightened?"

Krake had forgotten that Sue-ling had been under the memo disk through much of the incident. He said, temporizing, "If you just rest for a while now I'll fill you in later—"

"Now, Francis!"

What Krake knew best about Sue-ling Quong was that she could be just as stubborn as he. "All right," he said, and told her, as briefly as possible, everything that had happened, and everything the Turtles had said. She was wide awake long before he was through. "I'm sure they suspected it was these machines they call the Sh'shrane right away," he finished, "but Chief Thunderbird wouldn't tell us that. Maybe it was too frightening for him."

"You say they're supposed to be machines?"

He nodded. "If they're really the Sh'shrane they are. The Turtles found that out long ago, in that old war, when they captured a couple of shot-up Sh'shrane ships.

The crews inside were dead, of course. If you can say that
a machine is 'dead,' because that was what they were.
Litlun says they were really ugly things. Naturally, the
Turtles would be bound to think that anyway. But, from
what they say, the Sh'shrane do sound rather nasty—
pyramidal metal bodies, with a lot of tentacles—"

"Like Marco and Daisy Fay?"

Krake gave her a suddenly hostile look. "My friends
are *people,* Sue-ling!"

She was penitent. "I didn't mean anything by it.
They're my friends, too. I'm sorry I said that." Then she
shivered. "And it's these Sh'shrane things that are chasing us now?"

"They were. Maybe. I mean, if the things chasing us
really were the same Sh'shrane. But you don't have to
worry about them, Sue-ling. Whatever they were, they're
no danger to us now. You know we're safe as long as
we're in wave-drive—one photon can't catch up with another."

"You're sure of that?" He nodded, half amused, and
she sighed and closed her eyes.

He looked down at her, wondering if he ought to
leave—knowing the answer, unwilling to do it. In Francis
Krake's eyes at that moment, Sue-ling Quong appeared
to be the most beautiful woman he had ever seen. Not at
all an ordinary-looking one, of course. In particular, he
thought (remembering that long-ago love for the first
time without pain), not at all like the lost Madeleine Mc-
Kay. Sue-ling's eyes were almond-shaped and long, but
they were intensely blue. Her high cheekbones were Ori-
ental, but her hair was a lustrous coppery red. She was an
arresting blend of East and West, and Francis Krake,
who had missed the experience of the last few centuries of
interbreeding, thought her a startlingly desirable one.

Without thinking, he reached out curiously to touch
the rubbery lips of her implant socket.

Her eyes opened at once, looking up at him. "Please
don't, Francis," she said.

"I was just curious," he said, excusing himself, not
truthful.

"Does it repel you?" she asked.

"—No," he said, not sure that was truthful, either. "Does it hurt?"

"Of course not. . . . But I don't really like it, Francis. I wasn't always a memmie. I was an ordinary human doctor, but then, when I found myself working with memmie surgeons, with all those Turtle skills, I decided I had to be able to do the things they could do. So I made up my mind." She shrugged. She was particularly beautiful when she moved like that, Krake thought, her soft, warm shoulders moving so gracefully. "The next day I let them slot my skull."

"And now you're sorry?"

"Sorry? What's the good of being sorry? It's done, and there it is."

"It doesn't change anything. You're still very beautiful," he told her.

That stopped her. She looked at him in a different way. "Francis," she said seriously, "I'm sorry if I'm still giving you any wrong ideas, but please don't. That's the one thing I *am* sorry about. You're a wonderful man, and any woman would be proud to have you for a lover—but I've still got those other commitments." She smiled regretfully up at him. "I know I forgot them for a while. But I have to start remembering again."

———

When push came to shove, Sue-ling refused to stay away from her patient for the full hour. Krake was glad enough of that. It was frustrating to be alone in the sight and smell of her, and not be allowed to touch . . . and he was beginning to want to be back in the control room of his ship, too.

There seemed to be no need for that. As he stood behind Marco Ramos at the board, staring up at the screens, the dull coppery disk had long since dwindled to be just another coal in those hostile skies. "I don't see any trace of the Sh'shrane ships," Krake said.

"No, Captain. They just disappeared half an hour ago. I guess we're home free."

Krake made a noise in his throat. In lighter mood it might have been a laugh. "Free, probably. Home, I doubt," he said.

Marco twisted one eyestalk to regard him. "Have you got any new orders for me, Captain?"

Krake shook his head. "Continue as you are. I don't know where we're going, but we're certainly on our way." Feeling helpless, and angry at himself for the feeling, he turned to Moon Bunderan. "Any bright ideas from Thrayl?"

She sighed. "Nothing useful, I'm afraid. All he says is that the bad song is getting very loud. I'm worried about him, Captain."

Krake didn't respond. He didn't want to say the truth, which was that he was worried about all of them, himself included. He turned to the room at large. "Any ideas, anybody?" But Kiri Quintero merely looked politely apologetic, Marco and Daisy Fay were silent and the Turtles were muttering unhappily to each other, their transposers off, paying no attention to the others.

That left Sue-ling Quong.

She was ignoring everyone but her patient, crouched over Sork's silent form, methodically rolling the sensors over his body to check for pulse, temperature and other vital signs. Krake didn't like staring at her, but he couldn't help himself, though the sight brought him no more than a feeling of desolation. He had no right to Sue-ling Quong, he reminded himself . . . but it hurt just as much as though he had.

She looked up. "He's deteriorating, all right," she reported, her face drawn but determined. "I'm going to have to go in again."

"But you said you needed things you don't have here."

"That's right," she said, "but what choice have I got? He's going to die if I don't do something. Maybe I can patch him together a little better . . . but I'll have to have help. Daisy Fay, Marco—will you give me a hand with him?"

"I'll do it," Moon Bunderan offered, but Sue-ling shook her head.

"Not this time, Moon. You take care of Thrayl."

"Do what she says, Marco," Krake ordered, and slipped into the place before the board to relieve him, while Kiri Quintero silently took the other board over from Daisy Fay McQueen. Krake watched without joy as his crewmates carried Sork Quintero away. Francis Krake certainly did not wish Sork any harm. There was, it was true, a part of his mind that was calculating the effect Sork Quintero's death, if that happened, would have on his own chances with Sue-ling . . . but that was not a thought he wanted to concentrate on. It was ugly. It was also stupid, because whatever happened to Sork, there would be no practical benefit for Krake as far as Sue-ling was concerned while Kiri Quintero was still around. . . .

He turned when he heard Kiri call his name. Kiri was looking unusually agitated. "Francis?" he called. "Have you been looking at the screen? Is there something wrong with our instruments?"

Startled, Krake swung back to stare. Yes, there did seem to be something unusual there on the screens. It was no more than a faint, fuzzed appearance, hard to detect, much less to identify. It wasn't easy for Krake to be sure even that anything was actually there, for it was no more than the almost invisible haze of a summer morning's mist.

But it had not been there before.

Suddenly alarmed, Krake touched the board, switching frequencies for the sensors. One after another he scanned every octave of the electromagnetic spectrum. Infrared, optical, all the way down through microwave— yes, the fuzz was there in every frequency, all over the sky. And it was growing rapidly denser until it became a milky glow, like a bright fog, all around *The Golden Hind.*

"What the hell!" Krake snapped. But his voice was

drowned out by a simultaneous keening from both Turtles. "One knew it!" Chief Thunderbird moaned, and Litlun cried:

"It is surely the Sh'shrane!"

Krake looked at them, baffled. "What are you talking about? There's no way those ships could catch up with us in wave-drive!"

Chief Thunderbird was frantic. "One has told you their ships are better than ours!" he bellowed.

"But there's no ship there," Krake said reasonably, "only a kind of—"

"Smudge," he had been going to say. He didn't get the word out.

Suddenly there was a ship.

More accurately, there was a piece of a ship. The stranger did not appear on the screen at once. It began to show up bit by bit, like an ancient dirigible poking its nose out of a cloud. It kept on coming.

A ship it certainly was. A ship of unfamiliar design, football-shaped, and huge. When the last of it had emerged from the milky cloud, its bow was almost touching the hull of *The Golden Hind.*

"It is truly the Sh'shrane," moaned Chief Thunderbird.

Krake shouted in wordless startlement and anger. He pounded on the keys of the controls—trying to accomplish what, he could not have said—to do anything, to change the course, to come out of the wave state—it made no difference, for nothing worked. The *Hind* did not respond.

The strange vessel settled itself against the hull of *The Golden Hind* with a solid nudge and hung there. A hatch in its side opened. And out of it came—

Sh'shrane.

There was no doubt that that was what they were, metal monsters no larger than a cat, waving short, stubby, flexible members like arms. They collected at the hull of the *Hind* and then began crawling purposefully along it toward the lock of *Hind*'s scout ship.

"But we're in *wave-drive,*" Krake said stupidly. He

could not believe what he saw. Everyone knew that a ship in wave-drive was completely isolated from every material object in the universe. There was no way these things could have reached them!

But they had. He watched them, unbelieving, as they clustered around the exterior lock of the scout ship. It opened to them. They disappeared inside.

Then, a moment later, the interior hatch to the *Hind* itself swung open, and five of the alien machines boiled through.

Krake was frozen in astonishment, but others were not. Everyone in the control room of the *Hind* was shouting at once, and some were acting. Chief Thunderbird threw himself despairingly at the invaders, Kiri Quintero only a moment behind him . . . unfortunately for the Proctor, for it was his death.

The Turtle didn't have a chance. The leading Sh'shrane hardly paused in its advance. It simply raised a stubby tentacle and pointed it at him. A fat, violet spark leaped out from the end of the tentacle and flew at the Turtle. The spark was lethal. There was a horrid *splatting* sound, and a reek of chemicals and foulness, and the body of Chief Thunderbird burst like a child's balloon. Bits of Turtle flesh and chitin scattered horribly around the control room, splattering on the walls and furnishings and people like an awful rain. . . .

And behind Chief Thunderbird, Kiri Quintero was caught in the same blast. His arm and shoulder were ripped away, his head burned black on one side.

Litlun screamed in horror and pain. He dropped frantically to the floor, to scrabble in the butcher's offal that had been his Elder Brother. Moon Bunderan ran to Kiri's side, Thrayl painfully rising to follow her, his great horns questing from side to side.

Krake did not will any action from his own body, but his body had a will of its own. Before he knew it he was charging toward the Sh'shrane—not for any reasoned purpose, only to attack; knowing that no bare-handed attack could accomplish anything but his own death. He

could see death coming at him, as two of the machines
raised tentacles and pointed them toward him—

And then they stopped.

They froze in place, all five of the Sh'shrane. Every
one of them turned abruptly toward the passageway.

There the bouncing red form of Daisy Fay McQueen
had appeared, drawn by the commotion in the control
room. She stopped short in horror at what she saw.

The Sh'shrane seemed to confer inaudibly among
themselves. Then they simply ignored all the survivors in
the control room. They advanced on Daisy Fay and bore
her back, protesting, struggling, until the sounds of her
voice faded out and they were out of sight.

Then there was silence in the abattoir that had been
the control room, except for the sounds of weeping from
Moon Bunderan. "It's Kiri," she said, sobbing. "I think
he's dead."

Though the aiodoi sing on, they listen more intently now to the smallsongs from everywhere. Especially they listen to the song of that aiodos among them who sings lovingly of all, and yet intends to give up eternity for life. This is a grave concern to all the aiodoi, who seldom act but only are. Yet they sing on, and listen on, to the songs of the old Earth scientist and poet.

————

"Let's talk a little more about the fine structure of the universe, and what it contains. We'll start by talking about pi.

"You all know what pi is. It's the ratio of the circumference of a circle to its diameter, and when you measure it out it's a little more than 3. I can be more exact than that, though. To fourteen places, pi is 3.14159265358979.

"I hope I've impressed you by remembering all that, but so you won't get *too* impressed I'll let you in on a trade secret. An old-timer named James Jeans had trouble keeping that value of pi in mind, so he made up a mnemonic for it. You know what mnemonic is? It's a device to aid your memory, like the notes you scribble on your cuffs before a final. In this case, you use the mnemonic by counting the letters in each word—3, 1, 4 and so on—and it goes:

" 'How I want a drink, alcoholic of course, after the heavy chapters involving quantum mechanics.'

"You mustn't think that even that fourteen-place figure is *right,* though. It isn't. It's still an approximation. People with computers have carried pi out to thousands of decimal places now, and they'll never end, for pi doesn't have an end. It's an irrational number.

"Before computers, mathematicians used to amuse themselves calculating extra decimal places for pi by the method of inscribing polygons inside a circle. You can get as close as you like—up to a point—just by increasing the number of sides of the inscribed polygon.

"Now, we already know that they'll never get to the *real* value of pi, because it doesn't have one, being irrational. But let's make believe it isn't. A question for you all to consider is this:

"Assume the biggest circle you can imagine, with the maximum number of sides; and assume you have all eternity to count and measure the sides. Is it *possible* to get this mythical 'exact' value for pi that way?

"Answer: It is not. The reason is what we call 'space-time foam.'

"In order to get the maximum closest possible value for pi, the sides of your polygon would have to be very, very small. But smallness has a limit.

"You can't have anything smaller than Planck's ten to the minus twenty-seven centimeters, because below that size the concept of size itself doesn't exist; it is a philosophical abstraction, irrelevant to quantum considerations. Nothing *gets* shorter than that. There you are in the realm of quantum effects, and everything is dominated by the superforce.

"Which, you remember, is the force that lets you do anything at all to anything at all. If we could ever learn how to control the superforce . . . well, then you could forget all the 'can'ts' and 'impossibles' I've been saying to you, because nothing at all would be impossible ever again."

———

And some of the aiodoi sang:
"Of course."
*And some of the aiodoi sang as always, but listened
and listened for the song of that aiodos among them who
had chosen to be gone.*

18
~~~

Krake's first thought was to charge after the alien machines—"thought" was too intellectual a word for what he felt; actually it was only the atavistic adrenalin-rush of the attacked and enraged male—but he stopped himself. It wasn't cowardice that stopped him, though he was certain that attacking these mechanical murderers who had slaughtered members of his crew could accomplish nothing but his own quick death. What kept him in the control room was the urgent needs before him.

There was nothing that anyone could do for Chief Thunderbird. Litlun was squatting amid the noisome rubble that had been his Elder Brother, muttering dejectedly to himself, and, queerly, picking up the gobbets and bits—as though neatness could count here! But Kiri Quintero—

Kiri wasn't dead. Not quite. "His heart's beating," Moon Bunderan called from where she knelt with the scorched head in her lap. Krake took one frustrated look toward the corridor, then dropped to his knees beside her.

Yes, there was a pulse, faint but regular at the base of Kiri's throat. "Hold on," Krake said—not so much to Moon as to Kiri himself. While she dabbed at the crusted char, trying not to let the stench of burned flesh affect her, Krake ripped off his shirt and belt, wadding the shirt against the raw meat where Kiri's shoulder and arm had been, winding the belt around the torso to hold it in place. The blood was fountaining. But though the wadded shirt was soaked with it at once, the bleeding was at least slowed. It would be the wound to the head that would kill Kiri Quintero, Krake thought, and could only marvel that it hadn't done the job already.

He raised his head quickly, listening to a sudden new outburst of sound from the corridor. It was Marco's voice. He was shouting something—puzzlingly, sounding angry rather than in hurt or fear. Krake swore. "Can you hold Kiri?" he begged Moon Bunderan. "I have to go after them—"

As he tried to rise, the Taur rose beside him and gently, firmly, pressed him back down. He rumbled something that Krake could not make out. "Make him let go of me, Moon!" he snapped.

But she was listening to Thrayl rather than the captain. "No, Francis," she said. "He says you can stay here. It's all right, he says."

"All *right*!" Krake exploded, staring up at the Taur. The great head was lowered toward him, the eyes bright, the horns brighter still. The majestic head shook slowly as the Taur spoke again.

"He says no harm will come to Marco. The Sh'shrane are confused by them—they think they may be machines like themselves."

"What difference does that make? And how the hell would Thrayl know that?"

"He does know, Francis," the girl said with confidence. "And—oh, Francis! He's saying something else, too. I don't know what he means, but it's about help."

"Help! God, yes! I'd be begging for help, too, if I knew who to beg!"

"No, no, Francis, not like that. He says help is *coming*."

Krake turned his head to glare at her. "Now, where the hell would help be coming from here?" he demanded . . . and, off balance, almost fell as the Taur suddenly released him, straightening.

Krake stared up at the great shape, astonished, almost afraid. Something was happening to Thrayl. The great head was flung back, the strong arms lifted toward the sky; the Taur was rumbling deep in his throat, like a lion's purring. Suddenly Thrayl seemed even larger than before. The needle-sharp horns were almost crackling with internal fires, as brilliant shapes of gold and blue-white light chased each other across them.

Thrayl bent his head back down to regard them. His demeanor had changed—servile no longer, now almost commanding, though the purple-blue eyes were kind and reassuring.

"Help comes here vrom me, Francis Grake," he said, in a voice the captain had never heard from the Taur's mouth before.

Krake almost lost his grip on the belt that was holding Kiri Quintero's life in. The Taur reached down swiftly to place one great paw over Krake's hand, pressing the packing tighter.

"Do nod vear," he said, the voice deep and kind—and in English! In *perfect* English—or as perfect as the lips and throat of a Taur could make it. Some of the consonants seemed to drag, the vowels were rounder and more liquid than a human would have made them, but every word was perfectly clear. "This Taur's song has been heard vor a long time," the voice proclaimed, "and you are to be aided."

Litlun looked up from the butcher's offal that had been his Elder Brother, both yellow-red eyes startled and watchful. Moon Bunderan clapped a hand to her mouth.

"Who are you?" she wailed. "You're not Thrayl!"

The great eyes looked down benignly on her. "Thrayl is within, and never gone vrom you," the voice said. "All will be well."

There was a fresh racket from the hallway. The great head lifted, the horns thrusting toward the doorway. Then the Taur looked down again. He released his hold on Krake's hand and placed his paw gently on the faint stirring of heartbeat at the base of Kiri's throat. The horns blazed brightly for a moment.

"There is time," he said, "but Kiri Quintero musd have help now. Francis Grake, pick him up. Take him to Sue-ling Quong. Facilitator, you will assisd."

Moon sobbed, "But the Sh'shrane are out there!"

The great head nodded comfortingly. "The Sh'shrane," said the beautiful organ voice, with a note of sadness, "will nod intervere again. Come now."

And the being that had been Thrayl turned and moved quickly, dancingly, toward the door. Those sharp horns were now shining so bright that they made faint, shifting pools of light on the corridor walls as the Taur led the way.

There was no way to refuse those orders. Litlun set down the fragments he had collected of Chief Thunderbird's anatomy. With Krake, he lifted what was left of Kiri Quintero and, Moon Bunderan by their side, they followed.

Shock had robbed Francis Krake of imagination. He didn't question his orders. He didn't even try to guess where the thing in the body of the Taur was leading them, or what they would find when they got there. He expected no one thing more than any other. . . .

And yet when he entered that corridor and saw what was there he gasped.

Those violent, vicious murder machines, the Sh'shrane—they were lined up like statues against a wall. They did not move or threaten. They made no sound. Their stubby tentacles were still, as silent and motionless as though frozen. Their eyes did not even follow as the thing that had been the Taur passed them without a glance.

Marco was standing there—alive! Well! He dodged out of the way as Thrayl passed, rumbling softly, reassuringly. Marco's eyestalks were roving bewilderedly, and the expression of the face on his belly plate was incredulous. He turned the eyes on his captain. "Francis," he begged, "what the hell is happening? Those things looked like they were going to kill us—then, all of a sudden, they just *stopped*!"

Krake didn't even try to answer. "Give us a hand with Kiri," he ordered.

The machine-man gasped as he saw the wounds. He ran to obey, but even so couldn't help asking, "But what's happened to Thrayl?"

"We'll explain later," Krake promised, a promise that he had no confidence he could really keep. Thrayl was in the doorway of the operating room, speaking to those inside. Daisy Fay's red ball of a body squeezed through past him, her eyes peering down the corridor.

"Oh, dear heaven!" she cried. "What happened to Kiri?"

She got out of the way as the drafted corpsmen carried him through. The being in Thrayl's body said, its voice rich and reassuring, "You are to help him, Daisy Fay McQueen, and—" as Sue-ling looked up from Sork's figure on the operating table, her face expressionless in the memmie mask—"you, Sue-ling Quong, will do whad is necessary."

"Of course," she said, with neither surprise nor doubt in her voice. She made room on the operating table for Kiri to be set down beside his brother, and bent to study his wounds without haste or emotion.

"All of you," said Thrayl, "will assisd in this—" he gestured with a three-fingered paw at Krake, his crew and the Turtle—"excepd for Moon Bunderan. She is to come with me."

Moon shrank back. "But the Sh'shrane are out there," she sobbed.

The Taur head bent to gaze kindly down at her. "Yes, the Sh'shrane," said the rich voice, a note of sadness coloring it. "Do nod fear the Sh'shrane. I will arrange whad musd be done vor the Sh'shrane." He was silent for a moment, as though sorrowing, before he finished, "I musd, vor they are the other halve of we."

———

What Krake did then he did almost without the use of his mind. He followed orders. He didn't bother to think, because there was no way of understanding what was going on.

It was only Sue-ling, of all in that room, who seemed unaffected, businesslike, competent. The memmie disk insulated her from astonishment and worry. She said crisply, "Daisy Fay, prep the patient. You others, scrub up. Litlun, you're the only one who can wear a memo disk; there's a spare in my bag. Use it, because you're going to assist."

No one argued. Everyone seemed to be in the same semi-shock as Krake. They did what they were told—even when what they were doing was wholly outside any previous experience, as it was for Francis Krake.

After three tours of combat duty in the South Pacific, Krake was no stranger to blood. Still, this kind of controlled, deliberate bloodletting made shivers run up and down his back. He was given the task of sterilizing instruments, not a part of the operating team at all—not a disappointment to him at all. He could hardly see what was happening on the table, for all the figures crowded around it. Litlun was methodically cauterizing blood vessels in the hollow where Kiri Quintero's shoulder had been, with a stink of burning flesh rising from the operation. Simultaneously Sue-ling was opening Kiri's skull, concentrating on what she was doing and yet sparing enough thought to keep an eye on Daisy Fay, monitoring Sork Quintero's condition at one side of the table, while Marco Ramos acted as assistant to all three operations at once. It was a great blessing that the machine-bodies of his crew had so many limbs to help with, for both of them were doing a dozen things at once.

Krake was careful with all the instruments in the radioclave, giving each one its full time in the germ-destroying radiation, carefully setting each one down in a sterile bed of cotton with his gloved hand. But he could not help listening for sounds from outside. He had not forgotten that silent, petrified row of killer machines, immobile no more than a dozen meters away; he knew that

that huge, strange Sh'shrane spaceship was still just out-side the hull of the *Hind.* He knew most of all that *his* ship had been boarded by inimical aliens, and against them he had been as helpless as a child.

But it was all so incredible! No ship *could* have caught them in wave-drive! He could hardly accept the fact that he had seen what he had seen . . . especially could not believe that they had been reprieved by—by whatever it was that was living in the body of the Taur, Thrayl. It was all too much. Too many shocks. Too many marvels. . . .

He closed his mind to it all. He hardly even glanced at what was happening on the operating table. He took the soiled scalpels and forceps as Daisy Fay or Marco handed them to him, cleaned them, sterilized them, read-ied them for their next use—and went on doing that, for hours he did not count.

It was only when Sue-ling at last said, her voice bone-weary, hardly more than a whisper, "We can close now," that he gave himself the freedom to act on his own. He turned away from the table and toward the door. Half-way along the silent, empty corridor—where were the Sh'shrane?—he began to run.

When he burst into the control room, once again, he was ready for anything—anything but what he saw.

His first look was at the screens.

What he saw there made him swear in consternation and rage. The milky glow was gone, but the sky around *The Golden Hind* was not empty. It was littered with the great, gleaming eggs that were the Sh'shrane spacecraft. There were hundreds of them, all in easy optical range!

He turned toward the figures at the control board, and stopped short. The Taur was gazing at him peace-fully. "Do nod vear," said the voice that was not Thrayl's. "They are here by my will. They are to do whad musd be done vor you."

"And what's that?" Krake asked.

The Taur did not answer, but the horns were so bright that Krake could hardly bear to look at them. He turned and looked around the control room.

It was only then that Krake's mind registered the fact that the five Sh'shrane robots were no longer in his ship. "They're gone?" he said, meaning it as a statement, worry turning it into a question.

Moon Bunderan put her hand on his. "He made them go, Francis," she explained. "He even made them clean up first."

"Clean up?" And then he saw that some of the gore that had splattered the control room was gone. Moon Bunderan nodded toward a heap of something in a corner of the room, covered with a cloth. But from under the edge of the cloth one detached red eye was glaring sightlessly at the world.

The Taur was standing there, silent and benign, regarding them with kindness. Krake opened his mouth to ask a question, but the Taur was turning toward the doorway.

Flapping and squawking, Litlun came hurrying in, his memo disk in his hand. The Turtle's first look around was as startled as Krake's. He saw the little pile of parts that was all that was left of the Proctor for Humankind and snatched the cloth off, to make sure everything was there. Only after that did he look up at the screens.

Litlun shrieked, pointing at the vast fleet outside. Moon hastened to reassure him. "It's all right, Facilitator. See, they're doing what he wants them to do."

The Turtle turned both eyes on Thrayl, then back at the screen.

And Krake saw it too. Something was happening with that vast congeries of Sh'shrane vessels. They were not just a milling mob, nor were they assembling to attack. They seemed to be forming in a kind of pattern, two-dimensional, radially symmetric. They were taking position as though creating the nodes of an immense spiderweb in space near *The Golden Hind*.

And in the middle of that giant web, a faint discoloration was beginning to appear.

Thrayl spoke. "They are opening the way vor you," said the organ voice. "Id is whad they do. Id is the lasd

time they will do thad, vor anyone." The being was silent
for a moment, then, sounding almost regretful, said,
"This will take you where you wish to go."

Litlun cawed excitedly, "To the Mother planet? But it
was destroyed!"

"Id was destroyed *then*. Id is nod destroyed *now*. All
time is one time," the voice said, as the great purple-blue
eyes gazed once more around the room, and the huge
Taur face seemed to smile.

Then, "Id is finishd," the voice said. And Thrayl's
body slumped to the floor, the eyes suddenly sightless,
while the horns went almost black.

————

Moon Bunderan cried out and flung herself on the
body of her friend, hugging the huge head in her arms.
For a moment she looked desolated.

Then the eyes began to live again, and the great horns
once more became milkily opalescent.

The Taur sat up. Thrayl stretched, yawned, touched
Moon with an affectionate paw. He muttered something
to her . . . and then lay peacefully down on the floor of
the control room and went to sleep.

Francis Krake shivered, aware that there was one less
person in the room. "What did he say?" he demanded.

Moon looked at him wonderingly. "He said you can
take the ship through that wormhole out there now,
Francis," she whispered in awe. She looked down lovingly at her Taur, restored to her, and when she looked
up again at the captain her eyes were brimming with glad
tears. "Oh, Francis," she said, "I really think it's going to
be all right now!"

The songs of the aiodoi swelled in triumph and welcoming as the one who had gone from among them returned, and they listened to the old smallsongs from Earth:

———

"When we talked about that other dimension we call time, we noted that the strangest thing about it is that it only goes one way. We are always going toward the future. We never see time going from the future to the past. It's as if there were an arrow on a one-way street, an 'arrow of time,' as some people call it.

"That arrow has a name. It's called 'entropy.'

"The figure of merit for the entropy of a system is the logarithm of the number of microscopic states the system can assume. You have to remember that, because you might easily get it on a test, but there's a more common way of putting it.

"Entropy can be called a measure of increasing randomness. That's why my brother-in-law calls their two-year-old 'Entropy' for short, because when she enters a room disorganization begins at once.

"We *always* observe that things proceed toward increasing disorder. For instance, consider a watch.

"A watch is made up of hundreds of parts, all complicated. There are gears and springs and jeweled bearings and case and cover—remember, I'm talking about the *real* watch, the wind-up kind, not what you all have on your wrists these days. A watch is highly ordered. If anything changes in it, it has nowhere to go but downhill. It may rust, or fall apart, or be stepped on and crushed. Or it may fall into a vat of molten metal and cease to have any recognizable identity at all. And you know that any of those things can happen, and you also know that if they do there is no way in which the disordered parts can turn themselves into a watch again.

"Right?

"Wrong. There *is* a way in which a watch can spring from completely random materials—in fact, that's how all your watches came to be.

"It happens all the time. Random dust and gas clouds collapse into stars; big stars explode into supernovas; new stars and planets form out of the supernova residue—life appears—intelligence appears—*watchmakers* appear, and make your watch for you. But disorganized matter became organized, and thus entropy is violated—right?

"Wrong again.

"There's nothing in the entropy concept that says that some *part* of a system can't become temporarily more highly organized, only that the *whole* system must become more disordered with time. And the whole system, if you allow baby universes and all that other Hawking stuff, is very large indeed.

"That's an example of Treiman's theorem.

"Sam Treiman was a Princeton scientist, whose best-known theorem is 'Impossible things don't usually happen.'

"But some things we would like to believe impossible actually do happen now and then, and you can sometimes get a special dispensation from even the law of entropy.

"For instance, there is Bell's Theorem.

"John Stewart Bell says that there aren't any purely local effects in the quantum universe. Every last electron, no matter where it is located, is connected with every other one. As Nick Herbert puts it, in the cosmological model of Bell's Theorem, 'an invisible field informs the electron of environmental changes in superluminal response time.' Which means that Einstein's speed limit does not apply in the quantum universe as far as information is concerned.

"Startling enough for you? Then let's go a step farther. If you want a *real* exemption from the laws of entropy—and just about everything else—remember that 'superforce' we talked about a while ago. That will cheerfully break just about any law you can think of. Why not? It's a *superforce*. Within its own domain, entropy means nothing to it. The superforce will do anything at all, you remember, even reversing the flow of entropy. Even allowing time travel. Bell's Theorem lets you postulate that some kind of instrument, or person, somewhere, can be in instantaneous contact with everything else . . . but the superforce lets you be in contact with every*when*."

———

And the aiodoi, who knew well of the wholeness of all, sang on. Their song welcomed the one from among them who had gone but is gone no more, and the glad smallsongs sounded against their own song, and the harsh and hostile smallsongs of the others were no longer heard.

19

~~~~~

Once the world of Captain Francis Krake had made sense to him, but that time was long gone. Now his world had been turned topsy-turvy into a bewildering jumble of killer robots, alien visitors inhabiting the body of a docile Taur, ships that did what he had been quite certain that no ship could ever possibly do. The only sanity left for him was to be at the controls of his ship . . . and it was a measure of how crazy things had become that what he was doing with *The Golden Hind* was plunging it into the heart of a wormhole!

He had drafted Litlun for the second board. The Turtle was fidgety with the cranky nervousness of unexpected hope—over and over he was muttering to himself, disjointed phrases that the transposer picked up as references to the Mother planet, to the death of his Elder Brother. There was no problem with pilotage or navigation. The sweep of Sh'shrane vessels was like a firing-range target, aiming Krake directly into the shimmering distortion at their center.

Going through was almost routine. Krake breathed a long, silent sigh when he saw that on the other side of the wormhole was a normal sky—stars and distant galaxies, nothing threatening, nothing bizarre and unexpected. He sat back, almost at ease at last. He looked around the control room and beckoned to Daisy Fay. "Take this board over," he ordered. "I'm going to see if I can get Sue-ling to get some sleep for a change."

Litlun twisted quickly around to turn both eyes on Francis Krake. "Relieve me too, Captain," he asked. "One must place the remains of the Elder Brother in proper storage."

"Sure. Marco?" And when the machine-man had replaced the Turtle at the second board, Krake turned to Moon Bunderan. "Will you come with me?" he asked.

"Of course, Captain," she said, her mood lightened since her Taur was himself again. She took Thrayl with her to the operating room, of course. She wasn't willing to let him out of her sight, though it wasn't easy to wake him up long enough to make the move. Thrayl's tour of duty as host to—to whatever you might call the visitor which had taken his body over—had used up a lot of reserve strength. All the Taur wanted to do was to eat and sleep, by choice curled up against the feet of Moon Bunderan.

But when they reached the room the girl gasped, staring at the operating table. There was only one form on it, swathed in bandages that covered most of the head, even the eyes. "What happened?" she asked. "Did—did Kiri die?"

Sue-ling raised her head to look at her. She had long since removed the memo disk, and she was glassy-eyed with fatigue. She had to lick her lips before she was able to answer. "Kiri's body did," she said. "But Kiri's still alive—or part of him is, anyway—in Sork's head."

"Sleep," Krake ordered, taking her by the arm and leading her to the door. She hesitated, but obeyed, stumbling away. He turned to Moon Bunderan. "They're both in there," he told her, looking at the swathed head. "Part of both brains—the parts that weren't destroyed."

"But you can't transplant a *brain*!"

"You can if you're Sue-ling Quong with a memo disk, and if you have a Turtle with a disk of his own helping you," he said. "At least, he's alive now—or they are, whichever way you can say it. Sue-ling says there's no rejection problem because they're identical twins. They have exactly the same genetic chemistry."

Moon swallowed, and gazed apprehensively at the figure on the table. It did not look reassuring. The only proof that there was still life in the motionless body was the constant background sound of purrings and chucklings from the jury-rigged life-support machinery and the instruments monitoring vital signs. "And he'll—they'll—be all right now?"

Francis Krake crossed his fingers. "That's right," he said, hoping it was true. But Sue-ling had seemed sure of what she was doing under the memo disk. Even Litlun, wearing an identical disk as he shared the surgery with her, had never hesitated or shown any doubt that the procedure would work.

Moon caught him off guard with a sudden chuckle. Krake gave her a swift look, wondering if hysteria had finally caught up with her, but her smile seemed genuinely amused. "I'm sorry, Francis," she said, "but I can't help thinking that that solves one problem, anyway, doesn't it?" And explained: "Now Sue-ling doesn't have to worry about making her mind up between them any more."

"I suppose that's true," Krake said after a moment, and his tone was icy.

Moon gave him a startled look, then a remorseful one. She said quickly, "I mean, if she really still wants one of them—or wants him, I mean . . . I don't know what I mean, exactly," she said, knowing she was making a mess of what she had meant to be an apology. She thought for a moment, and decided to give it up. She sat down on a crate that had once held medical machinery, next to the sleeping Taur, and silently stroked the close-cropped fur between Thrayl's gently glowing horns.

It was Krake who changed the subject, as uncomfortable as Moon herself. "Tell me about that—what did you call him, a 'poet'?"

"Oh, yes," Moon said gladly. "Only 'poet' isn't quite the word. He told me the right word for Earth people to use was 'aiodos'—it's an old Earth word, he said, from the Mycenaeans. Whoever they were. It means a kind of a bard; Homer, he said, was an aiodos." Thrayl stirred in his sleep. She scratched the warm, broad skull, and the Taur made a sleepy rumbling sound and was asleep again.

"Some poet," Krake observed. "He tamed those Sh'shrane without even working up a sweat."

"I guess they're not *just* poets, Francis." She looked up at him wonderingly. "It's like a fairy tale, isn't it? When he was talking to me, it almost felt as though he should have started with 'once upon a time'. . . ."

———

Once upon a time, the aiodos had said, or almost said. . . .

Once upon a time, a *long* time ago (but, really, all time was one, the aiodos had also said), the aiodoi were organic creatures who lived on a planet in a galaxy within a universe very far from Earth's—the very universe they had just left, in fact.

"They were living people, like us?" Krake asked.

Moon shook her head. "He never said they were like us," she corrected him. "Only that they were biological creatures, the same as we." In physical appearance, she said, they hadn't looked at all like human beings. In other ways, though, they were very much like us. As with the human race, these people had been ingenious and forceful, and also sometimes thoughtful and sometimes wise.

But, as with the human race, the active and ingenious ones were not necessarily the same ones who were both thoughtful and wise.

These beings had evolved, as living things always do. They had sharpened their intelligence. As the millennia drifted by they discovered fire, and agriculture, and machinery—just like human beings—and, like human beings, they built cities and prospered immensely. When they had reached a stage of burgeoning science and technology, the wise ones among them studied the stars and planets out in space. The ingenious ones took that knowledge and used it. They built ships to venture out to explore these other worlds—and not just to explore them, but to *own* them.

"Those were the Sh'shrane?" Krake guessed.

"And the others the aiodoi? Not yet, Francis," Moon said, "but that's what they became—over a long, long time."

It took a long time. During all that time many things were happening. Among others, the explorers and conquerors went farther and farther into space. Now and then, at this time and that, their explorations encountered other races of beings, some of them almost as intelligent as themselves. The stay-at-home wise ones welcomed these discoveries with delight. The adventurers had other views. The other races they found were sometimes absorbed into their own growing empire. More often they were brushed aside . . . or simply destroyed.

The ones who became the Sh'shrane were great destroyers. Ultimately they even destroyed their own bodies. Simple organic flesh was not hard enough or strong enough to meet their desires.

At first they had sought out warm and fertile planets like their own, but those were rare. There simply were not enough of that kind to suit the wishes of the voracious Sh'shrane. That problem had a solution, though. The ones who became the aiodoi helped them find it; they showed the conquerors how to change themselves to adapt to harsher environments, with prostheses and mechanical supplements, until they were more than half machine—humans would have called them "cyborgs." Now they were truly fitted for the work of conquest and subjection they had chosen for themselves. They were exempt from the needs of flesh and blood. They could survive in any gravity or atmosphere, or even in none at all.

Ultimately (Moon Bunderan told the captain wonderingly) the Sh'shrane lost the organic component of their bodies entirely. Their minds were machine-stored, in rustless, ageless, computer-like things, and the machine bodies they were housed in never died. The Sh'shrane doubled in numbers, and doubled again and again, until one single galaxy was too tiny to hold them all—until, at the last, they came to believe that not even a single universe was large enough to contain the mighty and irresistible Sh'shrane.

While the aiodoi. . . .

The aiodoi, too, had transcended flesh and blood.

They chose a different pathway. Not into inorganic matter; not into matter at all. The intelligences who were becoming the aiodoi had long ago discovered the principles of the wave-drive. They had given it to the Sh'shrane, as they gave so much else—of course, for without the wave-drive the Sh'shrane could hardly have ventured outside their birthright solar system. But the aiodoi found a different use for the wave-drive.

As the wave-drive ships became more and more sophisticated, they no longer depended entirely on mechanical components. Finally they required no mechanical components at all. The aiodoi learned from their ships the freedom of matterless existence. They transformed themselves. From organic beings tied to a benign environment, they came to exist as standing waves of pure energy, self-sustaining assemblages that Earthly scientists would have called solitons. They were continually in motion; and they, too, became immortal.

Learning and learning, always learning, the aiodoi began to comprehend the mysteries of the quantal realm. They had long since recognized the plurality of universes. Now, bound by neither space nor time, the aiodoi reached out to them. Through the manipulation of their own energy spectra, through the fluctuating creation of new wavicles in the false vacuum that underlay everything, everywhere, the aiodoi were always in touch with each other. More than that. The aiodoi were always one great chorus, hymning the praise of the majestic wholeness of all.

The aiodoi were never alone. There was no space and no time between universes, and so the aiodoi in the far past were in intimate contact with those in the far fu-

ture—though, to them, there was no past or future. They
were the aiodoi, and they were everywhere and every-
when.

They knew that when they themselves reached out to
other universes the hard, hostile ships of that worser half
of themselves, the Sh'shrane, would be quick to follow.
Follow the Sh'shrane did. And when they discovered that
race of beings that humans called "Turtles" they did as
they had always done.

They waged war against them.

But that, in the end, the aiodoi would not permit.
They could not allow the great plexus of universes to be
polluted by the viciousness of those alter-ego personali-
ties they had left behind. The aiodoi acted. They abandoned that birth universe to the Sh'shrane. They drove
the Sh'shrane ships back inside it, and closed off its
wormholes, quarantining it. . . . For a time.

Francis Krake listened to all she said, hardly able to
believe, even less able to doubt. He asked, "So the
Sh'shrane wouldn't let it go at that? They just bided their
time, and then they tried again?"

Moon nodded somberly. "They didn't forget the Turtles. They couldn't forget the only war they hadn't won.
This time they attacked the Mother planet itself. They
dragged it through the wormhole and destroyed it. I suppose then they thought it would be easy enough to mop
up the rest of the Turtles. . . . But the aiodoi would not
let that happen, Francis."

"They did, though. They let them wreck the Mother
planet."

She nodded earnestly. "I think he was sorry about
that. He said, 'We were listening to other songs.' But
they've made up for it. It's really over for the Sh'shrane
now. The aiodoi won't ever let them out of their own
universe again. Not ever."

———

When they were back in the control room Krake took
his place at the board, listening to the fourth or fifth

repetition of Moon Bunderan's story. Naturally she had to repeat it for everyone else on *The Golden Hind*—once to each handful of them as they returned from sleep, or wherever they had been, and several times over for all of them, to answer questions—or, more often, to tell them what questions she couldn't answer. Krake listened without speaking, but at the other board Litlun was full of agitated questions. "That's all I *know*," the girl said at last, almost cross. "I've got to take care of Thrayl. Anyway, it makes no sense to keep on asking about things I don't know anything about. I think what I've said already is all the aiodos wanted us to know."

Daisy Fay spoke up. "But there are things we *have* to know. We need to set a course, Moon. Didn't the—aiodos—tell you where we're supposed to go?"

The girl shook her head, already on her way to the food warmer. "I think Thrayl will do that, when he's had something to eat. And the other thing I think—" She pursed her lips before she said it. "I think he wasn't talking about *where* we were going, so much as *when*."

That made the Turtle squawk excitedly. "One must ask more!" Litlun said, the voice from the transposer almost trembling. "Is it possible then that one can really return to the planet of the Mother *before* it was destroyed?"

Moon was already on her way to the warmer. "I think that's what he meant," she confirmed.

"But that is traveling back in time!" the Turtle barked.

Moon shrugged. "All I can tell you is what he said: 'There is no time. There is only an eternal now.' Whatever that means."

Tired of questions that had no answers, Krake rubbed his eyes wearily. It wasn't just fatigue, though there was plenty of that. It was the harsh, ammoniacal stench left by the destroyed body of Chief Thunderbird that made his eyes sting. Looking at Moon Bunderan popping a meal into the warmer reminded him that he was hungry, too—and made him wonder if he could get anything down in that pervasive stink.

Moon saw his expression. "You don't notice it so much after a while, Francis," she said. "The air circulators are cleaning it up."

"Not fast enough," he grumbled. He watched her give the first meal to the awakening Taur, who ate quickly—and fastidiously, too, as he always did; but mostly quickly, and held out his plate for more as soon as he was through. Moon ruffled his head affectionately.

"I'll have something for us right away, Francis," she promised. She glanced at the Turtle, glumly staring with both eyes. "I'm sorry I can't tell you more, Lit—I mean, Facilitator," she said, softening. "I'm sorry about your friend, too."

Litlun was silent, studying her. "One suffers pain at the loss of an Elder Brother," he said at last. "It is no more than that." Then suddenly he turned his whole body to confront Moon Bunderan. "The Taur is now fully awake!" he said, his tone abruptly peremptory. "Can he not now tell us what we must do?"

Moon stood up to confront him, one hand straying protectively to rest on Thrayl's broad head. "Leave him alone," she commanded. "He's had a hard time!"

"But one wishes to know," Litlun pleaded, both eyes rotating around the control room, seeking support.

He got it from the Taur himself. Thrayl paused in his delicate eating and looked up, the huge eyes kindly. He rumbled something to Moon, paused, added something else and then quietly returned to his meal.

"What did he say?" Krake demanded, as impatient as Litlun himself.

Moon glanced doubtfully down at Thrayl. "He said, yes, he will take us to your Mother planet, Facilitator, but we must use up many, many long years first. And he also said something for you personally. He said—" she hesitated, then finished—" 'The Facilitator should know that a fine, good thing may come of a selfish wish.' "

"What do you mean, 'use up' years?" Krake demanded, but Moon wasn't listening to him. She was looking at the Turtle, who was muttering agitatedly to himself.

"Do you want to tell us something, Facilitator?" Moon asked, her tone kind and friendly.

The Turtle drummed his claws on his belly plate for a moment, his eyes wandering. Then he engaged his transposer and said in a burst: "One was not selfish! One wished only for the privilege of doing a great thing for the Brotherhood! The Proctor was wrong!"

They were all looking at him now, fascinated by the spectacle of a Turtle experiencing an emotional outburst. "One perceives justice in the Proctor's death!" he cried. "One grieves, but he was at fault. It was this one, not the Proctor, who devised the plan to use this ship for the Mother's sake. It was improper of the Proctor to insist on coming along, when he knew that only one male could receive the reward of success and pair with a new Mother." He turned away, glaring emptily up at the whirling star patterns on the screens.

"Are you saying he forced you to bring him along?" Krake asked.

"Force?" The Turtle rotated one yellow-red eye back to gaze incredulously at the captain. "There is no intelligence in that question. How could one Brother ever force another?"

"Then why did you let him do it?"

The Turtle gave him both scorching eyes now. "Why? Because he was one's *Elder Brother*." He closed the parrot beak with a snap, and then, without a word, gestured to Marco Ramos to take his place and waddled away to his solitary room.

As Marco slipped into place he turned his eyestalks on his captain. The face on the belly plate was grinning wryly as he said, "Turtles, Francis. We'll never understand them, will we?"

———

No, Francis Krake knew, he would never understand Turtles. He could accept that equably enough. It was only one more failure of comprehension to add to all the others that had borne themselves upon him. If he did not understand what made Turtles do the things they did, he was certainly no better at understanding these things called aiodoi, or the Sh'shrane—or, most of all, women.

He found himself yawning. He knew that he should go off to his own room and sleep. He even wanted to. He simply did not have the energy to make himself get up and do it. He sat before the board, gazing wearily at the changing constellations outside the ship, and was all but asleep when he heard Marco Ramos calling to him from the other board. "Francis! I've got something to show you!"

Krake shook himself awake. He turned toward the second board, where Marco had thrown a grid of rainbow lines on a small screen. It was too far to make them out, but he didn't have to. Marco was pointing up at the outside view. "Notice anything about those external galaxies?"

Krake blinked up at them. You didn't expect to see much of external galaxies at normal magnification—the Magellanic Clouds, yes, and M-31 in Andromeda if you looked in the right place, maybe one or two others. . . .

But now there were fifty or a hundred in plain sight. Puzzled, he turned to Marco. "Why are there so many of them?"

"That's what I wanted to know, Francis. It isn't that there are so *many*. It's just that they're so *close*! So then I began checking spectra." He waved to the rainbow patterns. "Look at the elemental abundances, Francis. Out of the first fifty stars I looked at, every one was metal-poor. Almost pure hydrogen and helium, no matter what kind of star it was!"

That woke Krake up. "The stars are different? You mean, then this isn't our universe?" he asked, bracing himself for new trouble.

"Oh, no, that's not it, Francis. At least, I don't think so. I think it's our universe, all right, probably even our own galaxy—it wouldn't make sense for the aiodoi to have sent us into a different one, would it? But *early*. When the universe was *young*. It hasn't even expanded very much yet—that's why we see all those galaxies outside our own." The metal-man's tentacles were waving excitedly and the imaged face wore an expression of delight. "That explains what Thrayl was trying to tell us, skipper! We have to keep going at wave-drive speed—time-dilated, just using up time—until the universe gets *old* enough for our own planets to be born!"

Krake blinked at him. "But then—then—how will we ever find them?"

"Thrayl will find them for us," Marco assured him confidently. "He as much as said he would, didn't he?"

"Of course he will," Moon Bunderan put in as she entered the room, hand in hand with Sue-ling Quong. "Why did you ever doubt it?" She turned toward Krake. "And we've just looked in on the patient, Sue-ling and I, and he's doing fine."

"That's good," Francis Krake muttered, suddenly brought back to his loss. The glow on Sue-ling's face was a wound in his heart. He looked at her, trying to keep his face emotionless—or even happy for her, though that was hard. He did not want to see her like this, or to think of her being fiercely protective of Sork—or Kiri—or Kiri/Sork, whatever they might call this collective new person. He did not want to dwell on the picture of Sue-ling changing him, doing bedpan duty, hovering over him as he opened his eyes for the first time. . . .

He was, in short, jealous. He said, unaware of how revealing his words were, "I suppose he won't be out of danger for a long time, though—putting two brains in one skull—I guess it will be a miracle if he finally survives."

Sue-ling looked at him sharply. "Miracle? We don't need any miracle, Francis. He's going to make it."

He shrugged, unwilling to say more. She studied him for a moment before speaking. "Francis," she said, "that was an unusual operation, all right, but I had two unusual subjects. You know that Sork and Kiri were twins." He nodded curtly. "What you probably didn't know was that once they were what people used to call *Siamese* twins. They were a kind of genetic accident—not startlingly rare, but not common, either. Before they were born the doctors discovered they were physically linked together. In the old days, babies like that went to term and were born that way. Sometimes they had to go through their whole lives joined together—sometimes as circus freaks! But we're better than that now, of course. The Turtles helped. Their memmie doctors did some intrauterine surgery, separating the two babies while they still had a chance to develop normally."

"Normally," Krake repeated. His tone was neutral, but Sue-ling did not miss the sneer in the word itself.

She flared up. "You're damn right they were normal! Considering what they could have been, anyway. They were joined at the *brain,* Francis! They had only one brain between them. The surgeons had to separate them by cutting through the corpus callosum."

She had his full attention now. "Corpus—?"

"Callosum. It's the thing that links the right and left halves of the brain together. They did the operation while the embryos were still plastic, and so there was time for each to develop another half-brain to replace what was missing. But still—" She bit her lip. "You know there are differences between left- and right-brain types? That's what happened to them . . . only now the two halves are back together again. Francis, they won't only recover —they'll be better than ever, because they'll be one single person again!"

He looked at her in bafflement. It was all too much for him to take in.

"I hope so," he said. "I mean, I'm sure you're right, Sue-ling."

He stopped there, tugging fretfully at his beard, trying to think of something else to say. Congratulations? I hope the two of you—or the three of you?—will be very happy?

It was too much for him. He stood up, waving Daisy Fay to take over the board for him. "Call me when we've got some piloting to do," he said, to no one in particular, and lurched away toward his own room. He was too full of his own woes to notice the way Moon Bunderan was following him with her eyes, watchful, sympathetic . . . and confident.

In the great many-voiced rejoicing song of the aiodoi, as they welcomed the one who returned, there was a special joy for the beings of Earth. Those beings did not know how they sang, nor did they hear the songs of others. They had never learned to listen, as the Taurs had long ago, but such learning could not be far away. And so the aiodoi listened with delight to another faint, faroff song from that tiny, distant planet. It was not even altogether a real song. It was hardly more than a verse, a fragment; but even that the all-hearing aiodoi heard, and welcomed.

———————

"I'll tell you what Paul Davies says about those 'other universes' in the Everett many-worlds interpretation. He says that when we open the box on Schrödinger's cat what we find out isn't whether or not the cat died, but only which universe we are in.

"Remember, I am speaking of *universes*. Not just local groups, like a galaxy or a cluster, but *everything*. With their own spaces and dimensions and times. Every one of those universes is all the things any universe is. In their 'real time' the vacuum fluctuations will produce all the things any universe can exhibit—stars and metagalaxies and 'people'—oh, an immense number of people, or so one would like to believe, each of them of a kind but different from all others of its kind because they are individuals; each kind different from all the other kinds, but like them, too.

"At least in one respect they will all be alike.

"Eventually they will all die. And, sooner or later, so will their universes."

———

And the returning aiodos sang:
"And we will await them when they do."

20

〜〜〜

Because photons have no clocks, even the longest voyage in a wave-drive ship winds somewhen to its end. This particular voyage was, to be sure, a very long one—a matter of several billion years . . . or of several billion light-years, which as Einstein told the human world long ago are the same. Long before they had reached the end of it Krake was counting the remaining food supplies aboard *The Golden Hind* with the beginnings of real worry.

But there was still a reasonable margin left when the voyage ended. The external galaxies had receded to their proper remote places. The closer stars around them had swirled into nearly familiar constellations, and Marco's spectroscope confirmed that more and more of them had become the metal-rich objects of later generations.

When they came out of wave-drive at last, the space that surrounded the Mother planet was as Krake had first seen it, long and long ago. There was no great wormhole to threaten in the nearby sky. Instead, the baleful accretion disk of the old black hole hung on one side of their screens, menacing, dangerous, pocked with lightnings of hard radiation; the Sh'shrane-generated wormhole that had swallowed the Mother planet had not yet been formed. But the neutron star was in its proper place, looking no different, and the Mother planet itself swung just below them, to all appearances quite permanent there, exactly where Thrayl had promised.

The Taur gazed down at the stark, dimly lit planet in benign silence, his horns glowing with their milky light. Beside him Litlun was aquiver with excitement, his claws drumming on his belly plate. "It has really happened!" he rasped, almost like a prayer. "One can yet save the Brotherhood! We must land at once!"

Francis Krake didn't question that, but he had problems to solve. He had to plan a landing in the shadow of the planet itself, precisely navigated to avoid as much as possible of the deadly radiation from the black hole and the neutron star. More, he had to decide who was to make the trip down to the surface in the scout ship.

Two possible candidates were ruled out at once: There wasn't any way to bring the still unconscious Kiri/ Sork (or Sork/Kiri) Quintero down to the surface of the planet; so he was naturally excluded. So was Sue-ling Quong, who flatly would not consider leaving the wave-ship without him. "And we have to leave at least two behind in the waveship," Krake said, considering. "Marco, Daisy Fay—I want you two to stay aboard to crew the ship, in case—"

He stopped there. He did not say in case of what. It wasn't necessary, and he didn't have the opportunity. Litlun was already squawking urgently at him.

"That must be all, Captain Krake! No more persons are to stay aboard! One requires as many in the landing party as possible," the Turtle said peremptorily.

Krake stared at him. "Why? Are you looking for witnesses?" he asked. "Are you trying to tell us that the Turtle Mother would take our word for all this, and not yours?"

"It is not a question of doubting one's word," Litlun croaked, defensive, almost abject. "It is a matter of that which must be said. The things which one must tell the Mother are—" he hesitated. "Are shunned," he finished.

Marco Ramos put in wisely, "Because they're about quantum mechanics and all that sort of thing, right? I see his point, Francis. But since that's what we have to talk about, don't you think I ought to go, since I've been listening to those old lecture chips more than anyone else?"

Krake didn't answer that. He just shook his head. "Everybody else goes, then. Let's do it," he said to the others, and the four remaining—Moon Bunderan and her Taur, the Turtle and the captain himself—sorted themselves out and squeezed themselves into the scout ship. "Buckle in," he ordered as soon as they were all inside, and took the controls. And the little scout lurched away from the waveship, and began its long drop toward the surface of the great, dark planet, with its immense, faintly gleaming caps of ice. . . .

Then, suddenly, they were no longer alone in their descent.

Out of nowhere, a cluster of Turtle spacecraft appeared to orbit them, close in, escorting them—or threatening.

Moon Bunderan gasped, and the Turtle cawed incomprehensibly to himself. "It's all right," Krake said. "They were bound to detect us and they aren't going to harm us . . . I think." But then he took a second look and swallowed. The ships that surrounded them were not like *The Golden Hind.* They were of an older and cruder design, and they possessed something no Turtle ship of his experience had ever had.

Each one of the ships around them carried a cluster of ominous-looking housings on its hull.

"Those are weapons!" Krake said in astonishment. "They're armed."

And Litlun echoed, "They are armed, yes. Captain Krake, do you understand what that means? No ship of the Brotherhood has been armed since the war with the Sh'shrane! We are at a time before the Sh'shrane ever reached here!"

That was inarguably true, if fantastic. There were plenty of other proofs. The mere fact that they had to make a powered landing was evidence enough that they had wound up at a long earlier time, for everyone knew that the Mother planet had had a skyhook of its own for many Mother-generations. The only question was, *why*? Krake puzzled over that with part of his mind, while concentrating with most of it on the reentry of the scout ship into the atmosphere of the planet. He accepted the fact that *The Golden Hind* had been performing what was in fact a kind of time-travel, first reentering their own universe at a very early point in its history, then cruising at wavespeed until they approached their own present. That was crazy enough, but he admitted it was true. But then why stop short? Thousands of *years* short? He glanced at the Taur, who was purring contentedly. "Thrayl says it's all right, Francis," the girl whispered. Fatalistically, Krake put the question out of his mind.

In any case, it was taking all his skill to keep the ship from excessive turbulence. As the lurching vessel threw them all against the straps, Litlun squawked rasping complaints.

"Are you functioning properly, Captain Krake?" the Turtle demanded. "Shall one take over the controls for you?"

"Fat chance," Krake said shortly. Moon touched his shoulder from behind.

"I think you're doing fine, Francis," she offered. "And things will be all right when we land. Thrayl says so."

"Glad to hear it," he muttered. It was true that the Taur seemed quite relaxed where he was strapped in beside his mistress. His eyes were gently reassuring, and his horns now glowed softly in rainbow colors. It was obvious that Thrayl had completely recovered from his ordeal. All it had taken was a little sleep and a few meals and the Taur was back to normal. It was taking more than that for the rest of the *Hind*'s crew; Krake wondered if there would ever be a time when his world would be "normal" again.

But he didn't really want it to be normal—at least, he surely did not want to return to the kind of normal, empty existence he had been living through ever since the Turtles picked him out of the Coral Sea. The trouble was that what he wanted, he told himself with resignation, was out of his reach forever. He accepted the fact that his brief time with Sue-ling Quong was over and would never come again . . . but acceptance did not imply contentment. There was still a yearning space in his heart that cried out to be filled.

Then the scout ship was screaming through the less tenuous stretches of the planet's atmosphere, and Krake had no time to think of anything but guiding the little ship.

"Hold on!" he yelled, while Litlun was tugging at him with one clawed hand, pointing toward a mountain range near a pole of the planet. The turbulent atmosphere shook them all up, but it had one pleasing consequence. The guardian ships were unable to maintain station in the buffeting, and they fell away, out of sight.

Krake swore at Litlun to shut him up; he knew where he was meant to land. He dived the scout ship down and away, pouring on power, heading for the chosen point at the fringe of the northern ice cap. The Turtle was craning his leathery neck to see with one eye, while the other eye roamed around to see if the escort ships were following.

"There," he squawked through his transposer, waving one stubby arm. "On that plain, just before the ice!"

"I *know,*" Krake gritted, fighting the controls. It was not the proper way to land a scout ship. What you did normally was to orbit close in until you had spotted the best possible place, then come down to the surface in a long, careful spiral—halfway around the planet if necessary. But normally you did not have armed ships herding you along.

Krake swore as he scanned the images that were growing in the screen. "There's nothing there," he snapped. "Isn't there supposed to be a city somewhere?"

Even in that moment Litlun managed to sound indignant. "The Brotherhood does not huddle in *cities,*" he croaked, his wattles flushing. "Do as one instructs you now! Put this vessel down!"

Krake swore again—hadn't stopped swearing, really, for the last several minutes—and had reason to go on swearing, because his job was getting harder. This was a planet of high winds and rocky peaks, and the landing approach was bumpy. Only the rugged restraints kept him from flying off the control seat. In the window he saw the reflection of Moon Bunderan quickly raising a hand to her mouth, her face greenish in distress.

Krake thanked heaven that there were no clouds. At least he had unlimited visibility for the approach to the spot Litlun had chosen for landing. Krake caught a glimpse of an opening in the ice cap that yawned a few kilometers from the edge and blinked in surprise. Any gap in that massive ice cap was wholly unexpected; but he had no time to study it. He had no time for anything but landing the scout, for now the winds coming down off the ice were the strongest of all. Gusts tried to flip the little scout ship over as it came almost to the ground; Krake had to wrestle it level to get it down in one piece.

Then the ship touched down, skidding to a halt almost in the face of the giant cliff of ice.

Thunder above them told Krake that at least one of the escort vessels had managed to keep pace. Squinting out, he watched the Turtle ship slide to a halt on the ground a hundred meters away. Even before it had quite stopped its exit hatches were flying open.

At once a pair of giant Turtles leaped out of the ship, waddling rapidly toward them.

"Open the hatch," Litlun begged. "We must go out at once—hands raised—to show them we mean no harm to the Mother!"

"Not yet!" Krake snapped. "Radiation suits first—we'd be fried in a minute out there!"

"Then do it quickly and follow me!" the Turtle squawked. Needing no suit for himself, he was already scrabbling at the scout ship's hatch. The rest of them were struggling in the confined space to pull out the capes and hoods that would—that Krake hoped would—protect them, at least for a while, from the lethal radiation that drenched the Mother planet from the inferno in its sky.

By the time Krake got outside Litlun and the Turtles from the guard ship were already screeching raucously at each other. It didn't sound like a friendly discussion. In Krake's opinion, the two new Turtles weren't acting much like a welcoming committee. But at least no weapons had been drawn.

Krake was careful to stand a good, non-threatening distance away from the shouting match. Moon Bunderan was between him and Thrayl, their backs to the blast of dank, bone-chilling air from the ice cliff. The Taur's great, glowing horns swung watchfully from side to side, but there was no serious alarm on the broad face. Out of the corner of his eye Krake saw half a dozen more Turtles racing toward them from a new source—not from a ship, this time; the new ones were coming from a gray stone construction that seemed to penetrate right into the face of the glacier itself.

Krake stole a moment to look around. Overhead the sky of the Mother planet was a dusty pink, curiously brilliant. The black hole was out of sight, but near the horizon the neutron star blazed wickedly. It gave little heat. Krake felt the girl trembling beside him, and it was only when he looked at her that he realized he was shivering with cold himself. Their cloaks might protect them from the wicked radiation, but they were doing nothing to keep them warm. Thunder from overhead told him that another of the escort ships had finally managed to catch up with them. It landed as precipitously as the first, and two more of the mean-looking, ancient ships were following it down.

The odds were getting worse.

Krake grinned to himself at the thought. Of course that made no difference: the four of them against an entire planet, what difference did a few more Turtles make? He watched with resignation as more Turtles leaped from the ships and waddled toward them at high speed.

"Francis?" the girl whispered. "Isn't Litlun waving to us?"

He turned back and saw it was true. The rust-red little Turtle was gesturing frantically for them to join him. As they approached he engaged his transposer. "One has been granted permission!" he croaked in triumph. "We are permitted to see the Mother herself!"

"She'll help you, then?" Moon asked.

The Turtle's gestures slowed. "One does not know that with certainty," he said, the words coming with reluctance. "But we must not delay! These Brothers will take us to her at once!"

————

To be taken to the Mother meant first penetrating through that wall of ice, Moon Bunderan discovered as they followed the first pair of Turtles toward that old stone structure at its base. Two other Turtles swung in behind them—a guard of honor? Or a prison guard?

Moon didn't know the answer to that. There was so *much* she didn't know! For Moon Bunderan, all these experiences had been coming too fast and too unexpectedly. She took reassurance from the presence of her dearest friend, the Taur, not to mention that other rather dear person, Captain Francis Krake; whatever happened, at least they were all together.

All the same, she was glad to get into the tunnel through the ice. It was good to be out of the sight of that awful neutron star in the sky, though it was no warmer inside. She saw that the tunnel stretched a long way into the glacier, but there was little time for sight-seeing. The Turtles were herding them onto a thing like a farm cart. It had no motor that Moon could see. Nevertheless, as soon as they were all aboard it began to roll steadily into the tunnel, under the ice, in a gloom that was not quite total darkness.

There was light enough for Moon, though, and it came from the familiar, friendly glow of Thrayl's horns. In that illumination she could see Francis Krake's face, pinched in worry as he stared ahead into the gloom. Poor

Francis, she thought, though she could not have said why.

She burrowed closer to Thrayl's warm, firm body. At least, she told herself, there was something to be accomplished here. Litlun's dreams might be realized in this place, and obviously he was on tenterhooks about it. The Turtle was fidgeting nervously, muttering to himself, transposer off. She wondered what it might mean if the Turtle's hopes were realized. Suppose Litlun did persuade this ancient Mother to come with them. Suppose it meant that the Turtles had a new rebirth of life in their own time. Suppose they returned successfully . . . but what, she wondered, would they return to? Could she ever go back to her life on the New Mexican ranch again?

To her surprise, Thrayl bent his great head to nestle against hers. "Do not fear, Moon," he lowed gently, his warm, sweet breath stirring her hair. "Your wish. It is my wish, too."

She sighed, not asking for an explanation, committed to trust. She could not believe it was a guarantee of any kind—but if Thrayl told her not to be afraid, why, then she would not.

As the car came to a jolting stop Moon gasped and squinted as bright light struck her eyes. They had emerged from the tunnel into a brilliant vista.

They were in a vast, circular pit, like the caldera of an ancient volcano. All around them steep granite cliffs rose high above, shutting out the direct rays of that awful neutron star. There was no sign of the ice that she knew was all around them, held back by the towering granite.

The whole scene was as brightly lit as a summer day on the ranch, though there was no sun in the sky. When Moon squinted up she saw that the light came from shifting curtains of multicolored fire in the sky itself.

"An aurora," Francis Krake muttered, staring up at the pink sky. Energetic particles from those dead stars were making the heavens blaze. "A hell of a bright one, too! But I don't think we'll need the radiation suits anymore."

Not even to keep the cold out, Moon thought, because, astonishingly, in this sheltered place it was *warm*. As she looked at the sight before them she felt a sudden, unexpected stirring of pleasure. It was quite beautiful! In the center of the deep, round valley they were in there was a wide and handsome lake, dotted with islands.

It was no passive landscape, either. The scene was filled with activity. She saw that the meadows were alive with Turtles—all kinds of Turtles, tiny ones, medium-sized ones, even some very large ones with silvery carapaces, which seemed to be in charge of the others.

Krake was staring with marveling eyes as well. He said, "This must be their hatchery, Moon! I've heard of this place, but I never expected to see it for myself. What we're looking at is the next generation of Turtles, and the Mother herself must be somewhere near!"

The Turtles who had brought them this far got out of the cart and stood there, backs to their guests—or prisoners. They seemed to be waiting for something. Litlun was trying to question them, but they ignored his nervous cawing. They were looking across the meadow, where another Turtle was unhurriedly waddling toward them.

The newcomer was one of the huge, silvery-bodied ones, and Krake caught his breath at the sight. "Do you know what that is, Moon?" he demanded. "I think it's a *female*! It must be one of the nymphs!"

Moon stared at the new arrival. It was taller than most of the Turtles she had seen, but slimmer as well. The rudimentary winglets of male Turtles were well developed in this one, and its carapace gleamed like polished metal. Moon looked at Francis Krake in puzzlement. "A nymph?"

"It's an immature female," he explained. "I've heard that they're supposed to always keep a number of them around—in case anything happens to the Mother, you know. But nobody's ever seen one before."

One of Litlun's eyes wandered to them. "A nymph, of course," he agreed through the transposer. "They do not simply idle here. It is the honor of the nymphs that they tend the Mother in all her needs. How could it be otherwise? It could not be done by males, since very few males are permitted to see the Mother in person." He hesitated there, then added in a rush: "Or so it was in one's own time."

"You think it's different now?"

Litlun made the equivalent of a fatalistic shrug. "One does not know," he admitted. Then he added another admission. "One was unsure of the Taur's purpose in bringing us here at such an early stage," he said thoughtfully, "but perhaps that is best. This is a ruder, less sophisticated time in the life of the Brotherhood. It is possible that one's requests may be granted more easily now." He seemed to meditate for a moment, then roused himself. "Still," he said, "there are certain rules one must follow, even now, when one appears before the Mother—"

But he did not get a chance to explain them just then. The nymph was speaking to him, her voice a higher, softer version of his own. Hastily Litlun disengaged his transposer to answer her.

The conversation lasted for a few seconds, then the nymph gestured. Obedient to her wish, the male Turtle stepped back. She entered the cart and began to drive it directly toward the lake, with Litlun croaking and squawking deferentially to her all the while.

The closer they got to the lake, the younger and smaller the Turtles around them seemed to become. Then Moon saw that at the water's edge there were row upon row of ebon-colored objects like small footballs. Eggs! Basking in the light from the auroral display above, with nymphs moving among them and helping hatchlings to emerge as they cracked their enclosing shells. The tiny Turtles that emerged were damp-looking and soft, but they began to move their little limbs as soon as they were free.

"They're *darling*," Moon said, unable to restrain herself.

Litlun turned both eyes to give her a scorching look. He was making no progress with talking to the nymph; he turned on his transposer and addressed the others. "This nymph does not wish to discuss what the Mother may decide," he said worriedly. Then he added, "One has a concern."

"Which is?" Krake demanded.

Litlun drummed his claws fretfully on his platen. "She knows nothing of the Sh'shrane," he said, sounding disturbed. "Nor does she know anything of Taurs—she was quite startled to see this one, and to see you two, as well—or even of wave-drive ships. It is for this reason that one is concerned, Captain Krake. We are so many Motherlives in the past—thousands of years at least—that one may find it difficult to explain one's needs."

He scratched unhappily for a moment, then seemed to brighten as he glanced around. "Ah, but what a joy it is to see this place again! One remembers one's own hatching, and the cycles of growing and learning here before the great journey into the world beyond the ice, where we adapt to the radiation from the neutron star and the accretion disk. . . ."

The cart jolted and stopped for a moment, halting Litlun in mid-reminiscence. Then it slowly began to mount a bridge to the nearest island.

Litlun's claws drummed more ecstatically than ever. "We are almost there!" he cawed, his wattles suddenly pale. "See the glory of the way our Mother lives!" He turned off the transposer to speak pleadingly to the nymph.

But Moon wasn't listening. She had followed his instructions, gazing at the things the island held, and her eyes widened as her mouth formed a tiny O of surprise and delight. What she saw was *opulent.* Bright gems flashed everywhere in the aurora light. There was a sort of great tepee in the center of the island, its loosely draped sides encrusted with glittering stones. The drapes hid whatever was inside, but out of the far side of the tent Moon could see a procession of nymphs lovingly carrying eggs away, to be deposited in boats and taken to the lake shores. The paths the nymphs trod were paved with jewels! Diamonds, rubies, emeralds, sapphires—the treasures, Moon thought, of more than one world. All was beauty wherever she looked—

Almost all. She wrinkled her nose. "What's that smell, Francis?" she complained.

"It's not just Turtle," Krake told her. "I think it's sulfur compounds—probably from the water. Maybe that's why it's warm here; I think this lake comes from geothermal springs. A good place for the Mother to produce her eggs!"

Scandalized, Litlun broke off his attempts at conversation with the nymph and slapped his transposer back on. "Do not speculate in that offensive manner!" he barked, his eyes glaring reprovingly at them. "One requires that you show respect, for in that nest is the Mother herself! You must listen attentively to these instructions: In the event that you are admitted to the Mother's presence you will always stand. Never turn your back on her. Your arms must remain lifted in the position of her wings, which is the attitude of worship." He raised his knobby elbows to demonstrate.

Moon tried to follow his example. "When will we see her?" she ventured.

The Turtle gave her a hostile glare. "One has not promised that!" he screeched. "It is entirely her decision, but if it should come you must behave properly!"

The cart stopped, a dozen meters from the tepee. The nymph looked over the group with non-committal eyes, then spoke quickly to Litlun. He looked surprised, then engaged his transposer again.

"It seems that one is to have an audience with the Mother alone," he said, trembling. "You will therefore wait here for instructions."

And he waddled nervously away, the nymph at his side, to enter the sacred presence of the Mother.

———

Time passed.

No one came near them, though half a dozen tiny Turtles came waddling with tiny steps to the edge of the lake to stare at them, until a nymph arrived to herd them back to where they belonged. Moon Bunderan began to feel warm again, after so chilling a time in the outer world. The nasty sulfur stink began to fade—or she had become used to it. "What do you suppose is happening, Francis?" she whispered.

He gave up craning his neck in the effort to see what was going on in the tent. "We'll find out," he promised—an ambiguous kind of promise, she thought, but took comfort from the fact that Thrayl, beside her, was rumbling softly and contentedly to himself. Thrayl did not seem curious, though both Moon and the captain were doing their best to understand the occasional brief glimpses they caught. They could see figures moving around—Litlun, for certain, his elbows upraised in the worship gesture, others they could not identify. Though they could hear distant screeches and gurgles from within the Mother's birthing nest, they could not guess at meanings. Still no one came near them, though several nymphs loitered conspicuously near the side of the tent, talking among themselves and now and then glancing one-eyed at the visitors.

A new figure appeared as it moved behind the tent flaps, dimly seen. "Is that the Mother?" Moon whispered, pointing.

Krake tugged at his beard. "It could be," he said. Except for her bloated abdomen, she looked no larger than the nymphs around her. Her shell was yellowed, though, and cracked and bleached with time. "She looks like she's had a hard life. Well, I suppose she has. Giving birth to an entire race by herself can't be easy! . . . But I wish Litlun would come out."

"And I," Moon said practically, "wish I knew what time it was. I bet Sue-ling's worrying about us."

Francis Krake gave her a surprised look, then an amused one. "I imagine so. _I_ am."

She put her hand on his. "Oh," she said, her voice serene, "didn't you hear what Thrayl said? It's not necessary to worry. He told us there's nothing to worry about."

He managed an actual laugh at that. "No?" he asked, gently mocking. "Not even about whether they'll throw us out of here—or maybe even decide to have us for dinner, to feed the babies?"

"Oh, Francis," she cried in reproach. "How can you say that? They *wouldn't*. Anyway," she went on, "don't you remember that both Litlun and Chief Thunderbird gave us their word that things would be better when we got back?"

Krake didn't have the heart to point out that Chief Thunderbird, at least, would not be coming back anywhere. He couldn't help saying at least, "I remember just fine, Moon. But what has Litlun got to say about anything now?" She shrugged, serenely at ease. "And even if we do get out of here with everything Litlun wants, what then? We're still thousands of years from our own time, aren't we?"

"Thrayl said not to worry," she pointed out. "Not even about how we get back to our own time, I guess—after all, we can just do some more time-dilation travel and wait for our time to catch up with us, can't we?"

"Yes, but—" Krake began, and stopped himself. He did not want to cause any more worries for Moon Bunderan than the situation itself forced on her.

She patted his hand. "Thrayl would *never* disappoint me, Francis," she told him. "Please remember that."

"Of course," he said, to end the conversation. He could not share her childlike faith in the future, but it touched him in spite of himself. He looked at her curiously. Moon Bunderan was certainly not a child in any physical sense. Not in intelligence, either. She had proved that by the quick wit she displayed in learning her way around the waveship, her display of prompt skills in surgery—in everything she did. But to Francis Krake she seemed so hopelessly, helplessly . . . "naive" was the only word that fit the case. Perhaps it was because of her sheltered upbringing on the ranch. Perhaps it was simply her nature.

It occurred to him to wonder whether being naive was necessarily a bad thing.

He hadn't reached a decision on that question when Thrayl made a soft warning sound. Krake looked up to see Litlun coming out of the tent, followed closely by his silvery guardian nymph.

"Is something the matter, Facilitator?" Moon Bunderan called.

The Turtle turned both eyes to regard them. His wattles were purplish with suppressed anger, but his demeanor reflected hopeless gloom.

He engaged his transposer. "Something is the matter, yes," he croaked. "The Mother and her nymphs heard me out. But they do not accept what one has told them. They have refused to give any assistance at all."

Krake stared at the Turtle. "Maybe you didn't put it right. What did you ask her for?" he asked.

"For help simply," Litlun cawed dejectedly. "For a nymph which one could take back to our own time, so that the Brotherhood might be reborn. Nothing more!" He turned a resentful glare on his guard. "One thought the nymphs at least would be pleased to have the chance for one of them to become a Mother quickly, but they gave no support at all."

Looking at the particular nymph escorting him, Krake could well believe it. In fact, she seemed actively hostile. Her eyes cold with detestation, she peremptorily gestured them all into the cart, squawking harshly as she climbed in after them. She slammed the cart around in an especially rough turn as she headed it back toward the tunnel.

Clinging to the edge of the cart, Moon asked, "What went wrong, Facilitator? Did the Mother think that you were lying to her?"

Litlun gave the girl a full glare from both eyes. "That is a ridiculous question, and an offensive one! Members of the Brotherhood do not lie!" he screeched. "The Mother would never think such a thing. No, she—" He paused, wounded. When he went on his tone was hopeless. "It was worse than that. She stated that one is unfit," he said.

"Unfit?" Krake asked. "You mean she thought you were crazy?"

Litlun cawed wordlessly for a moment, then surrendered. "Perhaps a condition of that sort, yes. One suggested she interview you for corroboration, but she stated there was no value to be obtained from discussing matters with strange and possibly dangerous animals."

Krake bristled. "Animals! What does that mean?"

"One cannot say," Litlun wailed. "One cannot even say what will now be done. It is known that those who are unfit are not permitted to survive. Nor is it customary to permit dangerous beasts to exist where they might do harm."

There was a faint gasp from Moon Bunderan, and Krake demanded, "What are you trying to tell me? Do you think they might try to execute us?"

Litlun gave him a severe look. "That is not important, Captain Krake. Only one thing is important, and that is that one has failed in the attempt to preserve the precious Brotherhood!"

"The hell you say," Krake raged. "It's important enough to *me*. We're not beasts, and they can't slaughter us at will." Then he clamped his lips shut, planning. He watched the nymph at the control of the cart. There was a lever that seemed to control both direction and speed; simple enough, Krake thought. He could do that. So when the nymph got out and turned them over to the male Turtles, for whatever purpose they intended, it was worth a try for him to grab the lever, try to barrel their way through the Turtles, through the tunnel, out the other side, back to their ship—

What the chances of success were he did not bother to calculate. It didn't matter, though. Things didn't happen that way.

As the nymph stopped the car and rose, Thrayl rose with her.

The nymph turned toward the Taur, imperiously questioning. Thrayl simply reached out with one three-fingered paw and touched her shoulder. He bent the massive head to hers, the purple-blue eyes gazing into her pale ones. The nymph flinched, but then stood still and mute for a long second.

Enraged squawks came from the male Turtles, waddling hastily toward them. Krake turned to face them, the movement a reflex without hope of accomplishing anything, weaponless as he was—but not willing to submit tamely to whatever they might do.

What they did was quite unexpected. They stopped short as the nymph shrilled a peremptory word at them. She gazed into Thrayl's eyes for a moment, then at Litlun.

Then, without speaking, she turned back to the control lever and the cart began to move again. The male Turtles stood silent and confused, staring after them as the cart entered the tunnel and began to pick up speed.

As they were racing through the ice wall toward the outside world Krake held the side of the cart against the jolts and swaying. It took him a moment to collect his thoughts enough to gasp, "What—what did Thrayl do to her?"

"He simply let her know that Litlun was telling the truth," Moon Bunderan said comfortably. "I told you there was nothing to worry about, didn't I? And Thrayl never disappoints me."

Krake stared at her, hardly able to believe—hardly able then, as they came out onto the barren, cold plain and the Turtles there scattered before them, hardly even when they reached the side of their ship and the nymph hissed dismissal to the Turtles waiting there—hardly even when the nymph herself followed them into the ship and motioned Litlun to secure the hatch. But then Moon said, in a different tone, "Hurry, please, Francis. Let's get out of here before they change their minds!"

In the sweet songs of the aiodoi there are phrases and melodies of myriad other songs and myriad other singers. The songs of Einstein, Mach and Bohr join with the songs of the aiodoi, and are not found wanting. So do the songs of Dirac and Schrödinger, Newton and Aristotle, Davies and Thorne, Hawking and Heisenberg, Hubble and Higgs, Chandrasekhar and Anaxagoras, Foucault and Feynmann, Coleman and Carter, Klein and Kaluza, Gott and Guth, Planck and Pythagoras, Boltzmann, Wheeler, Alvarez, Eddington, Maxwell . . . it is only the aiodoi who can know all the singers, for their number, like the aiodoi themselves, is without end. There are myriad others known to the singers from Earth, as well as myriad not known to them, and myriad myriad never to be known at all until that timeless time when all songs and all singers sing together. . . .

Amd all the songs are sweet.

21

~~~~~

Twenty-four hours into the homeward flight, almost caught up on his sleep, Francis Krake made a discovery. The discovery was that there was something new and strange in the air inside the waveship *Golden Hind.*

The discovery puzzled Francis Krake. It kept nagging at him as he tried to identify just what it was—as he listened to smiling Sue-ling Quong rapturously reporting on the progress of her patient; as he saw the contentment on the face of Moon Bunderan, patting and cosseting her beloved (and wonderful!) pet Taur; as he watched the ecstatic Litlun tagging after the nymph while she delightedly explored all the parts and businesses of the spaceship; as he heard grinning Marco Ramos and happy Daisy Fay McQueen boast about the wonderful stories they would have to tell to the Earthbound humans when they got back. Everybody seemed so different . . . so, well, *happy.*

When Krake saw that he sat up straight, blinking in surprise. Why, of course! How could he not have seen it before? There was certainly something new and different all around them now, and the name of that new feeling that pervaded the waveship was simply *joy.*

What startled him most of all was that he was beginning to feel that same unfamiliar emotion himself.

It was not surprising that he didn't recognize joy

when it struck him. There had been very little of anything joyous in Krake's life for a very long time. Not much in the South Pacific, even less as he was being interrogated by the Turtles, very little in those years when he did the Turtles' work as pilot of their wavecraft. There had been one interlude, yes. . . . But that sweet, swift, joyous moment with Sue-ling Quong had ended almost as soon as it had begun.

Krake accepted the truth about that. It was a wonderful memory, but it was gone. He knew that where Sue-ling gave her love was for no one but Sue-ling to decide. He was even able really to rejoice with her when finally Sork/Kiri (or Kiri/Sork) at last opened his eyes for her. That was only for a moment; and it was true that those eyes were crossed, and he barely seemed to recognize Sue-ling's anxious face as it hung over him. The event delighted her beyond measure nevertheless, and she promised all who would listen that he would be up and walking in a week—well, no more than a month at the outside.

And in much less than a month—just a few days, really—they would be back on Earth. There every facility of any hospital would be at Quintero's service. There a whole new life would open ahead for them all, and it would all be very *soon*. After *The Golden Hind*'s mind-shaking voyages of billions of years, through far-off universes, the trip of a few thousand years to the "present" they had left behind seemed like nothing. A breeze, Krake thought, like everyone else on *The Golden Hind* abandoning himself to contentment and to pleasurable anticipations. . . .

Until second thoughts began to set in.

———

He was at the control board, finishing a meal, when Marco and Daisy Fay came purposefully into the room. He hadn't heard them coming, because he'd been idly listening to the distant, interminable squawks and raucous yowls that came from Litlun and his precious nymph as they roamed around the *Hind*.

Krake chuckled. "Listen to them," he said, grinning. "I guess that's what Turtle courtship sounds like. Are you hungry? Thrayl will get you something if you like, though God knows what it will be." He smiled at them as he said it, because it was amusing that the only foods left on the *Hind* were the bores and oddities that no one had particularly wanted to eat before—principally dried redfruit and a few obscure desserts. They would not starve before they got back to Earth, but they would surely get tired of their diet.

From the other board Moon Bunderan murmured, "I don't think they're hungry, Francis."

Then Krake looked more closely at the two. The expressions of the faces on their belly plates were unexpectedly solemn.

"What's the matter?" he asked.

Marco spoke first. "We've been thinking," he said, in a tone which said that what they had been thinking had not given them pleasure.

"About those aiodoi and the Sh'shrane," Daisy Fay added, equally grave.

"Ah, yes," Krake said, nodding, thinking he understood. "They were certainly pretty weird, but they're nothing to get upset about. We don't have to worry about the Sh'shrane any more. The aiodoi promised that they won't ever be let out again. As far as the aiodoi themselves are concerned—" His voice trailed off as he shook his head. Not in worry—he hadn't begun worrying yet—but simply at the unexpected marvel of those timeless and eternal beings.

"Thrayl says we won't see the aiodoi again," Moon put in. "They won't interfere in anything people like us do; the only reason one of them got involved at all was that what was happening was their own fault."

"No," said Krake, pursuing the discussion, "but we'll always know they're there, won't we?" He thought for a moment of the implications of that, chewing his leathery dried redfruit. "It's going to be hard for some people to take," he went on, meditating. "Knowing that there's something up there that's always there, knows everything, can do anything—"

He tugged at his beard, suddenly silent. He was frowning as he tried to capture some fleeting understanding that was hovering just on the verge of making itself clear to him when he saw the look of impatience on Marco's image. "That isn't what we've been thinking about," Marco said, interrupting. "It's the Sh'shrane."

"And the aiodoi, too," said Daisy Fay. "We mean, the way they got to be the way they are. They started as the same race, and they changed so *terribly.*"

"And, most of all," Marco finished, "what we've been thinking about is whether such a thing could ever happen to *us.*"

That really startled Krake. "What are you talking about?" he demanded. "We're all one race, aren't we? I mean, not counting the Turtles and the Taurs."

"I'm not talking about the Turtles and the Taurs."

"Well, then what? What happened with the aiodoi and the Sh'shrane was that some of them began supplementing their bodies with machine parts, and after a while— Oh," he said, staring at his machine-crew, with their machine-tentacles waving around their bright machine-bodies and their machine-made images on the belly plates patiently waiting for him to comprehend. "Oh, my God."

"That's right, Francis," Daisy Fay said, sternly sympathetic. "What we're afraid of is ourselves. What are we, Francis? Do you think it's possible that people like us could be just the beginnings?"

———

That was a notion that Francis Krake had never wanted to have. It lingered with him all through the day. Sh'shrane and aiodoi. . . . Why, he remembered, there had been an old story, an old *human* story, about something like that. He dredged it out of his memory: *The Time Machine,* by the Englishman H. G. Wells. The human race growing and evolving and, ultimately, splitting from two classes into two separate races, the sweet, mindless Eloi with their sunlit flowers and songs, while below ground there lurked the terrible, equally mindless Morlocks, who crept by night to the surface to feast on their distant cousins.

Krake shuddered.

Of course, he told himself, the aiodoi were nothing like those empty-headed flower children of Wells's invention. On the contrary. They were not merely intelligent, they were all but godlike in their powers. . . .

That was when the thought that had been escaping him finally made itself clear. Godlike! Of course! The aiodoi were as close as anything could ever come to the churchly notion of an all-wise, all-seeing, all-powerful—but always mysterious, and never clearly seen—Jehovah or Allah or Whoever.

That thought was a relief. The human race had managed to live with the notion of a God for most of its history without being destroyed by it—surely they could do as well with the knowledge that there were aiodoi. And as to the Sh'shrane, and the division that had brought them about, perhaps hinted at by the presence of his two half-machine friends—

Standing in the makeshift surgery, he told Sue-ling Quong grimly, "We'll just have to be careful. We know what can happen. We'll remember. We won't let the same thing happen to us."

She looked up at him wonderingly over the body of her patient, and he realized the woman had hardly been listening to him. "Of course, Francis," she said vaguely. "But don't you think he's looking much better?"

Krake looked down at the patient on the table. Better than what? he wondered, but was too sensible to ask. Most of Sork/Kiri's—of *Quintero's*—bandages were off, and the eyes, if not really open, were sometimes at half mast. "I've been telling him what's happened," Sue-ling went on. "I think he's been understanding me—well, part of it anyway. It's really hard to be sure when he's asleep and when he's awake."

Krake was willing enough to agree to that. Still, just at that moment at least one of the barely focused eyes seemed to be directed at him, and the lips were twisting as though he were trying to speak. Nothing but a sort of staccato groan came up, and Sue-ling bent swiftly over him. "What is it, dear?" she asked. And then as the trembling lips ceased their motion again, she was reassuring. "Don't worry if it doesn't come this time," she said. "You'll be able to talk soon enough—and everything else, too. I promise!"

She quickly checked the readouts and the various tubes and wires that were sticking out of Quintero at all angles, then fondly eased his turbaned head on the pillow. When she was satisfied that her patient was benignly asleep again she stood up, yawning. She cocked an ear to the approaching, but distant, squawks of the two Turtles. "What do you suppose they're doing, Francis?" she asked.

"Getting to know each other, I guess. It's got to be a pretty stressful time for both of them."

She nodded. "I think—" he noticed that she didn't use a name, only gestured toward the patient—"*he* wanted to say something to them a little while ago, when they looked in. But I wouldn't let them stay, because he was getting too excited, and I didn't really understand him."

"I didn't know he could actually talk!"

"Of course! Well, not very well yet, of course. But soon."

Krake grunted. "And you don't know what he was trying to tell them?"

"I don't even know if that was what it was, Francis. Still, it was definitely *something* about the Turtles, I think. I only really caught two words. One was 'Litlun.' And I'm pretty sure the other was 'promise.' "

Krake repeated the words, "Litlun. Promise." He was no more than mildly interested . . . until the meaning of them sunk in.

Then he shouted aloud. "Of course!" he cried, causing Sue-ling to make reproachful shushing noises at him.

"But he's right," he said, a little more softly, no less excited. "We've got to make sure of that before it's too late—Litlun's promise!"

———————

It took hours to do, and he talked every item of it over with everyone else on *The Golden Hind* except the Turtles to make sure he had left nothing out. But when he was through Francis Krake had taken the forty or fifty items anyone had suggested and reduced them to a list of five items. He read it over twice. Then he crossed his fingers before he sent Marco Ramos scuttling off to find the Turtles and bring them to the control room.

Then he read the list over one more time to make sure while he was waiting. Five items—and every one a document comparable to the Bill of Rights or the Magna Carta:

"The Brotherhood, in consideration of the great services rendered to them by the human race—"

(They had squabbled more over the wording of that than over any of the actual clauses, but that was the way it had come out at last.)

"—agrees to make the following changes in its policy, effective at once:

"1. The Brotherhood will never again attempt to interfere with human science, education or other activities in any way.

"2. The Brotherhood will provide the human race with examples of every instrument, machine and design requested, and will assist human scientists in duplicating them; this specifically includes wave-drive spacecraft.

"3. The Brotherhood will provide the human race with means to decipher the contents of the "memo disks" so that they can be learned by humans without the loss of such memories when the chips are removed.

"4. The Brotherhood will at once stop the practice of enslaving or otherwise trafficking in Taurs for any purpose, in particular the practice of using them as foodstuffs; and will allow Taur males to develop normally; and will free all Taurs now in its possession."

And then, the catch-all paragraph to take care of anything they might have overlooked:

"5. Finally, the Brotherhood will, on request, assist both the human race and the Taurs in any other way necessary to establish their sovereignty over their own territories and their equal status with the Brotherhood."

Krake looked up from it and saw Moon Bunderan's eyes watching him from the other board. He grinned ruefully. "I'm not used to high-level diplomatic negotiations," he confessed.

She looked around as she heard someone approaching. She had just time to say, "You're doing just fine, Francis," before Marco and the two Turtles came in.

Rust-red Litlun looked like the tiny pet of the vast silvery nymph, but he was almost whistling with excitement. "Facilitator," Krake said at once, "I want to remind you—"

But Litlun interrupted. "It is not proper to address this one as 'Facilitator' any more," he squawked, and even through the transposer his voice sounded elated. "She Who Is to Be the Mother has agreed, and now one is to be called He Who Is to Be the Consort."

"Right," said Krake, trying to get on with it. He held up the list. "Now, what you and the Proctor promised—"

But he couldn't finish that either. "Marco Ramos has spoken of this," Litlun squawked. "One has accordingly spoken to She Who Is to Be the Mother, and she has accepted the agreement. Is that your list? Give it to me!"

And he took it in one clawed hand and passed it to the nymph, cackling and cawing to her with the transposer off. She did not hesitate. She scratched at the bottom of the list with one sharp claw and handed it back.

Krake stared down at the sheet of paper, surgically sliced where the nymph had slashed it. "Is that it?" he asked. "Isn't there something else we should do?"

"There is nothing," Litlun stated positively, "except to get us back to our proper time safely, Captain Krake.

We must start our nuptial nest very quickly!" He hesitated, glancing at the nymph, who was showing signs of boredom with this conversation in another language. "One has a question, however. Since the Mother planet is destroyed one will need a new nesting place for the brood that is to be. What would you think of your planet Mercury? It is of no value to you. It is true that the temperature is greatly elevated, but there is ample radiation to feed the hatchlings—"

He broke off as he saw the expression on Krake's face. "What is it, Captain Krake?" the Turtle demanded. "Is there some reason the planet Mercury would not be appropriate?"

Krake shook his head, dismayedly contemplating the possibility of a world of Turtles as near neighbors. "Not that I know of," he said reluctantly.

But Litlun was hardly listening. "Yes, yes," he said, one roving eye following the nymph as she waddled around the room. "One need not think of these details now. A suitable planet can certainly be found once we have returned to our proper time—which, of course, must be *after* the disappearance of the old Mother, as you will understand."

"Of course," Krake agreed, and then scowled suddenly. "No, I don't understand," he said. "Why does it have to be after?"

The Turtle squawked in amusement. "Because there cannot be two fertile Mothers at once, to be sure! The idea is preposterous!"

"But if we stopped just short of the disappearance, perhaps we could prevent it from happening in the first place!"

The Turtle hissed in sudden shock. "That must not be!" he rasped. "What good would it do to stop short? We could not succeed! One cannot stop the Sh'shrane from stealing the Mother planet! The aiodoi will not interfere again; one would be helpless against their terrible weapons. One would surely perish—and, what is far worse, at the same time endanger the life of the Mother to be!"

"One could damn well try," Krake snapped, tugging angrily at his beard.

"One must not! Think, Captain Krake," Litlun went on persuasively. "Suppose, in spite of everything, one should somehow succeed, and preserve the old Mother from the Sh'shrane. In that case, what would be the value of this paper you treasure so much? It would be worthless, Krake! It could not bind the old Mother. It would mean nothing; your people would be in the same status as ever." He hesitated, turning both eyes proudly on the nymph, who had begun to drift toward the doorway. Litlun moved to follow her. "And, even worse," he finished as he waddled away, "this one would not be He Who Is to Be the Consort."

———

"So you see," Moon Bunderan told her captain with satisfaction, "everything's all right."

"You think it's all settled then?" Krake asked. He considered for a moment, then surrendered to success. He said, "I guess it is. I never heard of a Turtle telling a lie." Then he chuckled. "Well, almost everything. I think we'll have to make sure we talk Litlun out of the idea of locating his new Mother planet in our solar system. My opinion is that they'll be better neighbors when they're farther away."

"I suppose," she said thoughtfully, studying his face. Then she said, "There's one other unsettled thing, Francis. I hope you won't think I'm too forward."

He blinked at her as she left the other control board and walked over to him. He started to protest at her abandonment of her post of duty, then swallowed it—after all, if the state-of-the-ship instruments revealed that anything went most improbably wrong they would hear it at once and could act.

"Francis," she said, taking him by the hand, "this is the thing. I know you think I'm a child. Well, I am—almost. But I'm less of a child than I was. And, Francis, please remember that I won't be a child for long."

The most ambitious novel yet from the
award-winning author of
Bug Jack Barron and **The Iron Dream**

Russian Spring
by Norman Spinrad

"Norman Spinrad has built a career on challenges
few other writers...would take."--*Newsday*

Set in the near future but based on today's headlines,
Russian Spring is a sweeping novel of a new world order
that could very likely come true. It forecasts the success of
perestroika and the transformation of the Russian econ-
omy, culminating in the Soviet Union's entry into the
Common Market.

Against this turbulent background, Spinrad weaves a
powerful saga of one family caught in the heart of this
storm of change: American Jerry Reed's dream is to reach
space but that dream has a devastating price; Russian
Sonya Gagarin's love for Reed forces her to reconcile her
marriage with her ambitions; and their children, Bobby
and Franja, find themselves inextricably caught in the
complex web of the world's new structure, facing the
frustrations of their unorthodox parentage and the
hostility of an America turned belligerently isolationist in
anti-European backlash.

Russian Spring
A spellbinding novel so timely
we could be reading it in tormorrow's newspapers.

On sale now wherever Bantam Spectra
hardcovers are sold.

AN361 -- 10/91

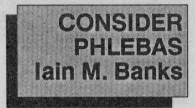
In the vast war between the Idrians and the Culture, one man is a free agent--his name is Horza. As a Changer, with the ability to transform himself at will, he works for the Idrians, and it's a fair exchange as far as he's concerned: his work is his most effective means to undermine the smug, sterile, highly advanced Culture that he despises.

Horza's latest assignment is to capture a renegade Culture mind--a form of artificial intelligence well beyond Idrian technology--hiding on a dead planet. Retrieving the mind is the easy part--it's the journey that's the challenge. He'll be facing cold-blooded mercenaries, a cannibalistic tyrant literally out for his blood, and a deadly game of Damage played out to the last minutes on a space habitat about to be blown to bits.

Star Trek®: The Classic Episodes

adapted by James Blish
with J. A. Lawrence

In the twenty-five years since it premiered on network television, bringing the voyages of the *Starship Enterprise* into America's living rooms and the national consciousness, *Star Trek* has become a worldwide phenomenon, crossing generations and cultures in its enduring universal appeal.

Now, in celebration of *Star Trek*'s 25th anniversary, here are James Blish's classic adaptations of Star Trek's dazzling scripts in three illustrated volumes. Each book also includes a new introduction written especially for this publication by D.C. Fontana, one of *Star Trek*'s creators; David Gerrold, author of "The Trouble With Tribbles"; and Norman Spinrad, author of "The Doomsday Machine."

Explore the final frontier with science fiction's most well known and beloved captain, crew and starship, in these exciting stories of high adventure--including such favorites as "Space Seed," Shore Leave," The Naked Time," and "The City on the Edge of Forever."

Now on sale wherever Bantam Spectra Books are sold.

AN332 – 9/91

With the fate of the world hanging in the balance, Elizabeth Devane must make a choice between the world she knows and the world that might have been....

The Trinity Paradox

Kevin J. Anderson and Doug Beason

Activist Elizabeth Devane wished for an end to nuclear weapons. She was certain that if they'd known what they were unleashing, the scientists of the Manhattan Project would never have created such a terrible instrument of destruction. But during a protest action, the unthinkable happened: a flash of light, a silent concussion, and Elizabeth wakes to find herself alone in a desolate desert arroyo...and almost fifty years in the past.

June, 1944: Los Alamos, New Mexico
While the Allies battle in the Pacific and begin the Normandy invasion, Nazi Germany deviates from the timeline Elizabeth knows and uses its new-found nuclear arsenal against America. Somehow, some way, Elizabeth has been given the chance to put the genie back in the bottle...yet could she--should she--attempt the greatest sabotage in history?

"Soberingly shows the perils of the sheep solemnly pledging themselves to vegetarianism while the wolves remain unconverted."
--James P. Hogan, author of *The Proteus Operation*

THE TRINITY PARADOX

On sale now wherever Bantam Spectra Books are sold.

AN362 – 10/91

privacy now and then—though never tell anyone *I* said that!

So I'll just wish them many years of happiness and sign off....

Romance is just one click away!

love scopes

- ➤ Find out all about your guy in the Men of the Zodiac area.
- ➤ Get your daily horoscope.
- ➤ Take a look at our Passionscopes, Lovescopes, Birthday Scopes and more!

join Heart-to-Heart, our interactive community

- ➤ Talk with Harlequin authors!
- ➤ Meet other readers and chat with other members.
- ➤ Join the discussion forums and post messages on our message boards.

romantic ideas

- ➤ Get scrumptious meal ideas in the Romantic Recipes area!
- ➤ Check out the Daily Love Dose to get romantic ideas and suggestions.

Visit us online at

www.eHarlequin.com

on Women.com Networks

HEUT2